USA Today bestselling auth̶
has a degree in journalism. She worked as a n̶ewspaper
reporter until she realised reporting 'just the facts' was
boring. Happier to report to her muse, Nancy writes
women's fiction and romance full-time. Critics have
deemed her work, 'funny, smart and observant.' She lives
in Tennessee with her husband and their crazy corgi. For
more, visit her website at NancyRobardsThompson.com

Christine Flynn admits to being interested in just about
everything, which is why she considers herself fortunate
to have turned her interest in writing into a career. She
feels that a writer gets to explore it all and, to her, exploring
relationships – especially the intense, bittersweet or even
light-hearted relationships between men and women – is
fascinating.

Charlene Sands is a *USA Today* bestselling author of
thirty-five contemporary and historical romances. She's
been honoured with The National Readers' Choice Award,
Booksellers Best Award and CataRomance Reviewers'
Choice Award. She loves babies, chocolate and thrilling
love stories. Take a peek at her bold, sexy heroes and
real good men! Visit her at charlenesands.com and on
Facebook.

Once Upon a Time

Once Upon a Time:
Charmed

NANCY ROBARDS THOMPSON

CHRISTINE FLYNN

CHARLENE SANDS

MILLS & BOON

First Published in Great Britain 2024
by Mills & Boon, an imprint of HarperCollins*Publishers* Ltd,
1 London Bridge Street, London, SE1 9GF

www.harpercollins.co.uk

HarperCollins*Publishers*
Macken House, 39/40 Mayor Street Upper,
Dublin 1, D01 C9W8, Ireland

Special thanks and acknowledgement to Nancy Robards Thompson for her contribution to the *Fortunes of Texas: All Fortune's Children* continuity.

Special thanks and acknowledgement are given to Charlene Sands for her contribution to the *Dynasties: The Montoros* series.

ISBN: 978-0-263-32268-2

FORTUNE'S PRINCE CHARMING

NANCY ROBARDS THOMPSON

This book is dedicated to Jennifer.
Never forget you're a princess. All my love, always.

Chapter One

"Zoe Robinson, you could have your choice of any man in this restaurant. Why must you fixate on the one guy you can't have?"

Zoe pursed her lips and tested her friend Veronica's theory, letting her gaze do a quick sweep of the people in the Gilded Pig's dining room. The rustic joint was jam-packed with its usual lunchtime clientele. Strains of a heartfelt country tune set the backdrop for the scene—mostly businessmen of varying ages, shapes and sizes who pushed up their shirtsleeves and tucked paper napkins into their collars to protect their white button-downs from what was arguably Austin's finest barbecue. Even though the room contained an appetizing smorgasbord of men, not a single one in the large barn-turned-restaurant piqued her interest. Each and every one of them probably had fine qualities and was certainly worthy of *someone's* love, but not a single one did anything for Zoe. Not even the cute guy who was grinning at her over his pulled pork sandwich.

As the music—Tim McGraw maybe?—asserted something about being a *real bad boy* who at the same time was a real good man—she flashed a noncommittal smile at the guy and turned back to Ronnie.

"Why fixate on Joaquin Mendoza? Because I can't get him out of my mind. That's why."

Ronnie scrunched up her face the way she always did before she stuck a big fat reality-check pin in Zoe's balloon of possibility. "That would be very romantic, Zoe, if only he would ask you out. Or even better, if he would talk to you about something other than business."

Okay. So, maybe Ronnie had a point.

Still, Joaquin Mendoza had swept her off her feet from the moment he'd first walked into Robinson Tech several months ago. Actually he'd captivated her the first time she'd met him when her sister Rachel married his brother Matteo, last year. They'd been paired as maid of honor and best man, but the focus of the weekend had been on the bride and groom and, at the time, Zoe had no idea her father would end up hiring him as a programmer at Robinson Tech to work on a special project.

It wasn't simply that he was older and tall and good-looking—no, scratch that—the guy was *gorgeous*. There was something about the cool way he held himself, and he had the strangest ability to put all of her senses on high alert the minute he ventured within five yards of her. It was like his superpower. Zoe had been ruined for other men since Joaquin Mendoza had walked back into her life three months ago. It was too bad he seemed more interested in work than in getting to know her better.

He hadn't messed with her equilibrium on purpose, of course. In fact, even after all this time, he didn't seem to recognize she was a woman who was interested in a man.

A very specific man.

"Okay, if you're going to be stubborn, maybe you need to take things into your own hands. Who says you have to wait for him to ask you out?" Ronnie continued, straining so that her voice was heard above the music. "I mean, if you like him, maybe you're the one who needs to break the ice—make sure he knows you're interested in him. In the past, you've never had a problem with making your intentions known."

Zoe sucked in a long, calming breath, blew it out in a measured gust and took in the Gilded Pig's decor. A decade ago the space had housed an antiques market. Keeping true to its roots, the Pig was decorated with vintage pieces such as the ornately carved church pews that served as seats for the booths, mirrors with light-reflecting mercury glass that seemed to double the already expansive space, and old wooden chests of drawers and sideboards that held napkins, silverware, condiments, steaming coffeemakers and sweating pitchers of iced tea.

"I don't know, Ronnie. This feels different."

"How so?" Ronnie asked.

Zoe thought about it for a moment, but she couldn't really put it into words. She knew Ronnie thought it was because Joaquin hadn't pursued her like the other guys. But putting that aside, he wasn't like anyone else she'd ever known. This was different. Even if she couldn't define it, she could feel it in her bones.

"Trust me. With him, I think the old-fashioned approach will work better than coming on like gangbusters. He's a little older than I am and I get the vibe that he likes to be the pursuer. So that's the new preamble to my Husband List. Let the guy be the hunter and stake his claim."

"You have a new preamble to the list?" Ronnie asked flatly.

Zoe lifted her chin. "Yes."

For as far back as Zoe could remember she'd had a list of deal-breaker qualities she wanted in a boyfriend. Over the years the Boyfriend List had morphed into the Husband List. It included things such as *must love animals; must make me laugh; must be passionate about his work but must not let work come before me.*

"Girl, you are no wallflower. You've never had any qualms about making the first move. I would so not sit at home and wait around for a man who can't seem to catch a clue."

"Who says I'm sitting around at home?"

"Didn't you just say you're waiting for Prince Charming to make the first move?"

"Just because I'm holding out for *Prince Charming* to ask me out doesn't mean I'm sitting around."

"All I'm saying is even Cinderella had to put herself out there to get what she wanted."

Zoe smiled and sat a little straighter. "I do feel like Cinderella. Only in reverse. Because I'm the one searching for the perfect fit. I'm the new-millennium Cinderella."

Yeah. She liked that.

Ronnie took a long sip of her sweet tea and then set it down and gave Zoe one of her *looks*.

"In my book, the new-millennium Cinderella doesn't even need a prince. She's her own woman and all she wants is a fun night out and a great outfit."

The two girlfriends laughed. But Zoe found nothing funny about the way Joaquin looked right past her unless she spoke first. When she spoke, he was always charming and amiable. So at least he didn't *hate* her. But there had to be a way to get through to him. Because these dead ends made her feel as though she was losing her mojo. She wasn't about to toss in the towel without a good try. Well, a try that involved getting him to make the first move.

The server refilled their iced tea and set a mountain of red-velvet cake and ice cream between them. The dessert was so big it could've easily fed four hungry adults. But in anticipation of a treat, Zoe had kept lunch light, ordering a salad with grilled chicken. She fully intended to do her fair share of damage to the Pig's signature dessert.

"Is there anything else I can get for you girls?" the server asked.

Yes, please. One surefire plan for how to get the guy?

"We're fine, thanks," said Zoe.

The server smiled. "Just holler if you need me."

She left them and went to a table across the way where a man was flagging her down.

Zoe settled back into the red-checked cushion that lined the booth's stark, hard wood.

"Okay, we are not leaving this restaurant until we

come up with a foolproof plan to get Joaquin Mendoza to ask me out."

Veronica sighed and propped her elbow on the table, resting her chin on her left hand and forking up a healthy bite of the cake with her other hand. "Why are you asking me? This is so not my department, Zoe. You've always been the one who gets the guys."

"You're only as good as your last victory," Zoe said. "Joaquin is always working, rarely looks up from his computer."

"Isn't that why your dad hired him?"

Yes, but…wait a minute…

"I think you're on to something, Ronnie."

"I am? Okay."

"I don't know why I didn't think of this myself."

"Um. You lost me somewhere between the first bite and the bit about Joaquin's computer obsession?"

"My dad. He mentioned that he loves Joaquin's work ethic, but he also said he wished he would get more involved around the office."

"Did he really say that?"

Zoe nodded.

"In so many words." She shrugged. "Actually, it was more like he thought Joaquin was sharp and hoped he could find a permanent position for him after he finished the consulting job. So you could interpret that to mean he should *get involved*."

Zoe shrugged again as she scooped up a forkful of cake. "Well, he *should* get involved. *With me*." She nodded resolutely and put the bite into her mouth.

"I don't know, Zoe. Don't you think you should be careful?"

Zoe swallowed. "What do you mean?"

"I mean, is this going to turn out like all the others?"

Zoe poked at the cake's white icing with her fork, leaving tine marks that looked like tiny bird footprints on a snowy lawn.

"The others?"

"Come on, Zoe, don't be coy. You know you love the thrill of the chase. Once you get the guy, you lose interest, you move on."

That was partially true, but not simply because she had a short attention span. She believed in happily-ever-after. She knew exactly what she was looking for in a man and she didn't intend to settle. What was the use of hanging on to a guy who was wrong for her? If she knew the relationship wasn't going anywhere, wasn't it better to not lead on a guy? So, when the relationship had run its course, it was time to move on. It wouldn't do anyone any favors, prolonging the inevitable.

"It may seem that way, but it's not what it seems like. I have my reasons."

Ronnie arched an eyebrow over a knowing smile.

It wasn't as everyone thought. She had her reasons for moving on. Reasons she didn't care to discuss with anyone—not even Ronnie—because it was a little too personal.

Why did everyone have to be so judgmental, anyway? Especially when they didn't know the full story. Even if she did like to flirt, she was young and free and she had high standards.

She wasn't sorry about that.

How would she ever meet her prince if she didn't do a little kissing? She was down with meeting her fair share of frogs to find Prince Charming.

And speaking of kissing— "I have a plan. I'm going to ask Joaquin to help me put together a new website for the launch of the new FX350 Tablet."

Ronnie frowned. "Doesn't Phil in design handle things like that?"

"Maybe, but not this time. Plus, Phil is swamped with other projects. He will probably welcome the help. Since Joaquin is such a computer geek, he has to know how to do a simple website. He can help out a damsel in distress."

She batted her eyes and fanned herself with her napkin. "What gentleman doesn't like coming to a lady's rescue?"

The project meeting lasted much longer than Joaquin expected, and he was behind schedule with his report. That meant he'd have to burn the midnight oil. But what was new? Late nights in the office had become a way of life since he'd come to Austin. In the three months since he'd moved from Miami, he'd traded dinners at South Beach restaurants for microwaved frozen meals eaten at his desk.

The sound of a knock on his open office door jolted him from memories of the Miami club scene back to his office at Robinson Tech.

Joaquin looked up at the sound of a knock on his open office door.

Zoe Robinson stood there like a vision in black and pink. Damn, she was a stunning woman.

"Are you busy?" she asked.

"I'm always busy." He minimized his computer screen, more out of habit than for privacy. "But come on in."

He could've set his watch by her visit. She seemed to find her way by his office most afternoons around this time. He really didn't mind, even if her reasons for stopping by were usually thinly veiled. He'd been around the block enough to know when a woman was flirting with him.

He had to admit he was flattered by her attention, but that was as far as it would go. She was a nice kid. And she was exceptionally easy on the eyes. Hell, she was innocently sexy with that long, honey-brown hair that hung midway down her back. Don't even get him started on those big gold-flecked chocolate eyes of hers that seemed to change colors with her moods and tempted him to stare a little too long.

Nope. She was strictly off-limits because, hypnotic eyes and short, flirty skirts aside, she was way too young for him. When he'd been hired on at Robinson Tech back in February, the entire office had celebrated her twenty-fifth birthday. That meant he was nine years her senior.

If the age gap wasn't enough reason to steer clear, all he had to do was remind himself that she was the boss's daughter. He knew better than to go there. Been there, done that back when he'd lived in Miami. He'd learned his lesson and he certainly didn't intend to make the same mistake again. Especially given that his brother was married to Zoe's sister Rachel. That could get very messy.

"What can I do for you, Zoe?" he asked as she entered his office. Today she looked even cuter than usual. Her skirt did a great job showing off her toned legs. Not that he noticed, because he kept his gaze glued to her eyes so that it didn't slip into forbidden territory.

"It's your lucky day, Joaquin," she said as she planted herself in the chair across from his desk. Her eyes sparkled and her broad smile was contagious.

"Is that so?" he asked. "Enlighten me."

She sat forward on the chair and leaned in conspiratorially.

"Out of all the people in the office, I've chosen you to help me with a project."

Her smile showcased perfect white teeth. She cocked a brow as though she was about to present him an offer he couldn't refuse.

The phrase "he who speaks first loses" came to mind. So, Joaquin arched a brow right back at her, leaned back in his chair and waited for her to give him the lowdown.

"So, you know the FX350, that new tablet that my father talked about at the staff meeting last week?"

Joaquin nodded.

"We are pushing up the launch date and I need someone to build a brand-new website for it."

He waited for her to laugh or at least crack a smile to indicate she was joking, but she didn't.

Okay. Well. This was interesting. He certainly wasn't above helping out with the project, but his pay grade didn't make that a very good use of his time for the company. Not to mention, Robinson Tech had a design department and he didn't want to step on anyone's toes.

He was trying to think of a way to say that without sounding pompous, but before he could find the words another big smile slowly spread over Zoe's face.

"Gotcha," she said. "I'm just kidding. I wish you could've seen your expression, though. It was priceless. I know that's not your department. Though you're more than welcome to be part of the web-site design project, if you'd like."

"You're quite the practical joker, aren't you?" he said.

Zoe shrugged. "As I said, you're welcome to join us. If you do, then it wasn't a joke at all. However, I did come to ask for your advice on something."

She was adorable and outgoing and sometimes she flitted from subject to subject so fast, he almost got whiplash. Like right now. But he really didn't mind.

"About what?"

Out in the hall the faint hum and purr of the copy machine provided the soundtrack to two coworkers discussing a sports match—sounded as if it might've been soccer, but Joaquin wasn't familiar enough with the local team to be sure.

"Do you mind if I close the door?" Zoe asked.

That probably wasn't a good idea, but Zoe was already on her feet. The door clicked shut, blocking out the extraneous office noise, and they were alone.

They'd be fine for a few minutes.

He had a meeting with Zoe's dad, Gerald, at three. No one was late to a meeting with the boss. He'd have to go soon, anyway. On his best days Gerald Robinson was gruff. Joaquin didn't want to know what he'd be like if someone kept him waiting because he was flirting with his daughter.

So that meant he could give Zoe fifteen minutes max.

Ten actually. He'd need a few minutes to gather his

thoughts and notes before he made his way to Gerald's office.

"What's on your mind?" he asked.

Zoe stared at her hands for a moment. Suddenly uncharacteristically somber.

"You've been here...what, three months now?"

"Something like that. I started in February."

Last December he'd moved from Miami to Horseback Hollow, Texas, a quaint little town just outside Lubbock. All but one of his brothers and his sister had moved there to be close to their father, who had relocated to work at the Redman Flight School. His dad had been mourning the loss of his wife, Joaquin's mother, and thought the change of scenery would be good for him. Horseback Hollow had agreed with his father so well that Joaquin had decided to leave Miami and give small-town living a try, as well.

Sometimes the grind of South Florida was just too much. Plus, he had accumulated too much excess baggage living there for so long. All he wanted to do was to lighten his load. But even though Horseback Hollow had been a good fit for his father and siblings—his dad was in love again, and his brothers and sister had met and married their future spouses there—the laid-back pace was way too slow for him.

He'd wanted to make a new start, but after being there only a couple of weeks he'd felt as if he was stuck in a different kind of rut in the small Texas town. When his brother Matteo's wife, Rachel, offered to put in a good word for him at Robinson Tech, Joaquin had jumped at the chance to move to Austin when Gerald Robinson, the man himself, had offered to bring him on to consult on a temporary project.

"Since you've been here," Zoe said, "you've worked pretty closely with my dad and you've had a chance to get to know him." Her words trailed off.

"I haven't worked directly with him that much. But your dad is a computer genius and I consider myself fortunate to have had the opportunity to work for Robinson."

Zoe raised a finger. "That's precisely my point. He is so smart. Sometimes too smart for his own good. How can I put this delicately? Because I adore my father, I just want what's best for him."

"Right," Joaquin said. "Everyone knows you and your father are close."

"Joaquin, will you please help me help my father improve his image? He's not exactly a diplomat or even a people person for that matter, and it's really starting to take its toll."

Oh, hell, no. That was a recipe for disaster if he'd ever heard one. He was a computer geek, for God's sake. Gerald probably knew more about diplomacy than he did. Well, that was stretching it, but not by much.

"Just the other day," Zoe continued, "I called a Robinson client who works with the South by Southwest Festival to see if I could interview him for that lifestyle blog I do for Robinson Tech. I was going to tie it into the calendar software program we have and, you know, have the event on the calendar. But you know what happened?"

Joaquin shook his head. "What happened?"

"The guy hung up on me. Before he did, he asked if this was Gerald Robinson's company and when I said it was, he called my dad a bunch of names I won't repeat and said he didn't want anything to do with anything that Gerald Robinson was involved with and he would be taking his business elsewhere. The he hung up on me. I mean, my dad has even started offending clients. So someone needs to stage an intervention. And quick."

"You want me to help you stage an intervention for your father?"

Gerald Robinson was a gruff, cranky old genius who certainly wouldn't appreciate a temporarily contracted employee butting in where he didn't belong. That was the quickest way to get him a first-class ticket out of there. Do not pass Go. Do not collect two hundred dollars.

Yet one look at Zoe's earnest face and he knew this time she was not kidding. He'd have to find a way to let her down easily.

He smiled and shook his head. "You must have me confused with someone else, Zoe. I'm the guy who's good with computers, not people. In fact, I could probably borrow some of those tips you're trying to gather up for your father. This is a delicate issue. You, his daughter, might be able to go there, but the rest of us need to tread carefully. If I got involved, I guarantee you it wouldn't be pretty."

She didn't say anything. Just stared at her hands in her lap. He hated disappointing her, but this was way out of his league.

"That website you were talking about a minute ago?" he said. "I'd rather do that. It's more my speed than making over your father's image."

She looked up and blinked as if her mind was changing gears.

"Are you saying you'll help me with the website?"

"Wait. What? No."

"But you just said you'd rather do that, and I was only half joking when I brought up the new site a minute ago. Phil in design is swamped and I could really use some help. Otherwise, I'll have to outsource the job. I can write the content, but all that technical HTML stuff is like a foreign language to me. Will you help me, Joaquin? *Please?*"

She wrinkled her nose and gave him a tentative smile that almost seemed as if she was holding her breath waiting for his answer.

The woman was a force of nature. He wasn't quite sure what she'd just done there, and he obviously didn't know what he was doing when he heard himself saying, "Sure, I'll help you with the website. Why don't we schedule a meeting?"

He thought he saw a flicker of surprise in Zoe's eyes. "Oh, thank you. Does tomorrow at three o'clock work for you?"

He called up the calendar on his phone. "I can spare a half hour."

"Well, we will just have to make the most of that time, then."

She smiled at him as she stood and smoothed her skirt. Before he could stop himself, his gaze followed the path her hands were tracing. When he realized what he was doing, his gaze skidded back up to her face so fast, if there'd been a music to accompany the moment it would've sounded like a needle scratching across a vinyl record.

Had she just played him? The treacherous waters of possibly hosting an intervention to teach Gerald Robinson manners had certainly made the thought of designing a website for the FX350 seem like a child's birthday party in comparison.

The victorious glint in her eyes tempted him to backpedal, but he didn't. And when the unspoken window of opportunity to back out closed, he knew he'd need to be careful.

He had to admit he was attracted to her. He'd have to be dead or barely breathing not to be. She was a stunningly beautiful woman, but he was not going to cross that line. He could exercise some self-control for the duration of their thirty-minute meeting.

"So, your place or mine?" The flirtatious note was back in her voice.

But before he could answer, someone knocked and opened the door. "Sorry to bother you— *Oh!*" Steffi-Anne Bunting, the office manager, stuck her blond head in but stopped midsentence when she saw Zoe standing there.

Her eyes narrowed as she looked back and forth between Zoe and him.

"Do you need something, Steffi-Anne?" Joaquin asked.

"I was just, uh—" She pointed at a clipboard in her hand. "I just noticed that we don't have your RSVP for the executive office trip to Cowboy Country. We leave this Thursday afternoon and we need a final head count. May I put you down as a yes?"

Steffi-Anne was another one who tended to pop into his office regularly. She could've emailed him about this. But since she was here now… "Actually, I sent my regrets last week. Didn't you get it?"

"Yes," Steffi-Anne said, "I got it, but—"

"You're not going?" Zoe cried. "You have to go."

Joaquin shook his head. "This is a team-building thing. I'm a temporary employee. I didn't think it was appropriate."

"It's completely appropriate," Steffi-Anne countered with a slightly condescending tone. "That's why you were invited. That's why I'm following up."

The truth was he just wasn't good at this rah-rah, team-building bull. It made him uncomfortable. No, *uncomfortable* wasn't a strong enough word. It made him feel like a caged animal. And all he wanted to do when he felt backed into a corner was get the hell out.

He looked at the two attractive women standing in his office and knew that he should've loved the fact that they both seemed to take extra interest in him. There was a time not so long ago when he would've dated both of them. At the same time, as a matter of fact. He would've reveled in the game of juggling them both, along with various other women he might've kept up in the air right along with them.

Not anymore, though.

He'd learned the hard way that office romances usually led to disaster, and he knew damn good and well that toying with emotions was the fastest way to earn an express ticket to hell.

"I'm sure you'll have a great time at Cowboy Country, but I have a lot of work to get done and a very short amount of time to accomplish it. So, thanks, but I'll have to decline."

"We'll see about that." Steffi-Anne's smile was out of context with the edge in her voice.

"Stop pushing him," Zoe said. "If he doesn't want to go, he doesn't have to."

Clutching the clipboard to her chest, Steffi-Anne

put her free hand on her thin hip. "Look, Mr. Robinson wants every employee in the executive office to go on this Cowboy Country retreat. If it makes you feel any better, Joaquin, it's for work. It's not for fun. Heaven forbid anyone ever force you to have fun. I think you'll want to clear your schedule."

His gaze snared Zoe's. Despite the way she'd defended him, there seemed to be something hopeful in her eyes. She'd be there, of course. Suddenly, the thought of attending the retreat seemed a lot more palatable.

Chapter Two

The next afternoon Zoe positioned two cappuccinos, red plastic stirrers and various packets of sugar and artificial sweetener on the corner of her desk. She turned the cups just so, then walked over to her office door and looked at them from the angle of someone just entering the room.

"That looks too posed," she murmured under her breath as she walked back to her desk.

Well, of course it did. "It *is* posed. Just be cool and casual about it."

She picked up one of the paper cups and took a sip, making sure to leave a bright red lipstick imprint before setting it closer to her computer keyboard. That way it would look less formal. Not as if she was waiting for Joaquin to drink her coffee.

For good measure she returned the other cup and

the condiments to the beverage carrier on the credenza behind her desk.

What if he didn't like cappuccino? What if it looked too presumptuous that she'd bought him a coffee? What if she drove herself crazy with all this second-guessing?

She placed her hand on her breastbone. Her heart was thudding. She took in a steadying deep breath—going in through her nose, releasing it through her mouth.

This wasn't a date, and it wasn't as if she was delivering a coffee to his office out of the blue. He was helping her with the website. It was a nice gesture. Of course it didn't seem presumptuous.

If he didn't like coffee, she would simply give it to someone else.

"What are you looking at?" The sound of Joaquin's deep voice made her jump. He was standing behind her, following her gaze with his own.

She turned to him with a sudden feeling of clarity. "You want to know the truth?"

"Of course."

"I got you a cappuccino when I went out to get myself one, and I just realized I have no idea if you even like coffee. Do you?"

"I love it," he said. "And, actually, I could use a shot of caffeine right now."

Zoe gestured toward the credenza. "Well, there you go. At your service."

As Joaquin helped himself to the lone cup in the holder, Zoe made a mental note that he didn't add any sweeteners to his coffee.

Good to know. For future reference.

"Thanks for this."

Joaquin took a long sip of his drink, set it on her desk and then proceeded to move one of her office chairs around to the other side of the desk so the two of them would be sitting side by side. She couldn't help but notice how his biceps flexed and bunched under the short sleeve of his white polo shirt. The light color showcased the deep, bronzy tan of his skin and she had a sudden mental picture of him on South Beach in Miami in a pair of board shorts and nothing else. She'd gone there for spring break when she was in college. Too bad she hadn't known him then.

It made her wonder about his life before coming to Robinson Tech. Had he dated a lot of women or did he have someone special?

"Shall we get started?" Joaquin gestured for her to sit. After she slid into her seat, he settled in next to her. He was close enough that she could smell the soap he'd used and the subtle herbal scent of his aftershave. She propped her elbow on the chair's armrest and leaned closer, breathing in a little deeper, savoring the scent of him as he pulled the wireless keyboard toward him.

Obviously he was oblivious because he was all business. With a few keystrokes he'd called up the page they needed and had signed in to a screen that looked utterly foreign to Zoe.

She centered herself in her chair, prepared to act like the consummate professional and not some lovesick puppy fawning all over him. That was the opposite of the tactics Steffi-Anne used. Zoe knew the woman had it bad for Joaquin. She and every other female in the office. But where Zoe tended to go all starry and wistful around him, Steffi-Anne became a dominatrix.

It was interesting how Joaquin didn't seem to be partial to either of them.

Professionalism was Zoe's safety net, her comfort zone. She'd gotten her job because of her ability and not simply because her father owned the company.

Steffi-Anne had made a few passive-aggressive digs about nepotism and, if Zoe were completely honest, it used to bother her, but she'd learned to let her job performance speak for itself.

That's why she needed this website to be top-notch. That's why she'd asked for Joaquin to lend his expertise.

She'd emailed him the specs and design ideas for the new site, as well as some images she'd procured for the project. Since she'd already turned in her homework and had no idea what all the numbers, letters and symbols he was keying in meant, she knew she would be no help right now.

What was the harm in making a little small talk?

"So, you like coffee," Zoe said. "What else don't I know about you?"

"What do you mean?" He kept his gaze trained on the computer monitor as his fingers tapped on the keyboard.

"I mean, I realized that we've been working together for three months and I barely know anything about you."

"I'm a private person," he said.

"So, does that mean that you won't even share basics with me? You know, the niceties that people share when they're getting to know each other? Even if it's just to make conversation?"

"Is that what we're doing? Getting to know each other? Or making conversation?"

"I'd like to get to know you."

When he didn't protest, she took it a step further.

"How about if I ask you one question and then you can ask me one after you answer mine?"

"Why do you get to go first?" he asked drily.

"If you feel strongly about it, you can go first. By all means. Please."

His hands stopped typing and he slanted a glance in her direction. So, he was going to humor her, after all. For the first time since Joaquin had walked through the Robinson Tech doors Zoe felt a glimmer of hope where he was concerned.

Casually, she shifted her weight to her right elbow and discreetly inhaled another deep breath.

"Ladies first. By all means."

"You're such a gentleman."

There were a million things she wanted to ask him, but she knew if she went right for the juicy, personal stuff, it might send him back into his shell.

So she opted for something that stayed on neutral territory to warm up the conversation.

"What did you decide about the Cowboy Country trip?" she asked. "Are you going?"

"Actually, I think I will."

"Really? Are you just trying to get Steffi-Anne off your back? The woman doesn't like to take no for an answer, does she? You'd think it was her own personal party."

"I don't know about that," he said. "But I have family in Horseback Hollow and I figured it would be a good chance to visit. But instead of riding the bus with everyone and staying with the group on Thursday, I think I'll drive down on my own and stay with my dad. I'll miss the dinner Thursday evening, but I'll catch up with everyone Friday."

"That's right. You lived in Horseback Hollow before you moved here, didn't you?"

"I'm from Miami, originally. I only lived there for a few months to be with my family before I moved here. Horseback Hollow was a little too sleepy for me."

He had a point. It probably was dull when compared to Miami. Even Austin had a different feel than South Florida. Granted, there was a lot more going on in Austin than in Horseback Hollow; Austin was edgy while Miami had more of a sultry, sexy feel.

Yes, sexy, sultry, like Joaquin Mendoza. With those brown bedroom eyes, he could've been the poster boy for everything that was exciting about Miami. She was certainly glad he'd brought that excitement into her world.

Her stomach fluttered.

Yes, she was very glad he was here now. Maybe if he continued to help with projects like this website, her father would find a permanent position for him after Joaquin had completed his temporary assignment. Then he could move here full-time.

"How do you like Austin?" she asked.

He shrugged, but just barely because his full concentration seemed to be focused on the computer screen.

"So far, so good."

Okay, that was a little noncommittal. His expression and body language were a little aloof. And he'd given a closed answer.

Maybe she should move on to another topic?

Horseback Hollow was too sleepy for him. He'd gone there to be closer to his family. She liked that. Family was everything to her, even if her siblings could be a little overbearing sometimes.

Like the way her older brother Ben had been harping on the fact that several members of the illustrious Fortune family lived in Horseback Hollow. He was obsessed with the Fortunes and the absurd notion that their own father was related to them. Between Ben and her sister Rachel who lived in Horseback Hollow, they'd managed to get their sisters and brothers on the bandwagon, too. It was causing a lot of strain with their father, who insisted there wasn't a drop of Fortune blood in his veins.

Even though Zoe was firmly on her father's side and respected his word that he wasn't related to the distinguished clan, she still thought it would be interesting to see what Joaquin had to say about them.

"So you know the Fortune family, don't you?" Zoe asked. "I mean you have a connection to them, right?"

He looked at her for a moment as if he were trying to read her.

"It's a huge clan, but I do know some of them since my brother Cisco is married to Delaney Fortune Jones, and my sister, Gabriella, is married to Jude Fortune Jones. But, honestly, I haven't spent much time around them. Why do you ask?"

Her stomach clenched and she suddenly regretted bringing up the subject. Still, she had, so she felt as if she owed him some sort of explanation.

"The Fortune name has been bandied about quite a bit these days among my family."

"Really? How come?"

Zoe sighed. "It's a long, complicated story."

Joaquin turned his attention back to the computer. "If you'd rather not say, that's fine. I really don't know them that well. If you think about it, my brother is married to your sister. So, really, there's as much of a connection between us as there is between the Fortunes and me."

She might have taken offense to that remark if he hadn't raised his brows and smiled at her in a way that sent ribbons of awareness fluttering in her stomach.

Zoe remembered the first time she'd met Joaquin. It was last year at Rachel's wedding. She'd been the maid of honor and Joaquin had been Matteo's best man. She guessed the special honor had been bestowed upon him because he was the oldest of his siblings. She wondered how he felt being the eldest and having three of his four younger siblings married before him. She knew about his family because she'd pumped her own sister for information. Then again, the order in which siblings married didn't seem to bother guys.

All she knew was that she was glad she was one of the youngest of her clan because there seemed to be something in the water in Austin, too. In addition to Rachel getting married last year, her brothers Ben and Wes had meet their soul mates this year and were living their very own happily-ever-afters.

At the rate she was going she might end up being the spinster sister, or at least the last one married. Her gaze swept over Joaquin's perfect profile and her stomach performed that somersault that was becoming all too familiar when she saw him.

"Were there any Fortunes in Miami?"

He shook his head.

"Not to my knowledge. It seems like this is bothering you a bit more than you're admitting. Sure you don't want to talk about it?"

As she looked into his eyes all she could think of was how much she'd love to talk to him about anything. Shoot, she'd even be happy sitting there discussing the complicated gibberish on the computer screen. Then again, she'd do more listening than talking since she knew so little about it.

"Can you keep a secret?" she asked.

He looked at her warily. "If this is something you shouldn't be telling me, then maybe you shouldn't."

"No, it's not really a *secret*. I mean, not one that shouldn't be told. If it was, I wouldn't talk about it. I guess what I was trying to ask is that you keep it between you and me. Of course, it's not as if you'd tell anyone here. You don't seem the type to engage in office gossip."

He chuckled. "No, gossip isn't really my thing."

He had turned his full attention on her now. As he sipped his coffee, watching her over the cup, her mouth went a little dry.

She followed suit and took a sip of her coffee before speaking. "All right. So, get this. My siblings have latched on to the absurd notion that my father is somehow related to the Fortunes."

Joaquin squinted at her, looking as confused as Zoe had felt when she'd first heard the news.

"Is he?" Joaquin asked. "It's a huge family. There are branches all over the place. It wouldn't surprise me if there were Fortunes in Austin."

"There aren't. I mean, at least there aren't any Fortune bloodlines tied to the Robinson family. My father has made that perfectly clear. I don't completely understand where my brothers and sisters got this notion, but I think they should drop the issue since our father has asked them to."

"But they keep pushing?"

"Right. My brother Ben went as far as tracking down a woman named Jacqueline Fortune. He's convinced that she is our long-lost grandmother. But get this. She had one son named Jerome—*Jerome*, not Gerald, mind you—and when Ben asked her about him, she told him that her son, Jerome, was dead. She said he died decades ago. But do you think that stopped Ben from moving ahead with this weird crusade? No, he just keeps pushing and pushing and hitting dead end after dead end. He thinks Jacqueline Fortune is mistaken."

Not only did Joaquin knit his gorgeous brows, he flinched at the notion.

"What?" he said. "Wouldn't a mother know if her son died?"

"I know, right? Apparently, Ben located Jacqueline in a memory-care unit of a nursing home. I think she is suffering from some form of dementia."

Joaquin was a good listener and Zoe appreciated it. He drew in a breath the way people do when they're weighing whether or not to say something.

When he didn't speak, Zoe asked, "What?"

"I can see that you are one hundred percent convinced that your father is telling the truth. But I still don't understand why you are asking me about the Fortunes."

"I'm not trying to dig up more evidence, if that's what you're getting at."

"No, of course not."

Zoe shrugged. "I guess I'm just curious. But, you know, let's just say even on the very far-flung chance my father was related to the Fortunes and for some reason he wanted to keep it from us... A—why would he hire you with your connection to that family? And, B—I mean, he's clearly made a new life for himself and he's asked his kids to drop it. I don't see why they're going against his wishes, continuing to doubt him and trying to dig up new evidence that proves he's lying. If he says he's not a Fortune, I think the family should respect that and leave the past in the past. What difference does it make who he used to be?"

As Joaquin sat back in his chair, his eyes darkened a shade.

"Are you asking my opinion or are those rhetorical questions?" he said.

"I'd love to hear your opinion," Zoe said.

Joaquin took in a breath and let it out slowly, as if weighing his words. "Personally, I believe a family has a right to know their roots and where they came from, even if one person thinks he has a good reason for hiding the information. I think it's better to get everything out into the open."

Now there was a faraway look in Joaquin's eyes. His expression and his words hinted that there might be something personal going on there.

"You sound like you're speaking from experience," she ventured.

"Me?" He shook his head. "We're not talking about

me. I'm just saying I believe it's not right to withhold important information like that."

For a moment he looked as if he was going to add something, but the moment came and went. Instead he said, "I also think it's nice the way you look out for your father. Everything else aside, your dad must have done something very right to raise a daughter like you."

Her heart did a strange little cha-cha-cha in her chest. Had Joaquin just complimented her? Maybe this *thing* she felt for him wasn't hopeless, after all.

Friday morning Joaquin arrived at Cowboy Country USA, a Western-themed amusement park that had opened a year ago in Horseback Hollow, ready to meet his coworkers at the Sagebrush Pavilion inside the park.

He'd made the six-hour trip from Austin to Horseback Hollow after work yesterday evening. He'd arrived at his father, Orlando Mendoza's, house around eleven o'clock, spent the night and had made it to the team-building retreat as everyone was finishing breakfast.

His coworkers had boarded a bus at the office just after noon the day before and had spent the night in Cowboy Country's Cowboy Condos. Joaquin had been relieved when Steffi-Anne hadn't hassled him about skipping the overnight portion of the trip. Sometimes the woman could be bossy and just this side of relentless, but at least she seemed to know when to back off and recognize that he was meeting her in the middle.

Inside the park's gates, he made his way down Cowboy Country's Main Street, past the old-fashioned restaurants and themed refreshment stands and gift shops. As he approached a rough-hewn wooden gate indicated on the map that Steffi-Anne had provided with the invitation, he heard gunshots and a loud round of whooping and hollering. About twenty yards down Main Street, a couple of cowboys, one dressed in white from his hat to his boots, the other clad in all black, tumbled out of the saloon, the doors swinging behind them.

"That's the Main Street Shootout show," said a park attendant who was dressed like a cowgirl and standing at the gates. "Right on schedule. Feel free to get closer if you'd like, but I must warn you, partner, they take innocent bystanders hostage from time to time."

He wondered if everyone who worked here had to stay in character day in and day out.

"Actually, I'm here for the Robinson Tech event. According to this map, I'm supposed to meet someone here who will point me in the direction of the Sagebrush Pavilion. Am I in the right place? Are you the person?"

"You certainly are and I certainly am. May I see your invitation, please? And I will direct you the rest of the way."

He scrolled up on his smartphone to the invite page and handed it to the woman. Finding it satisfactory, she handed him a map of the park that had his route sketched out with arrows. She opened the gate and ushered him through.

"Just follow the map and it will take you where you need to go. The Sagebrush Pavilion is right behind the executive office buildings. You can't miss it."

She shut the gate behind him and he was transported from the nineteenth-century cowboy town to the more modern backstage area. There, people not in costume went in and out of flat-roofed white buildings that looked like the portables that had served as extra classrooms when he was in elementary school.

In the distance he could still see the top of a huge roller coaster and hear the delighted screams of revelers as it turned a cart full of people upside down on a loop-de-loop.

Better them than me, he thought.

Then again, even though he hated roller coasters, maybe he would rather be upended on a theme-park ride than jump through the hoops of team-building exercises.

He hated rah-rah sessions like this. The forced proximity to coworkers with whom he had nothing in common had him grinding his teeth. Did retreats like this really work? Did people really grow closer after being strong-armed into mandatory fun and games?

Steffi-Anne had organized a full day of obligatory amusement for the Robinson Tech crew. She'd provided him with a schedule when he'd changed his RSVP to yes on the condition that he was released from the bus ride and overnight portion of the program. Actually, she'd thrown him a bonus when she'd told him he could arrive after breakfast because it was only provided to those who were staying in the Cowboy Condos. He certainly hadn't argued.

His dad had been glad to see him, even if it had been late when Joaquin had rolled in. They'd chatted for a few minutes before making plans to meet for dinner tonight at the Coyote Steak House just outside the Cowboy Country main gates. By that time, his coworkers would be on the bus and headed for home.

Cowboy Country was probably a fun place, but it

was quite a haul from Austin. He wondered why Gerald had chosen it for the retreat.

He thought about what Zoe had told him about her father's possible Fortune connection. Since Horseback Hollow was full of Fortune family members, it really didn't make sense that Gerald would agree to have the event here if he had anything to hide. Then again, the boss probably hadn't coordinated the event, and if the Fortune connection bothered Gerald, he probably wouldn't have hired him, either, given his own ties to the family. In addition to Cisco marrying into the family, his father was involved with Josephine Fortune Chesterfield. In fact, she would be joining them for dinner this evening. She was a wonderful woman and since his father seemed pretty serious about her, Joaquin was eager to get to know her.

However he also had some things he wanted to discuss with his father. Matters he had pushed under the rug for far too long. Funny, Zoe's confiding in him had actually brought his own family issues to the forefront.

What was behind his father's decades-long estrangement with his brother Esteban? Joaquin had a sneaking suspicion he knew. And it was high time everything was brought out into the open. Because if Joaquin was right, his father's alienation from Uncle Esteban was an issue that stretched further than a simple disagreement between the two of them.

Joaquin passed a group of modern-looking buildings and took a left at the last one. As he headed to the secluded area where the theme park hosted large groups for private events, he caught a glimpse of Gerald Robinson walking alongside one of the white buildings. It was odd that a CEO would attend a function like this, but Zoe had mentioned that her dad had meetings with Cowboy Country executives. Joaquin quickened his pace in an effort to catch up with him. It wouldn't hurt to say hello to the man who signed his paycheck and to let him see that he could be a team player.

Austin was growing on him. He liked how progressive the city was and he loved the creative freedom that Robinson Tech afforded him. If they had a permanent place for him, he wouldn't mind considering one once he completed the temporary project.

Gerald was just far enough ahead of him that he ducked into a building with a sign that read Guest Kitchen before Joaquin could catch up with him.

Joaquin veered from his path to stick his head in the door for a quick "good morning." It was a rare opportunity to get Gerald Robinson alone and probably in a good mood since he was away from the office at an amusement park, strengthening his team. Although Joaquin wanted to believe the boss hated events like this as much as he did.

That's why it paid to be the boss. You didn't necessarily have to practice what you preached. This might be a good time to ask him about specifics about the software he was writing for Robinson.

Joaquin pulled open the door and was hit by a blast of cool air. He blinked. First, to allow his eyes to adjust to the dimmer light, then out of surprise, because at the far end of the room he saw Gerald Robinson kissing a woman who was not his wife, Charlotte.

Chapter Three

Talk about being in the wrong place at the wrong time, Joaquin silently groused as he walked away. He didn't get a good look at the petite redhead in Gerald's arms because she was engulfed by his boss's large body, and Joaquin certainly didn't stay around long enough to see if he could identify her.

He quickly and quietly let himself out the same way he'd entered, hoping like hell that the sound of the door closing didn't break the couple's spell and alert them he'd witnessed their tryst.

Actually, scratch that. On second thought, part of him did hope Robinson had seen him so he would know he wasn't as sly as he thought he was. Because who brought his mistress to a team-building retreat?

Joaquin shook his head as he retraced his steps and returned to the path toward the Sagebrush Pavilion, a path from which he should've never strayed. As he turned the corner, Zoe was the first person he saw. His gaze had automatically zeroed in on her shiny dark hair and picked her out of the crowd of one hundred or so Robinson Tech employees who had gathered to become a stronger team. At the sight of her, his disgust for what he had just witnessed gave way to compassion for her. She was such a naturally kind, happy person who seemed to think only the best of people and especially saw only the good in her father.

Based on the conversation he and Zoe had had in her office the other day, she thought her father could do no wrong. The prospect of telling her what he'd seen made Joaquin's heart feel as if it would split in two.

Really, why would he tell her?

Zoe, I just saw your dad kissing a woman that wasn't your mom.

Yeah. No.

Actually he wasn't going to tell anyone. Because what good would it do? It certainly wouldn't fix anything or teach Gerald a lesson in morality. He'd only met Charlotte Robinson once in passing. For all he knew Gerald and his wife had an open marriage. Though why a woman would want to tie herself to a cheater like that baffled him.

He simply didn't get it. The whole point of marriage was to pledge your loyalty to one person. If that caused a hardship, stay single; play the field and be forthright about it. Just don't be a damn cheater.

He knew how it felt to be cheated on and it wasn't fun. He also knew playing the field was good in theory. Sometimes when you were open and honest about your intentions people still only heard what they wanted to hear.

He knew that from experience. He'd been on both sides of that relationship coin. It didn't make him eager to be in either place again.

He didn't see himself settling down and he didn't want to get back in the rat race of juggling multiple women—or making false promises to one woman, for that matter.

An image of Zoe with her beautiful, trusting smile popped into his head. Sure, he could date her. But he knew that was not what she wanted. Women like Zoe didn't take things casually.

There were too many odds stacked against them. Add in the fact that she was the boss's daughter and the tidbit about his not wanting to get serious right now—hell, he didn't even know where he'd be after this project wrapped up—and garnish it with the huge secret he knew about her father. A relationship with Zoe would never work.

He detested cheating and cheaters.

Not that he was such a do-gooder. Before he'd proposed to Selena, he'd done some things he wasn't proud of. He knew the damage deception like that could cause, and he didn't want to cause anyone that pain.

As he approached his colleagues, he shook his head to clear his thoughts. Because why was he even thinking about such ridiculous things as dating Zoe Robinson? Things like getting to know her better. Spending time with her. Kissing her—not to mention going to the places that kisses usually led.

She was the first person who saw him as he entered the pavilion. Her eyes flashed as she smiled and waved at him.

She looked adorable and bright and stylish in her pink shorts and orange top. Her dark hair was pulled back from her face with a pink-and-orange headband.

No matter the occasion, Zoe always looked as though she'd stepped out of a magazine. Not in a high-fashion sense, but in a fresh, cute, girl-next-door way.

He couldn't help but smile back at her, but he stopped short of going over and standing with her.

Yep, the only thing telling her what he'd witnessed would accomplish was heartbreak. He looked away.

Forget dating; this was precisely why Joaquin hated getting involved with his colleagues on a personal level. Knowing things about them. Now, every time he looked at Zoe, he would remember he was keeping a secret from her.

"Good morning, Joaquin," Steffi-Anne said. "Your timing is perfect. We are just getting ready to break into pairs and begin our first game. So, if you'll join group B over there under the pavilion, we'll get started."

Steffi-Anne called everyone to order.

"We're going to have a scavenger hunt," she said. "Each person in group A will draw a name out of this bag."

She held up a small brown bag with handles, the kind that you got when you purchased something in one of those fancy department stores.

"This will match you with your partner in group B. Zoe, how about if you start us off by drawing the first name?" Steffi-Anne smiled at Zoe, but the sentiment didn't seem to make it all the way to her eyes.

Joaquin had the sinking feeling she was up to something. The woman always had an agenda.

As Zoe reached into the bag to pull out a name, her gaze drifted over to Joaquin. He looked so darn good in those jeans and that white T-shirt. The color of the shirt showed off his tan, and the jeans weren't tight, but they hugged his butt in the most perfect way. It made her want to squeeze his buns to see if they really were as firm as they looked.

The naughty thought made her smile. How wonderful it would be if she pulled his name. Since she was the first to draw, she had a chance of being paired with him. However, since there were so many names to choose from, the odds were stacked against her.

She reached in and let her hand sift through the dozens of names handwritten on small slips of paper, willing her fingers to pull the golden ticket that read Joaquin Mendoza.

When Joaquin's gorgeous brown gaze connected with hers, it was like a lightning strike and she grabbed a piece of paper, sure it was the right choice.

She held her breath as she pulled it into the daylight and read, "Sissy Hanson."

Ugh. Sissy from accounting? No! Couldn't she have a do-over? No disrespect to Sissy. She was nice enough, but she wasn't Joaquin.

As Sissy came over to stand with her, Zoe did her best not to act disappointed. It would be fine. As long as Steffi-Anne didn't end up with him.

It took about five minutes before everyone had chosen a partner. Each time Joaquin's name wasn't called, putting him one step closer to Steffi-Anne, the tension in Zoe's chest wound a notch tighter.

Joaquin still hadn't been paired up by the time there were just two people left: Steffi-Anne and Jill Winski, who was the second-to-last person to draw.

After Jill drew a name, she knit her brows and looked into the bag. "I think we may be short a name. It felt like I pulled the last slip of paper."

"We should be fine," Steffi-Anne said a bit too fast.

The only people left standing in Group B were Homer Martin from IT and Joaquin.

Of course.

Zoe was willing to wager that the paper caught between Jill's forefinger and thumb read Homer Martin.

A slow burn began to simmer in Zoe's stomach.

Jill started to turn the bag upside down, but Steffi-Anne reached out and snatched it away from her before she could, poking her pointed nose into the sack.

"No, no. Look. Right here. Here it is. There's still one slip of paper left."

A vaguely victorious smile curled her lips. "Joaquin, you and I are partners for the scavenger hunt."

Oh. Well, will you look at that? What a surprise.

Before anyone could challenge the outcome, Steffi-Anne was barking orders about how they would execute the scavenger hunt, how it was important to work as a team and that there would be a nice prize for the team that won: lunch at the Copper Kettle.

As the scavenger hunt played out, Zoe noticed that the vast majority of her female coworkers were playing hard to win.

When Jill and Homer were the first to cross the finish line with their list completed, Zoe's partner, Sissy, quipped, "You know Jill didn't work that hard to have lunch with Homer. She did it to keep Steffi-Anne from winning the lunch with Joaquin."

Keep-away. Was that how this retreat had digressed? It had become one big game of keep-away. Well, in the name of team-building, Zoe intended to do her part.

Pretending not to be a sore loser, Steffi-Anne herded the group right into the next activity: the three-legged race. It would be cozy to have a legit reason to stand that close to Joaquin, arms around each other, their bodies becoming one as they reached climax—er— the *finish line*.

The *finish line*.

Good grief! Where had *that* come from?

Okay, she knew what had inspired the inappropriate thought, but she needed to get her head under control. It said a lot about the state of her love life when a three-legged race inspired thoughts of dancing the horizontal tango.

She risked a glance at Joaquin.

Then again, who wouldn't be inspired by him?

Heat began at the base of her neck and worked its way up to the tips of her ears. She took a deep breath to cool herself down before anyone noticed.

Yes, she had it bad for Joaquin Mendoza. So was she just going to stand around blushing over the predicament or was she going to do something about it?

"Zoe, would you please start us off again by pulling the name of your partner for the race?"

"You know what, Steffi-Anne? Since Jill and Homer won the last round, it's only fair that we let her draw first. Since they're such a power team, we need to make sure they don't get paired up again. Right?"

Steffi-Anne clapped her hands. "May I please have everyone's attention? We have just a few more teamwork exercises before we break for lunch and then we will have some free time in the park. Since it takes so long to draw names, why don't we make this round of pairings permanent partners for the duration of our drills? That will make things easier and give us more free time in the park."

As the bag made its way clockwise around the circle, Zoe drifted over to a picnic table a few paces behind the action. Keeping her back to the group and her ears open for the names each person announced as they drew, she took a pen out of her wristlet and retrieved the scrap of paper she'd drawn from the previous scavenger hunt round. Since she hadn't been near a trash can, she'd tucked it into the pocket of her shorts. Now, she was happy she'd done that.

Quickly and discreetly, she folded the paper, creased it and tore off the part with Sissy's name. She wrote Joaquin Mendoza on the small scrap.

If perchance he was called by one of the last few remaining people, Zoe would admit to herself that she'd been barking up the wrong tree and draw a new name from the bag. But her gut instinct told her this was rigged. She intended to draw right before Steffi-Anne and if her hunch was right, there would only be one slip of paper in that bag—and it wouldn't have Joaquin's name on it.

So she stayed back at the picnic table until the bag had made it all the way around the circle—and, oh, how interesting, no one had called Joaquin's name yet.

Zoe knew she was taking a chance by calling Steffi-

Anne's bluff. But what were the odds that out of fifty names his name was among the last two *twice in a row*?

Nah, something was definitely rotten in Cowboy Country.

Zoe held the brown bag with her left hand and, careful to hold the doctored slip of paper tight with her thumb against the palm of her right hand, she reached in and pretended to pull a name.

"Joaquin Mendoza," she said, reading the paper she'd forged. "Come on down."

"What?" Steffi-Anne pierced her with the look of death, confirming Zoe's hunch. She hadn't included Joaquin's name with the others. Since she'd gone last, she had pretended to pull his name. Did she really believe that no one would think it was odd that she drew Joaquin as a partner every single time? Worse yet, did she not think Joaquin might find it a little creepy that she'd rigged the pairings to throw them together?

It didn't matter now because Zoe would be the one getting up close and personal with Joaquin in the three-legged race and the remaining team-building exercises.

Now, he was walking toward her.

As Zoe turned to meet him halfway, she felt a hand on her shoulder.

"Well played, Zoe." Steffi-Anne's voice was low and venomous, completely at odds with that sickening smile that didn't reach her eyes. "Well played."

"What do you mean?" Zoe asked, all sugar with just enough spice mixed in to warn Steffi-Anne that she wasn't playing.

"You know exactly what I'm talking about. I know what you did."

"Oh, are you talking about how the pairings were rigged?"

Before she could answer, Joaquin walked up to them.

"Is everything all right?"

He looked back and forth between them, obviously sensing that something was off. But Steffi-Anne sprang into action.

"Everything is great. Are you having fun, Joaquin?" She reached out and touched his arm. "Aren't you glad you came?"

Zoe could tell by his expression that he wasn't buying her nicey-nicey act.

"Yeah. Sure. It's nice to spend a day outside. I don't get to do that often enough."

"Right. You know I was just telling Zoe that Cowboy Country's Main Street Shootouts are so realistic." She locked eyes with Zoe. "Almost makes you want to watch your back."

She laughed. "And, Joaquin, be sure to save me a ride on the roller coaster, okay?"

"Roller coasters?" He shook his head. "Sorry, I'm not a fan." He smiled at Zoe. "But I am looking forward to the three-legged race."

Chapter Four

"What was that about?" Joaquin asked Zoe as soon as Steffi-Anne was out of earshot.

Zoe looked as if she wanted to say something but instead opted for the high road.

"Nothing. She was just telling me about Cowboy Country. This is the first time I've been here. How about you? Did you spend any time here when you lived in Horseback Hollow?"

"No. It's my first time, too."

Zoe arched a brow. "Well, I'm glad we can share each other's *first time*. You know, make it special."

Phew! Did she realize the double entendre she was bandying about?

Of course she did. She could be a first-class flirt sometimes. When she was, it caught him off guard. He didn't quite know what to say. He didn't want to encourage her. But on the other hand, encouraging her—adding fuel to the fire—was exactly what he wanted to do.

And that latter won out handily.

"Please be gentle with me," he quipped. "I don't ride roller coasters. I'm not that kind of guy."

She locked gazes with him, her eyes sparkling.

"So, you don't like it rough and fast, huh?"

Damn, how far was she going to take this? She was killing him.

"No, I'm more of a smooth and easy kind of a guy."

"Really? Do tell."

A rush of awareness coursed through him.

Her smile was nothing short of wicked. Obviously she knew she was getting to him, but that seemed only to fuel her fire. And his, for that matter. For a moment he fought the urge to close the distance between them and show her exactly how easy things between them could be, but somewhere in the fog of his lust-hazy brain, he knew that would only muddy the waters between them.

Especially since he was already keeping a secret from her. If things became intimate between them— and God knew it was taking every ounce of restraint he could muster to not cross that line—he would have to tell her about what he'd witnessed as he'd arrived.

Or would he?

Hell, his brain was so fried with want right now, he didn't even know. The only way around it was to get out now.

He took a symbolic step back from her.

"I have a feeling Steffi-Anne is not going to go very easy on us if we hold up her race," he said. "She seems to have us on a tight schedule. Why don't we get over there now?"

Just as he'd predicted, Steffi-Anne was in a mood and she looked disheveled and frazzled, as if she was just about at her wit's end. She'd pulled her straight blond hair back into a haphazard ponytail and her yellow blouse had a dirty smudge on it. From this angle, the harsh daylight and the scowl on her face aged her about ten years.

"Yes. Let's go."

Zoe moved closer to him and pressed her pretty, tanned leg flush against his so that they were hip to hip. Well, they were in a sense. She was so petite that her hip hit his body in the upper thigh region. He loved how utterly un-self-conscious she was about invading his personal space. But the other good thing that came out of it was that he now knew for a fact that she seemed to fit perfectly under his arm. Just as if she belonged there.

And what her nicely tanned legs lacked in length they more than made up for in supple shapeliness. They looked strong and quite lovely, he thought as he bound the two of them together.

Being this close to her brought back the rush of awareness he'd felt earlier. He could smell her shampoo, something light and floral, and he could smell her soap—or maybe it was her perfume? Whatever it was, it was intoxicating and he wanted to lean down and bury his face in that sweet, delicate spot where her neck curved into her shoulder.

Being here with her like this, feeling how well she fit in his arms, was an unexpected surprise. Suddenly this team-building nonsense seemed a little more palatable.

Even though he knew getting involved with the boss's daughter was not a wise idea, it didn't mean he couldn't enjoy every single thing about being all tied up with Zoe Robinson. Win or lose.

It had been said the way a person danced revealed a lot about what kind of lover they would be. Zoe couldn't help but wonder if the same rule applied to the way a couple's bodies moved together and adapted to tests like the three-legged race and the water balloon toss. Because, if so, she and Joaquin were destined for greatness between the sheets.

They'd been beasts at the challenges that required them working together physically. Of course, it didn't hurt at all that they had permission—no, they were required—to get into each other's personal spaces and violate boundaries that were usually off-limits.

Could they please do team-building exercises every day?

Then again, if they did, Steffi-Anne would surely find some way to ensure she ended up paired with Joaquin.

Now that they were breaking for the barbecue lunch Cowboy Country was providing, Steffi-Anne was already weaseling her way back in to Joaquin's company.

It had only been natural for Zoe and Joaquin to fall into the buffet line together since they'd been partners. After they got their food—pulled chicken and barbecued brisket with baked beans, coleslaw, potato salad and ice-cold glasses of sweet tea—they'd found two spots at a table.

Steffi-Anne filled her plate and brought her lunch over to the full table where Joaquin and Zoe were sitting with six other coworkers. Zoe was sitting next to Joaquin, who was on the end.

"Scooch, please," she said, gently nudging Tracy from accounts receivable, on the opposite side of the table.

"There are plenty of places at the other tables," said Tracy.

"Yes, but this is the only table in the shade." Steffi-Anne had given the entire table the big, poor-me eyes and it had worked. Well, it had sent Tracy grumbling to another table where she could have more elbow room.

After Tracy left, Steffi-Anne zeroed in on Joaquin like a homing device.

"Aren't you glad you came today?" Steffi-Anne said.

Joaquin smiled at Zoe. "Actually, I am. I'm having a lot of fun."

The way he looked at her made Zoe's heart perform a quickstep.

"I've been dying to go ride the Twin Rattlers Roller Coaster," Steffi-Anne said. "I've been waiting for that all day."

"I've been looking forward to the funnel cakes," Zoe said. "I love them so much."

Steffi-Anne looked at her as if she'd just said she was going to go eat a bucket of fish heads.

"God, Zoe, funnel cakes are pure fat. Fat, carbs and sugar," she said. "You're young now, sweetheart, but if you keep eating things like that, you'll regret it sooner than you think."

Since when had eating a funnel cake become a capital offense?

"I enjoy the occasional one," she said. "One every five years won't hurt anything."

"Suit yourself." Steffi-Anne shrugged, her gaze scanning the picnic area. "Oh, Zoe, look. There's Ron Lowell. Didn't the two of you used to date? He's kind of cute in a bookish sort of way."

"We went out a couple of times," Zoe said, thrown by the non sequitur. "He's a nice guy, but it was nothing serious."

"Who are you dating now?" Steffi-Anne pressed.

"No one."

"I thought you had a boyfriend," she said.

"No, I'm completely free."

The way Steffi-Anne was moving the food around on her plate instead of eating it made Zoe think of a witch at her cauldron. At any moment she might pull out a poison apple and lob it at her because it was much healthier than a funnel cake.

"I'm surprised you don't have someone special by now," she continued. "You've dated a lot of really nice guys. Like Jake over there and George Simpson from marketing."

She pointed with her fork.

"And why didn't things work out with Frank? I thought you two looked especially cute together." Steffi-Anne turned her attention back to Joaquin. "I'm not saying this girl gets around. She's just very popular in the office. Joaquin, if you're interested, you'd better take a number."

Okay, so that was her game. Zoe had always known that Steffi-Anne was the queen of the backhanded compliments, but she'd never pegged her as a mean girl. Then again, she'd never gone head-to-head with her over a man.

"That's what dating is for," Zoe said, "trying out potential relationships, seeing how they fit. If they don't, there's no use in prolonging them."

Since the day Zoe had started working for her father at Robinson Tech, she'd made a point of not playing the daddy's-girl card. She realized, by virtue of birth, she'd been born with some privileges. She was deeply grateful for her blessings, and she didn't want to get the reputation that the only reason she'd gotten ahead at work was because she was the founder's daughter. It was important that she got her jobs and any promotions on the merit of her knowledge and expertise, because she was the best person for the job. Not through nepotism. She never wanted to come across as entitled. That's why she worked hard and went out of her way to be extra nice to people.

But sometimes when people like Steffi-Anne knew she wouldn't fight back, they tended to push her more than they would someone who would put them in their place.

Today, Steffi-Anne was hitting extra hard and low. Zoe wasn't about to get into a catfight with her, and she seemed to be spoiling for exactly that. Zoe really thought the woman was more professional than that. But she was dishing it out, and the others at the table looked eager to feast on a huge helping of juicy drama.

Zoe hadn't finished her lunch, but she'd lost her appetite. Maybe the best thing she could do would be to go get that funnel cake and enjoy every fat-laden bite. Part of her hated to leave Joaquin in Steffi-Anne's clutches, but if he sat back and allowed himself to be clutched, then maybe he wasn't the guy for her, after all. Better to find out now. Her heart sank at the thought.

Zoe tossed her napkin on her plate, stood and gathered the rest of her garbage. "I think I'm going to go get that funnel cake now."

To her surprise Joaquin stood, too. "I'm not surprised Zoe's popular. She's got a lot going for her. A guy would be lucky to get a date with her."

He turned to Zoe. "I'd love a funnel cake. May I join you?"

Zoe stopped at the garbage can to dispose of her trash. She took a deep breath and tried to shake off the sting of Steffi-Anne's words. Swallowing the urge to fight back when someone came at her swinging wasn't easy. It was human nature to want to defend oneself, but the perverse part was that doing so would've made her look just as bad as Steffi-Anne.

Joaquin must have read her mind because he tossed away his trash and said, "Come on, let's get out of here."

They walked in silence as they made their way toward the exit of the backstage area. But before they made it to the park, Zoe caught sight of her father and waved.

"Where are you two off to?" Gerald asked. He always came across so gruff, but Zoe knew he was a big softy on the inside. She wished more people knew him the way she did.

"We are going in search of funnel cakes." Zoe planted a kiss on his cheek. "When did you get here?"

"I drove down last night," Gerald said. "Had business to tend to."

"Joaquin." Gerald stuck out his hand and Joaquin gave it a firm shake.

"Hello, sir."

Her father liked him. That scored Joaquin huge points in Zoe's book. As if he needed extra ones.

It was another quality she could check off her potential Husband List. Suddenly things were looking a lot brighter than they had a moment ago.

"Is lunch over?" Gerald asked. "I wanted to say a few words to the staff."

"No, the group is still over there," Zoe said. "We're just sneaking away a little early to get some dessert."

"Good," Gerald said. "I'm glad I didn't miss it. I've been busy all morning. This is the soonest I could get away. I'll let you two go and get on with your business. Joaquin, you take good care of her. She is my little girl."

He sounded stern but Zoe knew he meant well. She liked the way Joaquin held up under his scrutiny.

Check.

"Yes, sir," Joaquin said.

Her father gave a curt nod and walked away.

Once they'd stepped out from behind the fence and onto Main Street, Joaquin said, "Your dad is pretty protective."

She wanted to say, *Yes, but don't let him scare you off.*

"You know how fathers can be. Don't you? Are you close to your family?"

Shrieks and whoops filled the air as log-shaped cars splashed down the final drop of the Gulch Holler Rapids water flume ride. The waterlogged merriment was set against the *pow-pow-pow* of pistols from the Main Street Shooting Gallery, which was located next door.

"We are pretty tight," he said as they strolled past Gus's General Store where a cute straw cowgirl hat caught Zoe's eye. She decided to look at it later so as not to interrupt what Joaquin was saying. "I stayed with my dad last night and I will again tonight. After we're finished here, I'm meeting him for dinner at the Coyote Steak House just outside the main gates."

So, not only was the guy smart and gorgeous, but he was family oriented, too. Could he be any more perfect?

Check. Check. Check.

She had to resist closing her eyes to revel in the thought and the smell of funnel cakes cooking somewhere nearby.

"May I ask you a personal question?" Joaquin said.

Zoe's heart leaped into her throat. She had to wait for it to settle back into her chest again before she could answer. Even then it beat a thrilling staccato.

"Sure. Ask me anything." And she meant it.

He could ask her out.

He could ask her to marry him.

He could ask her to—

"Why do you let Steffi-Anne get away with acting like that?"

Oh. Except for that.

She had hoped that they'd left Steffi-Anne back at the pavilion. But here she was again, virtually elbowing her way between them like a ghost they couldn't exorcize.

"I'm not letting her get away with anything," Zoe

said, making sure her voice was steady and matter-of-fact but not defensive. "I choose to not respond. Because when you react to a bully like her, you're playing right into her hands. Don't you see it? What she wants most is a reaction from me, and I'm not going to give it to her."

Joaquin watched her intently as she spoke, nodding his head as though he agreed with her.

"Actually, getting a reaction out of me probably falls second to getting one out of you," Zoe said. "Just sayin'. Because you know she wants you to ask her out."

She was happy when he flinched, as if the suggestion was the furthest thing from his mind. And her heart nearly leaped out of her chest when he frowned and said, "That's not going to happen. I'm not interested in Steffi-Anne."

She wished she could've paused the moment—that perfect moment when she knew exactly where her nemesis stood with the man of her dreams—but he ruined the moment when he said, "I don't date women I work with."

Well, why the heck are you sending me mixed signals? Why did you sit with me at lunch, defend me to Steffi-Anne, make me want you in the worst way, when it was all for nothing?

But before she could respond or even mask her expression to make sure it didn't expose the utter disappointment that had eclipsed all the joy she had been feeling a moment ago, a street performer dressed in period costume planted his feet in front of them. His big voice boomed, "Gather 'round, all ye good people. I do believe I have found the happy couple who will be the next victims—er—the next bride and groom I will unite in connubial bliss in the Cowboy Country Matrimonial *Extraaaavaganza*."

Somehow the man, whom Zoe now realized was wearing a sash that read Honorable Justice D. Peace, managed to hook his arms through Zoe's on the right and Joaquin's on the left and herd them toward a small stage raised about ten inches off the ground.

"What in the world—?" Zoe asked.

"Does our beautiful, blushing bride have cold feet? Please tell me I am mistaken. Honey, your groom looks bucking ready to go. I think he has the wedding night on his mind."

As he made a couple more jokes, a player–pipe organ started churning out a dramatic version of the "Wedding March." A woman dressed in period costume with a sash that read Matchmaker made an overblown show of fawning over Zoe and Joaquin. She shoved a wispy tulle veil onto Zoe's head, placed a bouquet of tattered-looking flowers in her hands and thrust a tall top hat at Joaquin.

The music and the fuss the performers were making over them drew a crowd.

"Oh, my gosh," Zoe said. "Like it or not, I guess we're part of the show."

"You only live once." Joaquin shrugged and placed the top hat on his head at a cocky angle, playing the good sport. "I said I don't date coworkers. I didn't say anything about not marrying them."

Chapter Five

The best souvenir that Zoe was taking home from Cowboy Country was being pronounced Joaquin's pretend wife. Even though the marriage wasn't real—obviously— for a few fabulous hours, it was fun to pretend she was his wife and they were on their honeymoon in Cowboy Country.

She even had the gaudy plastic ring on her left hand to prove it.

It was so romantic, in a kitschy-fun sort of way. Joaquin had been a great sport, playing along and even hamming it up a little bit. It was a side of him she'd never seen before.

As she waited in line to get on the charter bus that would take everyone back to Austin, her thumb found the back of the band. Joaquin had seemed pretty firm about not dating someone he worked with. But he had said that marriage was not out of the question. Okay, so that statement was as pretend as the plastic ring on her finger. It didn't change her feelings for him; if anything, it made her desire him more. It was evident to everyone else who was paying attention that Steffi-Anne was his for the taking. And there were also a dozen or so other women in the office interested in him. At least they'd had the good grace not to be so obvious.

But he didn't seem to be out for what he could get. That was a very attractive quality in a man. So was him having the good sense to know that office romances could get sticky. That's why Zoe was willing to take things slowly. As Steffi-Anne had so gleefully pointed out, Zoe had had her share of office romances that fizzled out for one reason or the other. She'd loved what Joaquin had said at lunch about it being okay to have dated a lot of guys. He was right. How would she ever find her prince if she didn't kiss a few toads along the way?

"Did you have fun, Zoe?" Steffi-Ann asked through her Cheshire cat grin as she checked in Zoe, ticking her name off the passenger roster.

"I had a great time, thank you," Zoe said, infusing a smile into her voice, determined to kill her with kindness. "Look at this cute cowgirl hat I bought."

As Zoe reached for the package, she realized her wristlet that held her phone, her credit cards and all her money wasn't on her arm. She looked in her bags and patted herself down, but it wasn't there.

Panic seared through her.

"Steffi-Anne, I don't have my purse," Zoe said as she excused herself past the others who were waiting in line to get on the bus. "I have to go find it. I'll be right back."

Mentally, she retraced her steps. She'd probably set it down during the wedding show. But no, she'd purchased the cute little straw hat with a pink gingham band at Gus's General Store. After that, she and Joaquin had ridden a couple of rides. Next they'd gone to the Patty's Cakes Funnel Cake stand and stopped by Foaming Barrel Root Beer to get something to drink before he said goodbye to go meet his dad. That meant she'd left it at either Patty's Cakes or the Foaming Barrel. But Joaquin had paid for the cakes and the root beer.

Her purse could be anywhere.

She jogged as fast as she could back to Patty's Cakes. It was almost at the farthest corner of the park, away from the entrance.

"Excuse me, I was here earlier and I think I may have left my purse and phone. It's small, pink, has a loop so I can wear it over my wrist." Zoe pointed to her arm. "Please tell me someone turned it in."

The kid shook his head. "Sorry, no one has turned in anything like that. You might want to try Lost and Found."

The woman behind her made a sympathetic noise.

Zoe's heart sank. It was getting late and she knew she was holding up the bus. Maybe she'd have to give up the search for now. She didn't want to keep everyone waiting. She would've called Steffi-Anne to let her know she'd be right there, but she didn't even have a phone.

"Where is Lost and Found?" she asked, just in case it was nearby.

"Up front," said the guy. "Right by the exit."

Well, that was good, but it didn't do much to calm the panic festering inside her at the thought of losing her phone. It contained all of her contacts—phone numbers, addresses, her schedule, her life. Without it, she wouldn't know her next move.

She swallowed the mounting hysteria.

She thanked the guy and jogged toward the main gates. She would tell her coworkers what she was doing and then run and check Lost and Found. If it wasn't there, perhaps they could assist her with calling the other locations in the park.

It had been a long time since she'd run this far this fast, and her lungs were about to burst when she finally made it to the front. She breathed in great gulps of air as she walked to where the bus was parked.

Or—where it was supposed to be parked?

It wasn't there.

Frantically, Zoe looked around, trying in vain to locate it. Cowboy Country wasn't that large. Not like Disney World. There was only one place for buses, and this was it.

But the bus wasn't there. Had they left without her?

Her heart pounded in her chest like a caged bird thrashing against its pen. As horror slowly morphed into fury, she realized that the bus had indeed taken off without her.

She had no money, no phone and no way to get in touch with anyone. Then her gaze found the Coyote Steak House, where Joaquin was dining with his father.

As much as she had wanted to spend more time with him, she didn't want to do it like this—barging in on his family time, prevailing upon him to be her knight in shining armor whether he wanted to be or not.

She would look so stupid—worse yet, this would look so contrived. So planned. Steffi-Anne-level manipulation. But she had no choice, unless she wanted to start walking back to Austin.

Instead she took a deep breath and prepared herself to take the interloper's walk of shame.

"The new job sounds like it's agreeing with you, son," said Orlando Mendoza as he helped himself to a dinner roll out of the basket and smeared a slab of butter on his bread plate.

"It is," said Joaquin. "I like it very much. Although it doesn't seem like a new job anymore. It's already been three months."

The aroma of grilled steak filled the dimly lit restaurant and Joaquin's stomach growled in anticipation. The place was decorated in upscale cowboy chic. The walls were painted a deep green color, which set off the various cow heads and longhorn trophies intermixed with framed photos of famous country singers and rodeo champions.

"Has it been that long already?" asked Josephine Fortune Chesterfield. Her proper British accent sounded crisp and neat. "Where does the time go? Don't get me wrong, we've missed you living in Horseback Hollow. But time does fly."

His father had been seeing Josephine for a while now—since Orlando had moved to Texas from Miami a couple of years ago. Not only did they seem happy, they seemed to be getting serious. Although, Joaquin didn't know what *serious* actually entailed for someone like his father. He couldn't imagine him married to anyone else but his mother, but he did want Orlando to be happy and he couldn't have handpicked a better woman for him than Josephine.

He felt that old familiar tug of apprehension. He had things he needed to discuss with his father. Questions that he'd kept buried for far too long that needed to be brought out into the daylight and have the truth shone on them.

His mother had been gone for four years now and it had been so long since he'd seen his father smile. He'd taken her death hard. It hadn't seemed right to add to his suffering by opening a can of worms.

He was holding Josephine's hand and they were exchanging a look that belonged to lovers who had made it through the uncertainty of a new relationship and were firmly grounded in a confidence of where they wanted to be, where they belonged.

Orlando had finally remembered how to smile again.

Now it didn't seem right to mess that up by telling him Joaquin knew he wasn't his birth father. Maybe Orlando knew the truth. If he didn't, it meant his mother—the love of Orlando's life—had cheated on him. Joaquin had a pretty good idea whom she'd slept with.

The issue was too important not to get some answers. But not tonight, of course. Not with Josephine here. Maybe this weekend. He'd have to gauge it.

"Have you given any thought to what you're going to do once this project is over?" Orlando asked.

Joaquin took a long pull of his beer. It tasted good after spending the day outdoors and it took the edge off his appetite. Even though he and Zoe had eaten their fill of funnel cakes and drunk a good amount of root beer, he was hungry for some real food.

Spending the afternoon walking and talking with Zoe had given him an appetite. And not for food. If he were completely honest with himself, he was hungry to see her again. He'd have to give that some thought this weekend, too. Given the way things had turned out back in Miami, he should've learned his lesson about messing with the boss's daughter, but Zoe Robinson was a far cry from Selena Marks.

Selena was another type of daddy's girl, a different brand than Zoe, who seemed much too sweet to sleep with her fiancé's best friend the way Selena had done. Selena took what she wanted when she wanted it, no matter whom she hurt. But Zoe seemed like a breath of fresh air compared to the suffocating pitch-black of Selena's darkness. That was probably why he was tempted to break his number-one rule: no inter-office romance.

"Funny you should ask," Joaquin said in response to his father's question. "I have been thinking about the future. I wouldn't mind taking a permanent position with Robinson if they had something for me. Gerald Robinson is an interesting guy."

He glanced at Josephine to see if she had any re-action to the mention of Gerald Robinson's name, but she didn't. She simply smiled at him and looked as if she were waiting for Joaquin to expound.

"Josephine, I heard something interesting about Gerald Robinson. Do you remember him from Matteo and Rachel's wedding? He's Matteo's father-in-law."

"Yes, of course," Josephine said.

"There's a rumor that Gerald is related to the Fortunes. Have you heard anything about that?"

Josephine cocked her pretty gray head to the right. "I haven't heard a thing about that. But the Fortunes are a large and ever-expanding clan. I wouldn't rule out anything. Look at my story, how I ended up finding out I was related to them."

She had a point. It was an interesting saga, like something out of a novel. After more than half a century spent growing up in England, she'd learned she was adopted. Not only that, but that she was part of a set of triplets—two girls and a boy. She and her sister, Jeanne Marie, had been put up for adoption when they were babies. All these years later their brother, James Fortune, had learned of the existence and stopped at nothing until he'd found his long-lost sisters.

When Josephine, a widow, had learned of her new family connections, she'd moved to Horseback Hollow to be closer to her family. That was when she'd met Orlando. From what Joaquin had heard, it had been love at first sight but a relationship slow to take root.

Could Gerald Robinson have a similar connection to the Fortunes that he didn't know about, the same way Josephine and her sister hadn't known all those years? Zoe was adamant that wasn't the case. He probably shouldn't even have brought it up to Josephine. It was best to let the subject drop.

"Robinson stays out of my way for the most part," Joaquin said. "He lets me do my own thing. Of course, I get my work done. So he has no reason to crowd me. But it's a good atmosphere. It's stimulating and I like my coworkers."

Zoe's face came to mind. Actually he hadn't been

able to get her out of his head. Those big brown eyes. That smile. The sound of her laugh. The way he'd wanted to kiss her when they had ridden the Ferris wheel today. And how, for a crazy second, he had thought about asking her to ditch the bus ride back and stay with him here in Horseback Hollow for the weekend. But just as fast, he'd come to his senses. He'd blamed it on the altitude of the Ferris wheel, which was a lame excuse, of course. Almost as lame as the idea of her spending the weekend with him.

Maybe not lame, exactly.

Unwise. Reckless.

Tempting as hell.

His reckless days of buckling under temptation were over. If he knew what was good for him and her—for both of them—he'd stop thinking about her right now, look at the menu and figure out what he wanted to eat. Then he would focus his mental energies on how he would broach the subject of his paternity and his father's estrangement with Esteban once they'd said goodnight to Josephine.

As he lowered his gaze to study the menu, he caught a glimpse of a woman across the dimly lit steak house that reminded him of Zoe.

Now he was imagining her. Hell, he was conjuring her—the woman could be her twin. Her identical twin. Dressed in an orange blouse and pink shorts—

Oh, for God's sake, that *was* Zoe. She looked a little frantic.

Joaquin stood and waved at her, and relief seemed to wash over her as she headed in their direction.

"Who are you waving at?" Orlando asked, looking in the direction Joaquin was facing.

"It's Zoe Robinson. Gerald Robinson's daughter. Hey, please don't mention anything about the rumors about his Fortune connection."

"I remember Zoe from Matteo and Rachel's wedding," Orlando said. "I won't mention anything."

Josephine nodded in agreement and Orlando stood as Zoe reached the table.

"Hi, I'm so sorry to barge in like this," Zoe said. She looked at Josephine and Orlando. "Hello, I'm Zoe. I work with Joaquin. I'm so sorry to interrupt your dinner. But I have a minor emergency. I need to borrow Joaquin's phone."

"Hi. Uh, no, it's fine," Joaquin said. "You're not interrupting. We haven't even ordered yet. What's wrong?"

Orlando cleared his throat.

"Zoe, this is my father, Orlando Mendoza, and Josephine Fortune Chesterfield. I believe you met briefly at Rachel and Matteo's wedding."

Zoe's eyes flashed at the mention of the Fortune name and her gaze swept over Josephine. It was so subtle that no one else probably caught it. Especially because she smiled sweetly and greeted them both.

"Yes. Of course, I remember you. Please, carry on with ordering. Don't let me interrupt. Joaquin, if I could borrow your phone, I'll just take it into the lobby and make my call."

He handed it to her. "Sure, but what happened to yours?"

She always seemed to have it with her. He knew she'd had it today in the park because she'd been afraid it would get wet when they rode the Gulch Holler Rapids log flume ride.

"I don't know." Her voice sounded shaky. "And—" She covered her face with her free hand for a quick moment. "This is so embarrassing. I must've lost it in the park. I realized it after I'd checked in to get on the bus. Before I went to look for it, I told Steffi-Anne that I'd be right back, but she must not have heard me because the bus left without me. Now, here I am stranded with no phone and no money and I'm just thanking God that you are here because I don't know what I would do if you weren't. Well, actually, Rachel lives in Horseback Hollow and before I bothered you I used the restaurant's house phone to call her, but she's not picking up."

"You are not bothering us," Orlando interjected. "The reason you can't get hold of Matteo and Rachel is that they're out of town for the night. But you have nothing to worry about. We will take care of you. Please join us for dinner."

Orlando gestured to the empty seat next to Joaquin.

"Oh, thank you. That's so kind of you to offer, but I can't impose like that."

"Looks like you don't have many other options," Joaquin joked. "So you might as well."

He gestured to the empty chair next to him. Zoe's face clouded and he realized his words might not have sounded as humorous as he'd meant them.

"Thank you," she said. "But I'll call Steffi-Anne and ask if they can come back and get me."

She squeezed her eyes shut for a moment and Joaquin knew even the thought was humiliating to her. What the hell was wrong with Steffi-Anne to go off and leave her stranded like that?

"Do you really want to do that?" he asked.

"No, of course not. But as you said, I'm sort of short on options."

"Do you know her phone number, because I certainly don't have it?" Joaquin said.

Zoe frowned. "No, I don't. Okay, time for plan C. Will you lend me some money for a place to stay tonight? I will pay you back as soon as Rachel gets home and she can take me back to Austin."

"Nonsense," said Orlando. "The closest hotel is the bed-and-breakfast in Vicker's Corners. There is no need for you to stay there when I have plenty of room at my house. I insist that not only you stay with us tonight but that also you join us for dinner."

Orlando flashed his trademark winning smile and it seemed to work on Zoe because she heaved a full-bodied sigh and her entire demeanor changed. She glanced at Joaquin as if to make sure he was amenable to his father's suggestion.

They would be sleeping under the same roof tonight. A frisson of awareness sparked inside him. What would her body feel like pressed against his? What would it be like to wake up with her in his arms? He blinked away the thoughts because he wouldn't find out tonight. She was in a vulnerable position right now. She was depending on him. He would never take advantage of her. The thoughts brought out a protectiveness he didn't know he possessed. "Please, join us," Joaquin tried again. "There's an empty place right here next to me, just waiting for you."

Chapter Six

What a way to meet the parents—or *parent*, in this case—Zoe thought as she bid Orlando good-night from the couch in front of the fireplace in the expansive living room of his ranch-style home. He was such a nice man. He'd made her feel so welcome. Not as though she was an idiot who had lost her purse, missed the bus and barged in on their dinner, which was all true.

Or worse yet, he had not suggested that she might be a manipulator who had manufactured the excuse simply to spend time with his son, which was 100 percent untrue, but still made her cringe thinking about how it looked.

No, both Orlando and Joaquin had been nothing but gracious, right down to opening an after-dinner bottle of wine and building a fire in the fireplace.

Even though it had been a pretty day with temperatures in the low seventies, the thermometer had dropped into the forties tonight. It was downright chilly.

Now that Orlando was retiring for the night, she and Joaquin would be left alone to finish the bottle of merlot. The realization left her nearly breathless. So, she turned her thoughts on expressing her appreciation to Orlando.

"Thanks, again, for the dinner and your generous hospitality, Orlando. I really don't know what I would've done without you and Joaquin."

After dinner the four of them had gone to the lost and found to see if anyone had turned in her wristlet and phone, but no one had. The manager on duty had taken her name and contact information and had promised to call her if they turned up.

"It was my honor and pleasure to welcome such a lovely guest," Orlando said. "I hope you will be very comfortable tonight. If you need anything, please don't hesitate to ask. Either Joaquin or I will be happy to get it for you."

He smiled warmly and gave a quick parting salute as he left the room. She knew instantly where Joaquin had gotten his good looks and gentlemanly manners.

Josephine had been wonderful, too. Kind, engaging and interesting to talk to. If she was representative of what the Fortune family was like as a whole, being related to them might not be such a bad thing, after all. But Zoe hadn't brought up the subject of her father's possible connection to the clan.

Given the way Gerald had so vehemently denied it, broaching it felt like a betrayal. Besides, who knew how Josephine felt about the rumors—if she'd even heard them. Why risk ruining what had turned out to be a perfectly lovely dinner with potentially upsetting talk of hearsay and speculation?

Zoe had been stranded and they had rescued her. She was touched by how warmly they'd included her and offered her a place to stay until she could reach Rachel, who, according to Orlando, was supposed to return tomorrow morning.

But that seemed light-years away.

Right now she and Joaquin were alone. Soft music played on the stereo and something electric vibrated between them. Was this really happening? Was she really *spending the night* with Joaquin?

The thought made her a little light-headed and it also scared her more than a wee bit. They hadn't even been on a date. In fact, until today, she hadn't even been sure Joaquin wanted to be her friend. He was a puzzle. Gruff and silent one minute, but then he showed up when it really mattered.

And now here they were. Alone, sharing a bottle of wine and conversation that, for once, wasn't about work.

She'd seen a different side of Joaquin today. A more human and personal side of him. She'd loved how relaxed he'd been. How natural things had felt between them.

But despite their easy-going good time at Cowboy Country, she realized that there was still so much about him that she didn't know.

Nothing else would happen between them tonight, as much as her body begged to differ. There wasn't going to be any hanky-panky, but she fully intended to leave here knowing him better.

"Would you like some more wine?" he asked, picking up the bottle and pouring more into her glass even before she had a chance to answer.

"Are you trying to get me drunk?" she joked. "Because I usually don't drink much."

One side of his mouth kicked up, just the hint of a smile. He refilled his own glass and sat back against the sofa cushions.

That was a good sign. It meant he was in no hurry to call it a night and head to their separate bedrooms, which were at opposite ends of the hall from each other.

When they'd gotten back to the house, Orlando had showed her to her room, which had an en suite bathroom. He had set out fresh towels and a new toothbrush. He'd asked Joaquin to get her a blanket from the closet in the room where he was staying. Joaquin said he would and also agreed to lend her one of his T-shirts to sleep in. But for now they sat on the couch in front of the fire, not so close that it might suggest crossing that line, but certainly close enough to edge right up to that line. Whether his interest was strictly platonic or more personal and much more exciting remained to be seen.

Now that they were alone, though, she felt as if she owed him some sort of explanation.

"I'm so sorry for this," she said.

He sipped his wine. "For what?"

"For barging in on your dinner and putting you in the position to have to take me in. My sister should be home tomorrow. I'll get out of your hair once she gets back."

"No worries," he said. "In fact, if you want, you can

hang out until Sunday. That's when I'm returning to Austin. You can ride back with me."

Another day in paradise and then a six-hour car ride back? It was so tempting.

"Rachel was planning on going to Austin tomorrow for some family business," she said. "We've been having regular meetings on that issue involving my father that I told you about. But thanks, anyway. I just want to make sure you didn't think I did this on purpose."

The second the words escaped her lips, the phrase "the lady doth protest too much" sprang to mind.

"You didn't?" he said.

She wanted to die until his mouth quirked up again and she realized he was kidding. Joaquin Mendoza had a sense of humor. Another checkmark in the sexy-as-hell column on the Husband List.

"For the record, *no*, I did not do it on purpose. I'm sure it might look that way. Especially after Steffi-Anne took such pleasure in pointing out all the guys I've dated."

"To put your mind at ease, I figured you wouldn't intentionally ditch your purse and cell phone just to spend the night with me."

"Another item for the record, I haven't spent the night with all the guys I've dated. Even though she made it sound like that, it's not true."

"Good to know."

"Well, personally, I was surprised you didn't have Steffi-Anne's phone number in your phone."

"I have no reason to call her. Why would I have her number in my phone?"

"I thought she would've at least punched in the digits herself. To make sure you could get in touch with her. You know, in case of an emergency. I guess she's falling down on the job."

"Guess so."

The two drank their wine as the fire blazed and music played in the background. Zoe recognized the song from a Ray Lamontagne CD she loved, but she couldn't remember the name of the track. She wanted to commit the melody to memory because it fit the mood so perfectly.

She had no idea where this was going, if it was even going anywhere. That's why she wanted to sip the moment slowly, savor it so it would last. Because this—being with him, just the two of them here with their defenses down—was something she could get used to.

"Do you need to call anyone to let them know you're here? Because once they realize you weren't on the bus, don't you think they'll worry? Especially if they try your phone and you don't answer."

"When I was at the restaurant, before I found you, I called my brother Ben. I left a message on his voice mail and told him I'd lost my purse, but I would catch a ride back to Austin with Rachel."

Joaquin frowned. "Won't he worry if he knows that Rachel isn't home and no one can get in touch with you?"

"Nah, it's just one night. It's fine."

Ah, this was a little tricky to explain. It dawned on her that while they were both close to their families, they were a *different* kind of close. His was obviously tightly knit. The kind of closeness she longed for one day. But her family—they were so busy going in opposite directions, racing toward their various goals and agendas, they probably wouldn't miss her if she was incommunicado for one night.

The thought was sobering. What did that say about the Robinsons? To outsiders looking in, they probably seemed like the family that had everything. And they really didn't want for much. But her parents were like two trains on different tracks. They shared the same station, but came and went on different schedules. The same could be said for her siblings. They worked together, yet maintained separate lives in the same city. Except for Rachel, who had made an enviable life for herself here in Horseback Hollow. Zoe had been completely unaware that Rachel and Matteo would be away tonight or even where they were going. Not that they needed to check in. It was just a different dynamic than Joaquin had with his family, and it made Zoe wish the Robinsons were a little more connected.

This "Fortune hunt" her siblings were on was turning out to be polarizing. Ben was at one end of the spectrum with his dogged determination and she was on the other end, the lone supporter of their father's wishes to leave well enough alone. The rest of her brothers and sisters were either on Ben's side or somewhere in the middle.

Maybe she could be the one to stop this nonsense and bring them all together at their family meeting on Monday.

"Where'd you go?" Joaquin's voice brought her back to the present. He was gazing at her intently and it unleashed a swarm of butterflies that performed a loop-de-loop in the pit of her stomach.

"I was just trying to think of how to say that even though my family is tight, we're *different*."

"What do you mean?"

Zoe shrugged. "It's hard to explain. They would certainly be concerned if they thought something had happened to me. But we're not the type to check in. But on the other hand, if I called my dad and told him that the bus left without me, he'd go ballistic. He would probably fire Steffi-Anne. I'm not kidding. He's superprotective of me. Maybe it's because I'm one of his youngest. Or maybe it's because, despite his gruff and bluster, we've always understood each other. Or maybe I should say, I understand him and he is protective of me. So, he can't know about the bus, okay?"

Joaquin cocked his head to the right. "Despite all the crap Steffi-Anne pulls on you, you're not going to put her in her place?"

"Don't get me wrong, I'm not afraid of her. I just don't ever want to contribute to someone losing her job. You never know what motivates people to act the way they do. Maybe it's insecurity. Maybe it's jealousy, though I'm not suggesting she's jealous of me. Although I can guarantee you she would be if she knew I was sitting here with you like this."

A lock of hair had fallen onto Joaquin's forehead and Zoe reached out and smoothed it back into place. Joaquin caught her hand and pulled her closer.

The next thing she knew, his lips were on hers. The kiss started whisper-soft, tentatively at first, as if he were testing the waters. When she leaned in and opened her mouth, inviting him in, he deepened the kiss. The world disappeared for a moment and the only thing Zoe was aware of was the feel of his lips on hers and that he tasted like something she'd been craving her entire life. She would've been perfectly content if the rest of the world had broken away, leaving the two of them to become one.

Time drifted and she had no idea how long the kiss lasted. It could've been a moment or a lifetime, but when it finally tapered off and they reclaimed their personal spaces, Zoe knew she was forever changed.

It was just a kiss, but it had been so much more than that. Because even as innocent as it had been, she'd given him a part of her she didn't want back. In fact, she wanted to give him more.

That was why it was probably a good thing when he stood, looking a little disoriented, and said, "We should probably call it a night. Let me get you that blanket and T-shirt."

He'd kissed Zoe. What the hell was wrong with him?

He couldn't shake the self-flagellation even three days later as he sat in his office on Monday morning. He was an idiot. He should've had more self-control than that. She deserved better. Certainly more than he could offer. But there was something about Zoe that rendered him stupid.

Her sister had called first thing Saturday morning. Before he and Zoe had been able to talk about what had happened and how they should move forward, Rachel and Matteo had arrived to say hello to Joaquin and whisk Zoe away.

He'd had the rest of the weekend to beat himself up and set himself straight. He hadn't seen her since she'd driven away with Rachel and Matteo, but he'd decided he'd gauge how she acted toward him and then see if they needed to talk and he needed to make things right. For all he knew, now that she'd had time to gain some distance and put everything into perspective, she might be just as sorry as he was that they had crossed that line. Yeah. It was unlikely, judging by her body language Saturday morning.

She had looked beautiful, all fresh-faced and natural. That's probably how she would look if they woke up together.

He leaned back in his desk chair, lacing his fingers behind his neck and looking up at the ceiling. *Sorry* was a strong word to describe how he was feeling. He *was* sorry he'd initiated the kiss and had put them in this situation, but he'd be lying to himself if he didn't concede that in the moment he had enjoyed every last second of it. But he'd been down this path before. He'd made the mistake of messing with the boss's daughter and if that experience had taught him one thing, it was that you don't play with people's emotions.

He should know. He'd been the biggest player in Miami until one spoiled, rich woman had played the player and taught him a lesson he couldn't forget. A lesson he'd be wise to remember now.

Zoe deserved someone who could offer her everything she wanted. He could not promise that right now. He didn't even know where he'd be when this project at Robinson ended. Knowing Gerald Robinson, if Joaquin hurt Zoe in any way, he'd have to deal with the big guy.

Joaquin had to figure out his own head before he'd be capable of knowing what he could offer anyone else. And, of course, there was the issue with his dad. He needed to get that out into the open and get to the heart of that matter before he could move on. If things turned out the way his hunch thought they would, it would be a game changer of unfathomable magnitude. He couldn't even wrap his mind around it yet. Because of that, he hadn't broached the subject with his dad after Zoe left. Josephine had come over and cooked a fabulous breakfast for them. And Orlando was smiling. Joaquin was pretty sure his dad was in love again. That was such a good thing since, when his mom died, it had seemed as if his father had lost his will to go on. Because Luz had been the love of Orlando's life.

The paternity bombshell Joaquin was about to drop was of nuclear proportions. Sometimes, such as when he saw the way Orlando had looked at Josephine, Joaquin wondered if exposing the truth was even worth it. Because if his mother had cheated, it might very well change Orlando's ability to love, similarly to how Selena had shattered the way Joaquin looked at just about everything.

But, he reminded himself, there was a lot more at stake than having a second chance at love or having the carpet yanked out from under him by a woman. The secret he harbored affected more people than Orlando and Josephine.

Even if they'd have a lot rebuilding to do after Joaquin dropped the bomb, it was something that couldn't be swept under the rug any longer.

He returned his attention to his computer, ready to get to down to business, when a message notification popped up in the bottom right corner of the screen.

It was from Zoe. His chest clenched as he clicked on it.

Are you still up for meeting about the website at 9:00?

The website?

That's right. Last week they had agreed to meet again today to work on it.

He knew darn good and well they'd have to talk about the weekend. He really didn't want to have this conversation here, because it was bound to make things awkward. But he couldn't put it off forever. The best thing he could do would be to show her that, as far as he was concerned, everything could still be normal.

My office or yours?

He waited for a response but it came in the form of a knock on the door.

"Come in," he said.

Zoe closed the door behind her and walked into his office looking bright and shiny and beautiful. Her long dark hair hung in loose waves down her back. She wore a red dress with a short black jacket. The outfit danced the fine line between professional and flirty. But if anyone could pull it off, she could. She had painted her lips bright red to match the dress.

His mouth went dry and his heart twisted a little. Because, though every bit as beautiful, this polished, professional Zoe was a sharp contrast to the freshly scrubbed, makeup-free beauty who'd greeted him Saturday morning.

That mental snapshot had his mind racing back to the kiss they'd shared, how those lush lips had tasted and how she'd fit so perfectly in his arms.

For a split second he longed to hold her again and his mind searched for something, anything, that would justify kissing her one more time.

Thank God, a moment later good sense took over and he gave himself a mental shake.

"Good morning." She flashed her usual warm smile and it made him feel a little more at ease.

"How was your weekend?"

"I had to spend a good chunk of time canceling my credit cards, but all that aside, it was great. It would've been even better if we would've had more time together."

His mind raced, trying to think of something to say that wouldn't hurt her feelings but wouldn't lead her on as he'd done on Friday night.

Before he could form the words, she said, "I got a new phone. I wanted to call you, but I didn't have your number."

She sat on the edge of one of the chairs in front of his desk.

"And you know what?" she said.

"What?" he asked because, well, why the hell not?

"Not knowing your number made me realize that that are a lot of things I don't know about you, and I figured out an easy way to remedy that."

He scowled as he picked up his cup of coffee and sipped it.

It burned his tongue.

That's what was wrong with him. He hadn't had enough coffee this morning. And along those same lines, he supposed he could blame his Friday-night weakness on the long day and the wine.

Lame. Yep. It was a lame excuse. But it was all he had. That, a cup of scalding coffee and woman right in front of him who was even hotter—too hot for him to handle.

"What I decided," she continued, undeterred by his silence, "is I'm starting a new column for the employee newsletter called 'Getting to Know You.' I'm going to interview a new employee every week, and guess who gets to go first? *You* do."

He winced before he could help it.

"Oh, come on. It's not that bad. In fact, it will be painless. I promise. It's five simple questions."

"Zoe," he said.

"Come on, Joaquin. This is me trying to show you that nothing has changed between us. So don't make it weird. Okay? I mean, unless you don't even want to be friends. Is that how you want it? Because that would make things very weird."

Their gazes locked across the expanse of the desk.

No. That wasn't how he wanted it. He still wanted to talk to her, joke around with her. She was fun and refreshing and optimistic. Exactly the type of person he needed in his life.

She was a million surprises. He had to admit, this take-charge, direct, professional attitude wasn't what he had expected from her this morning. Obviously he'd underestimated her.

"Of course, I want to be your friend," he said. "Since you brought up friendship, friends should be frank with each other. In that spirit, I owe you an apology."

"An apology? For what?"

"For kissing you."

She flinched. "Was it that bad?"

"No. It was fabulous, but it can't happen again."

Her face fell for a moment, but she recovered quickly. Held out her hand. "Okay. Friends, then?"

He nodded and shook her hand. "Friends. But I can't

do the interview right now. We have to make some headway on this website and then I'm in meetings all day. Tomorrow, too."

"Then meet me for a drink at Señor Iguana's tonight," she said.

He shook his head. "No. Zoe, that is not a good idea."

"Joaquin, *friends* meet for drinks all the time. Besides, we will have chaperones. Plenty of them. My brothers and sisters and I are having dinner there tonight. It's that family meeting I told you about."

"At Señor Iguana's? That doesn't seem very private."

Señor Iguana's had a cantina in the front where people could meet and order bar food, and a full-service Tex-Mex restaurant in the back. The casual atmosphere and good food made it a popular place, and it was busy seven days a week.

"There's a private dining room in the back. Ben reserved it. He thought it might be nice to meet on neutral territory for a change."

She shook her head.

"I am not looking forward to this. I don't know how many times my father will have to tell them he is not a Fortune before they stop this nonsense."

"Why do you go to these meetings?" Joaquin asked.

"Because I seem to be the only one who brings a voice of reason to this circus. It's not fun. So, will you please be a *friend* and meet me there? If nothing else it will give me a reason to escape the nonsense if they get long-winded. I can tell them I have to go because I'm meeting a friend."

She was right. *Friends* did meet for drinks, but he'd already seen what happened when he was alone with

her. That line between friendship and *more* had gotten so blurry he'd lost his way. Even though his brain
warned him against doing so with Zoe again, pure,
primal need shoved him toward the outer edges of that
boundary. And there didn't seem to be a thing his brain
could do to stop the momentum.

Chapter Seven

"Zoe, Rachel tells me you had dinner with Josephine Fortune Chesterfield this weekend?" Ben Fortune Robinson set down his fork and looked at Zoe expectantly.

The private dining room at Señor Iguana's suddenly became so quiet she could almost hear the questions swirling around in Ben's mind as her siblings, Wes, Graham, Kieran, Olivia and Sophie, gazed at her eagerly.

The only one whose attention wasn't trained on Zoe was Rachel. Her head was down and she was focusing on her enchiladas as though they were the most fascinating special in the world.

Yeah, thanks, Rach. That's the last time I share anything like this with you.

She tried to catch Rachel's eye, but her sister wasn't looking.

"I did," Zoe said. "But that's not why you called us together, Ben. Why don't you tell us what's on your mind? I need to leave in a few minutes. So can we please get started?"

Ben pushed away his plate and leaned forward. "I'll get to my thing in a minute. How did it go with Josephine?"

Zoe frowned and tried to dam a wave of irritation that was cresting and threatening to break.

"It went fine, Ben. How else would it go? It was strictly a chance meeting because Joaquin Mendoza and his father, Orlando, were gracious enough to take me in after I missed the bus in Horseback Hollow. I certainly wasn't going to barge in on their dinner and dominate the conversation by quizzing her about her family tree. Classless, Ben. Even the thought is classless."

Ben didn't seem to hear her or maybe he simply didn't care because he clamped down on the topic like a bulldog with a meaty bone.

All this talk about her father having a secret identity and being part of the Fortune family had become boring. Their dad denied it and Zoe chose not to believe it because it was yet another example of secrets harming relationships. Only these secrets belonged to her siblings, who kept on digging into their father's past behind his back and against his wishes.

Her words rolled right off her brother.

"You all are aware that Josephine Fortune Chesterfield was adopted and only found out a few years ago that she was a Fortune, right? I believe the same could be true for Dad."

Zoe sighed loud enough that everyone turned to look

at her. Even Rachel, who was the one who'd started this whole mess last year when she'd discovered evidence that she thought suggested their dad's real name might be Jerome Fortune. That's all it had taken to get Ben started on this "Fortune hunt." Never mind the way their father had denied the allegations, and the fact that the rest of the Fortune family claimed it was impossible. Ben was determined to uncover this so-called truth.

Zoe wished he'd put as much effort into his job as chief operating officer at Robinson Tech. The way he'd been going against their dad's wishes, bird-dogging this issue, she was surprised their father didn't fire him, or at least demote him.

Each new lead seemed to turn into a stone wall at a dead end. Most recently, after much wasted time and energy, Ben had located a woman named Jacqueline Fortune, who was this Jerome's mother and, as Ben insisted, their grandmother.

Never mind that the poor woman, who was in her nineties and living in a memory-care unit of a nursing home, suffered from dementia. Ben just kept pushing.

He almost took this one too far because when he brought up Jerome's name, poor Jacqueline had completely freaked out and started yelling that Jerome Fortune was dead.

Wouldn't he think that would be a sign that it was time to close this ridiculous case? *Nooo.* Ben still wouldn't let it go. He had to keep raking up the muck.

His latest allegation was that their father might have illegitimate offspring scattered all over the world. This stemmed from a British guy named Keaton Whitfield whom Ben had come across on this odyssey to drag their father through the mud.

The wave of anger that Zoe had tried to contain finally crested and crashed.

Until this point she had tried to stay out of the fray and do what she could to be the peacemaker. She attended these monthly meetings Ben insisted on holding to be the voice of reason. As a general rule, she preferred to take the kind approach and focus on the positive things in life. But now Ben had gone too far.

Zoe stood, her chair scraping loudly across the wooden floorboards. "Okay, Ben, if we're just going to rehash false starts we already know have led to dead ends, then I'm going to say good-night."

She grabbed her purse and fished out her phone, looking at the time…and to see if Joaquin had texted her to say that he was there.

He hadn't. Probably because he wasn't due to meet her for another half hour. But she had to get out of there. She couldn't stand one more minute of hearing her brother's desperate attempt to turn their father into a liar and rehash the rumors of his infidelity.

Even on the far-flung chance that their dad was this Jerome Fortune in another life, what difference did it make? He had always been a good parent. He had provided for his family, making it possible for his kids to not only have every material possession a person could ask for but also careers for each and every one of them if they wanted to be a part of the family business. He also gave them the freedom to not be part of it—with no prejudice—if they so chose. Rachel was a good case in point.

"Sit down, Zoe. That's not why I've asked everyone

to be here tonight. I have a new lead, and it just might be the breakthrough we've been looking for."

Zoe rolled her eyes.

Here we go again.

The only reason she sat again was that she wanted to know what inane tree Ben was barking up now. Since he had gone so far as to produce someone who claimed to be a half brother—and was making noises that there might be more—she needed to stay to make sure her siblings hadn't done something stupid like invite him to move into the Robinson estate. At this point, nothing would surprise her.

"I have found an old friend of Jacqueline Fortune's. Her name is Marian Brandt. She was Jacqueline's neighbor. She and I talked at length."

Zoe glanced at Ben. He was holding up a small photograph. Zoe squinted, but she couldn't tell what the image was since he was at the head of the table and she was toward the other end.

If he went to the trouble of bringing props, he would certainly show and tell. Zoe took one last look in her compact mirror, snapped it shut and put away her cosmetics.

"Her late son, Eddie, and Jerome Fortune used to play when they were very young. She even shared this photo."

Ben gave it to Olivia, who sat to his right.

"Jacqueline and Marian have a lot in common. Both of them were widowed at a fairly young age and both lost their only sons. It's no wonder that they bonded over their tragic losses."

The picture had made its way around the table to Zoe. Of course, it was hard to tell if one of the boys was their father because they were so young in the picture. Zoe realized she couldn't recall ever seeing a picture of her father as a child. But that didn't mean anything.

As she passed it to Wes, she considered asking him if he'd ever seen pictures of their father as a kid, but quickly decided not to because if he hadn't, it might give Ben more fuel for his fire.

"Even now that Jacqueline is bedridden, Marian is still a good friend and goes to visit her several times a week. When she heard that I had been to visit Jacqueline, she got my number from the nurses and called me and agreed to meet me for lunch."

"Did she give you this picture?" Kieran asked.

"She brought the original and allowed me to snap a shot of it with my phone. I had it printed out."

Of course, he would. Zoe wondered if Ben had a big evidence board similar to ones the FBI used when they were trying to solve a crime. Because he certainly was trying his best to turn their father into a criminal.

"Was she able to tell you anything new?" Sophie asked.

Ben grimaced and gave a palms-up shrug. "Technically, no. She said Jerome mailed his mom a suicide note and that the boat that had washed ashore without him in it was registered to the Fortune family. But, remember, even though he was presumed dead, Jerome Fortune's body was never found."

"Really, Ben?" Zoe groaned. "The neighbor woman confirmed what the police have already told you—that Jerome Fortune took out his family's boat and committed suicide—and that's still not enough to convince you it's time to end this ludicrous obsession?"

He ignored her.

"I'm going to see if the police have a copy of the suicide note in the evidence file. I'll get a graphologist to compare it with a sample of dad's handwriting."

"Jerome Fortune has been dead for more than thirty years," Sophie challenged. "Do you really think they'll still have his file?"

Again, Ben shrugged. "I'll never know unless I check into it. My gut still believes Jerome Fortune is very much alive and that he is our father. I will keep looking until I find irrefutable evidence to prove it— one way or the other."

That's enough.

Zoe slid her purse onto her arm and stood. "I think you're ridiculous and you need to stop this nonsense right now. It's your business if you want to waste your time chasing the ghost of Jerome Fortune, but until you have that irrefutable evidence, this is the last meeting I will attend. You all should be ashamed of yourselves for dragging our father through the mud when he has been nothing but generous to each and every one of you."

This time she ignored her siblings' attempted justifications and explanations and walked out of the meeting. They each had their own reasons for doing this to their father, but she didn't want to hear it. It was hurtful and disrespectful.

Sure, some might have considered Gerald Robinson a tyrant, and, yes, she knew she had always been his favorite, but they were a family. Even though she was aware of her father's indiscretions, she didn't want to know the gory details. That was between him and her mother. She knew their parents' relationship was strained enough. If Ben kept it up, they would eventually hit the breaking point. If her brothers and sisters would stop looking for trouble, it would go a long way toward strengthening family relations. Families stuck together; they didn't try to tear each other apart, because when one went down, they all went down.

Zoe wasn't going to sit there and watch them destroy the people who had given them life.

She made her way to Señor Iguana's crowded cantina area. It buzzed with the noisy music and energy of a beloved night spot. She squinted as she scanned the dimly lit room, past its neon signs and perennial Christmas-tree lights strung in draping swags, to see if Joaquin was waiting, but it was still a little early. She was tempted to leave and come back, but a quick glance at her phone revealed they were due to meet in fifteen minutes. She couldn't go anywhere and get back in that short amount of time. So she might as well stay.

She needed to change gears so that the irritation her siblings had stoked up in her was not rolling off her in waves when Joaquin arrived. Normally she didn't drink much, but right now nothing sounded better than a great big frozen-lime margarita. It would surely take the edge off.

She marched up to the bar and ordered, "One Iguana-rita, please."

In less than a minute the bartender set something the size of a fishbowl in front of her.

"Oh! This is enough for four people," she said as she handed him the cash to pay for it. "I didn't realize it was so large."

The bartender, a good-looking guy despite his man-bun and tattoo sleeves, said, "You've been here before, haven't you?"

Or maybe his bohemian look was what made him attractive.

"I have. I love this place."

"I thought I'd seen you around." He lingered, leaning his elbows on the bar. The tat on his right forearm was a skull with a clock face in one of its eyes. The more she looked at it, the more she saw how the individual images played into the bigger picture. It was a mesmerizing in a freaky Where's Waldo sort of way.

She'd never dated a guy with a tattoo. She wondered if Joaquin had any hidden pictures on his gorgeous body. *Mmm.* She'd like to find out. It would be like a treasure hunt.

"Have you never ordered the Thirsty Iguana?" Man-Bun asked.

She shook her head. "I've never ordered one. I asked for an iguana-rita. I think that's the much smaller version of this fish tank."

"My mistake," said Man-Bun. "It's on the house since I screwed up your order."

"No, that's okay. I can pay for it." She took her first sip. It was cold and delicious, and went down way too easy. Probably way stronger than it tasted. She'd have to be careful or she might be picking herself up off the floor.

While she was no stranger to the club scene and she certainly enjoyed partying on the weekends, she was not a big drinker and never did drugs. Some might say she didn't like to be out of control. She liked to think of it as being high on life.

Someone at the other end of the bar flagged down the bartender. "Enjoy it—what did you say your name was?"

"I didn't," she said.

"We'll enjoy it, *I Didn't*. May I call you *I* for short?"

Zoe laughed and sipped her drink. "Suit yourself."

"After things slow down, maybe I can help you finish that iguana?" he said.

"She won't need your help," Joaquin said as he slid onto the vacant stool next to her. "But thanks."

Joaquin didn't like the looks of that guy, with his tattoo sleeves and his long hair piled on top of his head. What kind of a guy wore his hair like that? He had *player* written all over him. He'd probably helped a lot of women finish their drinks. Probably a different one every night.

"He won't bother you anymore," Joaquin said. "But, hey, how are you doing? How was the meeting?"

Zoe frowned at him. "What makes you think he was bothering me?"

Her words and sharp tone made Joaquin do a double-take. "He was hitting on you."

She pursed her lips and her right brow shot up. That expression was starting to become a familiar challenge, even though her tone was a lot more intense than the Zoe he knew.

"And it bothers you that he was hitting on me?" she asked.

"What? You like him?"

"Don't answer my question with a question." She took a long sip of her margarita.

"He doesn't seem like your type."

She put her hands on her hips. "What is my type, Joaquin?"

Their gazes locked and for a moment something

electric passed between them. It was all he could do to keep from saying, "I am. I'm your type." But that was such a bad idea.

When he didn't answer, she said. "It seems like *you're* the one who is bothered by his flirting with me."

True. It did bother him. He knew he had no right because he had made it perfectly clear where they stood. He was probably worse for her than the tattooed bartender.

He glanced down the bar. The dude was talking and laughing with another woman. Zoe deserved better than that.

Better than the flirting bartender or better than a guy who kissed her and backed the hell up?

Better than both of them.

That guy was a player. But Joaquin was nine years her senior. She needed someone young, someone who was not preoccupied with his own issues.

When he turned back to look at her, he saw that she was watching the bartender, too. He couldn't tell if she looked disappointed or resigned.

"I thought I was doing you a favor by rescuing you from that one," he said.

"Thank you, but just because I missed the bus in Horseback Hollow doesn't mean I need you to keep rescuing me."

He nodded.

"No, you don't. You're a strong, smart, capable woman."

He almost added *beautiful* to the list, but he bit back the word before it escaped.

"Thank you for that." She sighed and looked a little defeated. "Look, I'm sorry. I'm in a mood and I don't mean to take it out on you. The family meeting didn't go very well. Why don't we start over?" She took a deep breath and extended her hand. "Hi, Joaquin. I'm glad to see you."

This was a different disposition for her. She was usually so happy and full of good spirits that her kindness and effervescence were contagious. But no one was perfect. She was allowed an off night.

"Do you want to talk about it?"

She looked at him for a long, silent moment filled by the loud salsa music playing in the background. He thought she was going to decline.

"Actually, yes, I would. I think that would help."

A four-top in the corner was just opening up. "Why don't we go grab that table over there?"

As soon as they sat, a server approached and Joaquin ordered a beer.

"Would you like anything else?" he asked Zoe.

She toasted him with her large glass. "Thanks, I think I'm all set for tonight—and possibly into next week. This drink is huge. There's no way I'll be able to finish it. So, please, help yourself."

"Why don't you bring us an order of chips and salsa?" Joaquin said to the server. Then he turned back to Zoe. "It might come in handy to soak up some of that alcohol."

As she pushed the drink aside, Joaquin felt an irrational satisfaction that he would be the one sharing Zoe's beverage, not the bartender.

After the server walked away, Joaquin said, "What's going on with your family?"

Her pretty eyes darkened a shade and she lowered her lids as she traced a crack in the Formica tabletop.

"I don't understand why Ben is so determined to prove that our father is lying about his identity. Now he's alleging Dad has illegitimate children scattered all over the place. Can't he see how humiliating this is for our mother? Though I don't think she's aware of this allegation. It seems like Ben is determined to tear our family apart. He keeps trying to dig up a past for our dad. When he doesn't find anything, he invents something. Ben just needs to hop off.

"But let's say by some fluke my dad *is* this Jerome Fortune person. He obviously doesn't want anyone to know. He has asked Ben time and again to stop. Why does Ben keep digging? What difference does would it make if our father actually did have a past that he isn't proud of? What good is it going to do if Ben uncovers buried skeletons and drags them out for everyone to see? What difference is that going to make except to hurt everyone involved?"

Joaquin wore his best poker face. He knew that Ben was on a mission to prove a Fortune connection, but he hadn't realized until this very moment how closely Zoe's family issues overlapped with his own. It gave him pause.

"I don't know Ben very well, but I can't imagine he's purposely trying to tear apart your family."

Zoe looked at him as if he'd spit in her drink.

"So, you're saying he's right to do this, even though my dad has asked him to stop?"

Joaquin shook his head. "I'm not saying anyone is right or wrong. What I was getting at is that I think it's natural to want to know your roots and where you came from."

"Well, he *is* tearing us apart. Or at least he's headed in that direction."

When there were issues—tough issues—that needed to be discussed, someone was bound to get hurt. But it didn't do anyone any good to ignore it.

"Before it gets any later," Zoe said, "we better start the interview. Since that's why we came here in the first place."

Good idea. Since they seemed to have opposite opinions about a similar family issue, it was bound to cause hurt feelings. As if to second the motion to change subjects, the server approached the table with his beer.

Since Zoe didn't want anything else, he paid for his drink rather than run a tab. Once that was taken care of, he said, "What's the first question?"

She pulled a small tablet out of her purse. As she typed, pink nails clicking on the built-in keyboard, her earlier tension seemed to ease.

"What do you like best about working at Robinson Tech?"

"The project I'm working on is interesting. I love the creative freedom I have at Robinson."

She glanced up at him and nodded before recording his answer.

"Favorite color?"

"How is that work-related?"

"Favorite color," she repeated. "I didn't promise that this was strictly about the professional you. That's boring, Joaquin. We have to spice it up with a little bit of personality. So, favorite color?"

He smiled and shook his head. "Blue."

"Really?" Zoe said as she tap-tapped away, typing

up his answer. "I had you pegged for a green man, but blue works. Favorite food?"

"There's not much I don't like. Everything from steak to sushi to all ethnic cuisines. I love good food. It's something I'm passionate about."

She propped her elbow on the table and rested her chin on the heel of her hand. "I think it's very sexy when a man is adventurous."

He laughed. "Are you going to put that in your article?"

"Maybe. How would you describe your perfect day?"

It had been so long since he'd had a perfect day that he had to think about it for a minute.

"Spending it with someone special. Maybe exploring new places, or if there was a somewhere we both liked, we could go there."

He remembered days spent on the beach and in a boat out on the ocean in Florida. He remembered the cruel way Selena had let him know their relationship was over. Funny, it was a fading memory now. He had been humiliated at the time, cut to the quick, but the pain was gone. He hadn't realized it until now.

"I haven't made it to the Driskill Hotel yet," he said. "I hear it's a quite a place."

Zoe reached out and put a hand on his arm. "Oh, my gosh. It's one of my favorite places in Austin. Maybe we could meet there for drinks some time?"

"Yeah."

And there it was again, that energy that coursed between them. If he wasn't careful, he might mistake it for chemistry. Aw, hell, who was he kidding? This was chemistry and it was undeniable. Admitting it was the best safeguard against crossing that line. That damn line. It kept tempting him closer and closer.

"What are you most grateful for?" she asked.

He was grateful she'd changed the subject. "That's easy—my family."

"See, you do know that family is most important over everything. *Everything.*"

The episode with Selena had underscored that. A lot of women had come and gone in his life, but his family was the one constant.

"Have you ever been married?" she asked.

"I agreed to answer five questions. That's number six."

She closed the tablet's cover and slid it into her purse. "That one is for me. Not for the newsletter."

He took a swig of his beer, debating whether he wanted to talk about this or not. But one look at Zoe's pretty face and he was putty.

"I was engaged once."

"Was?" Zoe asked.

Joaquin nodded.

"What was her name?"

"Selena Marks."

Zoe's eyes widened. "As in Marks Telecom in Miami? That's where you worked, right?"

"How did you know that?" he asked.

"I have my ways. Does your broken engagement have anything to do with why you won't date people you work with?"

For all of her fun-loving ways, she was pretty astute. He drained the last of his beer and set the bottle on the table.

"It has everything to do with that. On that note, I

think it's time to call it a night. Do you want me to give you a ride home?"

"No, of course not. I have my car here."

"Are you okay to drive?"

"I've had maybe three sips. I'm a lightweight. It was way too strong for me. So, I'm fine to drive."

"Come on," he said. "I'll walk you out to your car."

They navigated their way to the front of the cantina and he held the door for her.

When they got to her car, a sporty little red BMW convertible, she turned to him, her voice soft and little shaky. "I don't know what happened that caused your engagement to end, but I hate that it caused you so much pain. And I'm sorry that it may be keeping you from potentially good relationships."

A moment passed between them. She looked vulnerable and angelic standing there backlit by the glow of the streetlight. She was right. He had been letting Selena keep him from moving forward, but tonight Zoe had helped him see that he'd moved further ahead than he'd realized.

"May I be perfectly honest with you?" he asked.

"Of course. I'd expect nothing less from you."

He nodded. "The thing is, I like working at Robinson. I didn't realize just how much until I realized that this project is almost finished and I'm not ready to go."

Her eyes widened. "Are you saying you want a permanent position?"

"I have a meeting with Gerald later this week and I was going to talk to him about it."

"I have an idea," she said. "What are you doing Thursday night?"

"I don't know. Why?"

"My dad is hosting a dinner for a handful of high-level employees. You should come."

Joaquin laughed. "You are something else. I cannot crash your father's party. He didn't invite me. Thanks, but I'll talk to him when we meet at the office."

"He's going to invite you. So, be prepared to clear your calendar on Thursday night."

Joaquin shook his head. It was more of a head-clearing gesture than a negative response to her promised invitation.

"Just like that, your father is going to invite me? Because you said so."

She shrugged and nodded, making a face as if he'd just asked the dumbest question ever.

Joaquin couldn't help but smile at her self-assurance. It was one of the things he loved about her. She wasn't arrogant or mean; there wasn't a cruel bone in her body. She simply knew what was what and she wasn't afraid to own it.

"You always get what you want, don't you?"

She cocked her head to the side. "You say that like it's a bad thing, Mr. Mendoza."

"No, actually, it's not. I was thinking that you're pretty amazing."

"Really? You think so?"

It took everything he had not to lean in and taste those lips again. But he knew better and he pulled himself back from the edge.

"You're a good friend, a good daughter, and you're great at what you do. I'd say all that adds up to *amazing*."

"I'm a good friend, huh?"

He tried to ignore the way the disappointment in

her eyes belied the smile curving up the edges of those tempting lips. "Well, Joaquin, you keeping me in the friend zone proves I don't get *everything* I want. You need to know I won't give up on you."

God, she was killing him.

"You also need to know that people have told me that I'm passionate and persistent." She let the words hang between them. "So I'm not letting you friend-zone me, Joaquin."

He bent down and kissed her on the forehead.

"Good night, Zoe."

"Seriously? Is that the best you can do?"

"Were you expecting something else?"

"Joaquin, that was like getting a kiss from my brother."

"Since your sister is married to my brother, doesn't that make us related in some way?"

She put her hands on her hips. "No, it does not. You're a hot Latino from Miami. I expected more from you than a kiss on the forehead. You have *no* game."

Joaquin laughed. "You think I just made a move on you? That shows just how innocent you are. Because when I make a move on a woman, she knows it."

Chapter Eight

As an independent contractor who'd only had a minimal amount of one-on-one time with Gerald Robinson, Joaquin had mixed emotions when the big boss stopped by his office on Tuesday to invite him to the Thursday-night dinner party.

He knew Gerald wouldn't have done it if not for Zoe's prompting. But on the other hand, despite how much Gerald loved his daughter, Joaquin was certain the man wouldn't have been goaded into inviting anyone to something like this simply for his daughter's amusement.

There was a time for pride and then there was a time when someone didn't refuse a bona fide invitation that could change his career. Robinson Tech was the premier technology company. It was the wave of the future. It was the only place for anyone interested in designing cutting-edge software.

When Thursday night rolled around and Joaquin arrived at the Robinson estate with its stone walls and iron gates, he felt like a fish out of water the minute he started up the long, winding driveway. When the house, a Mediterranean number that looked like a castle, came into view in, it knocked him back into his seat. He'd led a perfectly comfortable life in Miami. He'd never wanted for anything, but he had never been exposed to quite this level of wealth.

Not even with Selena.

Not that it mattered. The last thing he was looking for was to get tangled up with another spoiled little rich girl. But giving credit where credit was due, the more he got to know Zoe, the more he realized she wasn't spoiled. Even though she usually got what she wanted, she was pretty damn down to earth. It sounded like a contradiction, but it wasn't. It was the truth. She was fresh and fun and bubbly, and everyone would be better off if they borrowed a page from her outlook on life. Even when she was down, as she had been the other night, she didn't wallow and she kept other people's best interests at heart.

As Joaquin got closer, he saw a couple of guys standing out in front of the house. Of course there would be valets. He had a feeling everything would be first-class tonight.

After he got out of the car and handed over the keys, he started to tip the guy, but the kid held up his hand.

"Thanks, but Mr. Robinson has taken care of us. Have a nice evening, sir."

Sir? The guy wasn't *that* much younger than he was. Then again, he was probably closer to Zoe's age than Joaquin, and it was probably just a show of re-

spect for anyone fortunate enough to be invited to the
Robinson estate.

The guy jumped into the car and carefully drove
away, leaving Joaquin to contemplate the huge wooden
front doors. He wondered if Zoe was somewhere inside.
Then he realized he didn't even know if she lived here
or if she had a place of her own. From the looks of this
house, she could have an entire wing and it would be
more space than most middle-class houses.

Joaquin ignored the knot in his gut. He squared his
shoulders and rang the bell. A middle-aged man in a
black suit answered, greeting him formally.

"Good evening, sir." Ha! *Sir.* There it was again.
"Mr. Robinson would like everyone to gather in the
living room for cocktails before dinner."

Joaquin followed the directions the butler gave
him—down the polished wooden hallway, first door
on the left—and joined a handful of men and women,
none of whom he recognized. Robinson Tech was
a huge business and Joaquin mostly kept to himself, keeping his head down, focusing on his work.
They were all mixing and mingling and seemed to
know each other. It wasn't any wonder that he was the
stranger here, since he hadn't made much of an effort
to get to know his coworkers socially.

His gaze took in the room from its hardwood floors
covered with Persian rugs to its high, arched ceilings.
The fine antique furniture and artwork, which looked
like an art lover's dream, gave the place an air of old-
world elegance that he'd only encountered in the finest hotels and the couple of mansion museums he'd
toured over the years.

But one important element was missing: Zoe hadn't

arrived yet. Earlier today she'd stopped by his office and said she'd see him tonight. He hoped something else hadn't come up. Until now, he hadn't realized how much he missed her. But as quickly as the thought registered, he shook it off. Tonight was about business, not about exploring odd feelings he didn't know how to process.

He needed a beer. That's what was wrong. He found his way to the open bar and ordered his drink, which the bartender poured from a tap into a frosted pilsner glass. When Joaquin turned around, Zoe was just walking into the room. She looked like something from his dreams in a short black dress and strappy sandals. She wore bright red lipstick and had swept her hair back from her face into a fancy ponytail. Somehow she always managed to look as though she'd just stepped out of the salon. The rush of emotion that hit him nearly knocked him to the floor.

Her face lit up when she saw him. He couldn't take his eyes off her as she crossed the room. It hit him that this beautiful woman, who could have any man she chose, wanted to spend time with *him*. *With him*. He'd be lying if he didn't admit that he wanted spend time with her, too. He'd spent so much time denying it, all for the sake of not dating the boss's daughter— but why?

It wasn't because of her family or because Gerald was her father. It wasn't this castle of a house or the fact that she had the power to connect him to the man who could define his future. All of those things were great, but what smacked him so hard that it forced his eyes wide-open was the way she looked at him, the way she lit up just for him. It shifted something inside him, tantamount to rolling aside a boulder that had sealed off a cold, dark cave that had trapped his soul.

Seeing her was like stepping out into the sunshine again.

After his broken engagement, after the hell Selena had put him through, tonight he realized he could still feel. It came like a lightning bolt because it had been a couple of years since he'd been able to feel anything remotely like this. That could only mean one thing: the past was behind him now. He'd left it inside that cave that had held him prisoner and rolled that rock back into place, so those difficult times could wither and die inside and never plague him again. He wasn't sure where this was going or if it would even go anywhere, but for the first time in a long time, he was ready to move forward.

"Hi, Joaquin." She leaned in and kissed him on the cheek and he kissed her back. She smelled good, like roses and honey and sunshine. He breathed in deeply, wanting to commit her scent to memory.

"You look handsome," she said after she pulled away, making no bones about giving him the slow, sexy once-over.

"You're not so bad yourself," he said. "May I get you a drink?"

"A glass of white wine would be lovely, thank you."

He made short order of fetching it, but by the time he returned to her side, Gerald had entered the room.

"Hello, everyone. Welcome and thank you for taking time out of your busy lives to join me for dinner tonight. I hope you all brought your appetites because the chef has prepared a delicious feast for us to enjoy. Without further delay, why don't we make our way into the dining room, because dinner is ready and I am starving."

The small crowd, about fifteen in all, made the appropriate adoring and convivial noises as they filed past Gerald. He took the time to greet everyone by name and express how happy he was to see him or her. The man seemed like a different person than the rough, gruff boss at work. Apparently he had different faces that ranged from dictatorial tyrant to beloved king of the castle. It was good to meet the more human side of him. Joaquin realized not everyone was privileged to glimpse the less gruff side of Gerald Robinson, whom one news magazine had named the Bully Genius and another had called the Attila the Hun of Technology.

Joaquin was beginning to understand why Zoe had come into his office that day and asked for help spinning her father's reputation in a more positive direction. It made sense after glimpsing the more benevolent side of Gerald Robinson. Zoe knew and loved this side of her dad and wanted everyone to see how great he could be. Still, Joaquin would wager that Gerald Robinson didn't give a rat's ass what people thought of him.

"Joaquin, good to see you." Gerald extended his hand and Joaquin gave it a firm shake. "It was short notice. I'm glad you could make it."

"Thanks for inviting me," he said, taking care to express his appreciation without gushing.

"Are we still on for that sit-down tomorrow? I'm looking forward to talking about what you want to do after you after you finish your current project." Gerald turned his attention to his daughter and Joaquin was dismissed. "Hello, princess. It's always a good night when we get to have dinner together."

"Hi, Dad." Zoe threw both of her arms around Gerald's neck. It was the first time Joaquin had ever seen Gerald's face go completely soft. But it only lasted a moment before he reclaimed his tough armor.

"Get in there to dinner," he said to Joaquin. "It's rude to keep everyone waiting."

Zoe looked at Joaquin and rolled her eyes goodnaturedly, but her father didn't see it. Joaquin wasn't sure if Gerald missed it by accident or design.

There were no place cards. The guests were free to sit where they wanted. By the time he and Zoe made it into the dining room, the places near Gerald were taken. Joaquin wished he'd gotten in there earlier. It would have been fun watching the others jockey for the prime real estate. The two seats available were at the opposite end of the sprawling table.

At each place setting there was a menu detailing the five-course feast: Oysters Rockefeller, cream of roasted walnut soup, surf and turf, salad of baby greens with vinaigrette, and flourless chocolate cake with raspberry coulis. Each course had its own wine pairing.

During dinner, everyone made small talk, but Gerald was quiet, hunching over his meal, paying more attention to the food than to his guests. While everyone except for Joaquin and Zoe tried to be the centers of attention, entertaining with their best anecdotes and worldly stories, they seemed to know better than to interrupt Gerald's rapturous dinner.

By the time dessert was served, Joaquin thought they'd have to roll him out of the dining room. But the after-dinner Calvados was the perfect ending to the delicious meal.

When he was done, Gerald commanded the stage and regaled his guests with a bit of his own history.

"As most of you know, I'm a self-made man," he said. "I built Robinson Tech from the ground up with my own two hands, starting with only the shirt on my back and the cash in my pockets. No one ever gave me anything, and I never asked them to."

There was an edge to Gerald's tone that bordered on bitter and Joaquin wondered if it had anything to do with the rumored Fortune connection. Joaquin glanced around the table, watching the others smiling and nodding and shaking their heads in solidarity. He wondered if they could hear the undercurrent in Gerald's words. It sounded a lot like hurt.

If the man really was a Fortune, as Zoe's siblings kept insisting, what must it have been like to walk away from that dynasty and start over? Or had he walked away? Maybe he'd been pushed. Or, as Zoe maintained, maybe it was all a moot point.

Zoe was facing questions about her family, questions about truth and lies and whom to believe, what was important and what didn't matter. Yet she still managed to see the good in life and give those she loved the benefit of the doubt.

She had questions very similar to the ones he was facing. For a moment Joaquin wondered if exposing the truth really mattered. Would it change anything for the better?

He cast a glance at Zoe, who was listening intently. In Gerald's case, exposing his past might not make things better. Of course, it would hurt Zoe and that in itself colored Joaquin's opinion on Fortune-gate. Because when he thought of his own situation, the devastating questions he needed to ask his father, it still seemed necessary.

"I respect hard work and dedication," Gerald continued. "It's what's gotten me where I am today. I want Robinson Tech to reflect that ethos of perseverance and independence. That's why I've asked each of you here tonight. Because I recognize a similar drive and determination in your work. I want this company to forge new paths. You don't get ahead in this business by regurgitating what your competitors have already created. So that's where you come in. You bring the fresh and the original to Robinson Tech. Over the next few weeks I'm going to meet with each of you one-on-one and we are going to map out your future with the company."

Gerald stood suddenly, tossing the linen napkin onto his dessert plate with the flick of his wrist. "But right now, it's time for you all to leave. Good night, everyone."

Zoe had never been so happy for a dinner to end. And even happier, since it was still early.

Stanley, who had been the Robinson's butler for as far back as Zoe could remember, herded the guests to the door, and it gave her a chance to grab Joaquin's hand and pull him toward the opposite door that led to the butler's pantry.

"Where are we going?" he asked.

"Away from here," she said, happy that he hadn't let go of her hand. Their fingers were laced and his palm felt big and warm against hers.

She led him through the butler's pantry and took a sharp left down a hall that led to the family room.

"Let's go outside," she said. "It's such a nice night."

Joaquin smiled. "That sounds like a great idea."

They walked hand in hand across the travertine porch, down the steps that led to the pool area and to a wooden bench that overlooked Lake Austin.

"This view is my favorite thing about this house," Zoe said. "Sometimes when I just need to think, I come out here and sit."

"It's a great view," Joaquin said. "What do you think about when you're out here?"

His thigh had drifted over into her space and was resting against her leg. She liked the feel of him next to her.

"Whatever's on my mind. Right now, I'm hoping to get a promotion. That's one of the reasons I was at the dinner tonight. Just because I'm the boss's daughter doesn't mean he automatically promotes me. I have to earn advancement like everyone else. And that's the way it should be. Why should I get special privileges? Shouldn't I have to earn my way just like everyone else does?"

Joaquin raised his brows and nodded.

"What?" she said. "Did you think I was here tonight just to see you?"

"I was hoping," he said.

She couldn't believe he'd said that. It made her stomach jump and her heart race, but she tried to play it cool, even though what she wanted to do was to wrap her arms around him and show him exactly how happy she was to be there with him.

"But you live here," he said. "Of course I'd expect you to be here."

"I don't anymore. I grew up here, but I have a place

of my own now. This is a great house, though, isn't it? It was fun growing up here. So, did you have fun tonight?"

Joaquin nodded. "It was interesting. I saw a side of your father I'd never seen before. I have acquired a brand-new appreciation for him."

"That makes me so happy, you don't even know. I wish everyone could see him the way you do."

"Thanks for having him invite me."

Zoe held up her hand. "Actually, all I did was ask him if you were coming tonight, and he's the one who decided to invite you. I didn't ask him to. He really likes you, Joaquin. And so do I."

She saw Joaquin's throat work. He was silent for a moment, just looking at her in way that she couldn't read. For a second she was afraid he was going to friend-zone her again.

"I like you, too, Zoe. You know what I like best about you?"

She shook her head.

"You always see the best in everyone, even in me. I know I haven't been the easiest person to get to know."

Zoe laughed. Even if he was hard to get to know, Joaquin obviously had no idea what a great guy he was.

"I wish I could claim that as a heroic quality," she said. "But it's not hard to see the good in you. I mean, good grief, half the women in the office are in love with you."

He made a face that said he didn't believe her.

"Or at least Steffi-Anne is," she said. "If you don't know that, then you're clueless. And if you are clueless, that's okay, because then I can tell you that it's true, but—"

She stopped, biting back her words before she said the wrong thing. But, really, what was the point of censoring herself now?

"Joaquin, I don't want to share you. Not with Steffi-Anne. With no one."

He answered her by lowering his head and covering her mouth with his. It was a kiss that she felt all the way down to her curled toes.

When they finally came up for air, he said, "In case you're wondering, I just made a move on you."

Chapter Nine

After the Robinson dinner, Zoe and Joaquin were inseparable outside of the office. The more time he spent with her, the more he wondered why it had taken him so long to get his head on straight. She made him so damn happy, he couldn't imagine a day, or a night, going by without seeing her.

That was why, when Zoe decided to show Joaquin some of her favorite places around Austin, he was psyched to let her be his tour guide. Once, they went to dinner at Botticelli's South Congress. Another night they headed to the SoCo area to hear a band that Zoe loved. They went for drinks at the Driskill Hotel. And that night after work, they'd visited the Harry Ransom Center, a museum on the edge of the University of Texas campus. The place was open until seven on Thursday nights. Afterward, they grabbed a quick bite to eat.

In the past, when Joaquin started dating someone new, this much togetherness would have made him itchy for his own space. But after dinner, when he took Zoe to get her car, which she'd left in the Robinson office parking lot, he didn't even hesitate when she asked him to come over.

In fact, the thought of saying good-night left him with an emptiness he didn't quite understand. So he followed her back to her place, a nice town home located about fifteen minutes from the office.

Once inside, he followed her past the small foyer and into the living room. She turned to him. The sensual way she looked at him made him crazy. He closed the distance between them and pulled her into his arms, weaving his fingers into her hair and kissing her deeply and soundly with all the pent-up passion that had been building in him since the first time he'd set eyes on her.

When they came up for air, she took a step back, looking a little disoriented. A piece of hair had fallen across one eye and he brushed it back, resisting the urge to pull her to him again.

"Have a seat," she said, gesturing toward a teal blue sofa. "I'll get us some wine."

The living area was an open design. He could see her in the kitchen, taking two wineglasses down from the cupboard.

"Do you need any help?" he asked.

"Nope. I'm good," she called. "I'll be right there."

He looked around, taking in everything. The high ceilings and the crown molding. The walls were painted light blue and the furniture was a perfect mix of formal and quirky, like Zoe herself. It was a nice place, tastefully decorated with feminine floral patterns and lots of color.

It was the first time he had been to her place. It was good to get a glimpse of Zoe's world. He hadn't had a mental picture of where she lived, but now that he was here, it was so her, somehow he couldn't imagine her anywhere else.

She came into the living room, carrying two wine-glasses and an open bottle of red, and set them on the coffee table so she could pour some into each glass. She handed him one, kicked off her sandals and curled up next to him on the couch.

They clinked glasses. The crystal pinged a melodic note and they each took a sip.

"I remember the first time I saw you," she said. "It was at Rachel and Matteo's wedding. You were late because your flight had been delayed—remember that?"

Joaquin nodded. He'd thought she was the most beautiful woman he had ever seen, with those large dark eyes and long brown hair.

"I guess it turns out that you really were the *best man*," she said.

They laughed and clinked glasses again.

"I just keep thinking how I had no idea at the wedding that things would turn out like this. But I'm glad it did. Little did we know."

He'd had no idea that Zoe had noticed him. It had been his own fault. He'd been so blindsided by the breakup with Selena that he'd turned inward, living inside his head and protecting his fractured heart. At that point, he had only been free a couple months. Thinking back to that time in his life, it had been sort of a blur. He was still reeling from the breakup, but he'd wanted to do right by his brother and be the best best man possible. Matteo was obviously so much in love with Rachel. What was it about these Robinson women that mesmerized Mendoza men?

"You're so quiet tonight," she said. "Are you okay?"

"I couldn't be better. I'm just enjoying being here with you like this."

She leaned in and rested her head on his shoulder. He put his arm around her, loving the feel of her next to him.

"So, if you count the wedding as when we first met," she said, looking up at him, "technically we've known each other for more than a year. Unless... You weren't engaged then, were you?"

He shook his head. "No, by that point we'd called it off."

"If it was that fresh, it must have been hard for you to be thrown into wedding festivities."

"It doesn't matter now. I was happy for my brother and Rachel. They're family. You do what you have to do."

"That's one of the things I like best about you. Your family seems so important to you."

Zoe reached out and trailed her thumb over Joaquin's bottom lip. He gently caught it with his teeth and drew it into his mouth, suckling it before he let it go.

"So... We've known each other a whole year. And this the first time we've been alone. I mean really *alone*."

Joaquin's hands locked on her waist and he pulled her close. "It's about time."

He inhaled in her scent and wanted to melt with the heat of her body. His finger traced the neckline of her blouse, teasing the valley between her breasts. She took a sharp breath, which he captured when his lips closed over hers.

She tasted like the most delicious delicacy and he couldn't help but want more.

As they kissed, his palm brushed over her breasts. Even through the fabric, he felt her nipples stiffen under his touch. Instinctively he ventured down and slipped his hand under her blouse, skimming her stomach until his thumb brushed the underside of one breast.

He ached for her with his entire being. The need quickly morphed into a ravenous hunger.

"I want you," he whispered against her mouth.

When he pulled back to look at her, he saw the dark desire in her eyes. That desire was for him. To realize she wanted him as much as he wanted her was a rush and it fueled his fire for her.

In a delirious rush, he claimed her mouth and she commandeered his sanity. He held her so close that he could feel their hearts beat in sync. Or maybe it was simply the rush of desire coursing through them, creating their very own rhythm. She slipped her fingers into his hair, and the need between them became so feverish it threatened to consume them both.

Without breaking the spell, he eased her back on the couch and made short order of ridding himself of his shirt. He wanted to feel her skin against his.

He undid the first two buttons on her blouse but then grabbed the hem and pulled it up and over her head. He was too impatient to work the rest of the damn things. At least he had enough of his wits about him to know better than to give it a firm yank and rip it off of her.

As he tossed her blouse aside, he felt her demeanor shift.

"Are you okay?" he asked. He probably needed to slow down. He wanted her so badly, but this was not a race. He wanted to savor every moment of the first time he made love to her. Most of all, he wanted her to enjoy it, too.

"I need to tell you something." Her voice was small. *Birth control.*

Damn it. Why hadn't he thought of that before now? Probably because he hadn't counted on this happening just yet. But it felt so right.

"If you don't have anything, I can go out and get something."

Her face was a question mark.

"Condoms?" he said.

"Oh. No, that's not it. Well, yeah, we would need those." Her voice was a little shaky. Joaquin lifted himself off her to give her some room. She wriggled out from under him and sat up, crossing her arms over the front of her.

"If we're moving too fast, we can slow down," he said.

"I know this might sound corny and old-fashioned, but for a long time I wanted to save it for my wedding night."

It?

Oh—

"So you've never—"

She shook her head. "Don't look at me like I'm some sort of unicorn."

"No. I'm not. Or if you thought I was, I'm sorry. I'm just surprised, that's all."

"Why?" she asked.

He probably needed to shut the hell up because everything he said was just making the situation worse.

She shrugged. "Actually, I'm sorry. I probably sounded a little defensive. I didn't mean to. All of Steffi-Anne's innuendos and her pointing out all the guys I dated probably gave you the wrong idea."

God, was that what she thought? "Do you think I'm here just because I think you're easy?"

A nervous hiccup escaped her beautiful lips. "That sounds so high school–ish. Are you trying to make it with the *fast girl*, Joaquin?"

"Zoe. Be serious."

"I'm just kidding. Please don't make this any weirder than it already is. And I'll stop making it weird on my end. So, I'll just say it. I have dated a lot of guys, but I've never slept with any of them. In fact, in the past when things have gotten to this point, I usually don't see them anymore."

Joaquin sat back against the couch. "Are you breaking up with me?"

"Am I your girlfriend?"

"Aren't you? I just assumed. But if we're reliving high school, do you want me to ask you to go steady? I know it took me a while to get here." He gestured between them. "But I'd like to see where this goes. We can take things slowly. That doesn't bother me at all. I just want you to be okay with…us."

Zoe looked uncertain and a little uncomfortable.

Joaquin reached down and picked her blouse off the floor and handed it to her.

"Thank you." But she held it in her lap. Sitting there

in her lacy bra, she didn't get dressed or try to hide herself.

"I hope you don't think I'm some kind of a weirdo," she finally said.

"No." He reached out and took her hand. "Of course not."

"When I was in college, one of my friends got burned by a guy who promised to love her forever. So, she gave herself to him body and soul. It lasted maybe three months. He broke her. I know people get hurt every day and lots of relationships don't last, but she was so devastated and I couldn't help but think that if everything was going to end, I didn't want to give myself to a guy who really didn't care that he was taking the most special gift I could give him. He'd just move on like it was nothing. If you think that's weird, it's okay, but it's who I am and I can't be anyone else."

He reached out and lifted her chin so that she was looking him in the eye.

"I don't take it lightly. As long as you'll have me, I'd like to keep exploring this thing between you and me. I want to spend time with you, but let's take it slow."

She smiled at him. "You really are a prince, aren't you?"

He bent down and kissed her, soft and tender.

After he said good-night with a plan for them to cook dinner together tomorrow night, the slow realization washed over him that they *didn't* need to rush things. Women like Zoe didn't fool around for fun. Before anything could happen, he needed to make sure he was ready for the type of serious commitment she was expecting.

* * *

The next day Zoe was relieved when Joaquin acted perfectly normal. She might not be ready to give him that ultimate part of herself just yet, but after he'd left she knew down to her bones that she didn't want to lose him.

She hadn't been kidding when she'd called him a prince. After kissing as many frogs as she had in her life, she would know.

She'd stopped by the coffee shop and picked up two cappuccinos. It was a peace offering, or at least a gesture that meant she truly wanted things to be okay between them.

She'd worried for a moment when she'd gone to his office and he had asked her to shut the door. She was afraid that he'd had time to think about things and change his mind. Because in her experience when guys discovered she was a virgin, they took it one of two ways: they either beat a hasty retreat or they took it as a challenge that they were going to be the one who would convince her she didn't want to save it for marriage.

But after she closed the door, Joaquin had taken the coffees from her and set them on the desk. Then he'd pulled her into his arms and kissed her until she was questioning whether waiting was what she really wanted.

That's how good they were together.

Crazy good.

Fireworks good.

I-want-to-wake-up-to-a-kiss-like-that-every-morning-for-the-rest-of-my-life good.

Zoe wasn't sure if the knocking she heard was her heart pounding or—

"Excuse me?"

Oh, God. It was Steffi-Anne.

After they broke the kiss, Joaquin kept his arm around Zoe.

"Good morning, Steffi-Anne," he said. "How can I help you?"

The woman looked as if she had been sucking on lemons.

"Elaine Baker from personnel and I need to see the two of you in her office right now."

That evening, Zoe sat at Joaquin's kitchen table, looking over the consensual relationship agreement that Elaine Baker and their good friend Steffi-Anne had insisted they sign.

Apparently if two employees were in a relationship, they had to declare it—even if one was an independent contractor and the other was the boss's daughter.

"It's policy set by Mr. Robinson's attorneys," said Steffi-Anne. "It's so people won't sue Robinson Tech for sexual harassment. Zoe, as Gerald's daughter, you of all people should understand how important this is."

"I'm not going to sue anyone," Joaquin said, clearly irritated.

Steffi-Anne pushed the document across the desk toward him. "Then you should have no problem signing this agreement."

"This is the first I've heard of this," Zoe said. "I've dated several Robinson employees, but why has this never come up before now?"

"That's not important," said Elaine. "But I do need both of you to sign these now."

"Neither of us is going to sign anything until we

have time to read through the document carefully," said Zoe. "I'm sure you will understand that we need to take the forms with us."

"Be my guest." Steffi-Anne sniffed. "In fact, take the weekend. But we need them signed and turned in first thing Monday morning."

Or what? Zoe wanted to say. *Are you going to fire us? I don't think so.*

Never in her life had she wanted to play the boss's daughter card so much. Never in the history of working for Robinson Tech had she been so tempted to tell both Elaine Baker and Steffi-Anne to back off or she'd have their jobs. And it had crossed her mind more than once to go to her father and sweet-talk him into letting her be an exception to the rule. And he probably would've done it. He liked Joaquin. He respected him.

Even though Zoe knew that the stunt was strictly fueled by jealousy, she refused to let it compromise her principles.

She had taken such pride in being like everyone else, in working her way up the ladder and proving her worth, that she wasn't going to buckle now. Even if Joaquin had seemed a little bothered by signing a statement that would essentially formalize their relationship. She didn't want to pressure him.

Could there be a case for sexual harassment when they hadn't even had sex? She almost made a joke about it but stopped. She couldn't quite tell if Joaquin was quiet because he was feeling boxed in by this agreement or if her lack of experience was finally sinking in. When she had tried to talk to him about it earlier, he had managed to put her off by changing the subject.

Since they were supposed to be cooking together tonight, it would probably be best to forget the form for now and spend time in the kitchen with him.

Zoe was glad she did because it seemed to be the right choice. Together they made one of Joaquin's favorite dishes: arroz con pollo, chicken and rice. But it was so much more than that. It had red bell peppers and peas cooked in a broth of wine, saffron and tomato paste. It was a little bit of Miami heaven on a plate.

Dinner was so delicious that it seemed to lighten the mood. She certainly didn't want to cause things to go south by pressing the darned consensual relationship agreement.

They had all weekend to deal with it. Right now, she was content to snuggle up next to Joaquin on the couch. While he watched some political show on TV, she read a magazine that she'd picked up on her lunch break because of the cover story about "Bonnie Lord Charlie" Fortune Chesterfield and his fiancée, Alice Meyers.

It was so cozy, she couldn't help but think, *This is what it would be like to be married to Joaquin.* It made her heart sing and the butterflies in her stomach fly in giddy formation.

Savoring the feeling, Zoe flipped the pages until she came to the article on Charles and Alice. Charles Fortune Chesterfield wasn't actually a prince, though that was what the media had dubbed him. But he did come from a long line of British nobility and was devastatingly handsome, if you liked the dark-haired, blue-eyed rakish type. Personally, Zoe preferred men who were tall, dark and Latin. Her appreciative gaze drifted to Joaquin and lingered for a moment before finding its way back to the article about Charles and Alice's whirlwind romance. Their story was enough to make a girl believe in fairy tales. And, of course, she adored those.

The other thing Zoe found so compelling about Charles was that he was actually the youngest son of Josephine Fortune Chesterfield, the same Josephine with whom she'd had dinner at Cowboy Country. Joaquin had cracked a joke about "Bonnie Lord Charlie" when he'd seen the magazine cover, but he hadn't said much else.

In fact, even though Joaquin had been gracious about introducing her to his father when she'd been stranded in Horseback Hollow, he'd told her so little about his family and his background that she had the feeling he might be holding back. As crazy as it seemed, reading about his potential stepbrother felt as though she was getting a glimpse into one facet of Joaquin's life.

Charles and Alice were so old-world chic it made her wistful. She stared at a picture of the couple with their baby boy, Flynn, who had Charles's dark hair and blue eyes. They made an adorable family. Alice was beautiful with her wavy blond shoulder-length hair and blue eyes; she was tall and thin, with long legs that went on for miles. A perfect *lady* for Bonnie Lord Charlie.

She tried not to think of the great Fortune hunt and how Ben kept pushing the issue against their father's wishes. She hadn't talked to her brother since the family meeting last week. But they'd be okay, once he finally accepted the fact that Gerald Robinson was not Jerome Fortune. She just needed to put some distance between them for now.

Yes, it was crazy, she thought as she flipped the pages in the magazine, looking at the photos, pausing to read the captions. Yep. It was all crazy and far-fetched and— She paused at one of the pictures, a close-up of the heirloom ring Charles had given Alice when they got engaged. She held the magazine up to get better light so she could get a better look. The caption said it was a present passed down to Charles from the famous Kate Fortune.

In the light, she could see it was an emerald ring with the letter *F* on it.

Zoe gasped. *No. It can't be. This has to be some sort of* Twilight Zone *coincidence.*

"What's wrong?" Joaquin asked.

Zoe didn't answer because she didn't quite know how to explain. Because if she was remembering right— She suddenly felt a little light-headed.

Joaquin turned off the TV with the remote. "Are you okay? You look like you've seen a ghost."

Zoe gave herself a mental shake. Joaquin was so levelheaded. He could probably help her process this. Besides, if their relationship was going to grow, they needed to share. Just a moment ago she had been thinking about how he didn't seem very open about his own family. Maybe she should encourage communication by example.

"Look at this ring." She pointed to the picture. "I've seen it before. Or one almost exactly like it. I found it when I was a little girl, playing around in my father's office. I thought it was such a treasure. When I asked my dad if I could have it, he snatched it away from me and yelled at me, asking me where I found it. I told him it was in a box on his desk. He asked me how I opened the box because it was supposed to be locked."

Joaquin was listening attentively. She paused, thinking about how to say this last part.

She took a deep breath.

"I remember what happened so vividly because it's the only time I can ever remember my father yelling at me. Even though he yells at everyone else on a daily basis."

She tried to laugh, but it turned into a sob and the tears began to meander down her face.

"Zoe, don't cry." Joaquin wiped her tears. "I want to help, but I'm not sure I understand."

It nearly broke her heart to explain. "This ring in the picture is exactly like my father's. I think I just found the proof that Ben has been looking for to prove—"

A sob caused her voice to break. She cleared her throat before she began again.

"Don't you see what the picture caption says?"

Joaquin picked up the magazine and read it silently.

Zoe found her voice again. "Kate Fortune gave Charles a family heirloom ring that is identical to the one I saw in my father's office that day. Are you doing the math with me, Joaquin?"

Joaquin's brow knit and he nodded as if the truth was slowly dawning on him. But what was he supposed to say? She knew he wasn't going to damn her father. Even after all of this, she didn't want him to.

"I think my father has been lying to us all this time. But why? I don't understand why."

He lowered his gaze, but not before Zoe saw the shadow that darkened his eyes. He was such a complex man that she didn't know what he was thinking. Maybe she shouldn't have told him.

"If it's true," he said, "the only one who can answer that question is your father. All I know is that all families have secrets. So this doesn't make your family any worse."

Zoe's mind was reeling.

"All families have secrets? What's yours, Joaquin?" she asked through her tears.

He frowned, shrugged, but he wouldn't look at her. She had to fight the urge to reach out and lift his chin, to force his eyes to meet hers.

The question seemed to catch him by surprise, but right before he spoke, he leaned in unexpectedly and dusted her lips with a kiss.

"My secret is…that I think I'm falling in love with you."

Chapter Ten

Joaquin was such a study in contradictions.

He claimed to be falling in love with her, yet when Sunday evening rolled 'round, he still hadn't signed the consensual relationship agreement. She'd mentioned it again later Saturday evening, thinking his declaration of love would make signing it a no-brainer. If they were a couple, didn't it stand to reason that they were in a consensual relationship? Then again, they hadn't had sex, so maybe his definition was different than hers. Because when she'd brought it up again, he'd hedged.

That was the last time she was going to mention it. She had other things to sort out right now. Questioning Joaquin's feelings wouldn't do anyone any good.

She had to figure out what she was going to do with the information she'd discovered about the ring Charles Fortune Chesterfield had given his fiancée. What were the chances it was a coincidence that it was identical to the one she'd found in that box that was supposed to be locked in her father's study? If it didn't matter, why had he gone off the rails the way he had? It was the one and only time he'd ever yelled at her. His anger had been so white-hot, it had burned the details of that moment into her brain. She remembered that ring as though she were looking at a photograph of it—and it was the same one she had seen on Alice Meyers's left hand in that magazine photograph.

The question remained, did Alice have his ring? Had her father sold it or pawned it? Although that wasn't his style. He certainly didn't need the money. So had he given it away? But how would it end up in the hands of a member of the Fortune family—the very one Ben had been insisting their father was related to?

The thoughts sent a shiver rushing up Zoe's spine.

She thought about calling a family meeting but two seconds later realized that if she told the others before she talked to her father she would be opening Pandora's box. She didn't want to be the one responsible for that. It felt as though she were letting her father down. No, worse than that. It felt as though she were betraying him.

That's how she came to find herself standing in a hallway in the Robinson estate, outside her father's study. She'd come over to talk to him, but he wasn't home, which she knew because his car wasn't in the garage. She'd checked when she arrived. When the stall had been empty, a great rush of relief had swept through her.

She probably should've called and asked when he would be at home, but she couldn't seem to make the call. Instead she'd come over hoping for the best. She wanted to see his eyes when she told him what she'd found. That way, she would know if he was telling the truth—or not.

Despite his car being gone, Zoe rapped gently on the study door. As she expected, no one answered. However, her knock had pushed the door ajar just a little. Enough for her to see that the lights were off and there were no signs of life in the room, which was lit only by the diffused daylight streaming through the slats of the closed shutters. Still, there was enough light to make out the bookcases that lined the walls, the fine leather furniture and his desk, where she had originally discovered the ring all those years ago. The timeless room with its classic elegance hadn't changed a bit since then. It was like stepping back in time.

Maybe this wouldn't be a wasted trip, after all. If she looked at his ring again, maybe she'd discover that she was mistaken. Maybe it was similar, but different from the piece of jewelry in the magazine picture. In fact, just to be sure, it would be a good idea if she snapped a photo of it with her cell phone. That way she could put the ring away and compare her photo with the picture of Charles Fortune Chesterfield's. She'd torn it out of the magazine and put in her purse, but she would need better light to compare the details.

Yes. That's what she'd do. Just to be sure.

After all, there was no need to upset her father unless she was 100 percent certain that the rings were identical.

She stepped into the study and quietly closed the door behind her. She went to her father's desk and found the fine mahogany box—the one Zoe used to think was a treasure chest, especially when she'd opened it and discovered the ring.

It had been such an unexpected delight, finding jewelry, of all things, in her father's office. She'd been so mesmerized by the gorgeous green stone and the fine gold-filigree setting. She thought it was a magic ring like the one in E. Nesbit's novel *The Enchanted Castle*. She'd put it on her finger and made a wish. Then she'd run to her father, shown him the great treasure she'd discovered and asked him if she could keep it. Of course, the last thing she'd expected was for him to come unglued.

Even though it had happened a long time ago and it hadn't taken long for her father and her to move past it, the incident had scarred her.

Now she tried to lift the lid on the box, but it wouldn't budge. It was locked up tight. She opened the top desk drawer to see if she could find a key. When that search proved fruitless, she picked up a paperclip to see if she could pick the lock. She'd never done that before, but it was worth a try.

She closed the desk drawer, lowered herself into her father's chair and moved the box closer to her. She had the paperclip in the lock and was actively working it when the door to the study opened.

Her father turned on the lights and started when he saw her.

"What the hell, Zoe? What the hell are you doing in here?"

All of a sudden she was six years old again, caught red-handed doing something that this time she knew good and well displeased him.

But before she could come up with an excuse—she

never had been able to lie—she had a moment of clarity. She cupped the paperclip in her hand and stood to face him.

"Dad, we need to talk."

"The only thing we're going to talk about is why the hell you are in here, trying to jimmy open my private lockbox."

Only this time his anger didn't shred her the way it had the first time.

He walked over to the desk, reached across and grabbed the box, turning it around to inspect the front of it.

"What are you doing, Zoe?"

Maybe she should've talked to him before entering his study. Despite the sickening feeling that she knew the answer to the question, she still needed to ask him. Even so, it would've been nice to have irrefutable proof before she opened this can of worms. The only way to handle this was to be direct.

"I'm looking for that emerald ring. You know the one I'm talking about, don't you? The one with the filigree setting and the *F* monogram."

"I have no idea what you're talking about. I think you'd better leave and don't you ever let me catch you sneaking around and snooping through my possessions again."

"You can't tell me you don't know which ring I'm talking about. It was the one I discovered when I was six years old. It was right here in this box." She reached for her purse and pulled out the picture of Charles and Alice. "It's just like this one that Charles Fortune Chesterfield gave to his fiancée."

"I said I have no idea what you're talking about. Are you deaf? I also told you to get out."

Zoe grabbed her purse. "Fine. If you won't talk to me about it, I'll talk to Ben. I think this might be the missing piece he's been looking for in his search to prove that we are, in fact, related to the Fortunes."

She walked past her father and out the door, knowing full well that he knew she was calling his bluff. She also knew that if he let her leave without talking to her about this, she fully intended to go straight to Ben's house and show him the photo.

Gerald let her get down the hallway before he called to her.

"Zoe, get back here."

She didn't wait for him to ask her twice. She came back into his office and shut the door. But she waited for him to speak first.

"Look, I don't want you to go away mad," Gerald said. "You know we've always had a special bond." His tone was softer now, the anger that had flown off his tongue in sparks and flames a moment ago diffused. Of course he was being nice and playing the favorite-child card again. He didn't want her to spill the beans about the ring.

At heart, she'd always been the consummate daddy's girl, the one who'd loved him unconditionally. She'd wanted nothing more than to please him. But his time his ploys weren't going to work.

"I know it's the same ring, Dad. Do you want to explain?"

He couldn't look her in the eyes.

"Come on, Dad. It's me you're talking to. I'm not

going to run out and tell everyone. You can trust me to keep your secret. But you do owe me an explanation."

It was the first time she'd ever seen her father look defeated. But he did. He stood there, slack jawed and confused, staring at the floor.

She resolved not to say a word until he spoke. She'd let him break the silence.

A couple of uncomfortable minutes ticked by before he finally spoke.

"I was never accepted by the Fortune family."

So, it was true.

Even though she knew it was coming, his confession knocked the air out of Zoe. It took all of her willpower to keep from demanding to know why he'd lied. But she managed to hold it in, despite the way her heart ached and all the questions that flooded her mind: Was he Jerome Fortune? If so, why did everyone think Jerome was dead?

Gerald motioned toward the couch. They both sat down.

Her dad rested his forearms on his knees and stared at the ground as if arranging his thoughts.

"My father was a brutal man." Gerald's voice was shaky. "I was an only child and he was dead-set on me following in his footsteps and going into the family business. He wanted me to be his protégé. So he could control me. He owned a brokerage firm. I had absolutely no interest in following in my old man's footsteps. And he couldn't stand that.

"Computers fascinated me. People did not. I couldn't deal with the all the phoniness and small talk you had to do to con people into giving you their money to invest. But I tried. I actually went to work for the

company, and I failed miserably. The clients didn't appreciate the way I spoke my mind. I didn't blow sunshine up their asses, and it cost my dad business. Every
day of my life my father reminded me that I was a disappointment. That I was a loser. He had no idea what I
was capable of. So, I decided to show him."

Gerald harrumphed.

Zoe sat rapt, afraid that if she made a sound she
might jar him out of this almost trancelike state.

"I had discovered how to breach some pretty sophisticated mainframe firewalls," he said. "I figured if
I could hack into systems and learn of pending deals,
my dad could have the jump on the average Joe. That
meant I could not only make up for the business I'd
cost him, but I could make it possible for him to have
unheard-of success. If I hacked my way to the information, could it really be considered insider trading?
So, I did it and for a few months things were better. He
couldn't believe I had made such a miraculous turn-
around. I hated myself. I felt like I was living a lie. I
decided to tell him the truth. When I did, the man went
ballistic and gave me an ultimatum—give up computers or leave.

"So, I left."

Zoe had heard rumblings that her dad didn't always operate aboveboard, that no one made the kind
of money he made by being on the up-and-up. She'd
figured it was envy and sour grapes. Maybe she was
naive, but having it confirmed that her father was just
as bad as everyone claimed was devastating. He was
supposed to be better than that. She'd always believed
in him.

"My mother said that if I walked out, I could never come back. I would be dead to them."

As stunned as she was by her father's fall from grace, her heart also ached for him. Obviously he hadn't had an easy time of it growing up. Her father was gruff and usually a little too focused on business, but he'd never called his children losers or made them feel bad about using their God-given gifts and talents. He had offered all of them jobs at Robinson Tech, but he hadn't taken it personally when a couple of them had wanted to explore their own paths.

What's more, he had built this company from nothing. The man was a genius and the things he had done with Robinson Tech had made a difference in the world. He'd never really hurt anyone. Maybe the good that he'd done canceled out his transgressions.

Zoe knew she was kidding herself again.

"So is that what Jacqueline Fortune meant when she said her son was dead?" Zoe asked.

Gerald's head snapped up and his nostrils flared. "How do you know Jacqueline Fortune?"

"Ben found her and contacted her. I thought he would've told you. She's your mother, right?"

"No. He didn't tell me. What exactly did Ben say to you?"

It didn't escape her that he'd evaded her question about his mother. She'd come back to that.

Zoe took a deep breath as she processed everything. Her dad had always said that his parents were dead. Yet her grandmother had been alive all these years. Alive, and she'd never had the chance to get to know her.

"Ben said she's in a nursing home and is suffering from dementia. When he asked her about Jerome Fortune, Jacqueline got hysterical and insisted that her son was dead. You sent her a suicide note and let her live alone all these years?"

Gerald hung his head.

"Why would you let your own mother think that? It must've broken her heart."

Her tone was a little sharper than she'd intended, but, come on. "How could you do that, Dad? Let all these years go by with her thinking you were dead?"

For that matter, how had he pulled it off?

Her father stared at her for so long that it felt as if he was looking through her, not at her.

Finally he shrugged. "I told you this much, I might as well tell you everything. After they told me I was dead to them and kicked me out, I *borrowed* some money from them. I was going to pay them back, but I was on the street. I needed some money to tide me over until I could find a job. We're talking food and shelter here. I wasn't funding a lavish lifestyle. I figured it was the least they could do. They brought me into this world and they kicked me out. I was barely eighteen. When my father realized I'd taken the money, he confronted me. We got into an argument. He said he was going to call the cops and have me arrested. I told him if he did, I would alert the authorities about the insider trading. The words had no sooner left my mouth when my father had a heart attack and died right in front of me."

Zoe gasped. "How awful. I'm sorry you had to go through that."

Her father shrugged. "If I'm being completely candid, I wasn't sorry the man was gone. His self-righteous attitude was like the pot calling the kettle black because not all of his business deals were honest. My old man had his own set of values. He hated technology and computers because he didn't understand them and couldn't control them. What he couldn't control pissed him off.

"I think the worst part of it was that my mom blamed me for his death. She said I murdered my father and that she never wanted to see me again. She accused me of killing him so that I could get my inheritance. The guy was loaded, but I didn't want his money. Her accusations cut me so deeply that I decided I wanted to make her pay. The way I did that was by leaving town. I used my hacking skills to create a new identity and I staged my own death so no one would come looking for me. I sent my mother a note saying I couldn't live with myself for causing my father's death and she would be better off without me."

"Oh, my God. Are you making this up?"

He shook his head.

"I launched an unmanned boat that was registered to my family and when the empty vessel washed ashore, Jerome Fortune was presumed dead."

Zoe wiped at the horrified tears clouding her eyes. "This is the saddest thing I have ever heard." A sob swallowed the rest of her words.

"As far as I am concerned, Jerome Fortune is dead," her father said. "He died the day I became Gerald Robinson. But don't be sad for me, princess. Gerald Robinson has had a wonderful life. I am a self-made man. I am successful beyond my wildest dreams. I have raised a family and I wouldn't change a thing."

Zoe was trying her hardest to stop the sobbing, but it had gripped her like a spirit possessing her body. "You wouldn't change the fact that you lied to your children about who you are? About who *we* are? Not the fact that you let your own mother believe you were dead? What pain she must've suffered."

Gerald shook his head. "She accused me of murder, princess." His voice was so resigned that it was spooky. "She told me she didn't want to be the mother of a murderer. She made it perfectly clear. She disowned me."

Zoe stood and held up her hands in a signal for him to stop talking. "I have to go. This is all too much. I believed in you, Dad. I defended you when Ben went against your wishes and kept pushing the Fortune connection. But he was right all along."

Zoe remembered the rumor about the legions of illegitimate children her father might have sired. But she didn't ask him because she really didn't want to know. At this point, she couldn't bear that it might be true.

Who was this man who used to be her knight in shining armor? She didn't even know him anymore. She opened her purse, fished for a tissue and blotted her eyes before she blew her nose.

"Are you going to tell your siblings everything?"

The walls suddenly felt as if they were closing in on her.

"No, I'm not. But it's not because I'm protecting you. You're the one who owes them an explanation. They need to hear it from you. So, this all on you, Dad."

Chapter Eleven

Zoe drove around Austin for a good hour, trying to process everything her father had told her. Her mind was on overload, with a pileup of thoughts converging and screaming all at once. On the one hand, her dad had suffered a terrible upbringing. It sounded as if his father had been unspeakably cruel. But, on the other hand, he had not only lived a lie, he also had lied to his family all these years, robbing his children of their own history and possibly a relationship with their grandmother.

Now Zoe faced the monumental task of deciding what to do with the information. To tell her siblings or not to tell? She'd been in such shock when she'd left her parents' house that she'd told her father she'd keep his secret. Not because she was protecting him or slighting her siblings—and definitely not because she was afraid to admit she had been wrong not to support their crusade—but because it was not her story to tell. It belonged to her father—it was his confession and it needed to come from him.

Still, Zoe couldn't quite make peace with that, either.

She needed to talk to somebody. Somebody who was unbiased. Somebody whose judgment she trusted.

Even before she was aware of what she was doing, she was steering her car into the parking lot of Joaquin's apartment building.

She pulled out her phone and texted him.

Are you home?

I am.

Look out your window.

She saw the blinds open in the second-story window of his apartment.

I'm glad you're here. I need to talk to you about something. Come up.

She felt better already because of how welcome he made her feel. He always brightened her days, especially when they got tough. It warmed her from the inside out.

When she got upstairs to his place, he was waiting for her at the door. He was wearing jeans and a brown Life is Good T-shirt with a picture of a dog next to a campfire. It struck her as funny because she didn't think of him as rugged or outdoorsy. He was more of a suit-and-tie, office sort of guy. Or better yet, a tangled-bodies-in-the-bedroom type.

The last thought made her blush. It was pretty amazing that she would even think that way because her relationships never made it to the point where her subconscious was contemplating getting—no, longing to get—naked and tangled up with a man. But this wasn't just any man. This was Joaquin.

Joaquin, who had said he was falling in love with her, which had opened the flood gates and allowed so many emotions to start pouring out.

As she fell into his arms, inhaling the delicious scent of him, she felt as if she'd finally found the place where she belonged.

"Hey, what's going on?" Joaquin asked. "Are you okay?"

He held her at arm's length for a moment, studying her face. When she didn't answer he said, "Come in. Talk to me."

He ushered her inside. He was leasing the furnished apartment for six months while he was working on the project for Robinson. The place was clean and, while the furniture wasn't fancy, it looked new and functional. He had told her not too long ago that if he stayed in Austin, he would look to buy. He'd even asked her to recommend good areas. While he hadn't said anything about them moving in together, it seemed as if they had a future.

In the midst of the family maelstrom, he was her touchstone, her beacon in the stormy night.

She took a seat on the couch and was a little surprised when he chose the chair across from her rather than sitting next to her, but the concern on his face was real.

"Zoe? What's going on?"

For a moment she couldn't speak. She didn't know where to start or how to tell him that the one man in her life she had always trusted had been lying to her and her siblings their entire lives.

Finally she forced out the words. "I'm confiding in you. Please promise me what I tell you will remain in the strictest confidence. Because I trust you, Joaquin."

He nodded. His brows knit with obvious concern. "Of course."

"It turns out that my dad is Jerome Fortune, after all."

His eyes widened and, for a moment, he looked as though she had just told him she had had a personal encounter with the Sasquatch. In a sense, Jerome Fortune did feel like a mythical creature.

"What do you mean?" he asked.

"I mean exactly what I said. Gerald Robinson is Jerome Fortune."

He shook his head. "No, what I meant was, how do you know this, or what makes you think this? You were always so adamantly against your siblings pushing to establish this connection. Did they find some evidence that supports their theory?"

"No. I'm the one who found it. Actually, it's not just evidence. It's irrefutable proof."

His eyes widened again and all of a sudden a look of realization passed over his face. "Is it the ring? Did you talk to your father?"

She nodded, and she hated herself, but the tears started falling and she couldn't stop them.

"I went to see him this morning and we sort of had it out. He tried to deny it at first, but when I threatened to take the picture to Ben, he told me everything. The ring is only the tip of the iceberg."

She didn't know if she could tell him, because relaying the whole sordid tale to someone else underscored the terrible things her father was capable of, the things he'd done. But she needed his advice. She needed to sort it all out and the only way she could do that was to review everything her dad had told her, detail by dirty detail.

She took a deep breath and told Joaquin everything.

"Now I don't know what to do. I told him I wouldn't say anything to my brothers and sisters. And when I came over here, I wasn't sure if that was the right thing to do—"

"Of course it is. You have to tell them, Zoe. You owe it to them."

She flinched at his words. "What I *started to say* was, after telling you everything, I think I've decided that it's not my place to tell them. He needs to be the one to do that."

Joaquin shook his head resolutely. "I don't agree with you."

Irritation sparked in her veins. Why was he being like this? She may have thought she'd come over here for advice, but she hadn't asked him for any. And as it turned out, she didn't want it; she just needed a trusted sounding board.

"I don't mean to be mean," she said, "but I didn't ask you if you agreed or not."

She saw his walls go up and his gate slam shut.

"Then why did you come over here?"

His words connected like a punch to the gut. Wow. And it hurt.

"It certainly wasn't to make you mad. I came over here because I needed someone to listen. I had no idea this would make you so angry and judgmental."

Yeah, why was he so angry about this? It really didn't have anything to do with him. That was one of the reasons she'd decided to talk to him about it. Well, that, and if things were getting as serious between them as they seemed, she needed to be able to share things like this with him. But what she didn't need was stern disapproval.

He drummed his fingers on the arm of the chair. "Look, Zoe, you said yourself that one of the reasons you were upset was that he had kept your heritage from you all these years. Because of that, you'll never know your grandmother. You know firsthand that it's wrong to keep someone's heritage from him or her. Now, no matter how painful it is for you, you owe it to your siblings to tell them what you've discovered."

"Joaquin, it's not my secret to tell."

He shrugged. "Since we're talking about your father and I'm advocating full disclosure, there's something I need to tell you."

"Absolutely," she said. "You can tell me anything."

"You might not want to hear this. But that day that we were at Cowboy Country, I saw your father getting pretty cozy with a woman who wasn't your mother."

Zoe winced. Her father's indiscretions weren't a secret. Even though it hurt her heart and was embarrassing, the issue was between him and her mother. She certainly didn't want to discuss it with Joaquin. Not on top of what she'd come to tell him. "I appreciate you telling me, but that's nothing compared to what I learned today."

Joaquin squinted at her. "Cheating is nothing?"

Zoe rolled her eyes. "You're putting words in my mouth. Don't."

The two of them sat there in stalemate silence. He wasn't going to budge and neither was she. She did appreciate his honesty, but the last thing she needed right now was another issue heaped on top of the mess she was already carrying. She couldn't even look at Joaquin right now. She couldn't even look at him. Actually she wished she hadn't told him. She wished she hadn't even come over.

She stood. "I need to go. Please just forget I said anything about this."

As she started toward the door, she spied his copy of the consensual relationship agreement lying on the bar area that separated the kitchen from the living room. He still hadn't signed it. Great. She wasn't about to remind him about it. He was a big boy and God knew a fight wasn't the right moment to bring that up.

Were they having their first fight?

"Zoe, I don't mean to be unsupportive. Secrets are never a good idea. Your siblings had a feeling that your father was Jerome Fortune and it turns out to be the truth. You keeping your dad's confession from them doesn't change the facts. It also doesn't mean that you're spreading gossip and rumors. You are not going to hurt them by telling them the truth. You are going to give them a gift of knowing who they really are. If anything, you're hurting them by not telling them."

Obviously they weren't going to solve anything. Joaquin may have had a point that keeping this to herself wasn't going to change the truth, but she stood by the fact that it wasn't her place to tell her father's story. Her dad may have proved himself to be a liar, but he was still her dad. He had always been good to her. Basically, without saying it, she had promised him he could tell his kids the truth in his own way and in his own time. She couldn't see how Joaquin could think he was being supportive by badgering her to break a promise.

"I'll talk to you tomorrow, Joaquin."

"I'm speaking from a place of experience, Zoe."

Before she could think better of it, she whirled around. "How in the world could you have had a similar experience to this? Your family is wonderful. I met your dad. He's great. I'm sure he never faked his death, created a new identity and pretended to be someone he's not. So please don't say that you've been here, because you haven't."

"It's true, Orlando is a great man. But sometimes things are not always as they appear on the surface. So, even though I haven't experienced verbatim what you're going through, I am facing the challenge of someone dear to me not being who they *think* they are." He softened his tone. "But you wouldn't know that because I haven't told you."

What in the world?

"What are you talking about, Joaquin?"

Those lips that she loved so much were pressed into a thin line and she could see the wheels in his mind turning. He looked just as upset as she felt.

She walked back to the sofa and lowered herself onto the cushion.

"Please tell me what's going on," she said. "Help me understand."

He looked at her with such heartbreak in his eyes that she wanted to take him into her arms and assure him that, no matter what it was, together they could make it better. But she didn't. Instead she sat there, letting him tell her in his own time.

"In a nutshell, I have very good reason to believe that Orlando is not my father. Or not my biological father, anyway. I don't know if he knows. I do know that once upon a time my mother had a thing for my uncle Esteban and apparently he led her on quite a chase. I don't know if my dad stole my mother away from my uncle or what happened. But I found a person with Orlando's blood type can't father a child with mine."

"How did you find out?"

"When my mother was sick. She needed a blood transfusion and Orlando was not a match for her blood type. I was, though. Of course. The doctor had mentioned Orlando's blood type in passing and it floored me. I remembered some basic genetics from high school biology, and there was no way that his blood type and my mother's blood type would produce a baby with my blood type."

Zoe reached out and squeezed his hand. "Have you talked to your father about this?"

"Not yet."

"How long has your mom been gone?"

"She died four years ago."

Zoe tried not to frown. "That was a while ago. Why haven't you talked to your dad about it?"

"That's a good question. I don't know the whole story. But I have reason to believe that my mother may have been cheating on him. He may be aware of it, too. And that could be why he brushed me off when I initially questioned the discrepancy at the hospital. But my mother was dying and my dad was grief-stricken. She was his soul mate and if he does know, he obviously forgave her.

"For a long time I brushed it off because I thought if he could forgive her, then there was no reason to talk about it. But the more time that went by, the more it weighed on me. If he's not my biological father, who is? I mean, Orlando was the best dad anyone could ever want, but I finally came to the conclusion that knowing about my birth father didn't necessarily have to take anything away from the love and gratitude I feel for Orlando."

"So...why are you having a tough time talking to him about it?"

"How do you ask your father if your mother—his wife, his soul mate—was unfaithful? It's even trickier than that. I think I know who my birth father might be."

Zoe's eyes widened and she leaned forward. "Who?"

"I have very good reason to believe that my mother may have had an affair with my uncle Esteban, my father's brother. I put two and two together and it just made sense. My dad and my uncle have been estranged for years—all my life. Nobody talks about the reason they don't speak. I've wondered if anybody even knows. My dad and my uncle aren't prone to holding grudges with anyone else. But the bad blood between them seems to run deep. It's the only thing that makes sense. So, for the last year or so, I've been pondering whether my uncle actually is my father. And wondering if Orlando has been keeping it from me all this time."

Zoe's heart ached for him. That would be a huge burden to shoulder. She understood why he might hesitate to bring up the issue after it had been buried all these years. Even though it wasn't a carbon copy of her own situation, it was parallel and she understood the angst he must be feeling. She just wondered why he couldn't seem to cut her any slack, since he hadn't yet faced his own demons.

"I've contemplated talking to Esteban about it, but I feel duty bound to discuss it with Orlando first."

"I totally get that," said Zoe. "So, are you going to talk to your dad?"

Joaquin shrugged. "I don't know. I've been waiting for the right time. At first Orlando was so grief-stricken I thought he was never going to get over my mother's death. The last thing he needed was for me to ask, 'Oh, by the way, did you know your wife may have been having an affair, *and* did you know that I'm not your biological son?'"

Zoe nodded her understanding.

"My sister Gabi had some medical problems. Her health was still fragile when my mom died. He had just lost his wife and he was afraid he would lose his daughter, too. It wasn't the time. After he was sure Gabi was stable, he moved to Horseback Hollow. Since I was still in Miami, I barely got to see him as it was. I didn't want what little time we had together to be overshadowed by the revelation that I'm not his son. Then I moved to Horseback Hollow, fully intending to get to the bottom of the situation, but he had just started coming out of his grief. He's so happy with Josephine. I just couldn't pull him back into the shadows again. He's happy. I can't remember a time when he was so happy. I guess it was before my mom and Gabi got sick."

"You do understand that there never will be a perfect time, right?" Zoe's voice was gentle. "Since it's weighing so heavily on you, I think you need to just go visit your father and talk to him. He is happy now. If he takes it hard, he has Josephine to lean on."

She shook her head and gave him a sad smile. "Now it's my turn to be the bossy one. Take it from someone who knows. You think it's going to be painful to dig up the past, but the truth is, it's worse to keep it bottled up. Silence is so corrosive. It eats away at you and your relationships. Look at the wedges that my father's lies have driven between my brothers and sisters and me, and between them and him. I know the truth and I still maintain that my dad needs to be the one to tell them, but there's no getting around it. The truth is the only thing that will set you free, and the only way you're going to find that truth is to talk to Orlando yourself. Otherwise, this baggage you're carrying around will keep coming between you and the life you deserve. The past doesn't change how Orlando has loved you and it doesn't have to change your relationship with him going forward. Take it from someone who is speaking from experience."

She'd meant the part about speaking from experience to lighten the mood, since she was echoing what he'd said earlier. But Joaquin wasn't laughing. He was sitting there with a blank look on his face that bordered on annoyance.

"Look, I think we are going to have to agree to disagree on these issues," he said. "I think you need to tell your siblings and I think there will be a better time to talk to my dad about my issue."

"You think I'm wrong for not breaking my father's

confidence, but you are not willing to talk to your father about your paternity?"

"Right," Joaquin said. "They are similar situations, but they need to be handled differently. The only reason I brought up my situation was because I know how it feels to be lied to about your heritage. Nobody deserves that, Zoe. I'm not the one keeping this from anyone."

"You might be if your father doesn't know. You're just assuming that he does."

Joaquin shook his head. "It's still different. You know and you're perpetuating the lie if you don't expose it."

Who is this person?

Just last night he told her he thought he was falling in love with her. Now he was condemning her and casting her into the same liar's arena as her father.

"So, you're pinning this on me? You are not even willing to fix your own situation, and you are judging me for keeping my father's confidence? Oh, that's rich, Joaquin. Neither one of us seems to be in a good place to talk about this right now. I'll see you at work tomorrow."

Tears stung her eyes. She swiped at them before they could fall.

She had just put her hand on the doorknob when he said, "I don't think it's a good idea for us to sign that form."

She looked at him over her shoulder and her heart clenched when she saw his face. "The consensual relationship agreement?"

He nodded. "I'm sorry to bring it up now. I know you're dealing with a lot, but Steffi-Anne is bound to ask us about it tomorrow and I thought we needed to be on the same page or even be proactive and go talk to her in the morning."

"Talk to her about what?" Zoe didn't even try to hide the irritation in her voice. She was too busy trying to recover from the emotional whiplash. First, he did the two-step about their family situations, saying she should tell when he had no plans to fix his own. He said he was falling in love with her, then he objected to signing a simple form stating that they were in a consensual relationship.

This day was becoming her worst nightmare. Everything was falling apart.

"I've been thinking about it this morning," he said. "I'm still not sure where I'm going to be when this project ends in a couple of weeks. Actually, I've been doing some thinking since Steffi-Anne thrust that consensual relationship agreement on us. I think the world of you, Zoe. You are one of the most amazing women I've ever met in my life. You are just sweet and unjaded. You still believe in fairy tales and happy endings, and you deserve someone who can give that to you. I meant what I said last night about falling in love with you, but I just don't know if I can be the man you need. The man who deserves you."

Standing there with her hand on the doorknob, Zoe felt her heart shatter into a million irreparable pieces. This was the first time she had found someone who seemed so right, someone who actually did make her believe she could have her happily-ever-after, and now he wanted out.

Through the tears and the fog in her head, she heard herself telling him, "Please don't do this, Joaquin. I love you. Take some time if you need to figure out what you want, but I won't give up on you."

She heard him say something about doing this for her own good, about protecting her from worse heartache down the road. But she simply opened the door and let herself out. He didn't come after her.

He let her walk away.

Even though it was ridiculous to keep pursuing a man who had made it perfectly clear he didn't want her, the tiny shard of her heart that held the illogical belief that love would triumph over all was still hanging on by a thread.

She meant what she'd said. No matter how hopeless it seemed, she loved him and she wouldn't give up on him.

Chapter Twelve

If Joaquin thought his heart had ached when he had caught his fiancée, Selena, in bed with his best friend, it seemed like nothing compared to the black tar of despair he sank in to Sunday night after ending things with Zoe.

One of the conclusions he'd come to during his sleepless night was that he had made a big mistake by letting her go. The conundrum was, it was a mistake for him to not have her in his life, but reason reminded him she was better off without him. She was such a light in this world. She didn't need him and all his darkness snuffing out her flame.

He felt like such a jackass for being so hard on her yesterday. She hadn't deserved that and he would apologize once he got back to work. She had come to him looking for support, but he had let the stress of knowing he had to tell her he wasn't going to sign the relationship document, and the nerve that her situation with her father had struck in him, turn him into a beast.

That in itself proved he didn't deserve her.

Who was he to tell her what to do—so arrogantly, too—when he couldn't even figure out his own screwed-up life?

Still that didn't mitigate the way he missed her. It hadn't even been a full twenty-four hours and his heart felt as if it would bleed out. He had plenty of time to think about it as he drove to visit his father in Horseback Hollow.

After stewing on Zoe's words all night, he realized she was right. There never would be a perfect time. The only way he was going to lose his baggage was by talking to his father.

Since Orlando was an early riser, Joaquin knew it was okay to call at five o'clock on Monday morning. In fact, it would probably be the best time to reach him, because it would be before he got to work at the Redmond Flight School.

When he'd asked his dad if he had plans for lunch, that he would like to drive up to see him, Orlando had said even if he'd had plans, he would've canceled them to have lunch with his oldest son. He sounded so happy that Joaquin would take the time to come visit him. As he got closer to Horseback Hollow, Joaquin started second-guessing his decision to finally ask his dad about the paternity issue, but Zoe's words echoed in his head.

There will never be a perfect time.

He may have already blown it with Zoe. The way he'd acted yesterday, he was certain he had. But he would never be at peace with himself if he didn't have this conversation with his father.

Rather than having everything unfold in a public place, Joaquin stopped at a gourmet sandwich shop in Vicker's Corners, a small, funky town located right next to Horseback Hollow. He picked up two roast beef, arugula and béarnaise sauce sandwiches, some red potato salad, a large bag of kettle chips and a gallon of freshly brewed peach iced tea.

He picked up his father from work and they went to Hanging Moss Park, a scenic little oasis not too far from Redmond Flight School. They sat at a picnic table and enjoyed their feast. Joaquin waited until they were both finished before he brought up the paternity question.

As Orlando gathered up his fork and the paper his sandwich had been wrapped in and stuffed them back into the empty sack the lunch had come in, he said, "Now, this was a treat and such a nice surprise. It isn't every day that I get to have lunch with my oldest son."

It seemed the perfect segue into what Joaquin had come to talk about.

"We don't get to spend enough time together, do we?" Joaquin said. "I was thinking the other day, I don't know that I've ever thanked you for the way you raised me."

Orlando looked slightly bemused. "You're welcome. But where is this coming from?"

It was now or never.

"You know, that no matter what, I love you and nothing can ever change that fact."

Now, Orlando was scrutinizing him through narrowed eyes.

"There's something I've needed to talk to you about for a few years now. I haven't, because the time simply never seemed right. And I finally realized that there never would be a perfect time. That's why I decided on a random Monday to drive six hours and have lunch and a heart-to-heart with my *father.*"

He emphasized the word, wanting to see if Orlando would have a reaction, but his demeanor didn't change. He still sat there, watching Joaquin, as if he wasn't quite sure where the conversation was going.

"Remember at the hospital when Mom needed the blood transfusion? I gave her blood because mine was a match and yours wasn't."

He saw a flicker in his father's eyes.

"I'll cut to the chase, Dad. Simple genetics show that there is no way your and Mom's blood types could've produced a child with my blood type. Mine is consistent with hers. That means you're not my biological father. I'm not sure what this means. But I've worried for years it meant that Mom was having an affair when I was conceived."

Joaquin held his breath as he waited for a reaction from his father. Each second that ticked by was a dagger in Joaquin's heart as he anticipated Orlando's response.

Finally his father said, "I'm sorry you've shouldered this burden for so long, son. I wish you would've come to me sooner. Ah, hell, I should have opened the dialogue with you after you gave blood for your mother. There's really no excuse, except that I knew you were grieving. I was grieving. We lost her so soon after that and then it seemed like everything, life as we knew it, had been sucked into a black hole. I didn't know how you would take the truth and since you didn't bring it up again, I figured you didn't want to know. I used the excuse of all the change in our lives, of all the grief that we were suffering, to chicken out of leveling with you. But if you would like to know the truth, I'm willing to tell you everything."

Joaquin's heart beat so fast and furiously he could hear it in his ears.

"I do want to know, but I don't want it to change anything between us. Someone else may be my biological father, but you will always be my dad."

Orlando forced a smile as he nodded. Joaquin could see his dad's throat work as he swallowed.

"Nothing could ever change the love I have for you," Orlando said as he picked at a rough grain of wood on the picnic-table surface. He was quiet for a long, excruciating moment before he continued.

"Esteban is your father, but it's not what you think. Your mother was not cheating on me with him. Nor did she deceive me about your paternity. I've always known that you were Esteban's son."

Joaquin's mind whirled. "I knew that Mom briefly dated Esteban, but I never knew what happened or how the two of you ended up together. It seemed like a taboo subject. I mean, the two of you were soul mates. It seemed like there was nobody else for her before you. Will you tell me what happened? Because if she didn't cheat on you, I don't understand how she could conceive a child with him."

Orlando nodded. "That's a fair question. It's sort of complicated, but I'll do my best to explain."

His dad took a long swallow of iced tea, set the glass down and looked him in the eyes.

"I'd always, always had a crush on your mother. We'd known each other since we were children. I think my first memory is of falling in love with her. But Luz always carried a torch for Esteban. Your uncle, he was kind of a scoundrel and a rake. He led your mom on a merry chase. She used to confide in me about her feelings for Esteban. I loved Luz so much it was enough for me to be her confidante because it was the only way I could be with her. Esteban used to always take Luz for granted. He knew he could have her, but he was a popular guy. He had all kinds of girls after him. But Esteban and Luz did eventually date. It nearly killed me. Because he was not really in love with her and he still carried on with other women. In fact, he and I used to fight about that all the time, but he justified it by saying that that he and Luz were not exclusive.

"Well, your mama wound up pregnant, but she didn't discover it until after Esteban had run off and eloped with somebody else. When Luz told me about the pregnancy, I married her and vowed to raise the child as my own. I knew I had enough love for the two of us. Esteban was married. What good would it have done to tell him? Your mama and I promised each other we would never tell a soul that the baby wasn't mine. And as far as I'm concerned, you are as much mine as your brothers and sister."

Joaquin knew Orlando was a good guy. He had always thought so much of his father that he didn't think there was room to idolize him any more than he already did. But in the moment following his confession, Orlando Mendoza—his father—became a saint in his eyes.

"What about the bad blood between you and Esteban? Does he know the truth? Is that why you two don't speak?"

Orlando sighed. It was the sound of discontent, resignation.

"Because of Luz's pregnancy and premature delivery, Esteban believes that Luz and I were sleeping together while he was still dating her."

Joaquin balked. "That's ridiculous and pretty damn hypocritical. He was cheating on Mom left and right, according to what you say."

Orlando nodded. "Yes, he was. But all he could see was that I betrayed him. I was never interested in anyone beside your mother, so I didn't date very much. Oh, I tried here and there, but my heart belonged to your mama. Since Luz and I were close, he automatically assumed that I'd been sleeping with her when he was dating her.

"You know, for years, I felt justified in not telling Esteban that you were his son. I wanted to protect your mama from further pain, because you know it was bound to get sticky once anyone found out. Luz was the love of my life. I worshiped that woman and I would've given my life to spare hers. I didn't think I was ever going to survive losing her, but over the past few years that she's been gone I've realized that we were wrong to keep the paternity from both you and Esteban. I didn't know how to undo that mistake. So much time had passed, I didn't know if it would make things better or worse. I don't expect you to ever forgive me, but I hope someday you will understand why I did what I did. When you love someone the way I loved your mama—the way I love you—you'd do absolutely anything to protect them. Life is short, son.

Way too short not to do everything in your power to take care of those you love. But, son, I will do whatever you want. If you want to tell Esteban, we can. We'll handle it however you think we should."

The midday sun streamed through the branches of the live oak tree that shaded their picnic table. Rays of light, like beacons of hope, streamed down and a gentle breeze blew in like a comforting kiss from his mother.

"There's nothing to forgive," Joaquin said. "You did the best you could with the situation you found yourself in. If not for you, who knows what might've happened to Mom and me? There's no way I could ever be anything but grateful."

The look of absolute relief on his father's face nearly did him in.

Joaquin cleared his throat. "However, Esteban needs to know the truth. When do you think we could go to Miami to talk to him?"

Orlando nodded. "If you're available, we can go right now. We can take one of the Redman planes and be there in a couple of hours."

"Let's do it," said Joaquin.

Three hours later Joaquin and Orlando landed at Miami Executive Airport. They had called Esteban before they'd left to make sure he was around and willing to see them. Joaquin told him they had urgent family business to discuss, and Esteban agreed to see them.

In Miami they rented a car, checked into the hotel they had booked after confirming their visit with Esteban— Orlando didn't like to fly at night—and set out to mend some fences.

It was strange how Miami, with its electric-neon

lights, royal palm trees and colorful bougainvillea, was so familiar yet felt so strange. On the drive to his uncle's home, they passed many places that used to be Joaquin's local haunts, but now they felt unfamiliar, like acquaintances from another lifetime.

He hadn't expected Miami to feel so distant. It definitely wasn't home anymore. Funny, sometimes you had to leave your own backyard to discover how much it meant to you. In this case, Austin was now his backyard.

They arrived at Esteban's brick ranch-style house right on time. As Joaquin killed the rental car's engine, he glanced over at Orlando, who looked a little green and subdued.

"You all right?" Joaquin asked.

Orlando gave a resolute nod. "I should've done this a long time ago. Even if he tells me he doesn't want to see me again, at least I know I tried. At least he knows the truth."

Both Joaquin and Orlando had been surprised by how happy Esteban sounded when they told him they were coming for a visit. Actually, they had been amazed by Esteban's warm greeting, which had made it much easier to get down to business and tell him what they had come to say.

"When my mother was sick, she needed a blood transfusion," Joaquin said. "My mom and I both had O positive blood, which meant I was a perfect match for her, but Orlando couldn't be a donor because he had type AB blood, which is incompatible with ours."

Joaquin paused and saw the flicker of understanding dawning in Esteban's eyes.

"I'm not a genetics expert," Esteban said, "but if

I remember high school biology, it's impossible for types O and AB to produce a child with type O blood."

Joaquin nodded.

Esteban's brow knit, and he stared at a space somewhere over Joaquin's shoulder for a moment before a look of resolute acceptance softened his bewilderment.

"Just last month, I had blood work done for my annual physical. The tech told me I should consider donating blood since I'm type O positive, and there's always a high demand for that."

His lips flattened into a thin line, but his eyes looked sad, rather than angry.

Orlando cleared his throat. "I should've told you a long time ago, but—"

Esteban shook his head. "No. I was already married to Ginger by the time you and Luz got married. It would've only complicated matters."

His apologetic gaze swung back to Joaquin. "That doesn't mean I wouldn't have wanted to be your father. It's just—" Esteban's voice cracked.

"It's complicated," Joaquin finished. "I know that."

"I'm sorry," Orlando said.

"You did the right thing," Esteban said. "You stood by Luz and raised Joaquin as your own. I don't know if I would've had it in me back then."

They stood in silence for a moment until Esteban broke the silence. "You weren't sleeping with her when we were together, then?"

Orlando shook his head. "Not until our wedding night."

"I'm ashamed of myself for thinking she was fooling around with you while she was seeing me. I should've known that you would never betray me, and Luz had too much class to do something like that."

Tears misted Esteban's eyes. "I wanted to come to her funeral. I almost did, but in the end, I was afraid it might make it harder on you, brother. After the way I treated her, I didn't think I deserved to be there."

"I wish you would've come," Orlando said. "I would have welcomed you with open arms."

He closed the distance between his brother and himself and enfolded him in a hug.

"Now we both know that we could've saved ourselves a lot of angst if we had only spoken sooner," Esteban said. "I'm so tired of fighting with you, Orlando. I don't have any animosity left inside me. The simple act of you reaching out means a lot."

Joaquin knew that the brothers mending their relationship had to come before talk of Esteban's newfound paternity. Orlando and Esteban had been estranged for as long as Joaquin had been alive. Even though there had been bad blood between the brothers, Orlando had never begrudged Joaquin spending time with his cousins and uncle. Esteban had five sons; he'd probably needed a minute or two to digest the addition of the sixth. Joaquin was prepared to give him as much time as he needed. He was in the unique position to sit back and contemplate the fact that now he had not one but two fathers. Because Orlando, the good man who raised him, would always be his father.

As he glanced around Esteban's living room, at the well-worn upholstered furniture and the stacks of *National Geographic* magazines lined up neatly on the coffee table, along with the *Miami Herald* sports section and four remote controls for various electronic pieces, it dawned on him that the place looked exactly the same as it had all the years he'd been coming over to hang out with his cousins. Hearing Orlando and Esteban reminisce so fondly about Luz made Joaquin's heart fill to the point of nearly bursting.

Before too long the conversation drifted to Esteban's regrets of losing Luz's love.

"She ended up with the best man," Esteban said. "I was too wild. When I had her, I couldn't stand the thought of being tied down. That's why I didn't realize she was such a gem until after I married Ginger. I suppose she deserved better, too. In those days I didn't know how to treat a quality woman. I was too busy romancing the bottom of my highball glass. God knows that's what held my attention. That's why Ginger eventually left me. She put up with my crap for way too long. I didn't deserve the years she gave me and I certainly didn't deserve Luz, but you did, Orlando."

Esteban was silent for a moment. The ticking of the grandfather clock and the AC clicking on were the only sounds in the room.

"Although, I must admit that knowing Luz didn't cheat on me is a huge, healing comfort. She had every right, but she was a good woman."

He turned, almost shyly to Joaquin. "Discovering that you are my son is like having part of Luz back in my life." He gestured to Orlando. "Your father is an honorable man for so fiercely protecting your mother. The dumbest thing I even did was to let Luz get away. I guess deep down inside I always thought she deserved more than me. In life, you get what you expect. I expected that I was bad for her and I was."

As the sun set, Esteban excused himself because he

had a previous engagement—a date with a woman in the neighborhood. They were going to a potluck dinner. No, it wasn't anything serious; they were just spending time together.

It was comforting that things hadn't changed.

He told Orlando and Joaquin that they were welcome to stay, but the two thanked him and said they had to be going.

Even though Joaquin had had a while to sit with the reality that Esteban was his father, he was still a jumble of emotions: satisfied that the truth was finally out in the open, happy that Esteban had taken it so well, ecstatic that this rift between the brothers was on the mend. But he couldn't ignore the jangling uncertainty rattling his equilibrium.

"Let's definitely get the entire family together for Christmas," Orlando said as he hugged his brother again. "But let's not wait until then. That's more than six months away."

As Joaquin backed the car out of Esteban's driveway, he thought about what had just happened and how, even though nothing had changed, everything was different—in the best way possible, he reminded himself. He and Esteban knew the truth. Orlando was still and always would be his father. He only wished he had done this sooner. But who knew? Maybe if they'd done it sooner things wouldn't have turned out as well as they had today. Maybe he and Esteban wouldn't have been ready.

Everything happened for a reason and in its own time.

All he knew was that he had Zoe to thank for making this happen. He thought about calling her when he got back to the hotel, but before he could share his good news, he had some making up to do for the way he had treated her.

He'd learned two things today. When you were lucky enough to find a good woman, you treated her like a queen. And time waits for no one. If you don't act when you have chance, you just might lose the love of your life.

On Monday, Zoe didn't even look for Joaquin. In fact, she seriously contemplated not even going in to work because she didn't want to see him. Then she decided she didn't want to give him the satisfaction of thinking she was home pining for him. Okay, so in reality, he probably wouldn't be satisfied that their argument had kept her away, but it was still the principle of the matter. She was embarrassed by the way she'd sacrificed her dignity, telling him she wouldn't give up on him when clearly he just wanted her to go away.

So she'd come into the office, holding her head high, purposely immersing herself in a project to keep from wandering over to his side of the building.

On Tuesday at around two o'clock she couldn't avoid that side of the building because she had to pick up printed samples of the new company stationery. She walked by, pretending not to look, yet she couldn't help but notice that his door was open and the lights were off. He had either not come in or was taking an exceptionally long lunch. Or maybe he'd left early?

Why hadn't he at least texted her by now?

Okay, so maybe she hadn't given up on him, but that didn't mean she wouldn't wait for him to make the first move toward reconciliation. If this was how he fought, she wasn't sure he was the right guy for her. She'd have to think about this.

When she still hadn't heard from or seen him by Wednesday morning, Zoe's anger had faded and she was downright concerned. Where was he?

This had gone too far.

She hoped he was okay.

She swallowed her pride and called Steffi-Anne. She hated to do it, but what if he was sick or something had happened? He didn't have family in town. What if he'd slipped in the shower and hit his head and had amnesia and was wandering around the streets of Austin lost?

Okay, that was a little far-fetched, but still, if she'd been gone for three days—okay, technically it was two full days and this was the morning of the third—she would want people to check on her.

"Yes, Zoe." Steffi-Anne's usual mildly irritated monotone assaulted her ear.

"Good morning, Steffi-Anne." She infused as much sunshine as she could into her tone. "I hope your day is off to a good start."

"What do you want, Zoe? I'm sure you didn't call simply to inquire about my morning."

"You're so smart." Effervescence and sunshine this time. "I didn't call to ask about you. When will Joaquin be in?"

She squeezed her eyes shut and gritted her teeth. Being humbled like this would be worth it if she could find out when he was supposed to be back.

"What? Is there trouble in paradise? I would've thought that you, of all people, would be able to keep track of lover boy. And speaking of, I have not received a signed consensual relationship agreement form from either of you. Have things changed?"

Zoe wanted to slam down the phone. But first she wanted to tell her it was none of her stinking business and then she wanted to slam the phone. Instead she said, "You are so funny. Are you still running with that gag? It's getting a little old, don't you think?"

"It's not a gag, Zoe. Unless you get special treatment because you are the boss's daughter, I need those forms on my desk by the end of tomorrow."

Sunshine, effervescence and chirping bluebirds— she sounded like Snow White, Cinderella and Sleeping Beauty all rolled into one. "Oh, Steffi-Anne, you're so observant. I *am* the boss's daughter and it will behoove you to remember that. We will not be signing your silly form. So don't ask me again. Am I clear?"

"Perfectly."

Zoe hung up the phone, feeling queasy and giddy at the same time. She hadn't gotten the information about Joaquin she needed, but she was pretty certain it was the last time Steffi-Anne would bully her.

By four o'clock on Wednesday there was still no trace of Joaquin. Zoe swallowed her pride and texted him.

Hey, stranger. Do you still work here?

Her heart nearly jumped into her throat when he answered immediately.

I do. I've been in Miami. Got back late last night. Meeting your father for lunch. Talk to you later.

Her father? What was going on?

Why in the world had Joaquin been in Miami? She remembered him saying he wasn't sure what was going to happen after his project ended in a couple of weeks. Had he been there on a job interview?

And why in the world was Joaquin having lunch with her dad? She hadn't spoken to either of them since Sunday. God, she hoped Joaquin wasn't giving him his resignation.

For that matter, Joaquin had been so upset by Gerald's confession, she hoped and prayed he wasn't going straight to the source to tell him exactly what he thought of the situation.

For a moment Zoe couldn't breathe. If he was leaving, he certainly had nothing to lose by giving her dad a piece of his mind.

Chapter Thirteen

Wednesday evening, the last thing Zoe wanted to do was to go out and socialize. But Veronica had called her at quarter to five and insisted they go for drinks at the Driskill Hotel that night.

The Driskill? Of all places? Even thinking of it made her sad, because the last time she was there she'd been with Joaquin.

Was this what life was going to be like from now on? Thinking of him as she turned every corner? Avoiding her favorite places because they reminded her of him?

"Thanks, Ronnie, but I'll pass."

"I don't think so." She was particularly sassy tonight. "There's this bartender at the Driskill. I want him to ask me out. Come on, Zoe. You owe me. Be my wing woman tonight."

So that was the reason she was insisting on going

to the Driskill. Zoe should've known this urgent plan would involve a guy.

Zoe knew when Ronnie got that way, there was no escaping her will. So she might as well go and have one drink. Okay, maybe two. Lord knew that Ronnie had been her wing woman plenty of times.

After she'd relented, Ronnie said, "Why do you sound so glum? Trouble in paradise?"

"For God's sake, is that the theme of the day?"

"I have no idea," Ronnie said. "Is it?"

When Zoe didn't answer, Ronnie pressed on. "Is everything okay with Joaquin?"

As Zoe went through the paces of shutting down her computer, she said, "We will have plenty of time to talk at the Driskill. But if I don't get out of here now, it'll be eight o'clock before I can meet you."

"Actually, how about if I swing by your place and pick you up?" Ronnie said.

"Why would you want to do that? You have to pass the Driskill to get to my place. It's way out of your way. I'll just meet you there."

"No, I don't mind. Really, I don't. I will be there to get you at six thirty sharp. Oh, and I feel like dressing up tonight. So wear something nice."

By the time they got to the Driskill, Zoe was glad Ronnie had insisted on taking her car because that meant her friend was the designated driver. She probably hadn't thought of that when she'd insisted on picking her up. That's what she got for being bossy.

Zoe knew the reason her friend had gone out of her way was that she was afraid Zoe would cancel. While Zoe wasn't prone to flaking out on friends, tonight she might've been tempted. But when she'd gotten home to her empty condo, all she could think about was the night she and Joaquin had made out on the sofa.

Maybe she would go shopping for a new couch this weekend. Her sister Sophie had coveted Zoe's teal sofa. No doubt she would be delighted to have it.

She had seriously considered making love with Joaquin right there on that sofa. A wave of nearly unbearable sadness washed over her. She *loved* him. And she had believed him when he'd said he was falling in love with her.

If she hurt this bad now, she couldn't imagine how she would've felt if she had slept with him.

That was when she knew that Ronnie was her lifesaver. This condo was the last place Zoe needed to be tonight. If she stayed in, she would wallow in her misery.

"So, drinks are on me tonight," Zoe said as they settled into an overstuffed leather sofa in one of the quiet nooks in the kitschy, ranch-themed Driskill bar.

"What? Why are you buying drinks?" As soon as the words had escaped her mouth, Ronnie held up her hand. "Never mind. Far be it from me to turn down free booze. Ohhh, I gotcha. You're buying the drinks because I'm the designated driver. *Clever.* But seriously, Zoe, what's going on with you tonight? You just don't seem like yourself."

Zoe waved her off. "I don't want to be a buzzkill. I'm your wing woman tonight. Speaking of, do you think we could sit any farther away from the bar? How can you work your magic a football field away from the guy?"

Ronnie wiped her wavy blond hair out of her eyes

and looked at her cell phone again for about the fiftieth time tonight. This time she replied to a text.

"Here and now, Ronnie." Zoe snapped her fingers. "I'm talking to you. Do I have to take that thing away from you?"

"Huh? Sorry, that was important."

Ronnie was an artist who specialized in abstract acrylic paintings. Zoe understood that her friend's career was not the typical nine to five. Sometimes Ronnie had to interact with clients after hours. Though tonight she was wishing her friend wasn't quite so distracted.

"That had better be a client or better yet, a hot guy," Zoe joked. "Speaking of, where is this guy you're interested in? I want to see him."

Ronnie craned her neck, looking around the sparsely populated bar. "I don't know. It looks like he might not be working tonight."

Zoe was surprised Ronnie hadn't called to ask if— "What's his name? And when did you meet him?"

"Oh…" She was still looking around the bar, a little distracted. "His name? Uh…John?"

"You're not sure?"

"Of course I am. But enough about me. Tell me what is going on with you and Joaquin. Last I heard, you were in love. And that's why I haven't seen you in a couple of weeks."

Zoe knew if she didn't tell Ronnie what was going on, her friend would keep asking questions. And on the flipside of that, if she did tell her, she knew Ronnie would be a good friend and listen.

"I don't know what's going on with Joaquin. We had an argument on Sunday. It was a pretty bad one. But arguments happen in relationships. I wanted to believe that just because we disagreed on something, it wasn't over. But I haven't heard from him since then. Well, actually, that's not true. I broke down and texted him today."

Ronnie looked at her sympathetically. "Did he text you back?"

Zoe shrugged. "Yes, but it was a very short and to-the-point answer. He told me he's been in Miami for the past couple of days. That's where he is from. Then he told me he was having lunch with my dad. He said, 'Got to go.' And that was it. I thought he might have texted me back after lunch. But he didn't, and then you called and here we are."

"That's odd," said Ronnie.

"Ya think?"

"Why do you suppose he and your dad were having lunch?"

Zoe shrugged. "I don't know. Sunday, he was talking about not knowing what he was going to do or where he was going to be after his project here was finished. I know my dad wanted to talk to him about staying on in a permanent position at Robinson. So maybe that's what they were talking about today. But it's odd that he missed two days of work to go to Miami. That has 'job interview' written all over it. I hope he wasn't telling my dad he was going back to Miami."

Or worse.

Although, if Joaquin had said anything to her father about the Jerome Fortune stuff, her dad would've undoubtedly called and given her a piece of his mind about sharing personal issues with nonfamily members. So she felt a little better about that, and actually kind of silly that she had doubted him. That wasn't Joaquin's style and she knew it.

"Why would he want to go back to Miami when Robinson is the place where most software designers would give their firstborn to work? It doesn't make sense. Oh, God, Ronnie, I love him. I don't know what to do."

Nothing made sense anymore.

"Just give him space. I have a feeling he's crazy for you, too. Everything will work out. Mark my words, because you know my gut feelings are usually right. Where in the world is the server? Do we have to go to the bar and get our own drinks?"

"Why would you not want to go to the bar?"

"Yeah, I guess I could ask if Steve was working tonight," Ronnie said.

"Steve? I thought his name was John?"

Ronnie got another text. "Oh, crap. I have to go make a phone call. I'll be right back."

As she walked away Zoe called to her, "What do you want to drink? I'll order it while you're on the phone."

Ronnie pulled the phone away from her ear. "No, don't get up. We'll lose our seats."

Before Zoe could point out the fact that there were plenty of other places and most of them closer to the bar, Ronnie disappeared around the corner.

Ronnie was acting so weird tonight. She was distracted and now that they were here to see this John or Steve or whoever he was, she wasn't excited about it and they weren't even sitting near the bar.

Then Zoe sighed. She would admit she was a little hypersensitive right now. Maybe she was simply projecting her own antsy-ness onto her friend.

She thought about the adage that when the rest of the world felt like it was out of step, there was a pretty good chance the rest of the world wasn't the one with the problem.

Zoe needed to chill out. Ronnie was allowed to make a phone call. She would be back in a minute. Zoe didn't have to be anywhere and she certainly didn't want to go home to her teal couch.

She leaned her head against the back of the leather sofa. Looking up, she could see the stuffed head of a big steer. Not enjoying that view, she sat up and looked around the bar.

There was a couple getting cozy at a table across the way. She looked in the other direction and saw a group of six women clustered in another of the nooks. It looked as if they were either celebrating a birthday or out on the town for a bachelorette party. When she looked past them, she saw a guy sipping a beer and checking her out. When he realized she was looking, he flashed a seductive smile and waved her over.

Uh, no, thank you.

Since looking around appeared not to be a safe means of distraction, she took her phone out of her purse. Maybe there would be a text from Joaquin.

Nope.

She was just starting to check her email when a text from Ronnie popped up.

Come outside. I need you.

Zoe's heart lurched. What the heck was going on?

You okay? Be right there.

Zoe grabbed her purse and made her way out of the bar and into the Driskill's grand lobby with its splendid staircase and stained-glass ceiling. She rushed out the front doors, looking around for Ronnie. That's when she saw the horse and carriage and a guy who could've been Joaquin's identical twin standing next to it.

Oh! That is Joaquin.

Zoe stopped dead in her tracks, suddenly afraid that she had stumbled into something she wasn't supposed to see—like maybe he was here on a date. Had Ronnie seen him earlier and that's why she'd been acting so squirrely? But why would she call her outside?

Her gaze performed a quick check of the horse and carriage, but it was empty and Joaquin was walking toward her. And he was smiling and holding out his hand. And there was a single, long-stemmed red rose in his hand.

Her heart pounded so hard, she was afraid it might burst.

"Go to him." Ronnie was nudging her. "You can thank me later."

Zoe did a double-take because she hadn't realized her friend was standing next to her.

All of a sudden it hit her that this night had not been about being Ronnie's wing woman. Not at all. Ronnie telling her to dress nicely, insisting on picking her up, her being so distracted with her phone and then getting up and leaving.

This was a plan, and quite a well-orchestrated surprise.

Joaquin was standing in front of her now. He handed her the rose.

"Zoe, I'm so sorry for everything that happened on

Sunday. You have every right to not want to see me again, but I love you, and on Sunday you told me you loved me, too. If you can find it in your heart to forgive me, will you take a carriage ride with me? I have so much to tell you."

Zoe stood there paralyzed by emotion.

"This is where you say, 'Yes, Joaquin, I would love to take a carriage ride with you,'" Ronnie said in a stage whisper. "And this is where I leave. Have fun, kids."

As Joaquin thanked Ronnie, all Zoe could manage was a nod because she was still trying to process everything. Surely the things he wanted to talk to her about were good, because why would he have gone to the trouble to contact her best friend, whom he'd never even met, and get her to help him coordinate this surprise if they weren't good?

And then there was the horse and carriage. Had she told him how much she loved carriage rides? She couldn't remember.

But it didn't matter because here they were here and he was helping her into the carriage. That's when she noticed the silver ice bucket holding a bottle of champagne and the two crystal flutes in a special holder next to the bucket.

Joaquin signaled the driver and the carriage took off down the Driskill's driveway.

"Zoe, before I went to Miami, I went to Horseback Hollow to see my father. I did it because you made me realize I would never be able to unload all the baggage I was carrying until I had talked to him. You are absolutely right and I feel like a new person."

"That's great, Joaquin," she said, finally settling

back into her senses again. "So I take it that it went well?"

He nodded. "It couldn't have gone better."

"Tell me about it."

"I would love to, but before I do, I need to know, are we okay?"

All it took was one look at his gorgeous, anxious face and she knew that there was nowhere else she wanted to be. She felt whole again for the first time since she'd left his apartment on Sunday. Granted, the past three days had been hell, but if he'd needed that time to figure things out, it was all worth it. Obviously he had put it to good use.

"I told you I wouldn't give up on you, and I meant it. But if this is going to work, and I really want it to, you realize this isn't going to be our last fight, right? Even the best relationships have arguments."

He nodded.

"I need you to promise me this is the last time that we will go three days without talking."

Zoe saw his throat work beneath the white shirt and blue tie he wore with his black suit. "I promise you that and so much more, because I don't want to spend another day without you. I realized that over these last three days."

He told her about driving to Horseback Hollow on Monday and what his father had told him. He told her about Orlando flying them to Miami and how his father and his uncle had been estranged and how they had both loved his mother.

"But my uncle—my dad? Er, *Esteban* was too wrapped up in his own issues and too busy chasing skirts to realize he was losing the best thing that ever happened to him. However, my dad, Orlando, loved my mom so fiercely he was willing to sacrifice himself to protect her.

"If I learned one thing while we were apart, it's that you deserve to be loved just as fiercely as Orlando loved Luz, and I now know I can love you that way if you'll let me."

When he leaned in and kissed her, Zoe melted into him. His lips were a touchstone, grounding her in love.

"So, I saw your father today."

Zoe tensed for a second, but only for a second, because she somehow knew that he wasn't going to ask her if she'd talked to her siblings about the Jerome Fortune issue. And she was right.

"Were you talking about a permanent position at Robinson Tech?"

Joaquin smiled. "You might say that."

"What do you mean?"

"I asked his permission to propose to you."

Zoe's mouth fell open and she covered it with her hand. That's when she realized she was shaking. "What did he say?"

"He said it was fine with him, but it was up to you."

Joaquin reached into the pocket of his jacket and pulled out a small light blue box. The world moved in slow motion as he managed to position himself so that he could get down on one knee in the swaying carriage.

"Zoe Robinson, will you do me the honor of being my wife? If you say yes, I vow to bring you as much happiness as you have brought me."

Tears streamed down her face as she threw her arms around his neck. As the carriage rolled along, passersby realized what was happening and cheered and applauded.

When he sat next to her, he placed the gorgeous, traditional round diamond on her left ring finger and opened the bottle of champagne.

"I don't want to wait long to get married," Zoe said. "In fact, how would you feel about Memorial Day weekend? It's a long weekend. We should be able to gather all of our family. Do you think that will work?"

He put his arm around her. "It should, but as far as I'm concerned, we could elope."

She snuggled closer to him. "I want a wedding. I've always dreamed of that special day. In fact, I've been planning our wedding since I was about nine. So it will be no problem to get everything ready in a couple of weeks."

"I want you to have that wedding of your dreams," he said. "The only thing that matters to me is that you're happy."

If this was a dream, Zoe hoped she would never wake up.

Chapter Fourteen

When Zoe and Joaquin announced their big news, everybody was elated. Rachel and Matteo even decided to come up from Horseback Hollow to take them out for a celebratory dinner, which soon turned into a family meal at the Robinson estate.

For the first time in a long time the Robinson siblings had something else to focus on besides "the great Fortune hunt."

Not only was the pending wedding romantic and exciting, it had offered a much-needed breath of fresh air for a family on the brink of civil war.

It was as if they had hit the reset button.

At least for now.

If the engagement hadn't already made Zoe's heart so full it was overflowing, she might've been relieved that the secret her dad had saddled her with had been pushed into the background. But she wasn't even thinking about it.

Of course, that didn't mean the conundrum about whether to keep his secret was gone. She still didn't know what she was going to do. What had changed was that the problem simply wasn't the first thing she thought about when she opened her eyes in the morning and the last thing on her mind as she drifted off to sleep.

Now her mind was full of wedding dresses, flower arrangements, cakes and signature wedding cocktails, dinner menus and invitations, because there wasn't enough time to send out a save-the-date card.

While it was a lot of work, it wasn't as hard as it seemed. Because she really had been planning her dream wedding since she was nine.

Until recently, the only thing missing from her well-thought-out plan was the groom. Now that she'd met her prince, everything was complete.

As she and Rachel walked arm in arm up the front steps that led to their parents' front door, they talked about bridesmaids' dresses and upon whom, out of her three sisters and best friend, she would bestow the honor of serving as maid of honor.

As Joaquin and Matteo trailed along behind them, talking about Orlando's newly mended relationship with Esteban—Joaquin had told his brother about his paternity issue, and it had turned out to be a nonissue because nothing had changed except for Esteban and Orlando ending their feud—Rachel said, "I have the perfect solution to your problem. I can be the matron of honor since I'm married. Olivia, Sophie and Ronnie can duke it out for who will be the maid of honor.

Or if you want an easy way to settle it, since I am the oldest of the sisters, I should get special distinction and they can all be bridesmaids. Since I have already been through this, I have the most experience. I know what the perfect matron of honor needs to do."

Maybe Joaquin had been onto something when he'd suggested they elope.

Oh, who was she kidding? She loved every single second of agonizing over every single tough wedding decision she'd faced so far. She was only doing this once and she intended to do it right.

A cluster of nerves knotted in her stomach, catching Zoe by surprise. *This is really happening, isn't it?* She had dreamed of this time for so long, it was hard to believe it was finally here.

"We will figure something out," Zoe said. "I don't want to hurt anybody's feelings. So we will make it work."

She glanced over her shoulder at her fiancé, who was still laughing and talking with Matteo, oblivious to the wedding plans being discussed right in front of them. This time the butterflies swooped and circled in her belly for a completely different reason.

That handsome, incredible man was the one she would spend the rest of her life with, the man for whom she had waited her whole life.

He is the one.

The one.

Matteo was in the middle of saying something, but Zoe caught Joaquin's eye. The smoldering exchange made her ache for him.

Since he'd proposed, when Zoe wasn't thinking

about the wedding her thoughts were consumed with giving herself, body and soul, to Joaquin.

She had waited so long for everything to be just right, and he was being such a good sport about honoring her wish to wait for their wedding night to make love. But it hadn't been easy for her to resist him. There were times when she was with him that it took every ounce of willpower she possessed to not give in to her desire.

Rachel opened the door and motioned for Zoe and Joaquin to enter first. Zoe breathed in the aroma of something delicious and it suddenly occurred to her that they must be the first to arrive because the driveway had been oddly absent of cars.

As she made a mental note to talk to her siblings about punctuality, since they would all be part of the wedding party, she turned the corner into the living room, into the thunderous sound of a crowd yelling, "Surprise!"

This was no family dinner. Some very sneaky people had apparently invited every single person she and Joaquin had ever met—and then some—to a surprise engagement party/wedding shower.

Good grief, the wedding was right around the corner, but Zoe was touched and a little taken aback by the generous, loving gesture that their friends would come out on a Saturday night to celebrate Joaquin's and her love.

She truly felt like Cinderella as she received good wish upon good wish. She fully intended to talk to each and every guest in attendance and to tell each and every one of them how much she appreciated them being here tonight.

About an hour into her mission, the waitstaff began circulating with trays of champagne flutes, and her father, with her mother, Charlotte, standing at his side, called everyone to order.

"I love all my kids," Gerald said. "But it's no secret that Zoe and I share an extraspecial bond." Her father's gaze snagged hers and Zoe couldn't quite tell if he was simply nervous or if something else was going on, because something in his demeanor didn't quite match the tone of the father-of-the-bride-to-be speech he was giving.

No one else probably noticed because Gerald Robinson was not known for being an emotional, warm and fuzzy kind of guy. Maybe it was because the two of them hadn't spoken since the showdown in his study nearly a week ago. Maybe this was his way of sending her a message, like a male peacock who fans out his feathers in splendid glory when the gesture was really meant to serve as a warning.

Whatever the case, everything that had gone out of her mind elbowed its way back into the forefront. She'd resolved not to think about the situation until after her wedding, because it upset her. She still hadn't wrapped her mind around the fact that her father was, despite how vehemently he'd railed against it, Jerome Fortune. She hadn't come to terms with the fact that her knight in shining armor had lied to his family all these years.

No! She wasn't going to think about that now. Joaquin's arm was around her waist and when she looked up at him, his smile turned the butterflies loose again. Boy, they were really swarming tonight amid all the excitement. She took a deep breath and raised her glass to his, refusing to let Jerome Fortune spoil any part of

Joaquin's and her party. No, Jerome Fortune was not welcome at anything that had to do with their wedding. The next two weeks would be a Jerome Fortune– free zone.

She mustered the appropriate smile and made all of the coos and sighs expected of a consummate daddy's girl and bride-to-be.

As everyone raised their glass and said, "Cheers!" Zoe scanned the crowd of happy faces, letting the merriment of celebration wash through her.

That's when she noticed an unfamiliar face among the crowd. A nice-looking guy was standing in the back, holding a glass of champagne and engrossed in conversation with her brother Ben.

She hugged her father because that's what everyone expected and kissed her mother on the cheek. Then she said to Joaquin, "I'm going to say hello to Ben. I'll be back in a moment."

Resuming her mission to greet everyone, Zoe headed toward the two men. Her brother had kept a relatively low profile tonight, or maybe there were just so many people here this was the first she'd seen him.

As she approached, she heard the stranger's proper British accent. "Why don't I come to your next family meeting and we can tell everyone about the others?"

Zoe stopped in her tracks, trying to figure out what they were talking about. Because surely Ben wouldn't discuss their family's dirty laundry with a stranger and air it at her engagement party.

Zoe stood there, intending to listen to their conversation, hoping to hear something that proved this wasn't what it looked like, but Ben looked over and saw her.

"Zoe." He motioned for her to come closer. "I want to introduce you to Keaton Whitfield. Keaton, this is my sister Zoe."

Keaton Whitfield?

Was he kidding? He had better be kidding.

"Ah, yes, Zoe. It is lovely to meet you. Congratulations on your engagement. I am delighted to celebrate with you."

The British accent confirmed Zoe's nightmare.

This was *the* Keaton Whitfield. The guy Ben had found who claimed to be a half sibling and supposedly knew of *others*.

Was that what he meant a moment ago when he said he would come to the next family meeting and they could talk about *the others*?

"What are you doing, Ben?"

Her brother gave her an odd look. "I'm introducing you to Keaton?"

"Don't be a smartass," Zoe said. "You know what I mean. Why did you bring him here tonight? Tonight of all nights, Ben? Why would you do this?"

Keaton transferred his weight from foot to foot, looking uncomfortable. "I see that this is upsetting you, Zoe. I am terribly sorry. I will say good-night."

Zoe couldn't even look at Keaton as he walked away. Her angry gaze was glued to Ben's. Her brother stood there looking just as annoyed.

Zoe lowered her voice to a whispering growl. "Why would you pull a stunt like this at my engagement party? What are you trying to prove? Did you see this as your chance to rub your crusade in Dad's nose? What about Mom? How do you think she would feel about you bringing Keaton Whitfield into her home?

Did you ever think that maybe at least until after the wedding is over you could give it a rest? It's only two weeks, Ben. If you don't have enough empathy or common sense to know what's appropriate and what's not, then maybe you just need to stay away from me for a while. I'm going to leave for a bit. When I get back, I want you to be gone."

She didn't give him the chance to answer. Tears were welling in her eyes. She had to get out of there before anyone noticed.

She ducked her head so that her hair fell in her face, hiding her tears until she'd made it to the hallway and out the front door. She couldn't leave her own party, so she would walk around until she got her emotions under control and her brother had time to leave.

What was he thinking, bringing Keaton Whitfield to a family event? Their mother was there. Did he have no regard for her and the pain it would cause if she had discovered her husband's illegitimate son in her own house?

As Zoe stepped out into the humid night, she saw that the valets were there now. They must've had instructions to lie low until she and Joaquin were inside. The two young men stood as Zoe approached.

"Good evening," said the tall one. "May I get your car?"

She was grateful that the light was low and hoped he couldn't see her misty eyes. She mustered a smile to give the impression that everything was okay.

"No, thank you. I'm just out for a short walk."

Because everyone leaves a party to take a walk.

He nodded. "Have a nice evening."

Zoe walked toward the garden on the west side of

the property, where she knew she could have some privacy.

Try as she might, she couldn't find the strength of spirit to give her father the benefit of the doubt on the cheating accusations and proof of illegitimate children Ben had dug up.

She was still coming to grips with the fact that her father had lied about his past and had asked her to keep it a secret.

Lying and cheating went against everything Zoe believed in. She certainly didn't want it paraded around at her engagement party, or her wedding, for that matter. But the damage had already been done. And she could no longer ignore the stark reality that had burrowed into the pit of her stomach: because of her father's actions, she now doubted everything she'd ever believed to be true.

These sickening doubts were dredging up all sorts of unwelcome memories of incidents she'd rationalized in the past.

Such as that time with her father and their neighbor Mrs. Caldwell. Zoe hadn't thought about it since she was six or seven years old.

Her parents had hosted their annual New Year's Eve party. At least one hundred and fifty people dressed in their finest evening wear had converged on the Robinson estate. It was a party worthy of Jay Gatsby.

Zoe was supposed to be in bed, but she'd gotten up to get a drink of water and seen her dad embracing Mrs. Caldwell on the second-floor landing of the main staircase. Now it dawned on Zoe that they'd probably thought they were tucked out of sight. The woman had been crying and Zoe thought she'd heard her whimper something about a baby. When they'd seen Zoe, Mrs. Caldwell had gasped and descended the stairs like a weeping Cinderella racing against the strike of the clock.

"What's wrong with Mrs. Caldwell, Daddy?" Zoe had asked as her father filled her princess cup with water from the bathroom faucet.

"She's sad and I was comforting her." Her dad's voice had sounded so kind, Zoe hadn't imagined he could be telling her anything but the truth. Still, as he'd tucked her into bed, Zoe had persisted. "Did a baby upset Mrs. Caldwell?"

"Why would you think that, princess?"

"Because I heard her say something about a baby."

"Sweet girl, you must've misunderstood."

"Then what made her so sad, Daddy?"

Zoe remembered how he'd gently brushed her bangs off her forehead and smiled down at her with sad eyes. "I'm not allowed to tell, princess. It's Mrs. Caldwell's secret. She would be very upset if I betrayed her confidence. You understand, don't you?"

Zoe had nodded even though she hadn't understood. She *knew* she'd heard the word *baby*.

"I think Mrs. Caldwell was embarrassed that you saw her crying. Will you promise me that you won't say anything to anyone? Because that would make her cry even harder. I know you're too sweet and kind to make anyone feel sad. Besides, this can be our secret. Something that you and I share that no one else knows. Just like the fact that you are my favorite of all my children."

He'd planted a kiss on her forehead and then plucked at her nose, which had made her giggle.

"*You* know you're my favorite and *I* know it, but if you tell your brothers and sisters it would make them sad. So, that's our secret, too. Right?"

She'd loved having secrets with her father. It made her feel special. So they'd sealed her promise with a pinkie shake.

When Zoe was a little girl, a pinkie promise was sacred and her father's word meant everything. She'd been his princess and he'd been her steadfast knight. So, naturally, she'd believed him because heroes didn't lie.

She'd kept his secret all those years ago. Now, even when he'd admitted to telling a lie of staggering proportions, he had asked her to cast aside what was right and good and keep another one. Only this time his knight's armor was tarnished and she didn't believe in fairy tales anymore.

If, in fact, he had fathered children outside of his marriage, that meant the situation was worse than she'd originally thought. Even though her parents weren't prone to public displays of affection, she'd always thought their marriage was strong, that it was impenetrable, rock solid.

Given her father's confession and Keaton Whitfield's talk about "the others," Zoe couldn't help but wonder whether Mrs. Caldwell had been pregnant with her father's baby. Was yet another half sibling out there somewhere, too? Had every word her from father's mouth been a bald-faced lie?

She didn't know what to believe now. She wasn't sure what was real and what was an illusion built on naive dreams...or delusions.

All she knew was that she had to leave. She couldn't

stay and pretend that everything was fine when it felt as if her whole world was crumbling around her.

Apparently nothing was sacred anymore. Apparently her tendency to see the best in people amounted to nothing more than naïveté. How could she have been so stupid? So blind?

Was she rushing into things with Joaquin? How well did she really know him? For all the joking about knowing each other for more than a year, really, it had only been a few weeks. He hadn't even wanted to ask her out. She'd had to all but cajole him into it. And then he'd disappeared for three days and come back with a ring.

Zoe's head was spinning.

The proposal had been lovely and romantic and everything she'd ever dreamed a proposal would be, but it had happened so fast.

Maybe she needed to take a step back and think about what they were doing. The wedding was less than two weeks away. If they canceled everything tomorrow, they could still get partial refunds.

Zoe only intended to get married once. She wanted a life with one man who wanted to spend the rest of his life with one woman: her.

In the wake of all that had happened with her father, happily-ever-after suddenly felt like the biggest fairy tale a naive woman could buy into. It was high time she removed her rose-colored glasses and saw the world and people for who they really were.

Out of the corner of his eye Joaquin caught a flash of Zoe's long, golden-brown hair as she turned into the hallway. Something about the way she moved warned him something wasn't right.

After the toast she had said she was going to say hello to Ben. Now she looked as if she was leaving in a hurry.

"Please excuse me," he said to the small group of well-wishers who were clustered around him asking about his and Zoe's plans for the future. "My bride needs me."

By the time he made it to the hallway, Zoe was nowhere to be found. On instinct he went outside and saw the same valets who had been working the night of the Robinson Tech dinner, but Zoe was nowhere in sight.

"Did a beautiful woman come through here a few minutes ago?"

"Long brown hair, white dress?"

"That's the one," Joaquin said.

"She went that way." The guy pointed toward the far side of the grounds.

"Thanks," Joaquin said and took off in that direction.

Once he had cleared the driveway, he called, "Zoe? Are you out here?"

He heard something rustling near a vine-covered arbor and headed in that direction. As he passed through, he caught a glimpse of something white a few feet ahead.

"Zoe? It's me. Are you okay?"

He passed through another arbor, this one heavy with pink wisteria, and saw Zoe sitting on a stone bench, her head bent so that her hair shielded her face.

"Zoe? What's wrong?"

When she didn't look up, that was when he noticed her shoulders were shaking. Was she crying?

He walked over and put his arms around her. "Hey, what's wrong?"

When he tried to lift her chin, she shrugged away from him.

"What's wrong?" he repeated.

"I don't think I can do this," she said.

"What are you talking about?" he asked.

"The wedding." Her voice broke on a hiccupping sob. "I think we need to postpone everything."

"No," Joaquin insisted, his heart thudding at the thought.

"Okay, then we can call it off," Zoe said. "I can't marry you right now, Joaquin. It's all happening too fast."

"Can we talk about this?"

"What's there to talk about?"

"I love you. That's what there is to talk about. Did I do something to make you change your mind?"

She took in a shuddering breath. "You didn't do anything wrong. You've been nothing but wonderful."

"And that's why you want to call off the wedding? Because I've been wonderful?"

"No—" Her voice broke and she shuddered out a sob.

He hated to see her cry. It cut him down to the quick. "You don't want to be part of this family. I love you so much that I don't want you to have to deal with them. I'm stuck with them, but you're not. So, get out while you can."

"That's crazy. If you're going to call off the wedding, the least you can do is talk to me." He had driven the four of them to the Robinsons' house tonight. "My car is still in the driveway. Can we go somewhere and talk?"

With tears still rolling down her cheeks, she gave a faint nod. He took off his jacket and draped it over her shoulders and they made their way back to his car.

The valets had the decency to not stare and stayed on the other side of the driveway, giving them some privacy. Joaquin opened the passenger-side door and helped Zoe inside before sliding behind the wheel.

They drove in silence. The only sounds were the hum of the engine and an occasional sniff from Zoe. Finally, when they arrived at a spot overlooking Lake Austin where Joaquin could pull off onto the side of the road, he killed the engine and turned in his seat to look at her.

"I love you more than I've ever loved anyone in my life, Zoe. I don't want to lose you. I'm not afraid of your family."

"I just don't even know what I believe anymore," Zoe said.

She told him about the encounter with Ben and Keaton Whitfield.

"Every day something that had defined my life is shattered. I don't even know my own mind anymore. This relationship has happened so fast. I love you, but what if we're moving too fast? What if I wake up and discover this had all been a lie, too?"

"It's not a lie. I have never been so sure of anything in my life," Joaquin said. "But if you're not ready to get married, I'm not going to force you into anything. Just say the word and we can call the wedding off. It's the last thing I want to do, but if that's what you need, that's what we'll do. Whatever happens, I'm going to tell you what somebody wise once told me—take some time if you need to figure out what you want, but I won't give up on you."

Epilogue

Two Weeks Later

Joaquin hadn't given up on her.

When it came right down to it, she couldn't give up on him, either.

Now she knew she could never give up on *them*. They were too good together.

He'd taken her breath away the moment she'd first set eyes on him. She experienced the same reaction when she stood at the back of the chapel sanctuary, saw him standing at the altar, looking so handsome in his tux.

Her prince.

The love of her life.

They'd scaled some challenges through their whirl-wind romance and had come out stronger on the other side of those thorn-covered walls.

Now here they were making the ultimate commitment in front of God, family and friends. Today they'd put aside their differences. She'd even told Ben he could invite Keaton Whitfield on the stipulation that Keaton would blend into the background and steer clear of her mother, Charlotte.

After giving the situation some time and space, she had realized that since Keaton probably was her brother, she'd eventually want to get to know him. Inviting him to the wedding was a way to test the waters. However she had made Ben promise that there would not be any surprises or family drama caused by his stirring the pot. She'd also asked him to relay the message to Keaton and tell him that she didn't want to hear a word about "the others" until after the wedding. The two of them could talk about things as soon as she returned from her honeymoon. But not before.

She wondered if the stipulation might inspire Keaton to turn down the invitation, but as she stood there, waiting for her sister Rachel, who had persevered in claiming the matron-of-honor job, to make her way down the aisle and take her place at the altar, Zoe spied Keaton sitting in the very back row, blending in, just as she had asked.

He smiled at her and nodded. Zoe offered a tentative smile before glancing at her father to see if he realized Keaton was there. Actually she didn't know if her father even knew about Keaton. Because just as she was keeping her dad's secret—at least until after her honeymoon—she hadn't said anything to her father about Ben locating Keaton Whitfield.

As the harpist transitioned from "Pachelbel's Canon" into the traditional "Wedding March," Zoe exiled all thoughts of family drama. She'd waited so long for this day and had almost let family issues cost her the love of her life. But with Joaquin's love and support and a little time, she was able to put everything into perspective.

And here she was.

And there was Joaquin waiting for her, just as he'd promised.

She floated down the aisle on her father's arm, feeling like Cinderella in her dream dress—a ball gown fit for a princess. The chapel was lit by hundreds of white candles and decorated to perfection with white and pale pink roses, peonies, lilies and cymbidium orchids interwoven with smilax garland and variegated ivy.

It looked like a wonderland.

When she and her father reached the altar, the minister asked, "Who gives this woman in marriage?"

Her father answered in a proud voice, "Her mother and I do."

As he lifted her veil, kissed her cheek and put her hand in Joaquin's, she realized she was no longer daddy's little girl, and that was okay. She was about to marry the love of her life and become his wife.

The ceremony went by in a romantic blur.

What she remembered best was when she and Joaquin had promised to love and protect each other for the rest of their lives.

And, of course, there was that kiss.

Oh, that toe-curling kiss.

When the minister pronounced them Mr. and Mrs. Joaquin Mendoza, their friends and family had broken into a round of applause that drowned out the harpist's recessional, but the sound of them clapping was the most beautiful music Zoe had ever heard.

A short while later, after taking pictures with family and the bridal party—they'd even gotten a picture of Orlando and Esteban with their arms around each other's shoulders, beaming at the camera—she and Joaquin made their way to the reception at the Robinson estate.

The wedding planner had erected a large white tent with dozens of linen-covered tables around the parquet dance floor. From its position on the lawn, the tent had a stunning view of Lake Austin.

As the bandleader introduced Zoe and Joaquin, they took to the floor and had their very first dance as man and wife. As Joaquin led her around the floor, Zoe saw her father talking to Keaton Whitfield. If she weren't so happy, she might have wondered what they were talking about, but the funny thing was, it really didn't bother her. It was just as well because the next time she looked, they were gone.

That was fine, too. Because she had more important things to focus on: her wedding night. No matter what her father said to Keaton or who her family turned out to be—Robinson or Fortune—she had just married her soul mate; she was Joaquin Mendoza's wife. They were a family now and that was all she needed to be happy.

Later that night, a Rolls-Royce whisked Joaquin and Zoe, who was still in her wedding gown, away from the reception to the Driskill for their wedding night.

They'd sent their luggage to the hotel ahead of their arrival, and early the next morning they would catch a flight to Paris, but right now, it was just the two of them. They had the entire glorious night ahead of them.

Giddy nervousness danced in Zoe's stomach as Joaquin unlocked the door to the Yellow Rose Bridal Suite. He lifted her into his arms with a decisive sweep and kissed her soundly, a preview of what was to come. It was a good thing he finally carried her over the marble threshold and nudged the door shut with his hip, because for a crazy moment, Zoe'd felt the urge to have him right there in the hallway.

Well, not really, but that was how much she wanted him.

With one last kiss, he set her down, but their bodies remained flush against one other, arms entangled, as they stood in the middle of the suite's living room. Everything about him—his touch, his taste, his scent—was so familiar tonight. It was like a touchstone anchoring her in the here and now; yet, at the same time, everything seemed brand-new. It was invigorating and it hit her soul in a way that rendered her weak in the knees.

Joaquin pulled away just enough to murmur, "Hold that thought. We need some champagne."

Zoe quirked a brow. "There's only one thing I want right now." Playfully, she nipped at his bottom lip. "Maybe we should save the champagne for later. I have a feeling we're going to be extra thirsty."

His forehead was pressed against hers. The way he looked at her with those dark, dark eyes melted her insides. "Pace yourself, my love." He kissed her again and the passion of it ran contrary to his suggestion to take things slowly. "In a moment I'm going to love you into incoherence. We should probably enjoy the champagne now."

His promise had desire spiraling through her again. As she watched her handsome husband open the champagne, his strong hands gently coaxing the cork from the bottle of Krug Grande Cuvée, she couldn't help but anticipate the feel of those hands on her body. Her skin prickled with intense longing, and heat pooled in her most intimate places.

She didn't quite know what to do with herself. So she walked over to the bedroom to have a look. It was decorated in cream and pale yellow. Tiffany lamps graced marble-topped nightstands. But it was the romantic canopy bed in the center of the magnificent room that made Zoe sigh. Draped in yards of sheer fabric swagged and tied to the bedposts by tassels that looked as if they were made of spun gold, her wedding bed was perfect.

Almost as perfect as her husband.

Joaquin Mendoza may have been her last first kiss, her prince who never had been a frog, but he would be her one and only love. She would give herself to him right here in this bed.

This was forever.

It was worth the wait. *He* was worth the wait. She knew without a doubt that he felt the same way, too. He'd proved it by his actions so they could have this… this first night together—this first time together. It would be heaven. She already knew.

She'd loved him from the depths of her soul the moment she'd first seen him. He'd been so patient, waiting for her so they could have this fairy-tale night. The wedding had been a dream come true. Now it was just the two of them, alone at last. To make their wedding night as magical as possible, she'd started birth control pills a few days after Joaquin proposed. The doctor had assured her that they would be protected after the first week. She was eager to start a family with Joaquin, but they wanted some time together as a couple first.

She sensed her husband behind her and turned. He handed her a flute of champagne. They clinked glasses, but only managed a couple sips before they were in each other's arms again.

Liquid spilled, glasses were forgotten and a moment later, they were tangled up again and he had taken possession of her body. That was good because nothing mattered but being joined together. "Make love to me, Joaquin."

They made short work of ridding themselves of fabric barriers. Finally, nothing stood between them. He eased her onto the bed. Smoothing a lock of hair off her forehead, he searched her eyes. Radiating love, he looked so earnest as he gazed deep into her eyes, asking the unspoken question.

Yes, I'm ready.

She answered him with a kiss.

They took their time exploring each other, getting to know each other's most intimate places. Joaquin's deft hands touched her with such love that she wanted to cry out from the ecstasy of it. Finally, when she was ready, he claimed her with one slow, gentle push. It didn't hurt. In fact, it was as if something that had been missing in her had finally clicked into place, making her whole for the first time in her life.

Joaquin feathered kisses over her lips and whispered gentle words of love as he slowly pulled out and tenderly thrust into her again. Instinctively, she matched his rhythm. Together, their bodies created magic. Finally, ecstasy, the likes of which she'd never dreamed possible, seized her body and rippled through her, lifting her to such an exquisite peak before they went over the edge together.

She was sure she would never be the same again.

Of course not. She was in love and forever changed in the best possible way.

As they lay there together, sweaty and spent, she relished the warmth of his solid body. He shifted to his left elbow and gazed at her with such reverence. "Zoe Mendoza, I love you."

As she reached up and brushed a wayward lock of dark hair off his forehead, a deep peace filled her entire being. "I love you, too."

In that perfect moment, she gave silent thanks to the heavens for leading her to her very own handsome prince.

* * * * *

HER HOLIDAY
PRINCE CHARMING

CHRISTINE FLYNN

For the lovely ladies who have made the 'Hunt' happen, and everyone who believes in the fairy tale.

Prologue

"What's on your Christmas list this year? No matter how big or how small, you're sure to find what you're looking for at Seattle's one-stop answer to all your holiday—"

With a quick flick of the dial, Rory silenced the cheerful voice suddenly booming from her car radio. In an attempt to drown out her worries while she waited to pick up her son from kindergarten, she'd turned the music to a decibel she'd never have considered had her five-year-old been in the vehicle.

The ad had just brought to mind the one thing she'd been desperately trying *not* to think about.

She'd hoped to make the holiday special for her little boy this year. Not just special, but after last year's unquestionably awful Christmas, something wonderful. Magical.

As of three days ago, however, she was no longer sure how she would keep a roof over their heads, much less put a tree under it. Due to downsizing, her telecommuting services as a legal transcriptionist for Hayes, Bleaker & Stein were no longer required. She'd needed that job to pay for little things like food and gas and to qualify for a mortgage.

Without a job, she had no hope of buying the little Cape Cod she'd thought so perfect for her and little Tyler. She had no hope of buying or renting any house at all. Since the sale of the beautiful home she'd shared with her husband closed next week, that left her four days to find an apartment and a job that would help her pay for it.

A quick tap ticked on her driver's side window.

Through the foggy glass, a striking blonde wearing studious-looking horn-rimmed glasses and winter-white fur smiled at her. The woman didn't look at all familiar to Rory. Thinking she must be the mom of an older student, since she knew all the moms in the kindergarten class, she lowered her window and smiled back.

Chill air rushed into the car as the woman bent at the waist to make eye contact. "You're Aurora Jo Linfield?"

Rory hesitated. The only time she ever used her full name was on legal documents. And she rarely used Aurora at all. "I am."

"I'm Felicity Granger." Hiking her designer bag higher on her shoulder, she stuck her hand through the open window. The cold mist glittered around her, clung, jewel-like, to her pale, upswept hair. "But please, call me Phil. I'm an associate of Cornelia Hunt. You've heard of Cornelia, haven't you?"

Rory shook the woman's hand, watched her retract it. "I've heard of her," she admitted, wondering what this woman—or the other—could possibly want with her. Nearly everyone in Seattle had heard of Mrs. Hunt, the former Cornelia Fairchild. She'd been the childhood sweetheart of computer genius Harry Hunt, the billionaire founder of software giant HuntCom. Rory recalled hearing of their marriage last summer, even though she'd been struggling within her fractured little world at the time. Media interest in their six-decade relationship had been huge.

"May I help you with something?"

"Oh, I'm here to help you," the woman insisted. "Mr. Hunt heard of your situation—"

Harry Hunt had heard of her? "My situation?"

"About your job loss. And how that affects your ability to purchase another home."

"How does he know that?"

"Through your real estate agent. Mr. Hunt knows the owner of the agency she works for," she explained. "Harry bought a building through him last month for his wife so she'd have a headquarters for her new venture. When he learned why you couldn't move forward with the purchase of the house you'd found, he remembered Mrs. Hunt's project and thought you'd be a perfect referral. So we checked you out." Her smile brightened. "And you are.

"Anyway," she continued, anxious to get to her point. "Cornelia knows of a property for sale that you might want to purchase. She's aware of your current unemployment," she hurried to assure her, "but she said you're not to worry about that little detail right now. Just look at the place. If you're interested, suitable arrangements can be made for you and for the seller.

"It's not exactly what you told your agent you want," she cautioned, reaching into a pocket of her coat. "But it could be perfect for you and your little boy. You really do need to keep an open mind when you see it, though," she warned. "Don't judge it as is. Look for the possibilities.

"You'll be met at the address on the back." She held out a white, pearlescent business card. "The owner's representative will be there at ten tomorrow morning. A man by the name of Erik Sullivan. He's quite knowledgeable about the property, so feel free to ask him anything that will help you decide whether you want the place or not. You should keep an open mind about him, too.

"I have to run now. Double-parked," she said, explaining her rush but not the warning. "If you like what you see, I'll see you tomorrow afternoon."

Rory took the pretty little card. Neatly hand-printed on the back was an address outside Port Orchard, a short ferry ride across the sound from Seattle.

With questions piling up like leaves in the fall, she glanced back up.

The woman was gone.

Seeing no sign of her in the Pacific Northwest mist that was closer to fog than rain, she looked back to the shimmery little card.

The past fourteen months had left her without faith in much of anything anymore. The sudden, devastating loss of her husband to an uninsured drunk driver who'd run a red light. The whispered and crushing comments about their marriage that she'd overheard at his funeral. The exodus from her life of people she'd once thought of as family and friends. Each event had been shattering in its own right. Together, they'd made her afraid to trust much of anything. Or anyone.

And that had been before she'd lost the job Harvey Bleaker had said was hers for as long as she needed it.

The lovely woman with the bookish glasses had appeared out of nowhere. As if by magic, she'd disappeared into the mist the same way, like some sort of a fairy godmother dressed in faux fur and carrying Coach.

Dead certain her sleepless nights had just caught up with her, Rory dropped the card into the open compartment on the console. Whatever had just happened had to be either too good to be true or came with a spiderweb of strings attached to it.

Probably, undoubtedly, both.

Still, she, Tyler and the for-rent section of the newspaper were going apartment hunting in the morning. Having just picked up a check for the small down payment she'd put on the house she hadn't been able to buy, less fees, she had enough for three or four months' rent and expenses. In the meantime, feeling a desperate need for either magic or a miracle, she figured she had nothing to lose by checking out the address on that card.

She just hoped that this Erik Sullivan would be as accepting of her circumstances as Mrs. Cornelia Hunt seemed to be.

Chapter One

"Are we lost, Mom?"

"No, honey. We're not lost." Parked on the dirt shoulder of a narrow rural road, Rory frowned at the building a few dozen yards away. "I'm just not sure this is the right address."

"If we can't find it, can we go to the Christmas place?"

"We'll see, sweetie. We're looking for a new place to live right now."

"I don't want a new one."

"I know you don't," she murmured. Freckles dotted Tyler's nose. His sandy hair, neatly combed when they'd left the house, fell over his forehead, victim of the breeze that had blown in when she'd lowered his window to get a better look at the address on the roadside mailbox.

Nudging wisps back from his forehead, she smiled. "But we need one. And I need you to help me pick it out. It's our adventure, remember?"

"Then can we go to the Christmas place?"

They had seen a banner for a holiday festival in nearby Port Orchard when they'd driven off the ferry. Tyler had been asking about it ever since.

Everything she'd read last night on the internet made the area around the shoreline community a few miles around the bend sound nearly idyllic. The part of her that didn't want to get her hopes up knew that could simply have been good marketing by its chamber of commerce. The part that desperately needed this not to be a wild-goose chase focused on getting them moving.

"Not today, I'm afraid." She hated to say no, but housing had to be their first priority. "We don't have time."

It was nine fifty-five. They were to meet the seller's representative at ten o'clock.

Reminding Tyler of that, and agreeing that, yes, they were still "exploring," she pulled his hood over his head and glanced to the structure surrounded by a few winter-bare trees, dead grass and a wet patch of gravel that, apparently, served as a parking lot.

The address on the mailbox matched the one on the card. The structure, however, bore no resemblance at all to a residence. The two-story flat-roofed rectangle of a building faced a partial view of a little marina two city blocks away and backed up to a forest of pines.

A long, narrow sign above the porch read Harbor Market & Sporting Goods. Signs by the screened door read Fresh Espresso and Worms and Closed Until Spring.

Mailboxes farther up the road indicated homes tucked back in the trees. The only vehicle to be seen, however, was hers. With no sign of life in either direction, she was about to pull out her cell phone to check the address with Phil Granger when she remembered what the woman had said.

She'd warned her to keep an open mind when she saw the place. To look for possibilities.

The potential goose chase was also, apparently, a scavenger hunt.

A narrow driveway curved around the back of the building and disappeared down a slight hill. Thinking there might be a house or cottage beyond the gate blocking it, she grabbed the shoulder bag that held everything from animal crackers to a Zen meditation manual and gamely told her little boy they were going to look around while they waited for the person they were to meet to show up.

The damp breeze whipped around them, scattering leaves in their path as they left the car. With a glance toward the threatening sky, she was about to reconsider her plan when the relative quiet gave way to a squeak and the hard slam of a door.

Tyler froze.

Across twenty feet of gravel, she watched six feet two inches of broad-shouldered, purely rugged masculinity in a fisherman's sweater and worn jeans cross the store's porch and jog down its three steps.

"Sorry about that." His apology came quickly, his voice as deep as the undercurrents in the distant water. "I didn't mean to startle you. I keep forgetting to fix the spring."

The breeze blew a little harder, rearranging the otherwise neat cut of his slightly overlong dark hair. He didn't seem to notice the wind. Or the cold bite that came with it. All lean, athletic muscle, he strode toward them, his glance shifting between her and the child who'd smashed himself against her leg.

That glance turned questioning as he stopped six feet from where she'd rooted herself in the driveway.

"Are you Mrs. Linfield?"

Surprise colored the deep tones of his voice. Or maybe what she heard was disbelief. His pewter-gray eyes ran from the wedge of auburn hair skimming her shoulders, over the camel peacoat covering her black turtleneck and jeans and up from the toes of her low-heeled boots. His perusal was quick, little more than an impassive flick of his glance. Yet she had the unnerving feeling he'd imagined her every curve in the brief moments before she realized he was waiting for her to speak.

"I didn't think anyone was here." The admission came in a rush. "I didn't see a car, so we were just going to look around—"

"I flew over. Floatplane," he explained, hitching his head in the direction of the water. "It's down at the marina.

"I'm Erik Sullivan." Stepping closer, he extended his hand. His rugged features held strength, a hint of fearlessness. Or maybe it was boldness. Despite its lingering shadow, the square line of his jaw appeared recently shaved. He looked hard and handsome and when he smiled, faint though the expression was, he radiated a positively lethal combination of quiet command and casual ease. "I'm handling the sale of this property for my grandparents."

"You're a Realtor?"

"Actually, I build boats. I'm just taking care of this for them."

Her hand had disappeared in his.

She could feel calluses at the base of his fingers. He worked with his hands. Built boats with them, he'd said. What kind, she had no idea. The white-gold Rolex on his thick wrist seemed to indicate he was successful at it, though. The words *capable* and *accomplished* quickly flashed in her mind, only to succumb to less definable impressions as she became aware of the heat of his palm, the strength in his grip and the deliberate way he held that strength in check.

What she felt mostly, though, was a wholly unexpected sense of connection when her eyes met his.

Everything inside her seemed to go still.

She'd experienced that sensation only once before; the

first time Curt had taken her hand. It had been a fleeting thing, little more than an odd combination of awareness and ease that had come out of nowhere, but it had dictated the direction of her life from that moment on.

As if she'd just touched lightning, she jerked back, curling her fingers into her palm, and took a step away. The void left in her heart by the loss of her husband already felt huge. It seemed to widen further as she instinctively rejected the thought of any sort of connection to this man, imagined or otherwise. Because of what she'd learned since Curt's death, it was entirely possible that what she'd thought she'd had with her husband—the closeness, the love, the very rightness of the life they'd shared—hadn't existed at all.

Having struggled with that awful possibility for over a year, she wasn't about to trust what she'd felt now.

Conscious of the quick pinch of Erik's brow, totally embarrassed by her abrupt reaction, she rested her hand on her son's shoulder. Just as she would have introduced her little guy, the big man gave the child a cautious smile and motioned her toward the building.

"The main entrance to the living quarters is around back, but we can go through the market. Come on and I'll show you around."

Whatever he thought of her reaction to him, he seemed gentleman enough to ignore it.

She chose to ignore it, too.

Living quarters, he'd said?

"There isn't a separate house here?" she asked, urging Tyler forward as the sky started to leak.

"There's plenty of room to build if that's what a buyer wants to do. The parcel is a little over three acres. Living on premises has certain advantages, though." He checked the length of his strides, allowing them to keep up. "Shortens the commute."

If she smiled at that, Erik couldn't tell, not with the fall of cinnamon hair hiding her profile as she ushered the boy ahead of her.

Mrs. Rory Linfield wasn't at all what he had expected. But then, the new owner of the building next door to Merrick & Sullivan Yachting hadn't given him much to go on. He wasn't sure what the elegant and refined wife of Harry Hunt was doing with the building Harry had apparently given her as a wedding gift—other than providing Erik and his business partner an interesting diversion with her total renovation of its interior. It had been his offhand comment to Cornelia, though, about a place he'd be glad to sell if Harry was still into buying random pieces of property, that had led him to describe the property his grandparents had vacated nearly a year ago.

The conversation had prompted a call from Cornelia yesterday. That was when she'd told him she knew of a widow in immediate need of a home and a means to produce an income.

When she'd said *widow,* he'd immediately pictured someone far more mature. More his parents' age. Fifty-something. Sixty, maybe. With graying hair. Or at least a few wrinkles. The decidedly polished, manicured and attractive auburn-haired woman skeptically eyeing the sign for Fresh Espresso and Worms as she crossed the wood-planked porch didn't look at all like his idea of a widow, though. She looked more like pure temptation. Temptation with pale skin that fairly begged to be touched, a beautiful mouth glossed with something sheer pink and shiny, and who was easily a decade younger than his own thirty-nine years.

He hadn't expected the cute little kid at all.

He opened the door, held it for them to pass, caught her soft, unexpectedly provocative scent. Following them inside, he had to admit that, mostly, he hadn't anticipated the sucker punch to his gut when he'd looked from her very kissable mouth to the feminine caution in her big brown eyes. Or the quick caution he'd felt himself when she'd pulled back and her guarded smile had slipped into place.

What he'd seen in those dark and lovely depths had hinted heavily of response, confusion and denial.

A different sort of confusion clouded her expression now.

He'd turned on the store's fluorescent overheads when he'd first arrived. In those bright industrial lights, he watched her look from the rows of bare, utilitarian grocery shelving to the empty dairy case near the checkout counter and fix her focus on a kayak suspended from the ceiling above a wall of flotation devices. Sporting goods still filled the back shelves. After the original offer to buy the place fully stocked had fallen through, he'd donated the grocery items to a local food bank. That had been months ago.

The little boy tugged her hand. "Why is the boat up there, Mom?"

"For display. I think," she replied quietly, like someone talking in a museum.

"How come?"

"So people will notice it." She pointed to a horizontal rack on the back wall that held three more. Oars and water skis stood in rows on either side. "It's easier to see than those back there."

With his neck craned back, his little brow pinched.

"Are we gonna live in a store?"

"No, sweetie. We're just..." From the uncertainty in her expression, it seemed she wasn't sure what they were doing at the moment. "Looking," she concluded.

Her glance swung up. "You said this belongs to your grandparents?"

"They retired to San Diego," he told her, wondering what her little boy was doing now as the child practically bent himself in half looking under a display case. There were no small children in his family. The yachting circles he worked and played in were strictly adult. Any exposure he had to little kids came with whatever family thing his business partner could talk him into attending with him. Since he managed to limit that to once every couple of years, he rarely gave kids any thought. Not anymore.

"They'd had this business for over fifty years," he explained, his attention already back on why the property was for sale. "It was time they retired."

The delicate arches of her eyebrows disappeared beneath her shiny bangs. "Fifty years?"

"Fifty-three, actually. They'd still be running the place if Gramps hadn't hurt his back changing one of the light fixtures." Erik had told him he'd change the tube himself. Just as he'd helped with other repairs they'd needed over the years. But the Irish in John Sullivan tended to make him a tad impatient at times. "He can be a little stubborn."

"Did he fall?"

"He just twisted wrong," he told her, conscious of the quick concern in her eyes, "but it took a couple of months for him to be able to lift anything. Grandma picked up as much slack as she could, but those two months made them decide it was time to tackle the other half of their bucket list while they could both still get around."

Her uncertainty about her surroundings had yet to ease. Despite her faint smile, that hesitation marked her every step as she moved farther in, checking out the plank-board floor, the single checkout counter, the old, yellowing acoustic tiles on the ceiling. Watching her, he couldn't help but wonder how she would do on a ladder, changing four-foot-long fluorescent tubes in a fixture fourteen feet off the floor. Or how she'd wrestle the heavy wood ladder up from the basement in the first place.

Since Cornelia had specifically asked if the business was one a woman could handle on her own, he'd also thought his prospective buyer would be a little sturdier.

Rather than indulge the temptation to reassess what he could of her frame, hidden as it was by her coat, anyway, he focused on just selling the place.

"The original building was single story," he told her, since the structure itself appeared to have her attention. "When they decided to add sporting goods, they incorporated the living area into the store, built on in back and added the upstairs.

"The business is seasonal," he continued when no questions were forthcoming. "Since summer and fall recreation provided most of their profit, they always opened in April and closed the first of October. That gave them the winter for vacations and time to work on their projects."

It was a good, solid business. One that had allowed his grandparents to support their family—his dad, his aunts. He told her that, too, because he figured that would be important to a woman who apparently needed to support a child on her own. What he didn't mention was that after the first sale fell through, the only other offers made had been too ridiculously low for his grandparents to even consider.

Because there were no other reasonable offers in sight, he wasn't about to let them pass up Cornelia's offer to buy it—if this particular woman was interested in owning it. He hadn't even balked at the terms of the sale that required his agreement to help get the business back up and running.

Selling the place would rid him of the obligation to keep it up. Even more important than ending the time drain of weekly trips from Seattle to make sure nothing was leaking, broken or keeping the place from showing well was that his grandparents had been the last of his relatives in this part of the sound. Once the place was sold, he had no reason to ever come back.

Considering all the plans he'd once had for his own life there, nearly all of which had failed rather spectacularly, that suited him just fine.

His potential project had yet to ask a single question. He, however, had a few of his own.

"Have you owned a business before?"

He thought the query perfectly reasonable.

She simply seemed to find it odd.

"Never," she replied, sounding as if she'd never considered running one, either. Still holding her little boy's hand, she set her sights on the open door behind the L-shaped checkout counter. "Is that the way to the living area?"

He told her it was, that it led into a foyer.

Wanting a whole lot more information than she'd just given, he followed her with the child looking back at him over the shoulder of his puffy blue jacket.

The instant he met the child's hazel eyes, the boy ducked his head and turned away.

With a mental shrug, Erik focused on the mom. She looked very much like the spa-and-Pilates type married to some of his high-end clients. Yet the car she drove was a total contrast—economical, practical. "Are you into outdoor sports?"

"We have bicycles," came her distracted reply.

"Mountain or street?"

"Street."

"For racing or touring?"

"Just for regular riding."

"Do you know anything about mountain bikes?"

"Is there a difference?"

That she'd had to ask had him moving on. "What about hiking or camping?"

"Not so much."

"Water sports? Do you windsurf, paddleboard, water ski?"

"Not really."

He took that as a no. "Do you know anything about sporting goods?"

Clearly on a mission of her own, she answered his last query with a puzzled glance and moved past the stairs, one set leading up, the other down, and into a spacious living room.

The empty downstairs space was interrupted only by the kitchen's long island near one end and anchored by a ceiling-high stone fireplace at the other. The bare walls all bore a pristine coat of latte-colored paint.

It was toward the kitchen that she motioned. "Mind if I look back there?"

Not at all pleased with her responses, he told her he didn't and watched her head for the glass-faced cupboards.

Her sandy-haired son darted straight to one of the large picture windows lining the opposite wall.

"Have you ever worked retail?" he asked her.

"Never," she replied once more.

"Wow, Mom. Look! It has a park!"

Rory's glance cut to where her little boy pressed his nose to the wide window near the fireplace. A large meadow stretched to a forest of pines. Between the dawning potential in the place and the feel of the tall, decidedly distracting male frowning at her back, she hadn't noticed the expansive and beautiful view until just then.

What she noticed now was her son's grin.

That guileless smile added another plus to her escalating but decidedly cautious interest in what surrounded her. "It sure does, sweetie. But stay with me. Okay?"

Yanking his unzipped jacket back over the shoulder of his Spider-Man sweatshirt, he hurried to her, his little voice dropping as he glanced to the man who remained on the other side of the white oak island.

"Does he live here?" he asked, pointing behind him.

She curled her hand over his fingers. "It's not polite to point," she murmured. "And no. He lives somewhere else."

"Where?"

"I don't know, honey."

"But it's a long way, huh?"

"Why do you say that?"

"'Cause he said he came in a plane. It floated here."

From the corner of her eye, she noticed the big man's brow lower in confusion.

"He came by *floatplane,*" she clarified, easing confusion for them both. "It's a plane that can land on water. It flies just like any other."

"Oh." Tyler screwed up his nose, little wheels spinning. "Why didn't he make him a boat?"

He remembered what Erik had said he did for a living.

There wasn't much Tyler heard that he ever forgot. She'd come to regard the ability, however, as a double-edged sword. While her bright little boy absorbed information like an industrial-strength sponge, there were things she knew he'd overheard that she truly hoped he'd forgotten by now. Things certain relatives had said that had confused him at the time, hurt him and made her even more fiercely protective of him than she'd been even before he'd lost his dad.

Since no response came from the other side of the island, she told Tyler it was possible that Mr. Sullivan did have a boat, but that it was really none of their business. Right now, they needed to look at the rest of the house.

There were certain advantages to a five-year-old's short attention span. Already thrilled by the "park," Tyler promptly forgot his interest in the boat their guide did or did not have and, like her, poked his head into the pantry, the mudroom and downstairs closets.

There was no denying his attraction to the cubbyhole he found in one of the upstairs bedrooms. Her own interest, however, she held in check. A person couldn't be disappointed if she didn't get her expectations up to begin with.

The property was nothing she would have considered even a week ago. It had none of the little neighborhood atmosphere she'd looked for. None of the coziness she'd craved for herself and her son. It felt too remote. Too foreign. Too…unexpected.

Her option was an unknown apartment in an as yet undetermined area near a job she still had to find.

Her hopes rose anyway, her mind racing as Erik led her back down from the three bedrooms and two baths that would be more than adequate for her and her son.

Phil had said to keep an open mind about this place.

Despite its drawbacks, it was, indeed, full of possibilities. But it wasn't just Tyler's surprisingly positive reactions or the idyllic views from some of the windows that tempered her misgivings. What Phil hadn't mentioned was that this wouldn't just be a place to live. It would be her source of income.

She could have her own business. Be her own boss. That meant the means to support her son would be dependent on her, not on someone else with obligations or agendas of their own. It would be up to her if she succeeded or failed. And while the thought brought as much anxiety as anticipation, mostly it brought a surprising hint of reprieve.

She could start over here. She could finally, truly move on.

By the time they'd worked their way back downstairs, Tyler knew which room he wanted to be his. He wasn't quite so sure what to make of their tour guide, though. Every time he'd looked over his shoulder to see if Erik was still with them, he'd moved closer to her or tightened his grip on her hand.

Considering the man's easy self-assurance, it struck her as odd that he appeared equally undecided about Tyler. Because he'd yet to say a word to her son, she wasn't sure if he simply didn't know how to relate to small children or if he was one of those people, like her father-in-law, who felt a child was to be seen and not heard and otherwise ignored until they became of an age to engage in meaningful conversation.

Maternal instincts on alert, the moment they reached the foyer, she asked Tyler to see if he could spot deer in the woods from the living room window. He was barely out of earshot when she felt Erik Sullivan's disconcerting presence beside her.

"Your son seems to like the place," he pointed out, joining her by the mahogany newel post. "What about you? You haven't said much."

Erik would admit to not being particularly adept at deciphering women, even when they did speak. *No* often meant *yes. Don't* often mean *go ahead. Nothing* always meant *something,* though finding out what that something was could be akin to pulling an anchor out of dried cement. But this woman hadn't given him so much as a hint about any conclusion she might have drawn.

"Do you have any questions?" he prompted.

"When did you say the store usually opened for business?"

"April. The first or second week."

She lifted her chin, her thoughts apparently coming in no particular order.

"Phil Granger said you know I can't qualify for a mortgage just now."

"We're aware of that," he assured her.

"Were your grandparents planning to carry the mortgage themselves?"

"A second party will carry it. So," he prodded, "you're interested, then?"

She wanted to smile. He could see the expression trying to light the flecks of bronze in her deep brown eyes. She just wouldn't let it surface.

"That depends on what they want for it. And the terms. How much are they asking?"

He should have been relieved by her interest. Would have been had she been even remotely qualified to take on the store.

"That's...negotiable."

"But they must have a price in mind."

"Do you have *any* business experience?"

It was as clear to Rory as the doubt carved in his handsome face that he had serious concerns about her ability to make a go of the store his grandparents were selling. Unflattering as his obvious skepticism was, she couldn't fault him for it. They had run the business for decades. They'd probably poured their hearts and souls into the place that had defined them for years. This man hadn't had to tell her for her to know how much the store and their home had meant to them. The shelving in the spare room upstairs—his grandma's sewing room, he'd said—had been built by his dad. The beautiful, lacquered banister beside them had been lathed by his grandfather.

He'd casually mentioned those things in passing. With his big hand splayed over the grapefruit-size mahogany ball atop the newel post, his thumb absently rubbing its shiny finish, she realized this place mattered to him, too.

Her only concern now was that he trust her with it.

She took a step closer, lowering her voice so Tyler couldn't overhear.

"It's not that I've never had a job," she informed him

quietly. "I was a file clerk while I worked on an associate's degree. After that, I spent four years as a legal secretary before Tyler came along. I went back to work transcribing documents at another law firm ten months ago. I'd still be doing that if they hadn't let me go because the firm merged and they cut my job."

Skipping over the five-year gap in her résumé, she aimed for the heart of his concern. "I've just never owned a business. Or sold anything other than whatever the PTA was selling to raise money for school projects.

"I'll admit that when I got here," she hurried on, hoping he'd overlook that last part, "the last thing I expected was a store. But you said it's a good, solid business. If your grandparents didn't usually open it until April, that would give me four months to figure out what needs to be done and how to do it." All she had to do was get past the daunting little fact that she had no idea where to start.

"Look," she murmured, too tired after too many sleepless nights to care how much of herself she exposed. "I'll admit I don't know a…a…"

"A bivy sack from a bobber?" he suggested.

"Exactly. And until now," she said, muscling on, "I'd honestly never thought about owning anything like this. The only sports I know anything about are tennis and golf." And that was only because her husband had wanted her to fit in at the club. She was so not the rugged, outdoors type. "But I'll do whatever I have to do to provide for my son.

"This could be a good place to raise him. He could help me in the store. I think he'd love that. He'd even have his own park," she pointed out, thinking of how badly she wanted them gone from the exclusive community that had come to feel like a prison. She'd hoped for a normal neighborhood, but breathing room would be a good thing, too.

"I'll never be able to replace the security he had before his dad died, but it's up to me to give him as much stability as I can." Her voice fell with her final admission. "I think I can do that here."

Her last words were as soft as the utter conviction in her eyes. Erik saw a plea there, too. Quiet. A little raw. And a lot uncomfortable for him to witness in the moments before he glanced to where her son seemed to be counting something at the window.

He'd been about that age—five or so, if he had to guess—when his grandfather had put him to work stacking canned goods on shelves. After that, he'd practically begged to come over so he could help.

He'd once thought this would be a good place to raise a child, too.

"There's one other thing," she admitted, her voice still quiet. "Tyler has never lived anywhere other than in the house we're leaving. We have to be out in three days. Until the job thing happened, I'd thought we'd be settled in our new house well before Christmas. He didn't have a very good one last year and it would be really nice to find a place that I don't have to move him from again." Practicality, or maybe it was weariness, kept her tone utterly matter-of-fact. "So how much is it?" she asked. "And how do I make this happen?"

He didn't know which struck him more just then: her absolute determination to do whatever she had to do to care for her child or the naked vulnerability lurking in the depths of her eyes.

As if she knew what he saw, her glance hit the floor.

Her determination to hide that vulnerability pulled at something unfamiliar deep in his chest, even as he steeled himself against it.

He hadn't been told how she'd been widowed. Or how long she and her child had been on their own. He had no idea if her marriage had been as good as his parents', as much a failure as his own had been or some form of tolerable in-between. He knew only from what she'd said about her child's loss that it was entirely possible she still grieved the man she'd lost, too.

He wasn't a particularly sensitive or sympathetic man. Or so he'd been informed by his ex-wife and certain of the arm candy who trolled the circles he moved in. But he wasn't at all comfortable being privy to something so personal. It disturbed him even more to find himself wondering what it would be like to mean that much to a woman.

Equally unsettling was the fact that an hour ago, she hadn't even known the store existed. "I can't give you the terms."

She hadn't a clue what she was getting into.

He knew for a fact that he was no longer comfortable with what he'd agreed to do himself.

"My agreement with Cornelia...Mrs. Hunt," he corrected, "is that she or her assistant will discuss those details with you."

Reaching into the back pocket of his jeans, he extracted one of the same pearlescent cards Phil had given her yesterday. "Did you take the ferry or do the loop through Tacoma?"

"Ferry."

"Which one?"

"Southworth. It lands at Fauntleroy."

By land or water, either way it would take her a while to get back to Seattle.

"Then I'll give you directions to their office from the dock. I have another meeting in Seattle at noon." Card in hand, he pulled his cell phone from another pocket and keyed in a number.

With the instrument to his ear, he turned away, started to pace.

Rory glanced at her watch. It was already after eleven o'clock.

She was about to mention that when she remembered his mode of transport was infinitely faster than hers. He was already into his conversation with Phil, anyway. She couldn't hear what he said, though. She knew only that he looked oddly resigned when he turned a minute later to inform her that Phil wanted to talk to her.

By the time the woman who had appeared out of no-where yesterday told her everything was ready to proceed with the sale and confirmed their meeting that afternoon, Rory couldn't shake the feeling that nothing could possibly be as simple as Phil had made it sound—and that Erik Sullivan had more of a role in the sale than anyone was letting on.

Chapter Two

The directions Rory had been given led her to the Ballard neighborhood in northwestern Seattle and a weathered, two-story redbrick building much like the others along an old business section of the waterfront. What distinguished the structure was the trail of plaster dust and debris leading from the open front door to the Wolf Construction Dumpster at the curb.

Inside, sheets of milky construction plastic masked two stories of interior scaffolding and what appeared to be something grand under construction. The filmy barriers did little to deaden the occasional clatter and boom of interior demolition. The noise was muffled considerably, however, behind the closed door of the only completed space—an unexpectedly feminine and elegant ground floor corner conference room in shades of ivory and pale taupe with a view of a marina, Shilsole Bay and snow-capped Hurricane Ridge beyond.

The long banks of ivory-draped windows caught Tyler's

attention the moment they'd walked in. Rory had thought the boats in the inlet had drawn him. Until she noticed Erik.

A walkway ran behind the buildings. She could see him outside, pacing past the rows of windows, bare-masted sailboats bobbing in the background. Apparently oblivious to the chill, he had one hand in a front pocket of his jeans, his head down against the breeze as he talked on his cell phone.

He did not look happy.

Logic told her he could be talking about anything. But the unease joining her curiosity and uncertainty over this meeting made her fairly certain his scowl had something to do with her.

"We're so glad you liked the place," said Phil, leading her across the floor, the click of her heels on polished oak suddenly hushed by the pale blue Aubusson rug. "With everything so unsettled for you, we didn't know if you'd see the advantages of taking on a business right now. Especially one that you might not ordinarily have considered."

Wearing a cream blouse and slacks slung with a thin gold belt, the woman Rory met yesterday took her and Tyler's coats and motioned to one of the Queen Anne chairs at the circular conference table. The light from the ornate crystal chandelier above it made the mahogany surface gleam like glass. "Cornelia did feel you'd consider it, though," she added, "given your circumstances."

"Which are very close to what mine were at one time," came a voice from a small alcove.

A statuesque, elegantly mature lady in pale lavender cashmere emerged from the washroom, carrying roses she'd just freshened. Her silver-blond hair was coiled in a chic chignon at her nape. Diamonds glinted from her ears. The rock on her left hand, a huge pink diamond surrounded by a dozen of brilliant white, flashed in its platinum setting as she set the vase on a marble credenza with a quiet clink.

"Please pardon the mess out there, Rory. We're a work in progress at the moment. I'm Cornelia Hunt," she said, intent on putting her guest at ease as she held out her hand. "It's a pleasure to finally meet you."

Feeling a distinct connection to Alice after she'd slipped down the rabbit hole, Rory clasped the woman's hand. She had dressed that morning in a casual black turtleneck and skinny denims to look at properties and apartments, not to meet well-dressed ladies in what could have passed for a drawing room in a palace.

"The pleasure's mine," she returned, fighting the urge to curtsy.

"You only met briefly, so I'll officially introduce you to Felicity Granger. Phil is my assistant. She's also an academic counselor at the university. She's really rather brilliant at helping others with their life decisions, so I brought her in to help me with my work." Her green eyes seemed to twinkle as she smiled. "What have you been told about the arrangements so far?"

"Hardly anything. The man who showed us around... Erik," she identified, still aware of him pacing, "wouldn't even give me the price."

"I don't doubt that you have questions," Cornelia conceded. "I'll have Phil start answering yours and explain the details while I get us some coffee. Or would you prefer tea?"

Rory told her coffee was fine, thank you. And that yes, cocoa for Tyler would be nice. Even as she spoke, she wasn't at all sure what struck her as more incongruous just then: that Cornelia Fairchild Hunt, the very pleasant wife of a reportedly eccentric computer-genius billionaire, was getting her coffee. Or the mound of dingy canvas mail sacks piled beside a delicate French provincial writing desk.

On the desk's surface, dozens of what appeared to be opened letters teetered in stacks.

Phil took the chair next to Rory. Seeing what had her attention, she adjusted her overlarge glasses and leaned toward her.

"There was an article in the Seattle *Washtub* recently about how Cornelia helped a young entrepreneur get the break she needed with her business. Ever since then, requests have poured in by email and snail mail for her in care of the newspaper and the offices of HuntCom asking for her help from other young women. And for them. Like you," she explained. "The reporter who wrote the article said she's bringing another sackful over this afternoon."

"A reporter is part of this?"

"Don't worry," Phil hastily assured. "Cornelia wants to stay under the radar with her project and she trusts Shea Weatherby to help her with that. As for anyone else we might need to talk with, we only identify our clients to those directly involved in her situation."

The assertion was hugely reassuring to Rory. She'd already supplied enough fodder for gossip in certain social circles to last a lifetime. Nearly every member of those circles would have sold their summer homes to mingle with a Hunt, too. But all that mattered to her just then was that this meeting was confidential. Her relationship with her in-laws was strained enough without word getting out and embarrassing them because their son's widow apparently needed to be bailed out by strangers. For Tyler's sake, she needed to make as few waves with them as possible.

Thinking about her in-laws reminded her that she needed to call them about Christmas.

"The volume of requests Cornelia is receiving," Phil continued, mercifully sidetracking her from the stomach-knotting thought, "is why she needed to hire help. I just love what she's doing."

"I really am at a loss here," Rory admitted. "What *is* she doing?"

"She's being what the first woman she helped called her," her assistant replied. "A fairy godmother."

She had a fairy godmother?

"On to the details." Phil pushed a pale blue folder toward her, the snowflake polish on her nails glittering. "If these terms are agreeable to you, Cornelia will purchase the property you saw from the owners and you will purchase it from her for the amount stated on line one. To keep everything legal and as simple as possible, your down payment will be one dollar. Your balance will be interest-free with the first payment due September first. You'll have had five months of cash flow by then."

Disbelief held Rory's tone to nearly a whisper. The number couldn't possibly be right. "The property has to be worth three times this."

"Oh, it is. And that's what Cornelia will pay the owners for it. But that's your price. Of course, there is more to the sale."

Ah, yes, Rory thought, unable to understand why Cornelia would take such a loss for her. The strings.

"Cornelia has added a few perks," Phil chose to call them. "She believes the best route to success is to have a good adviser. Since it's understandable that you'd know little about this particular business and since the Sullivan's grandson is reasonably acquainted with it, she arranged for Erik to be your mentor for the next six months. He'll help you with your inventory, suppliers, getting part-time help and whatever else it will take to get your new venture up and running.

"The two of you can determine how often you need to meet, but there will be a status meeting here once a month.

Of course, I'm available to both of you together or individually at any time. At the end of the six months, if you're on track with your business plan, Erik will have fulfilled his mentor agreement, and you'll be on your own. All we ask," she concluded, as if she'd rather expected the stunned silence coming from beside her, "is for your discretion in discussing the work we do here."

Phil sat back, smiling.

Rory couldn't seem to move.

Poof. Just like that. The property her little boy had fallen in love with that morning—and the business that came with it—could be hers.

The reality of it didn't want to sink in. Yet even in her disbelief what registered most was that her new life included a man who she strongly suspected didn't want to work with her at all.

"This Erik," she said, caution competing with amazement as Cornelia joined them with a tray of tall porcelain mugs. "May I ask the terms of his agreement with you?"

Taking the chair on the opposite side of her, Cornelia passed mugs to her and Phil. "It's nothing complicated. I just requested that he help you with the business if I buy the property for the Sullivans' asking price."

"But why did he agree to that?"

"Because he wants a decent price for his grandparents and I offered him one. He's been taking care of the property for them, so I also imagine he'd like to be free of that responsibility. I don't think he begrudges his grandparents his time. He sounds quite fond of them," she offered, approval in the soft lines of her face. "But he's a busy man."

Rory remembered his strong, workingman's hands, the calluses she'd felt brush her palm. Right behind the thought came the disquieting memory of what his touch had elicited. "He said he builds boats."

"Oh, they're more than boats. He and his business partner build world-class sailing sloops. Their boatworks is down past the marina, but their sales and rental office is next door. J.T., one of my stepsons," she said, identifying Harry's second oldest, "commissioned one from him years back. He said Erik is the only man he'd ever do business with on a handshake. If you knew my stepson, you'd know that respect for someone's character doesn't get any greater than that."

Her carefully penciled eyebrows arched as she offered cream and sugar. "Did you find him disagreeable?"

Disturbing, yes. Disagreeable? She couldn't honestly say they'd disagreed about anything. "No."

"Are you not wanting help?"

Rory shook her head. She'd be a fool to turn it down. "I'm sure he has far more information about how the market is run than anything I can even begin to find on my own."

The unguarded admission brought Cornelia's smile back. "Then it's a win-win for everyone."

Baffled by the woman, more uncertain than she wanted to admit about her mentor, Rory touched the handle of her mug. "Please don't think I'm not beyond grateful, Mrs. Hunt—"

"It's Cornelia," the woman said graciously.

"Cornelia," Rory corrected. "But I'm having a hard time making sense of all this. I understand from Phil that you helped someone else when she needed it. But why do you want to help *me* like this?"

"Because I can," she said simply. "My Harry gave me a ridiculously large amount of money for a wedding gift. Since I have the means, I decided to make it my mission to offer deserving young women a hand up when the going gets rough for them, or when they just need the right break.

"In your case," she admitted, "I know all too well what it's like to be financially strapped and the only parent. My first husband was a dear, but he left me in a real financial bind when he died. I had to sell my home, just as you've had to do. And I had to work hard to raise my girls."

She gave Rory's hand a pat, drew back her own. "From what we learned about you from your real estate agent—and other resources," she admitted, making it clear she thoroughly vetted the recipients of her largesse, "I don't doubt that you'll do what you must to make it work. Erik has proven himself to be an excellent businessman," she assured, as the opening door let in the back-up beep of a truck. "I'm sure you can trust him to help you succeed.

"Can't she, Erik?" she asked the man himself as he walked in.

Seeming oblivious to the way his presence suddenly filled the space, much less to the faint tension leaking from him in waves, Cornelia raised an eyebrow in his direction.

"Can't she what?" he replied.

"Trust your business judgment."

"It hasn't let me down so far."

The disarming smile he gave Cornelia and Phil seemed to come easily. The wattage, however, lowered considerably when it settled on her. Having met her eyes long enough to make her heart jerk, Rory watched him lower his glance to the older woman's coffee.

"Mind if I get some of that?"

"Not at all. The pot is fresh."

His heavy footsteps muffled by the carpet, Erik headed for the coffeemaker in the alcove. Behind him he could hear the elegant matron and the bookish blonde he'd met last week explaining that the paperwork for Rory's mortgage would be handled at a title company Monday afternoon. Since he had power of attorney for the sale for his grandparents, he and Cornelia had already agreed to take care of their business there that morning.

The Hunt name tended to eliminate delays.

He could hear the low, soft tones of Rory's responses, but he had no idea what she said. He was too busy telling himself that the next six months wouldn't be as bad as he'd feared.

They'd probably be worse.

He didn't question the sincerity of the rather shell-shocked-looking young woman reading the papers in front of her. Her determination to do what she had to do for her child had been nearly tangible to him. But her impulsiveness had raised about a dozen red flags.

Women spent more time making up their mind about buying a pair of shoes than she had about taking on something that would require a nearly 24/7 commitment. Especially at first. He knew. He ate, slept and breathed his own business. And that business was something he'd wanted since he was a kid. She'd only wanted the store since she'd learned about it that morning. She'd even admitted to knowing nothing about what she'd agreed to get herself into—which meant she'd take far more time than he'd planned on devoting to the care and feeding of her education.

It was that last part that he'd explained to his business partner when he'd called a while ago to tell him he'd still be tied up for a while. Pax had said not to worry about what he'd committed himself to. He'd cover for him if he needed time during the day to work with the store's new owner.

Though they'd never talked about the reasons for it, Pax knew how badly Erik wanted to be out from under that property. And why. They'd grown up together. Pax had been his best man. He'd also gone through the ugliness of his divorce with him by letting him take on however many projects it took to keep him too exhausted to think about anything else.

It had been seven years since the demise of his eight-year marriage, and Erik had long since recovered from what he had no intention of ever repeating again, but he already felt guilt about the time he'd be taking away from work. Especially with an April delivery date on their present work under construction, another client waiting for his final blueprints and two others hovering in the wings to get on their list.

Then there were their evening commitments with past and future clients. The holiday party season had just started—and Merrick & Sullivan Yachting never missed a business or philanthropic commitment.

With the women still talking, and feeling the tension creep up his back, he took his filled mug to the nearest window and rubbed at his neck. He'd do what he had to do where the woman behind him was concerned, and hope she wasn't the sort who required a lot of hand-holding to come up to speed. Heaven knew he wasn't a coddling sort of guy.

Erik took a sip of the coffee that was infinitely better than the sludge he and his partner had been brewing since their secretary had gone on maternity leave. It didn't help the situation that Mrs. Rory Linfield had a son. He'd made it a point over the past several years to avoid women with children. They tended to want more of a commitment than he was interested in. But that deliberate lack of exposure left him feeling less than capable when it came to anyone under four feet tall.

With his pretty little project deep in conversation, he looked out over the blue-tarped sailboats yawing in their slips. He and Pax had pulled their rental fleet out of the water last month, but farther up the shoreline, he could see the point that anchored the rest of their operation: the boatyard where they stored their boats over winter and the boatworks where they built their custom sailing yachts, one sloop at a time.

"How come that boat has a Santa on it?"

The little boy had walked over from two windows

down. Now, with his chin barely clearing the window-sill, the sandy-haired child pointed to a row of decorated sloops in the marina. Several had colored lights anchored fore and aft from the mainsail mast. One had a blow-up Santa at the helm.

Erik gave a shrug. "Some people just like to decorate their boats this time of year."

"How come?"

"Because they entertain on them," he said, thinking of the cocktail parties he and his partner had hosted on their respective sloops for their clients over the years. They had one scheduled next week. "Or maybe they're going to be in one of the boat parades." The floating parades were legend around the sound during the holidays.

The little boy's brow furrowed. Digesting what he'd been told, he said nothing else. For about five seconds, anyway.

"Do you have a boat?"

"I do."

"Do you decorate it?"

"I have."

"Do you put a Santa on it?"

"No."

"Oh," the child said.

He took another sip of coffee, waited for another question. When none was forthcoming, Erik tried to focus on the conversation behind him.

The small voice immediately cut in.

"I'm glad your house has a fireplace. So Santa can come down," Tyler explained, still looking out the window. "Mom said he can visit without one, but it's easier when he has a chimney."

It took a moment for the boy's conversational leap to make sense. Apparently since Santa was on his mind, any context was fair game.

"I've heard that about chimneys, too," he assured him. "And the house you saw isn't mine. It's my grandparents'."

The distinction apparently didn't matter.

"We have a fireplace in our house. But we didn't have a tree last time for him to put presents under." The small voice sounded utterly matter-of-fact. "Mom said this year won't be sad. We get a tree no matter what."

His mom had mentioned that he hadn't had a very good Christmas last year. Sad, the child had just called it. Yet Erik didn't let himself consider why that had been. Telling himself that her personal business was none of his, he murmured a distracted, "That's good," to her son and focused on the only business of hers he needed to be interested in. The store.

Cornelia had asked for his presence in case Rory had questions for him. He figured now was as good a time as any to see what those concerns might be.

The three females at the table glanced up as he approached.

It was Rory's dark eyes that he met.

"Is there anything you want to ask me about the property?"

Her shell-shocked look had yet to fade. With her ringless hand at the base of her throat, she slowly shook her head. "I don't even know where to start right now."

"Make a list as things occur to you," he told her. "I'll come by the market next week and we can go over it.

"The sale is being expedited," he told her, knowing now that part of the appeal of his grandparents' home, for her son, anyway, had been the fireplace his own family had gathered around at Christmas. "You can move in whenever you're ready. I'll check my schedule and Phil can set us up with a day and time next week to go over inventory."

He set his coffee on the table with a decisive clink and pulled his business card from his pocket. Walking around the table to give it to her, he watched her rise. As she did, his glance slid over what her coat had hidden earlier. The long black turtleneck she wore skimmed her feminine curves, molded the sweet shape of her hips.

She had the body of a dancer. Long, lithe and sexy as hell.

Masking his misgivings about having to deal with her, feeling them mount by the minute, he ignored the vague tightening in his gut. "Do you need help moving in?"

"No. I'm… No," Rory repeated, hating how flustered she felt. "But thank you." The last thing she wanted was to impose on this man. Considering what he'd been asked to do for her, she'd be obligated enough to him as it was. "I'd planned to be out Monday, so I've already arranged for movers."

She pushed back her bangs, revealing the pinch of her brow. "You really don't mind if I take things over before the sale closes?"

"You said you want to be settled before Christmas." He assumed now that that desire had something to do with putting up a tree. "The earlier you start, the sooner you can be."

Rory swallowed. Hard.

"Thank you."

He held out his card. "My office and cell numbers are on here. Call me if something comes up. I'll leave a key under the rock by the back porch. You'll get a full set at closing." His fingers brushed hers. Her skin felt cool to him, soft, and though he was trying not to notice anything in particular about her, he could have sworn he felt her trembling.

Without looking up, she palmed his card and clasped both hands in front of her.

"You're sure you're covered on the move?" he asked

"I'm positive. I arranged everything a couple of weeks ago."

Standing as close as he was, he caught the tremor in her

breath as she eased it out. He didn't doubt she felt overwhelmed with all that was happening for her. Yet she managed to maintain the composure that had her graciously assuring Cornelia that she truly needed nothing else as far as help was concerned. Something about that composure seemed practiced to him, though. It was as if she'd found herself in overwhelming or uncertain situations before and wasn't about to let anyone see how unsettled she really was.

She wouldn't look at him again. She seemed to know what he'd seen, and felt totally embarrassed being so exposed. A huge burden was being lifted from her slender shoulders, but she wasn't letting herself feel the relief of that weight. It appeared that admitting the scope of that relief would be admitting how truly desperate she'd begun to feel. So she just kept it all in, as if that was what she'd become accustomed to doing anyway, and turned to the women.

With a choked little laugh, she said she had no idea how to thank them.

Leaving her to figure it out, he looked to the matriarch running the show, thanked her for the coffee and headed for more familiar territory.

He'd given his word that he'd help. And he would. He never promised anything he didn't intend to deliver. But when he showed up for the meeting Phil arranged for him with Rory the following Wednesday, he discovered something about his charge that he hadn't anticipated.

The young widow with the sweet, sharp little boy might have looked as fragile as sea foam, but she had a stubborn streak as wide as Puget Sound.

Chapter Three

Erik hesitated at the store's front door. For years he'd simply walked in when the business had been open. After his grandparents had moved, he'd let himself in with his key. Since the sale had closed two days ago, he no longer had the right to come and go as he pleased from a place that had been part of his life for as long as he could remember.

The odd sense of having been displaced lingered as he rapped his knuckles on the frame of the screen door, and promptly disappeared the instant the inside door swung open. Even with her pretty features schooled into a smile of greeting, the unease in Rory's guarded expression made him suspect she was already having second thoughts about what she'd taken on.

Or so he was thinking when she let him in and his glance cut from the black hoodie and yoga pants molding her curves to the furniture behind her.

It looked as if every possession she owned sat piled in the interior of the market. Bedroom sets, tables, chairs, boxes.

"You said you didn't need any help moving in."

Good morning to you, too, Rory thought. "I didn't think I did," she said, stepping back for him to pass.

Deliberately overlooking the accusation shadowing his rugged features, she crossed her arms over her hoodie and the teal turtleneck and thermal undershirt layered beneath it. She wanted to believe her shiver had more to do with the chill in the large space than with the big man in the waffle-weave pullover and charcoal cargo pants. After all, the thermometer by the dairy case did read forty-nine degrees.

The man should wear a coat, she insisted to herself. It was easily ten degrees colder outside.

She turned on her heel to lead him inside where it was warmer. "The college kids I hired were only available long enough to drive the U-Haul over and unload it into the market," she explained, heading between the packing boxes that formed an aisle to the interior door. "It wasn't until we got here that they told me they wouldn't have time to carry everything to the rooms. They did take one of the beds upstairs, though." The thud of heavy hiking boots echoed behind her. In running shoes, her footsteps barely made a squeak. "A mattress, anyway," she qualified. "And a box of bedding." That had been huge.

Spending the past couple of nights on a hard floor would have guaranteed even less sleep than she usually managed. Even with a reasonably comfortable place to rest, she'd spent most of both nights trying not to disturb Tyler and listening to the building's unfamiliar creaks and groans while hoping to heaven she could make this store work.

"They'll come back to finish sometime next week," she continued, "so I've been taking in what I can by myself. Tyler's helping." Boxes too heavy to carry she'd emptied one armload at a time. The method wasn't the most efficient, but she now had one bathroom in order and the kitchen organized, except for the table and chairs. The old refectory table weighed a ton. She knew—she'd tried to move it last night.

She chafed her arms along her sleeves, winced a little when she rubbed a spot above the elbow that now sported the bruise she'd earned in the attempt. She had a matching one on the back of her shoulder. No longer hearing Erik's footfalls, she glanced around to see that he had stopped.

Across ten feet of worn plank flooring, she saw his dark eyebrows merge. "Isn't the furnace working?"

"It's working just fine."

"Then why is it so cold in here?"

"Because I'm not heating this big space until I have to. Fuel's expensive. By the way," she added, gratitude slipping into her voice, "thank you for having the tank filled. You saved me from running out of oil." She'd always had electric heat before. Not accustomed to an oil furnace, she hadn't realized the need for fuel until the man who'd performed the building inspection Sunday had showed her the tank and pointed out the gauge.

"The driver of the truck wouldn't leave an invoice," she told him. "So if you'll tell me what I owe you, I'll give you a check."

"You don't owe me anything."

"Yes, I do."

"No," he insisted, "you don't. Just think of it as a move-in present."

He obviously considered the matter settled. There seemed no doubt of that as he turned away to ponder the height and breadth of the obstacles blocking his view of the back of the store.

As appreciative as she was for his thoughtfulness, she couldn't accept his gift.

"Look." Hugging her arms a little tighter, she stepped in front of him. "I'm already not sure how I'll repay you for helping me get to know the store. I know you agreed to do it to help your grandparents sell this place," she conceded, which meant his benevolence definitely wasn't personal, "but I'd rather not be any more obligated to you than I already am. Or will be," she qualified, because other than make her acutely aware of his reluctant and very male presence, he hadn't done anything yet. "Okay?"

For a moment, he said nothing. He just let his deceptively easy glance slip over the quiet determination in her eyes before he headed to the checkout counter.

"Then don't accept it as a gift. Accept it because I'd rather work out here with heat."

Confusion preempted further defense. "I thought we were going to go over the inventory."

"That's the plan."

He carried a briefcase. A rather hefty one of scarred butterscotch leather and straps with buckles that had far more character than the sleek, unscuffed ones carried by other men she knew. As he set it on the scratched counter, she could see his burnished initials, worn shiny in places, above the equally worn lock. A section of stitching on the side looked new, as if it had recently been repaired. The case was old, she thought. It had history. And part of that history seemed to say that he'd rather keep and care for what he had than replace it.

Not appreciating how he'd dismissed her attempt to establish an understanding, she didn't bother to wonder why she found that so appealing.

"I thought we'd work where it's already warm. Inside," she pointed out, ever so reasonably. "We can sit at the island and go over the books in there."

"I meant the physical inventory. The stuff that's on the shelves and in the bins back there." He hitched his thumb over his shoulder. "I have a printout of what came with the sale, but those items have been sitting around for a year. You'll want to discount some of what you have and replace it with new merchandise. Things like sinkers, bobbers and leaders are fine, but creels and some of the stock that isn't packaged looks shopworn."

Rory hadn't a clue what he was talking about.

"Fishing gear," he explained, apparently sensing that.

Undaunted, she picked up a couple of the boxes from the cracked surface. She'd already decided the old laminate needed to go. "Then we'll work here at the counter."

The boxes had been emptied, Erik realized when she easily lifted two marked *Dishes* from where his grandfather had once kept displays of bug repellent and sunglasses. She removed two more, adding them to the only space available without blocking either doorway: the tops of three tall stacks of red-and-green bins marked *Christmas*.

She had to stretch to get them there. Jerking his glance from the enticing curve of her backside, he reached past her.

"Let me get that."

"Already have it," she insisted, and having placed the boxes, turned right into him.

Rock had more give to it.

The thought occurred vaguely as she bumped into his chest. Promptly bouncing back, she gasped a breath when his quick grip tightened on her upper arms. Her heart had barely slammed against her ribs when he pulled her forward to keep her from hitting the bins behind her and bringing the empty boxes down on their heads.

The freshness of soap and sea air clung to him. With her pulse scrambling, his grip tight on her bruise, she had no idea why the scents even registered. Her hand shot up, covering the back of his where it curved over the tender spot on her arm.

The pressure of his fingers eased.

With their bodies inches apart, she went as still as stone. Or maybe he froze first. She just knew that one moment she'd been intent on doing whatever she needed to do to make it clear that she wouldn't waste his time, and the next, the tension in his body and the warmth of his hands had seeped through to her skin, making her conscious of little more than…him.

Erik's eyes narrowed on hers an instant before she ducked her head. Slacking his grip, he dropped his hands. There'd been no mistaking the way she'd winced when he'd grabbed her.

Without thinking, he reached toward her again, touched the back of her hand where it now covered where his had been.

He hadn't thought he'd grabbed her that hard.

"Are you okay?"

At the concern in his voice, the caution in his touch, her head came back up. "I'm fine." Wanting to convince them both, she smiled. "Really."

His brow pinched as he drew his hand away once more.

Rory's breath slithered out. That small contact had been far too brief to elicit the loss she felt when he stepped back. Yet that sense of loss existed, sinking deeper into her chest with every heartbeat—unexpected, unwanted and feeling far too threatening under his quiet scrutiny.

A certain numbness had protected her since she'd lost what had felt like the other half of herself. Yet, as with the first time this man had touched her, something about him scraped at the edges of that barrier, made her conscious of things she truly didn't want to consider.

Out of nowhere, the need to be held sprang to mind. It was such a simple thing, so basic that she'd never truly considered it until it had been found and suddenly lost— that need for security, comfort, a sense of oneness. But she knew how rare it was to find that sense of belonging, and the need didn't feel simple at all. Not when she realized she was actually wondering what it would feel like to be folded against Erik's broad, undeniably solid chest. A woman would feel sheltered there. Safe from what troubled her. And for a few moments, anyway, free of the need to stand alone.

Shaken by her thoughts, by him, she started to move back, as much from the need behind the unexpected admissions as from the man who'd prompted them. The stacks behind her allowed her no escape at all.

His scrutiny narrowed. "If you're okay, why are you still holding your arm?"

She was holding in his touch. Realizing that, hoping he didn't, she promptly dropped her hand.

"It's nothing." Rattled, trying not to be, she shrugged. "It's just a little sore."

"Why?"

"Because I landed against the corner of a dresser." She was just tired. Tired and apparently in need of some downtime with her yoga mat. If she could find it. Or, even better, some fudge. The one thing she did not need was to think about this man's chest, his arms or the way he was scowling at her. "I was trying to move a table and lost my grip.

"So," she said, fully prepared to move on so he'd move himself.

He didn't budge. "Which table?"

Trapped between the counter, bins and boxes, she leaned sideways and pointed toward the eight-foot-long, solid oak-and-iron refectory table jammed between a bedroom set and the dairy case. "That one."

His scowl deepened as it swung back to her. "You tried to move that yourself?"

"It wasn't going to go inside on its own."

Forbearance entered his tone. "You said you were going to wait for the kids who moved you here to help with the heavy stuff."

"What I said," she reminded him, just as patiently, "is that they'd be back next week."

"When next week?"

"When they can fit it in."

"Meaning this could all be here a week from now," he said flatly. "Or the week after that."

She didn't particularly appreciate the cynical certainty in his tone. Especially since she was trying not to dwell on that discouraging suspicion herself.

"What about your friends?" he asked, clearly prepared to pursue other possibilities. "Have you asked any of them to help you?"

"I'm sure everyone's busy."

"Do you know that for certain?"

She could omit and evade. No way could she lie. Thinking of the few people she still thought of as friends, she muttered, "Not exactly."

"Then ask."

She started to say that she didn't want to. Fearing she'd sound like a five-year-old, not liking how he prodded at her defenses, she ignored the command entirely.

Since he had yet to move, she ducked around him. "I'll go turn on the heat."

She would do her best to cooperate with him for his help with the store. She could cut corners somewhere else to keep expenses down.

"I only took two bar stools inside, so there are a couple more back there we can bring up to sit on. I'm going to tell Tyler I'll be out here. He's watching a DVD on my laptop."

Erik watched her slip behind the counter, his focus on the resolute set of her shoulders as she disappeared inside. Her son was undoubtedly watching her laptop because her television was buried somewhere in the stacks beyond him. He also gave the guys she'd hired about a fifty-fifty chance of returning to finish their job.

He didn't care what she said. She did need help here. She just didn't want to ask for it.

Considering that she hadn't wanted to accept his little housewarming present, either, he couldn't help but wonder if the woman was always unreasonable, impractical and stubborn, or if some less obvious trait compelled her to refuse assistance when she clearly needed it.

What she needed now was some serious muscle.

Judging from the size of the decidedly upscale sofa and armchairs, sections of wall units, tables and a huge mirror sitting between the rows of shelving, there had been significant space in the house she'd left behind. The larger of two armoires was the size of a king-size mattress. He had no idea where she was going to put that. It might have fit in the largest of the bedrooms upstairs, but it would never make the bend at the top of the staircase.

He pulled his cell phone from his pocket, checked the time before scrolling through his contact list.

He'd just ended his call when she hurried back through the door.

"I have a friend on the way to help with the heavy stuff," he announced. "You and I can take care of the rest of it." Pushing up his sleeves, he motioned to an overstuffed, roll-armed, oatmeal-colored chair blocking a bedroom set. "Where does that go?"

Beneath a dusting of dark hair, his forearms were roped with sinew and muscle. They looked every bit as strong as she imagined them to be, but it was his left arm that had her staring. A silvery scar, hook shaped and wide, slashed from wrist to elbow.

"Just part of a collection. Caught a jib line when it snapped," he said, seeing what had her attention. "It couldn't be helped." His glance slid pointedly to the sore spot on her arm. "Unlike banging yourself up trying to move something you had to know was too heavy for you.

"So where do you want it?" he asked. "The living room?"

His presumption made her let the table reference go.

"You don't need to do this." *Part of a collection,* he'd said. He had more injuries like that? "And you definitely didn't need to call your friend."

Unease over what he'd done had collided with a hint of concern for the scar. Or maybe what he saw was embarrassment warring with interest. Whichever it was, he could practically see her struggling to decide which should take precedence as she moved with him toward the chair. The process, he thought, was rather fascinating.

"Yeah," he muttered, undeterred. At least she now had some color in her cheeks. "I did. I can't get those dressers up the stairs by myself."

"I meant, you didn't need to impose on him at all. I can't ask you to do this," she stressed, only to have him hand her the chair's seat cushion.

"You didn't ask," he pointed out.

"You know what I mean," she muttered back, arms wrapped around the awkward bulk.

"What I know is that there's no way to go over the inventory when we can't even get to it. So, yeah. I do need to do this." Challenge lit the chips of silver in his steel-gray eyes as he pulled one of her arms free and handed her the wide back cushion, as well. His glance slid to her biceps. "You're skinny, but you have more muscle than I'd thought. This'll go faster if you help."

Over the tops of the pillows, Rory could have sworn she saw challenge shift to a smile. Too disconcerted by him and what he'd done to stand there and make certain of it, she turned with the cushions and headed for the door.

She'd admit to having lost a couple of pounds in the past year or so, but no one had called her skinny since sixth grade.

"Which room do you want the twin bed in?" she heard him call.

"The one next to the master," she called back.

She had no intention of arguing with him. Not just because she didn't want to appear difficult. Or because he had a valid point about not being able to get to the inventory. As unsettled as her life felt—would always feel, she feared—getting the visible chaos under control would be huge. Tyler having his own bed that night would be nice, too.

Focusing on her son distracted her from the man carrying up her little boy's bed. For all of five minutes. The moment Tyler saw his bookshelf going up the stairs, he wanted to help. Wanting to keep him out of Erik's way, since she was trying to stay out of it herself, she waited until the piece was in place, then put him to work filling the shelves with his toys. While Erik moved on to tackle the living room furniture, she carried in lamps, pictures and, now that she could get to it, her box of potted herbs for the kitchen windowsill.

They didn't work together so much as they worked around each other. Erik clearly just wanted to get the job done so he could get on with the job he was there to do. Hating how she'd inconvenienced him, she just wanted to get it done, too.

An hour later, she'd returned to the base of the stairs for the rolled-up dinosaur posters she'd left there when muffled male voices drifted from inside the store.

"No way is this thing going up the stairs," she heard Erik insist. "Not without a saw."

"She might take exception to that," came the sensible reply. "How about through the bedroom window? Aren't there picture windows on that side of the house?"

"We'd have to take the window out and bring over a

crane, but it might be doable. The boys could load the EZ-Rig on a trailer and one of them can drive it over."

"That would do it." The unfamiliar voice paused. "There just isn't enough time to do it today. Not if you want the rest of this cleared out. That party starts at six."

Not totally sure what had the men talking about bringing in heavy equipment, equally concerned by mention of a prior obligation, Rory left the posters and poked her head inside the store. In the bright overhead lights, she saw Erik facing the large cherry armoire that blocked one of the grocery aisles. He stood in profile to her, his arms crossed over his broad chest, his wide brow furrowed.

He seemed totally occupied with logistics. She just couldn't see whom he was talking with. Whoever it was remained hidden by the sizable piece of furniture.

Needing to remove the apparent complication, she scooted past the checkout counter. "If it can't be carried up, just leave it. Or move it out of the way if you need to. I'll figure out what to do with it later."

Erik's glance caught hers as an athletic-looking male in worn denims and a plaid flannel shirt stepped from behind the armoire. The man had a scant inch on her mentor in height, which put him in the range of six-three or so, and the same imposing, broad-shouldered, leanly muscular build that spoke of intimate familiarity with hard physical work. Or a gym.

Beneath his wavy, wood-brown hair, his eyes narrowed an instant before he smiled. That smile seemed as easygoing as the man himself when Erik introduced him to her as Pax Merrick.

"My business partner," Erik added.

Pax reached out. "And partner in crime."

Shaking her hand, he gave her a quick once-over, the kind men who enjoy women often do, along with a rakish wink. "We go back a long way. You're Rory," he said, sparing his partner the introduction, along with whatever he could have added about their apparently extensive history.

Her glance bounced between the two unquestionably attractive, undoubtedly successful, probably rather fearless males. With the sense that their history might be rather intriguing, she offered Pax an apologetic smile of her own. "I'm really sorry to cut into your day like this."

"Not a problem. He'd do the same for me," he admitted, eyeing her with no small amount of curiosity. "You're really taking over this place?"

Something in the man's tone gave her pause.

"I am," she replied. "Why?"

"It'll seem really different, is all. I used to hang out here with Erik when we were kids. We built our first boat in Gramps's garage down there. And this store… It was just the Sullivans here all those years. They had sort of a mom-and-pop thing going," he explained, looking her over as if to verify some preconceived impression. "Down-to-earth. Comfortable, you know? I never thought about it being run by someone…"

Like you, she was sure he'd been about to say, only to be cut off by the quick-but-subtle slicing motion Erik made across his own throat.

"…else," he hastily concluded. "But if Erik's going to teach you the ropes," he hurried to add, "I'm sure you don't have a thing to worry about. The guy's got the patience of Job."

Meaning he thought she was going to require…what? she wondered, swinging her glance to Erik. Patience of biblical proportions?

Erik pointedly ignored her. "Are you going to help me move this, Merrick?"

"Absolutely. I'm on it."

As if wanting to muffle his partner, Erik motioned to the furniture the large piece blocked. "As soon as we get this out of the way, we'll take up your son's dresser," he told her. "Where do you want those bookcases?"

"In the spare room across from Tyler's." *Please,* she might have added, but his friend's insinuation still stung.

"Is there a bed that goes in there?"

"I don't have a spare bed anymore." She nodded toward the headboard and nightstands an aisle over with the same carving as the armoire. "That's a set we had in a guest room. I'll use it for my room now."

She'd sold the bed she'd slept in with Curt for so many years. Its new owner had picked up all the master bedroom furnishings the morning her movers had come. She'd sold the bulk of her other possessions to an estate broker she'd met at the country club to which she no longer belonged. Had it not been for Tyler, she'd have sold everything and bought only what she'd need to start over. But too much had changed for him already for her to indulge the need she felt to shed all the reminders of a life that no longer was.

Taking a deep breath, she pushed her hand through her hair and looked over to see Erik still watching her.

"I take it you've downsized."

"You have no idea," she murmured back.

She couldn't imagine what he saw in her expression, but she saw something in his that looked remarkably like understanding. It was as if he knew what it was like to walk away from the trappings and reminders of a former life. Whether he'd had no choice or the choice had been solely his, she had no idea. All she felt with any certainty as he shoved up his shirtsleeves to get back to work was that he wanted no part of those reminders now.

The realizations gave her pause. As she turned away herself and headed inside to pick up the posters, so did her disquiet over his partner's unwitting revelations. The fact that Erik had obviously implied to his friend that she would require considerable patience was merely annoying. She also questioned just how patient he actually was, given his steamroller approach to getting her things moved out of his way. But what truly troubled her was what his friend had said about her mentor's grandparents having been there for so long.

She hadn't even considered what her neighbors and customers would think of someone new running a business that might well be some sort of institution in the area. She'd already been wondering if she could keep it open year-round, and added that to her list of questions for Erik. Her newly heightened concerns about fitting in she'd have to add later, though, when she wasn't busy keeping Tyler out of the way of all the testosterone hauling bedroom furniture up the stairs.

Every time they clamored up the stairs and down the hall with another piece of something large, he'd dart to the door of his new bedroom to watch them go by.

Pax joked with him, noticeably at ease with small children. Erik, preoccupied, said even less to him than when he'd been around him before. He'd given him a half smile on their first pass, which had put a shy grin on Tyler's face, then barely glanced at him at all.

Because her little boy continued to wait in his doorway for "the man with the boat," it soon became painfully apparent that Tyler was hoping Erik would acknowledge him again—which had her feeling even more protective than usual when he asked if he could help him.

"I don't think so, sweetie. They're in a hurry," she explained, brushing his sandy hair back from his forehead. "When people get in a hurry, accidents can happen."

"If I be careful can I help?"

Erik heard the tiny plea drift down the hallway. Focused on getting Rory's possessions out of the way of the inventory, he'd paid scant attention to the child other than to make sure he wasn't where he could get something dropped on him.

But now they needed tools. Deciding to save himself a trip and do something about the dejection he'd heard in that small voice, he called, "Hey, Tyler. Can you do something for me?"

A nanosecond later, little footsteps, muffled by carpeting, pounded down the hall.

Tyler appeared in the doorway of the master bedroom, shoving his hair back from the expectation dancing in his eyes. Rory was right behind him, unmasked concern in hers.

Erik crouched in his cargos, his forearms on his thighs, hands dangling between his knees. Behind him, Pax continued squaring the bed frame to the headboard.

Rory's glance fixed on his as she caught her son by his shoulders. "What do you need?"

Whatever it was, she seemed prepared to do it herself. She had mother hen written all over her pretty face.

"Let him do it. Okay?"

The little boy tipped his head backward to look up at his mom. "Okay?" he echoed. "Please?"

For a moment, she said nothing. She simply looked as if she wasn't at all sure she trusted him with whatever it was he had in mind, before caving in with a cautious okay of her own.

It didn't surprise him at all that, physically, she hadn't budged an inch.

"There's a red metal box at the bottom of the stairs," he said to the boy. "It has socket wrenches in it. It's kind of heavy," he warned. "Do you think you can bring it up?"

With a quick nod, Tyler turned with a grin.

"No running with tools!" Rory called as he disappeared out the door.

"'Kay!" the boy called back, and dutifully slowed his steps.

Caught totally off guard by what Erik had done, Rory looked back to the big man crouched by her bed frame. He was already back to work, he and his partner slipping the frame parts into place and talking about how much longer it would take them to finish.

Not wanting to be in their way herself, she backed into the hall, waiting there while Tyler, lugging the case with both hands, grinning the whole while, made his delivery.

When he walked back out of the room moments later, his expression hadn't changed. She couldn't remember the last time her little boy had looked so pleased. Or so proud.

"Erik said I did good."

She knew. She'd heard him.

"Can I show him my boat?"

"Maybe some other time. He's really busy right now," she explained, then added that *she* really needed his help finishing his room.

Helping his mom wasn't nearly the thrill of helping the guys. Especially when Erik called for him again ten minutes later, this time to carry down the tools he'd had him bring up.

From where she stood on a chair adjusting the ties on a primordial-forest curtain valance, she watched Tyler walk by his bedroom door with both hands again gripping the handle of the red metal box. Right behind him came Erik, telling him he'd take the box when they got to the stairs so he wouldn't lose his balance with it.

Right behind Erik, Pax paused and poked his head into the room.

"I've got to run, Rory. No need to stop what you're doing," he called, because she'd done just that. "We have a client's Christmas party tonight or I'd stick around and help. Erik's going to finish up."

She'd forgotten they had plans. Groaning at the lapse, she left the last tie undone and headed for the door.

Erik had disappeared into the store. Tyler, now empty-handed, stood in the entryway as Pax passed him, ruffling his hair on the way.

"What can I do to repay you?" she called.

"Do you bake?"

"What's your favorite cookie?"

"Any kind that goes with coffee." Grinning, he disappeared, too.

Erik eyed his buddy as Pax walked into the store. "If she has any spare time," he insisted, setting the toolbox on the counter, "she'll need to spend it out here."

"Hey," his shameless partner said with a shrug, "if she wants to bake me something, it'd be rude to refuse. So how much longer will you be?"

Erik flatly rejected the odd sensation that hit out of nowhere. It almost felt like protectiveness. But just whom he felt protective of, he had no idea. The woman wasn't Pax's type at all. "Half an hour at the most."

"You taking a date tonight?"

"Yeah," he muttered, the word oddly tight. "What about you?"

"I'm leaving my options open. I'll cover for you if you need more time," he added, his smile good-natured as he headed out the store's front door.

Erik wished he'd left his options open, too. Though all he said to his partner was that he'd catch up with him at the party and turned back to what was left of his task.

The aisles were finally clear. The inventory visible. Except for the large armoire they'd moved to the empty space near the front door and the boxes and bins Rory had said she didn't need just yet, mostly those marked *Christmas,* nothing else needed to be carried in. Except for her monster of a dining table, which they'd put in place, he and

Pax had carried the rest of the furniture in and left it all wherever it had landed in the living room.

His briefcase still lay on the checkout counter's marred surface, its contents untouched.

Burying his frustration with that, he glanced up to see her watching him uneasily from the inner doorway. More comfortable dealing with logistics than whatever had her looking so cautious, he figured the furniture in the living room could be pushed or shoved into place. It didn't feel right leaving her to do it alone. It wasn't as if she'd call a neighbor for help with the heavier pieces. She didn't even know them. And she'd seemed inexplicably reluctant to call in a friend.

"Where do you want the sofa? Facing the window?" That was where his grandparents had always had theirs.

Rory wanted it to face the fireplace. She just wasn't about to impose on him any more than she already had.

"I'll take care of it," she insisted, because he had that purposeful set to his jaw that said he was about to get his own way. Again.

"What about the big cabinet?"

"It's fine where it is. For now," she conceded, not about to tell him she wanted it moved across the room to the stair wall. "I'm hugely grateful for your help with all this, Erik. And for your friend's. But I'd just as soon not feel guiltier than I already do for having used your time like this. You came to work on the business. Not to help me move in. You need to go now."

One dark eyebrow arched. "I need to go because you feel guilty?"

"You need to go because you have a date."

She'd obviously overheard his conversation with his partner. Not that it mattered. Like Pax's unveiled allusion to the care and feeding Erik had told him he was sure she'd require, nothing had been said that he'd rather she hadn't heard. He'd bet his boat she already suspected he wasn't crazy about being there, anyway.

"Right." He wasn't in the habit of leaving a woman waiting. "We'll get to the inventory later this week. I won't have time until Friday."

"Friday will be fine. I'll be here. And thank you," she added again, touching his arm when he started to turn away. The moment he turned back, she dropped her hand. "For letting Tyler help," she explained. "I haven't seen him smile like that in a really long time."

Thinking the cute little kid had just wanted to be one of the guys, he murmured, "No problem," and picked up the toolbox and his briefcase. There was no reason for her to be looking all that grateful. Or all that concerned.

Still, as he told her he'd call her later and turned for the door, adding, "Bye, sport," for the little boy who'd just appeared behind his mom, cradling a toy boat, he really wished he didn't have the date with the bubbly event planner he'd taken out a couple of weeks ago. He didn't know the striking blonde all that well, but she'd been easy on the eyes, into sailing and, had he been interested in pursuing her hints, not at all opposed to a little casual sex.

He just hoped she'd need to make it an early evening so there'd be no awkwardness at her door. His head wasn't into games tonight. He wasn't much up for a party, either, though he wasn't about to stand up a client.

For reasons he didn't bother to consider, what he wanted to do was stay right where he was.

Chapter Four

The last thing Rory wanted Friday morning was to be late for her meeting with Erik. Or for him to be on time.

As she turned her car into her gravel parking lot, she realized she wasn't getting her wish on either count.

She'd also just confirmed her suspicions about the gleaming white seaplane she'd seen tied to the dock at the bottom of the rise. It was Erik's. He was on her porch, leaning against a post.

The fact that her mentor flew his own plane meant that he hadn't had to queue up for the ferry or get caught in traffic the way she and the rest of the mortals had crossing the sound and navigating surface streets that morning. It also meant that it had only taken him minutes to make the flight that was now a ninety-minute-each-way expedition for her to Tyler's school.

Hating that she'd caused him to wait, she left her little car in the otherwise empty lot in front of the store rather than park it in her garage and hurried toward where he'd straightened from the post. "I'm sorry I'm late. I was the last car off the ferry," she called, praying he hadn't been there long. They'd agreed on eleven o'clock. It was only a few minutes after. Still… "How long have you been here?"

The ever-present breeze ruffled his dark hair as he pushed his cell phone into a front pocket of his jeans and picked up his worn briefcase.

"Long enough to figure out you weren't going to answer the back door or the one to the mudroom. I didn't realize you'd be gone. I was just going to call you."

His cloud-gray eyes slid from hers as a muscle jerked in his jaw. His skin looked ruddy from the chill. In deference to the cold, he wore a leather flight jacket—open, though, as if in defiance of the need for it.

She hadn't thought of him as defiant before. Or rebellious, or rash, or anything that might even hint at irresponsibility. He seemed too much in control of himself for that. Yet the finely honed tension surrounding him alluded to a sort of restiveness that implied far more than his impatience with her, and made her acutely aware of how restless a man with flying and sailing in his blood might be. Restless. Daring. Bold.

She couldn't remember the last time she'd felt anything that wasn't tempered by the numbness that lingered deep inside her. And she'd never felt bold in her life.

What she felt most was simply the need to keep pushing forward. Especially now. Forward was good. Looking back made it too easy to fall apart.

He didn't need to know that, though. As she crossed the porch planks, searching her crowded key ring for the unfamiliar key, she figured all he needed to know was that she would make this venture work. Exactly how she would do that was as much a mystery to her as the dawn of creation, but she figured the basics would be a good place to start. And basically, she knew she needed this man to help make it happen.

His footsteps echoed heavily as he came up beside her, his big body blocking the wind whipping at her hair. "Where's your son?"

"At school. He only has tomorrow and next week before winter break, so we're commuting."

"To Seattle?"

Conscious of him frowning at the top of her head, she tried to remember if the key she'd just selected was for the store's front door, its emergency exit, the door to the house or the side door to the garage.

"I don't want him to miss working on the holiday projects with the other kids. He already missed the first of the week because of the move and he really wants to help decorate the school's big tree." He wanted a big tree, too, he'd told her. A *huge* one. How she'd make *huge* happen currently fell in the mystery category, too. "Since he won't be going back there after Christmas, it's about the only thing keeping his mind off the need to change schools right now."

"How long does that take you?"

"An hour and a half, if you include queuing up for the ferry."

"You're spending three hours over and back in the morning, and another three hours every—"

"That's just today," she hurried to assure him. "I'll usually only make the round-trip once. Kindergarten is only four hours, so I'll run errands while he's there." And maybe see if she could slip into her friend Emmy's yoga class, since seeking calm seemed more imperative by the moment. "A friend is picking him up with her son this afternoon. He'll play at their house until I get there."

His tone went flat. "So you came all the way back just to keep this appointment."

"You said it was the only time you had this week."

"You could have told me you'd be in Seattle," he insisted. "I never would have expected you to come back here for this."

"You said we had to go over the inventory. We have to do that here, so there was no point in mentioning it."

The key didn't work. Her head still down, his disapproval doing nothing for her agitation, she picked out another.

Before she could try that one in the lock, Erik reached over and snagged the wad of keys by the purple rhinestone-encrusted miniflashlight dangling below them.

"That's to the garage." He paused at the practical bit of bling, chose one beside it. "You want this one."

He held a duller brass key by its blade.

"Next time something like this comes up," he continued, biting back what sounded a lot like frustration, "mention it."

All her rushing had left her jumpier than she'd realized. Or maybe it was the edginess in him that fed the tension she did not want to feel with this man. Taking the key, conscious of how careful he'd been not to touch her, she forced the hurry from her tone.

"My schedule is my problem, not yours. I'll make sure it doesn't interfere with what you need to show me here. Not any more than it has already," she concluded, since last time he'd wound up hauling in her furniture.

Trying not to give him time to dwell on that little failure, she slid the key into the lock.

As the lock clicked, he moved behind her. Reaching past her head, he flattened his broad hand on the heavy wood door.

His heat inches from her back, the nerves in her stomach had just formed a neat little knot when he muttered, "Then let's get to it," and pushed the door open.

Intent on ignoring the knot, disconcerted by their less-than-auspicious start, she hurried into the store to the warning beeps of the alarm system.

With the front display windows shuttered for the winter, the only light came from what spilled in behind them. Relying on that pale shaft of daylight, she headed straight for the checkout counter and the inner door behind it, mental gears shifting on the way.

Feeling his scowl following her, she deliberately sought to shift his focus, too.

"I'm going to start the coffee. While I do that, would you look over the floor plan I came up with? It's right here on the counter." Fluorescent lights buzzed and flickered as she snapped switches on. Punching the security code into the pad by the inner door, the beeping stopped. "I'll be right back."

In less than a minute, she piled her purse, coat and scarf onto the dining table, flipped on the coffeemaker she'd already filled and grabbed the tape measure she'd left on the island.

She'd barely turned back into the store when the hard line of Erik's profile had her freezing in the doorway.

He'd tossed his jacket over the far end of the U-shaped counter's now-bare surface. Without it, she could see *Merrick & Sullivan Yachting* discreetly embroidered in sky-blue on the navy Henley hugging his broad shoulders. Ownership, she thought. He had a definite sense of it. He had it stitched on his shirt. His initials, she'd noticed before, were on the latch of his briefcase.

On the scarred beige countertop lay the file she'd left open. His frown was directed to the new floor plan she'd come up with.

"You did this?" he asked.

With a vague sinking feeling she walked around to him. She might not know anything about the little doodads in the bins and on the Peg-Boards hanging in her new store, but she was a consumer with her fair share of shopping hours under her belt. If the interior didn't have some appeal, people might run in to buy what they needed, but they wouldn't stick around to browse and buy more.

"The store needs updating," she said simply, certain he could see that himself. "I thought it might make the space more interesting to have three shorter horizontal shelving units in back than that one long one down the middle. The floor space along here," she said, pointing to the front and back walls on the drawing, "would be a little narrower, but the endcaps would allow for ninety-six more inches of display space. I could use part of the longer piece—"

"I'm not asking you to defend this," he interrupted mildly. "I'm just asking if you drew it."

Erik's only interest when he'd first arrived had been in tackling the task they hadn't even started the other day. As far as he was concerned, they were already behind schedule if she was to open in April. Not wanting to fall further behind and risk her not making a success of the business, he'd just wanted to get in, get out and get back to work until the next time he had to meet with her. It had been that ambivalent sort of annoyance eating at him when he'd realized what she'd done to accommodate him.

The trip by air between the store and Seattle was nothing for him. Minutes from takeoff to touchdown, depending on head- or tailwinds and whether he left from his houseboat on Lake Union or the boatworks in Ballard. The drive and a ferry ride for her was infinitely less convenient. People commuted from the inner islands every day. But she had actually come back from Seattle just to meet with him, and would have to return later that day to pick up her son.

Even the time it would normally take her on other days seemed an enormous waste of time to him. She was right, though. How she did what she needed to do was her problem. Just as it was his problem, not hers, that he didn't want to consider changing the store from exactly as it had been for decades.

The need to play nice so they could reach their respective goals wasn't what had his attention at the moment, however. It was the detail in the drawing. It hadn't been generated using a computer program. The floor plan had been drawn with pencil on graph paper. While the layout was admittedly simple, the measurements and identity of the elements were all perfectly drawn and precisely printed. It had the touch of a professional.

"Oh," she murmured, apparently understanding. "I took a drafting class a few years ago. We'd thought about building our own home and I wanted to understand what the architect was talking about." She gave a shrug, the motion nowhere near as casual as he suspected she intended it to be. "We never got to the blueprint stage, though. We bought instead."

We.

The freshness of her soap or shampoo or whatever it was clinging to her skin already had him conscious of her in ways he was doing his best to ignore. He'd caught the light herbal scent of her windblown hair when she'd pointed out the walls on the drawing. He caught it again now. Whatever it was she wore seemed too subtle to define. But the elements managed to hit his gut with the impact of a charging bull.

Telling himself he didn't need to know anything about her that didn't apply directly to his reason for being there, he deliberately overlooked her reference to the man she'd married—along with the subtle havoc she wreaked on certain nerves—and indicated a rectangle she'd drawn by the front door.

"So what's this?"

"That's the armoire over there. It just needs to be moved

back against that wall and down a few feet and it'll be perfect. A couple of neighbors stopped by to welcome me yesterday. Actually, I think they came to check me out," she admitted, because their curiosity about the "single woman who'd bought the store" had been so obvious. "But one of them mentioned that she makes organic soaps and creams. She has a friend up the road who makes candles for craft shows. I thought I'd see what else is made locally and put a gift display in it."

He eyed her evenly. "This isn't a boutique."

"Are you saying it's a bad idea?"

He wasn't going to commit to anything yet. He was still back on her having taken a drafting class just because she'd wanted to understand her architect.

"When did you do this?"

Realizing he hadn't shot her down, a hint of relief entered her eyes. "After Tyler went to sleep in the evening. And between 1:00 and 3:00 a.m."

Sleepless nights, he thought. He'd once been there himself. Having one's world turned upside down did tend to promote a certain degree of restlessness. He figured it didn't help matters that she was trying to sleep in an unfamiliar house, in a bed she apparently wasn't accustomed to, either. She'd said the one she was now using had been in a guest room.

The thought of her in bed, tossing, turning or otherwise, had him reaching for his old briefcase.

"Let's get to the inventory. Once you know what you have to work with here, you'll know what you need to order and how much shelving space you can actually use."

"So you think this floor plan might work?"

The layout of the shelves his grandfather had built had served its purpose effectively for years. Changing anything about it hadn't even occurred to Erik. The old-fashioned footprint of the place was simply part of the store's personality. It always had been.

He'd thought it always would be.

He gave a mental snort, blocking his reaction to the change as irrelevant. No one knew better than he did how transient "always" could be. The store was hers now, he reminded himself yet again. She was free to do anything she wanted as long as she could turn a profit.

"It might. Probably," he conceded, because her plan would certainly better define the grocery section from the sporting goods. Using the big armoire to promote local artisans wasn't a bad idea, either.

Still, there was no denying the reluctance in his agreement. He could practically hear it himself. He also couldn't help but notice the small smile Rory immediately stifled.

It pleased her to know that her first instincts and efforts toward her new business were good ones. It didn't feel good to him, though, to know he'd deprived her of sharing that pleasure with the only person available. He was her mentor. He was supposed to be encouraging her. Showing a little enthusiasm.

Before he could tell her just how good her instincts probably were, she'd crossed her arms over the glittery designer logo on her hoodie and moved on.

"Before we start the inventory," she prefaced, "would you tell me about the customs your grandparents had here? One of the ladies I met said she hoped I'd have a farmers' market on the porch like the Sullivans did every summer. The other one said that the Harbor Market lighted walking kayak was missed in the Chimes and Lights parade last week."

She hadn't realized such an object even existed until Edie Shumway, the fortysomething community volunteer and, Rory suspected, neighborhood busybody, had explained what it was. Apparently Erik's grandfather and one of his cronies from the local lodge provided propulsion for the Christmas-light-covered kayak—which explained the two holes she'd finally noticed in the bottom of the one hanging from the ceiling in the back of the store.

"I'm going to call the lodge and see if I can get a couple of volunteers to walk it in the parade next year. I'll provide candy for them to throw to the kids, and get elf hats like Edie said they wore. But I need to know what else your grandparents did that I should do, too."

Erik hesitated.

"I'm not totally sure what you're after."

"Anything they did for holidays, or for community events. Or things they did every year that people looked forward to."

"Like the kayak and the elf hats," he concluded.

"Exactly. I want to belong here," she explained, as if that need meant as much to her as financial success. "I want us to fit in. The other day, your friend implied that this place was sort of an institution around here. If there are customs your grandparents had that their neighbors and customers looked forward to, then I'll keep them up the best I can."

"You want to maintain my grandparents' traditions?"

"If you'll tell me what they were."

Erik was not a man who impressed easily. Nor was it often that a woman caught him so off guard. Even as the businessman in him commended her approach to public relations, a certain self-protectiveness slipped into place.

Resting one hip on the counter, he crossed his arms over his chest, conscious of her honest interest as she waited for whatever he might be willing to share.

"They always gave suckers to the little kids." A few innocent memories would cost him nothing. And possibly help her bottom line. "And ice cream bars. Locals always got a free one on their birthday." His grandma had kept a calendar under the cash register with the regular customers' birthdays written on it. Anniversaries were there, too.

He told her all that, ignoring an unwanted tug of nostalgia as he began to remember traditions he'd taken for granted, then forgotten. Or noticed but overlooked.

"They always opened the week of the spring sailing regatta in April, so they hung nautical flags along the porch and a life preserver by the door. For the Fourth of July they hung bunting and handed out flag stickers," he said, memories rushing back. He'd loved the Fourth as a kid. Lying on his back in the grass to watch the fireworks over the sound. Or better, being out on the water in a boat, watching them explode overhead.

"And every fall," he continued, thinking her little boy would probably like it, too, "the porch would be full of pumpkins and hay bales and they'd serve cups of cider."

With her dark eyes intent on his, she seemed completely captivated by the small-town customs he hadn't considered in years. She also appeared totally unaware of how close she'd drawn to him as he spoke. As near as she'd come, all he'd have to do was reach out and he would know for certain if her skin felt as soft as it looked.

As his glance slid to the inviting fullness of her bottom lip, he wondered at the softness he would find there, too.

Her lips parted with a quietly drawn breath.

When he looked back up, it was to see her glance skim his mouth before her focus fell to his chest and she took a step away.

"What about Thanksgiving and Christmas?" she asked, deliberately turning to the file on the counter. "Aside from the kayak."

Forcing his attention back to her question, he stayed right where he was.

"Thanksgiving was just the fall stuff. But the day after, Gramps would string lights along all the eaves and porch posts and set up a Christmas village with a giant lighted snowman." There had been a time when he and his dad had usually helped. That was back when Thanksgiving dinner had always been here. Christmas had been at his parents' house, around the bend and in town a couple of miles. After the aircraft company his dad worked for had transferred him to San Diego a few years ago, he'd headed south for that particular holiday.

"The store was closed for the season by then, so I don't think they gave anything out. At least, not the past several years." He hadn't been around to know for sure. Seattle was only twelve miles as the crow flew, but he lived his life what felt like a world away. Unless his grandparents had needed something before they'd moved south, too, he'd given this place and the areas around it as little thought as possible. And he'd never given it as much thought as he had just now. "But a lot of people drove by to see the light display."

Whatever self-consciousness she'd felt vanished as she glanced back to him. "Where are the lights now?"

"They were sold."

"The snowman, too?"

"Everything. They had a garage sale before they moved."

For reasons he couldn't begin to explain, he wasn't at all surprised by her disappointment. What did surprise him was that he actually felt a twinge of it himself.

"Tyler would have loved to have a big snowman out there," she said. "And the village. He gets so excited when he sees Christmas decorations."

Threading her fingers through her hair, she gave him a rueful smile. "Unfortunately, I'd thought I was moving somewhere a lot smaller, so I sold everything for outside except a few strings of lights."

With the lift of her shoulder, she attempted to shrug off

what she could do nothing about now, anyway. "What else is there I should know?"

From the pensiveness in her voice, there wasn't a doubt in his mind that she was still thinking about how her little boy would have loved what his grandparents had done.

"I can't think of anything right now." Wanting to get her mind off what she couldn't do for her son, and his thoughts off her mouth, he rose from his perch. "But if I do, I'll let you know."

"One more thing," she said as he turned to his briefcase. "Everything I've heard so far tells me this will be a good place to live. But what do you think about it? The community, I mean."

Just wanting to get to work, he opened the case with the snap of its lock. "It is a good place. I grew up in town, but I was around here a lot, too. I even came back after college." Paper rustled as he pulled out a sheaf heavy enough for a doorstop. "Pax and I first went into business about a mile down the road." The stack landed on the counter. "You and your son should be fine here."

Considering that Erik had apparently lived much of his life there, it seemed to Rory that the entire area had to mean a lot to him. "Why did you leave?"

He pulled another stack of paper from his scarred briefcase. For a dozen seconds, his only response was dead silence.

"Didn't your business do well?" she prompted.

"The business did fine."

"Then if this is a good place to live and your business was doing well, why did you go?"

The defenses Erik had attempted to ignore finally slammed into place. He knew her question was entirely reasonable. It was one he'd want answered himself were he on the other end of their agreement. Yet as valid as her query was, it bumped straight into the part of his life that had led to an entirely different existence than he'd once thought he'd be living by now.

His plans had been unremarkable, really. No different from half the guys he knew: a good marriage, build boats, a couple of kids, maybe a dog. The one out of four he did have was 90 percent of his life. It was a good life, too. The rest he'd written off completely years ago.

"It has nothing to do with here."

"What did it have to do with, then?"

"Nothing you'd need to be concerned about."

"How can I be sure of that if I don't know what it is you're not telling me? If you were getting your life established here," she pointed out, "it's hard for me to imagine why you'd leave. You seem too much in command of yourself and everything around you to do that if you'd really wanted to stay. That's why your reason for leaving is important to me." She tipped her head, tried to catch his glance. "Was this place lacking something?"

She'd stated her conclusions about him more as fact than compliment. As if she saw his influence over his surroundings as basic to him as his DNA. He'd have been flattered by her impression of him, too, had it not been for how much control he'd actually given up to save the marriage that had ultimately ended anyway. He could see where she deserved something more than he'd given her, though. After insisting his business had been fine there and that she would be, too, he did feel somewhat obligated to explain why he hadn't stuck around himself.

"It didn't lack for anything," he admitted. At least, it hadn't as far as he'd been concerned. "I left because my ex-wife wanted to teach in the city for a few years before coming back to raise a family. Those few years led to a few more and she changed her mind. About coming back and about the family," he admitted, making a long story as short as possible. "When we left here, the business had barely gotten off the ground. But by the time I realized we weren't coming back, Pax and I were established in Ballard. We had a good location. We had good people working for us. So it made sense to stay there. Like I said, my leaving had nothing to do with anything around here."

Thinking he'd covered all the bases, he added two more stacks of papers to the first.

"She was a teacher?"

"Kindergarten," he said without looking up. "She was great with kids."

Her voice went soft. "You wanted children?"

A folder landed on the pile. "Let's get to this, shall we?"

He'd said as much as he was going to. He'd closed the door on all the excuses Shauna had come up with to delay having a baby, and on how he'd hung in there because he'd promised to be there for better or worse. She'd kept asking him to bear with her on the baby thing. Especially after his business took off. She'd eventually changed her mind about a baby, but only after they'd divorced and she'd remarried. He'd realized then that it wasn't that she hadn't wanted children. She just hadn't wanted his. She'd had no problem, however, keeping the house and a hefty chunk of their assets.

Frowning at his thoughts, he turned the whole stack of what he'd unloaded toward Rory. The past was just that. Past. Over. Done.

Rory saw a muscle in his jaw jerk.

The demise of his marriage evidently hadn't been his choice.

She thought that an incredibly sad thing to have in common. She'd had no choice in hers ending, either.

"I'm sorry about your wife."

"Ex."

"Ex-wife," she corrected. She spoke quietly, feeling bad for having pushed, worse for what she'd discovered. He'd once had plans to build his life in the fiercely beautiful surroundings where he'd grown up, but circumstances had forced him to move away, and move on. Just as circumstances had forced her in an entirely different direction than she would have chosen, and led her to the very place she strongly suspected he truly no longer wanted to be.

"Marriage can be complicated," she said, beginning to appreciate the roots of his restiveness. "That must be why it's never easy no matter how it ends."

The furnace kicked on with the rattle of the floor vent behind the counter. His head down, his hand on the printout, Erik slowly ruffled a corner of the pages with his thumb.

He'd heard understanding in her voice, suspected he'd see it in her fragile features were he to look up. She seemed to think they shared the same kind of pain.

He didn't want that kind of sympathy. He didn't want to poke around at what he'd finally grown so far beyond, or into what was undoubtedly fresher and more painful territory for her. And he definitely didn't want to be as curious as he couldn't seem to help being about her, or the man she'd married. She'd once spoken of her child's loss. There'd been no doubt in his mind at the time that she hurt for her son. He just hadn't considered how the boy's pain could easily compound the depth of the loss she felt herself.

Mostly, though, he didn't want her getting so close, or to get close to her. Emotionally, anyway. Physically would be just fine. Heaven knew he was aware of her in ways he had no business considering. But she didn't seem anything like many of the women he knew, those looking for a good time, no commitments involved. Not that he'd been intimate with anyone in longer than he cared to remember. He didn't want any commitments, either. Still, he'd grown tired of the games, the shallow conversations and walking away feeling little more than…empty.

He gave the top folder a nudge. "I'm sorry about yours, too," he admitted, because he didn't need to know the details to feel bad for her. "And you can have a good business here," he assured, because it was his job to help her make that happen. "We just need to get to work so we can make sure of it.

"This is my grandfather's business plan," he said, opening the folder. "Since you're new to all this, it'll be your bible. We can tweak it as we go, but to get you up and running, it'll be simpler not to deviate from it too much at first. This—" he pulled the top printout forward "—is a stock list of the groceries they kept on hand, divided by type and vendor. Dairy, produce, snacks, staples, that sort of thing.

"This printout," he said, indicating the tallest stack of paper, "is your sporting goods department. There are certain vendors you'll need to order from weeks or months in advance. Others can ship in twenty-four hours. You'll want to get their new catalogs. Gramps said they're all online, but some will mail hard copies. You'll need to establish accounts in your name with all of them."

He handed her a CD. "It's all on here for ordering and bookkeeping purposes. Look through it, list your questions and we'll go over them later. I want to get you started on the physical inventory. You need to know what you have on hand, so it's as good a way as any to get your feet wet."

The change of subject was as subtle to Rory as the slam of a door. He would share anything that would help her make a success of the business. But his personal life was now off-limits. Despite how deftly he'd closed off his past, however, he'd revealed wounds that might well have taken years to heal. Family mattered to him. His dreams had mattered. Once.

She'd give anything to know how he'd survived knowing that the woman he'd married had no longer loved him.

For her, even harder than Curt's death was the knowledge that he might not have ever loved her at all.

The deep tones of Erik's voice somehow overrode the sick sensation that inevitably came with the thought. Or maybe it was simply his no-nonsense presence that managed to keep that awful feeling at bay.

"We can start with things you can probably identify even if you've never used them. Camp stoves, lanterns, backpacking gear," he said. "Or go with something that might be more of a challenge. Your choice."

He was there to teach her what she needed to know to reopen the store, not about how to live with questions that could now never be answered. From his deliberate allusion to her lack of knowledge about certain outdoor activities, she had the feeling, too, that he intended his baiting to pull her out of her thoughts. If not for her sake, definitely for his own.

Since he had far more experience with both the store and self-survival, the least she could do was follow his lead.

"More of a challenge."

He said he wasn't surprised.

First, though, she brought them each a cup of coffee, his black, hers with milk, which they took with a section of the printouts and a notepad to the back of the store. It was there that he told her he needed to leave by two o'clock, which, thankfully, was a few minutes before she needed to leave to catch the ferry to pick up Tyler. So for the next hour, she learned to identify lures, hooks, rods, reels, creels, the difference between a bobber and a sinker and the different weights of leader—which would be important to know, he told her, if a customer came in asking for twenty-pound test. At least now she'd know they were asking for fishing line.

"If someone wants fish, wouldn't it be a whole lot more convenient to buy it from a grocery store?"

Towering beside her, he remained focused on a column of item numbers. "Might be convenient, but it wouldn't be nearly as much fun."

"I take it you've never been to Pike Place Fish Market." She focused on a page of her own. "You pick out the fish you want and the guys behind the cases toss it down the line to the scale. You get it wrapped, packed, you don't have to gut it and the show is free. That's fun enough for me."

With that even-eyed way he had of looking at her, he slanted her a tolerant glance. "You're missing the point."

"The point being?"

"Being in the great outdoors. The thrill of landing a thirty-pound salmon, or pulling an eight-pound rainbow trout from a freshwater stream."

"The guilt of taking Nemo from his mother," she muttered.

"What?"

"Never mind. I doubt that you know him."

"Please tell me that's not the approach you're going to take with your customers," he muttered back, just before his glance dropped to her mouth—which had the odd effect of shutting her up and getting her back to verifying counts.

They didn't have time to move on to the modest sections of hiking, camping or boating equipment before she noticed the time. Since she had to drive right past the marina at the end of the street, and he'd tied his floatplane there, she asked if she could give him a ride and save him the two-block walk in the misty rain.

Conscious of the time himself, he told her that would be great. She could go over the rest of the inventory on her own and call him with any questions. They'd meet again next week after she'd gone over the business plan. He also asked if he could take the drawing of her new floor plan with him.

Thinking he intended to give the layout she wanted some thought, she handed it over, along with a travel mug of coffee since he seemed to like hers. Minutes later, he'd just tossed his briefcase into the back of her fuel-efficient little car and folded his big frame into the passenger seat when her cell phone chimed.

One glance at the caller ID had her bracing herself an instant before she dropped the phone back into her bag, started the engine and backed up. The phone continued to chime as she pulled onto the wet two-lane road and headed down the rise.

Erik's glance cut from her purse to her profile.

"I'll call her back," she said. "It's Audrey. My mother-in-law. She's calling about plans for Christmas." The woman was actually returning Rory's call, something it had taken her three days to do. The conversation would be short, but it wasn't one she wanted to have with Erik in the car.

"She *was* my mother-in-law," she corrected. Technically, Rory was no longer related to the Linfields. Audrey had apparently pointed that out to Lillian Brinkley, the wife of the country club president, who had ever so thoughtfully shared it in the ladies' room with two other members of the socially connected among the mourners at Curt's funeral. Rory had been seeking a few minutes of quiet while closed in a stall at the time.

According to Audrey, via Lillian, Rory's vows with her son had been "until death do them part." They'd parted, however sadly. End of legal relationship.

As strained as her relationship with Curt's parents had always been beneath the polite manners and civility, Rory hadn't doubted the remarks at all.

"She's really only Tyler's grandmother now." That was the only part that mattered, anyway.

The wipers swiped at the heavy mist on the windshield. Through the veil of gray, the little marina came into clearer view. Erik barely noticed. For a couple of hours he'd caught glimpses of a woman whose guard with him had begun to ease, a smart, savvy woman who possessed no small amount of determination, ingenuity and a remarkable willingness to step beyond her comfort zone.

What he saw now was a woman doing her level best to mask disquiet. He'd seen her do it before, for her son's sake. Her attempts seemed to work fine on her five-year-old, but Erik recognized strain when he saw it. With her eyes on the road, he watched her take a deep breath, slowly ease it out.

Whatever was going on with Tyler's grandmother had her hands going tight on the wheel.

The heater whirred in its struggle to produce warmth, gravel crunching beneath the tires as she pulled to a stop by the wooden stairs that led to the long floating dock. In the choppy, chill water of the sound, his white Cessna Amphibian floated and yawed where he'd secured it at the end of the pier, well away from the few sport boats moored there this time of year.

He almost always felt better flying from this place than toward it.

"Thank you for your help today," she murmured, her hands now tucked at her waist, her shoulders hunched against the still-cold air. "I'll come up to speed on everything as fast as I can. I promise."

The bravado behind her smile pulled at protective instincts he'd rather ignore. He knew she wanted to belong there, in a place she'd known absolutely nothing about until last week. He knew she wanted to make a good home for her son. He suspected, too, that she could use a little reassurance on both counts.

After all, she was pretty much on her own here.

"I'll pass that on to our benefactor," he promised back, wanting to keep his purpose there in perspective. "And for what it's worth, Rory, you and your son really should do well here." He hesitated, perspective faltering. "I'd always thought it was a good place to raise a child."

He reached for the door, cold salt air blasting in as he opened it. "I'll call you next week. In the meantime, call me if you have questions." He climbed out, then ducked his head back in to retrieve his case from the backseat. "Thanks for the ride."

Rory had barely opened her mouth to tell him he was welcome before the door closed. In the space of a heartbeat she'd swallowed the words and was staring at his broad, leather-covered shoulders as he headed for the weathered stairs.

He'd made it halfway down the dock, his long stride sure and certain despite the drift and roll beneath his feet, when she finally put the car into gear. Even with the surface beneath him shifting with the unpredictable current, the man seemed as steady as a rock.

I'd always thought it was a good place to raise a child.

The admission had cost him. She felt as certain of that as she did of her gratitude for his having shared it. He knew his opinion mattered to her. She'd told him so herself. But sharing that particular thought had also demanded a hasty retreat back to the world he now lived in, back to a world so different from what he'd once wanted.

What stung, though, wasn't how anxious he'd been to retreat to the life he'd created for himself. It was the sharp, undeniable feeling that he had quite deliberately retreated from her.

Chapter Five

Rory returned the call to Curt's mother within a minute of dropping off Erik at the dock. When Audrey didn't answer, she left a message saying she was sorry she'd missed her and asking her to please call back as soon as it was convenient.

Despite two other attempts to reach her, it apparently hadn't been "convenient" for four days.

The conversation they'd had still had Rory reeling three hours later. Thanks to the distraction a text from Erik provided, however, at that particular moment she didn't have to struggle to mask the resentment, offense and indignation she wasn't about to impose on her little boy, anyway.

"Is Erik at our new house now, Mom?"

Following the beam of her headlights through the steady rain, she murmured, "Probably, honey."

"Can I help him again?"

"We'll have to see. I'm not sure why he's coming."

The text she'd received from Erik that morning hadn't given her a clue.

Am in mtgs. Need to know if you will be home around 6.

She'd texted back that she'd be there by 6:15 p.m.

His reply had been a wholly unenlightening See you then.

Since he'd indicated he'd be in meetings, she hadn't called to see what he wanted. She hadn't talked to him at all since he'd closed her out at the dock last week, even though he'd told her to call if she had any questions.

She had dozens. Between online catalogs and searches, she'd figured out the answers to most of them, though, and talked herself out of contacting him about the rest. Those she simply added to her list to ask at their next meeting. Partly because they weren't urgent. Mostly because she suspected that what she really wanted was more of the relief she'd so briefly experienced when he'd assured her that she and Tyler would be all right. The sensation hadn't lasted long enough to do much more than tease her with the hope of finding the security she hadn't truly felt in forever, but she desperately needed to feel something positive about the more personal aspects of her life—and that wasn't something she should be seeking from him at all.

There also existed the unnerving little fact that she'd just wanted to hear his voice—something she insisted she shouldn't even be thinking about, considering that she was nothing more than an obligation to him.

That glaring bit of reality mingled with her turmoil over her in-laws as she turned onto the gravel drive just past the store. Through the silvery drizzle, her headlights illuminated a black, bull-nosed pickup truck loaded with something large covered in plastic.

She'd barely pulled into the garage and gathered her

groceries from the backseat when Erik strode up and plucked the heavy sack from her arms.

"Anything else back there?" he asked.

Raindrops glistened in his dark hair, beaded on his leather jacket. His impersonal glance swept her face, his brow pinching at whatever it was he saw in her expression.

Not about to stand there trying to figure out what that something might be, she turned away. "Just one bag. I can get it."

Ignoring her, he reached into the car as Tyler raced around the back bumper and came to a screeching stop.

One strap of his green dinosaur backpack hung over his shoulder. The other dangled behind him as he looked up with a shy "Hi."

Erik straightened, looking down at the child looking up at him. "Hi yourself, sport."

Anticipation fairly danced in her little boy's hazel eyes.

As if unable to help himself, Erik smiled back and held out the bag of apples he'd snagged off the seat. "Do you want to take this?"

At Tyler's vigorous nod, he waited for the child to wrap his arms around the bag, then nudged him toward the warmth of the house. With Tyler doing double time to match Erik's long strides, Rory punched the remote to close the garage door and hurried to catch up, clutching her shoulder bag and keys.

She couldn't believe how pleased Tyler looked to see him.

"Were you on the ferry?" she asked, torn between her son's growing fascination with the man and trying to imagine why he was there.

"I took the long way around. I had a meeting in Tacoma," he told her, speaking of a town at the south end of the sound, "so I drove. Jake was on it, though. He should be right behind you."

"Jake?"

"One of our craftsmen." Rain glittered through the pool of pale yellow light that arced from the neat back porch. Even in that spare illumination, Erik could see strain in the delicate lines of her face, could hear it in her voice. "I'll explain when we get inside."

He watched her hurry ahead of him. Her head down, she unlocked the door and ushered Tyler inside, reminding him to wipe his feet on the way.

The mudroom, with its pegs for coats, cabinets for storage and the double sink his grandmother had used for re-potting plants, opened into the kitchen. The warmer air held the same welcome it always had, but no longer did it smell of the pine disinfectant his grandmother had used with abandon when mopping the floors. Now lingering hints of lemon soap gave way to scents of cinnamon and orange as Rory distractedly flipped on lights and told him to set the bags anywhere.

The island of the neatly organized kitchen seemed as good a place as any. As he set the bags on the laminate surface, his glance cut to where she'd left on a lamp at the far end of the long, open space.

She'd just moved in last week, yet everything appeared to be in order. Furniture had been pushed, pulled or shoved into place. Drapes and pictures were hung. Not a box remained in sight.

Not a hint of what had once been familiar remained, either.

The walls had been bare for over a year. Having walked through that empty space a dozen times, it no longer felt strange without the chaos of floral patterns and knick-knacks his grandparents had acquired living there. But with that blank canvas redecorated, the sense he'd had the other day of no longer belonging there, of having lost a piece of himself, threatened to surface once more. He didn't doubt that it would have, too, had the unexpected ease of what she'd created not distracted him from it.

The well-defined spaces now bore his student's decidedly understated stamp. The heavy wood pieces he'd carried in were dark and substantial enough to make a man feel comfortable, but balanced by shades of ivory and taupe that felt amazingly...restful.

The rustic refectory table with its high-backed chairs held a large pewter bowl filled with glittered pinecones and cinnamon potpourri. Beyond it, the deeply cushioned sofa faced the stone fireplace at the end of the room. A long, narrow sofa table behind it held a trio of thick cream-colored candles. The two armchairs he'd brought in had been positioned to one side, a heavy end table stacked with books and a chrome lamp between them.

He turned to see that she'd left her raincoat in the mudroom. The apples and her shoulder bag had landed on the desk by the now child's-art-covered refrigerator—mostly red-and-green construction paper bells. Sinking to her heels in front of her little boy, she worked his jacket's zipper.

"You've been busy."

Oblivious to what had his attention, conscious only of his presence, Rory understated considerably.

"A little," she replied, thinking of the day she'd had and how desperately glad she was for it to be nearing its end. "I had a meeting with the probate attorney." Now that the house had sold, she'd had more paperwork to sign. "And I had to go to the bank to close the safe-deposit box, then go straighten out my medical insurance."

The good news was that she could pay the attorney's fees and increased insurance costs from the proceeds of the sale of the house. The not so good part was that both cost more than she'd expected—which meant she'd have to forgo the new sign and new shelving she'd hoped to have for her store's grand opening. And buy a considerably smaller Christmas tree than a version of the megadollar, floor-to-ceiling noble fir that had so mesmerized Tyler at his school. She'd already ruled out buying more outdoor lights to pay for the ferry rides.

Budget concerns, however, had taken a backseat to the varying degrees of anger and hurt she'd been busy stifling all afternoon. Thanks to Curt's mother.

"After I picked Tyler up from school," she continued, "we dropped off library books and went grocery shopping before we caught the ferry."

"And saw Santa ringing a bell at the store," supplied Tyler, still in Christmas mode. "Not the real Santa," he explained. "Mommy said he was a helper." He gave a sage little nod. "The real Santa has lots of helpers."

"Be tough to do all he does alone," she explained. Her little boy's zipper now freed, she rose and headed for the bags. "I hope the milk stayed cold."

Erik had never seen her in a suit and heels before. A crisp white blouse peeked from beneath the black jacket that curved at her waist and hugged the hips of her slim pencil skirt. Black tights covered the long, shapely line of her legs. As he glanced up from her spike-thin heels, he had to admit he hadn't seen her truly upset before, either. Though she definitely was, and trying hard to hide it.

"I meant you've been busy around here."

Apparently realizing the extent of her preoccupation, she met his eyes and promptly closed hers with a sigh.

"Can I have an apple?" Tyler asked.

She forced herself to brighten. "You'll ruin your appetite, sweetie." Taking his head between her hands, she kissed the top of it, hard, and tipped his face to hers. "Hang up your jacket and empty your backpack. Dinner will be ready in a few minutes."

With Tyler dragging his jacket into the mudroom, she reached into the nearest bag to unload groceries. She'd just put the milk in the fridge and grabbed two boxes of cereal when she turned on her stylish heel.

The boxes landed on the counter three feet from where Erik watched her with his hands in the pockets of his cargos. The stance pulled the sides of his jacket back from the navy pullover covering his chest and made his shoulders look broad enough to bear the weight of the world.

It seemed terribly unfair just then to be taunted by the memory of how very solid his chest had felt. Especially when she so badly wanted to be held against it. But fair hadn't been a big part of her day.

"I'm sorry." She shook her head, the neat wedge of her hair swinging. "You didn't drive all the way here to watch me put away groceries." She tried for a smile. "May I get you something? Juice? Milk?" Neither sounded very adult. "Coffee?"

He took a step toward her. "I didn't come to interrupt. I just want to drop off your shelving."

"My shelving?"

"The three units for the back of the store. I had a couple of the guys work on them with me over the weekend. With Christmas coming, they were up for the overtime. One of the units is in the back of my truck. Jake is bringing the rest."

Disbelief cut through the anxiety that sat like a knot beneath her breastbone. They'd barely discussed her layout to update the market. Though he'd said it would probably work, he hadn't even bothered to tell her whether or not he liked the idea. All she'd done was show him her sketch, explain why she wanted it and all of a sudden the shelving she'd felt certain would now have to wait had materialized. He made it happen just like that, as if he was some sort of...fairy godfather.

The man fairly leaked masculinity. As utterly male as he was and so *not* fatherly in the way he'd checked out her legs, the thought would have made her laugh had she not felt like crying.

"You made my shelves?"

"You wanted them, didn't you?"

She wanted world peace, too, but that didn't mean she expected it to happen.

She raked her fingers through her hair, wondering if they were a gift, which she couldn't accept without reimbursing him. Wondering, too, how much he'd paid his men, since it was undoubtedly more than she could afford.

"Yes. Absolutely. I'm just…" *Speechless,* she thought. "Thank you," she concluded, because she had no idea what else to say before the ring of his cell phone had him pulling the instrument from his pocket.

After two short beeps and a glance at the text, he muttered, "Jake's out front," and dropped the phone back into his pocket. "I'll be back in a few minutes. Then you can tell me what's wrong."

Certain he was referring to her less than gracious reaction, she said, "Nothing is wrong. You just caught me off guard. I never expected you to make the shelves—"

"I meant what was wrong with you when I got here."

Oh. That.

Thinking him far too astute, uncomfortable with that, too, she turned for the cereal. "It's nothing."

Moving with her, Erik stopped scant inches from her back. With Tyler just around the corner, he lowered his voice to nearly a whisper. "Lying is a bad example to set for a child."

Conscious of his warm breath moving her hair, her head still down, she lowered her voice, too. "Then how about it's nothing I can talk about in front of him?"

"That's better." Taking a step back, he indicated the door near the stairway. "I need to get into the store. Mind if I go in through the living room?"

Since he tended to do what he wanted to do anyway, she was a little surprised that he'd asked. Mostly, she was just conscious of how close his muscular body still was to hers. All she'd have to do was turn around…

She shook her head, swallowed hard. "Not at all."

"Give me half an hour. I'll be back."

Twenty minutes was actually all the time it took him and his employee to unload the sections of the three shelving units from a company vehicle and the back of Erik's truck. It wasn't long enough, however, for Erik to question why he couldn't leave well enough alone with the woman he'd spent the past few days trying not to think about at all. Not beyond her needs for the store, anyway. He'd told her to call him if she needed anything. Since she hadn't, he'd assumed she was doing fine.

Except she clearly was not. Even when he let himself back inside, greeted by the scent of something delicious, there was no mistaking the disquiet she was still trying to hide.

Tyler smiled from where he sat on the dining room side of the island. Beyond him, light glowed through the glass-paned white cabinets, revealing neat stacks and rows of plates and glasses.

"Mom's making mac and cheese. It's my favorite. You want some?"

"Mom" had shed her jacket and heels. She stood across from them in her stocking feet, stirring a pot on the stove. The cuffs of her white blouse had been folded back. A green dish towel had been tied into an apron at the waist of her skirt. Erik knew she'd heard him come in, but it was her son's innocent invitation that had her looking over her shoulder with apology in her expression.

"I told him you probably already had plans," she said,

sounding as if she fully expected his refusal and had already prepared her son for it. "But he wanted to ask anyway."

Had this been any other woman, any other child, Erik knew without a doubt that he'd have done what she obviously expected and come up with some excuse for not being able to stick around for dinner. With just the three of them, the beat of the rain against the windows and the cozy warmth of the kitchen countering the cold outside, the scenario felt entirely too domestic for him.

He wanted to know what had upset her, though. If for no reason other than to be sure it wouldn't impede her progress with the store. Or so he told himself. He also knew she wasn't going to say a word about whatever it was as long as her son was present.

Then there was the little boy himself. With Tyler looking all hopeful, he simply didn't have the heart to say no.

"Mac and cheese, huh?"

Again, the quick nod. "It's really good."

"Then I guess I'd better stay." He looked to the woman at the stove, caught the strain countering the softness of her smile. "That okay, 'Mom'?"

Her hesitation held uncertainty, and collided with something that looked suspiciously like gratitude for indulging her child. "Of course it is. Tyler?" she asked. "Let's move your place mat to the table and get another one from the sideboard for Erik."

Erik tossed his jacket across the stool next to where Tyler sat. As he did, the boy scrambled down and grabbed his pine-green place mat from the island. Intent on his mission, he laid it on the heavy oak table, then pulled a matching one from a long drawer in the printer's cabinet his mom had pushed to the wall by the stairs.

He'd just set the mat across from the other when he looked back to the man tracking his progress. "Do you want to see my boat?"

Erik hadn't a clue what had prompted the question. Seconds ago they'd been talking about food. With a shrug, he said, "Sure," and the little boy was off.

Wondering if the kid's energy ever ran low, he walked over to where Rory spooned dinner into two shallow pasta bowls.

"What can I do?" he asked.

"You've already done it," she said quietly. "He's wanted to show you that boat ever since you said you build them. After you told him about the boats outside Cornelia's office, it was nearly all he talked about." She turned, a bowl in each hand. "But if you want, set these on the table for the two of you while I slice another tomato. That would be great."

Handing them over, she slipped past him to take two salad plates from the cupboard.

"Where's yours?"

"I'm not hungry. What do you want to drink?" she asked, pointedly avoiding his scrutiny as he set the bowls on the table.

Walking toward them with his toy, Tyler announced that he wanted milk.

Rory told him she knew he did. As she set salads of tomatoes, herbs and olive oil above their place mats, she also said she knew he really wanted to show Erik his boat, but right now he needed to sit down and eat his dinner before it got cold.

She appeared as calm and unruffled to Erik as he'd always seen her with her son. Still, he recognized restlessness when faced with it. There was no mistaking the nerves that had her too keyed up to sit down herself. She seemed to be using motion as a means to keep that tension under control as she started pulling measuring cups, flour and a big wooden spoon from cabinets, cupboards and drawers.

Intimately familiar himself with the cathartic effects of

movement, specifically his usual morning run or sanding teak until his arms ached, he said nothing about her joining them. While she moved about the kitchen side of the island, he turned his attention to the boy who'd docked his little blue plastic boat on the table between them.

His fork in his fist, Tyler stabbed a noodle. "It's my Christmas boat."

It certainly was.

The miniature ski boat held a hunk of clay middeck. A peppermint-striped straw stuck up from the little blob like a mast. More clay anchored a bit of pencil-thin neon-green tinsel from bow to mast and mast to stern.

He'd rigged the tinsel on it just like the lighted boats they'd talked about in Cornelia's office.

Erik couldn't believe how deeply touched he was by the boy's innocent desire to share something of his with him. Or how humbled he felt by the innocent expectation in the child's eyes.

The silence coming from the table had Rory nearly holding her breath as she waited for Erik to acknowledge what her son had shared.

He finally picked up the toy, turned it in his big hands.

She could have hugged him when he said, "Now that is one awesome sailboat."

Tyler beamed.

Rory felt her heart squeeze.

Setting the child's handiwork back on the table, Erik pointed his fork at the bow. "Do you know what that's called?" he asked.

"The front?"

"That, too," came his easy reply. "But in nautical terms, the front of a boat is called its bow."

"What's 'not-cul'?"

"Nautical," Erik emphasized with a smile. "It means things relating to boats and sailors," he added, which led

Tyler to ask what the back was called. That led to a discussion of stern, port, starboard and keel, the latter of which his ski boat didn't have, but which Erik fashioned out of a paper napkin just so Tyler would get the idea of what one looked like.

When Rory casually mentioned that she was going to have to reheat their dinner if they didn't start eating, conversation turned to the merits of shell-shaped pasta over elbow while they cleaned their bowls. Over pudding for dessert, talk then turned back to the boat—specifically the differences between sail and motor.

Her child ate up the attention her mentor so generously bestowed while she put cranberry muffins into the oven to have with breakfast and cleared their dishes. By the time she'd finished cleaning up the kitchen and removed the muffins from the oven twenty minutes later, it was nearing Tyler's bedtime, and she didn't want to impose on Erik any further.

"It's time to put the boat away," she finally told him. "Say good-night to Erik now, okay? And go brush your teeth. I'll be up in a few minutes to tuck you in."

She'd thought he would do as she'd asked and simply say good-night. Instead, with his toy under one arm, he walked to where Erik stood by the island and wrapped his free arm around the man's thigh. "'Night, Erik," he said.

She wasn't sure who was caught more off guard by the unexpected hug—her or the man who went completely still a moment before his big hand settled on Tyler's head.

"'Night, sport," he murmured back. "Thanks for showing me your boat."

Tyler tipped back his head, gave him a smile. "You're welcome."

Her conversation with her former mother-in-law already had Rory's maternal instincts on high alert. Torn between allowing the draw her child obviously felt toward someone who would be out of their lives in a matter of months and the need to protect him from it, she took him by his little shoulders and eased him back.

"Teeth," she reminded him, and turned him around to get him headed in the right direction.

"Can I read?" he asked on his way.

"Until I get there," she called after him.

"'Kay," he called back and disappeared up the stairs.

"He's a neat kid." The admission came almost reluctantly, as if he hadn't wanted to be as impressed—or touched—as he was by a five-year-old. "I don't know how long it's been since he lost his dad, but you seem to be doing a great job with him."

It had been fourteen months that sometimes felt like mere weeks. Sometimes, strangely, as if it had been years.

"It was a year ago in October. And thank you," she offered at the compliment. "Thank you for being so nice to him, too. I'm sure you had other things to do tonight, but you just made his week. He's not around men very often," she said, compelled to explain why her son had monopolized his evening. "And he really misses his dad."

"I imagine he does." The agreement brought a frown. "What about relatives? Grandfathers? Uncles?"

She shrugged. "My parents are in Colorado." This month, anyway. Heaven only knew where they'd be this time next year. "I'm an only child. So were my parents. So that's it for my side. Curt's family is in Seattle, but his parents aren't…available." Pushing her fingers through her hair, she could practically feel the hurt building in her chest. Even with Tyler out of earshot, her voice sank at the heartlessness of what had been said. "Actually," she conceded, "they don't want anything to do with him."

He took a step closer, his brow dropping right along with his voice. "Why wouldn't they want to see their grandson?"

The need to restrain her resentment pushed hard. The

hurt pushed back. It was Erik's expression, though, the unquestioning disapproval in it, that urged her on.

"Until a few hours ago, I'd thought it was just because of me," she admitted, pride biting the dust. "I don't care about having a relationship with Curt's parents for myself. I gave up wanting their acceptance a long time ago. But they're family. Tyler's, anyway," she clarified, reminded again of how succinctly her change in status had been pointed out to Audrey's friends. "For his sake, I did want him to have a relationship with them. I wanted him to have traditions.

"Especially this time of year," she hurried on. "Curt and I barely had time to start our own and my parents never had any." None that counted, anyway. None she wanted to pass on. "But as much as anything, I'd hoped he'd have a sense of being part of more than just him and me."

This wasn't the first time she'd mentioned traditions to him. The last time he'd been there, she'd made learning those his grandparents had maintained over the years a huge priority. But discovering why she apparently lacked those bits of history herself—and, if he had to guess, the sense of belonging that came with sharing them—would have to wait. He was far more interested in what had her looking agitated enough to pace the walls.

Until a few hours ago, she'd said.

"Does this have something to do with that call from his grandmother when you dropped me off last week?"

It had everything to do with it. It also surprised her that he remembered it.

"I finally talked to her this afternoon. I already knew she didn't want me to be part of their Christmas Day," she told him, hating how she'd even let that matter to her. "But I'd hoped I could stop by for an hour or so with Tyler on Christmas Eve so he could spend some time with them. Audrey hadn't sounded thrilled with the idea when I first asked," she admitted, understating considerably, "but she'd said she'd get back to me. She called while I was on my way from the lawyer's to pick up Tyler at school."

Rory would be forever grateful that Tyler hadn't been in the car at the time. She had known for years that the senior Linfields hadn't approved of her. She'd just had no idea until that call how little they'd cared about the child their son had so dearly loved. "She and Curt's father decided it best that there be no further contact between us. She said it was just too painful for them to see me or 'the boy.'"

The hurt she felt for her son shadowed her eyes, filled her hushed voice as slights of past years could no longer be ignored.

"I should have seen this coming." She turned toward the rack of muffins cooling on the counter. Turned right back. "Nothing about this ever came up while Curt was alive, but since his death they haven't wanted to spend any time with Tyler at all." Twice she had arranged to meet them. Once for Curt's father's birthday so Tyler could give him the present he'd made for him, a collage of photos of Tyler and his dad. Once for a trip to the zoo. Both had been canceled by last-minute calls from Audrey. "I'm just glad I hadn't told him we'd be seeing them at Christmas. It's so much easier on him to not get his hopes up at all than to have him be disappointed all over again."

She turned back to the muffins, brushed a couple of crumbs from the counter into her palm, took two steps to the sink.

"What are you going to tell him if he asks about seeing them?"

"I don't know. I haven't had time to figure that out."

"Maybe they'll change their minds."

With a glance toward him, the crumbs landed on white porcelain.

"Only if you believe in hell freezing over."

The rush of water in pipes told her the child under discussion remained occupied in the upstairs bathroom. Still, her voice grew quieter as agitation had her turning away, turning back once more.

"Audrey said that they feel no bond with him." She spoke bluntly, as Audrey had. "That they never have. She said they tried while Curt was alive, for Curt's sake, but with him gone, there was no need to keep up the pretense. He's not their son's blood, so they want nothing to do with him. Apparently, they already amended their will to delete Curt's 'legal offspring.' Heaven forbid 'the boy' should get a penny of their precious money."

Caution crossed the hard angles of Erik's face.

"Not their son's blood." He repeated her words slowly, as if to make sure he hadn't misunderstood. "He's not Curt's child?"

As upset as she was, as insulted and offended as she was for her son, that caution barely registered. "Not biologically. We adopted him. We've had him since he was two days old," she explained, going with the bonds that really mattered. To her, anyway. "We didn't know until after a year of trying that Curt couldn't have children. It wasn't anything we ever discussed with anyone," she added in a rush. "We just said that the opportunity to adopt came up and we couldn't say no. After nearly four years and no other children, I'm sure his parents figured the problem was with me.

"Not that it matters," she muttered, hugging her arms around her waist. "And not that I'll ever tell them otherwise. They hadn't liked me the minute they found out I was Curt's secretary and not a lawyer myself. You could actually *see* them withdraw when they found that out. It got even worse when they found out my 'people' weren't the right pedigree. But Tyler's a *child*," she insisted, only to forget whatever else she'd been about to say when she realized all that she'd said already.

Erik looked as if he wasn't about to interrupt her. Though one dark eyebrow had arched significantly, at which detail she couldn't be sure, he was clearly waiting for her to continue.

Appalled by the scope of personal detail she'd just dumped at his feet, she closed her eyes and turned away. Rubbing her forehead, she muttered, "I cannot believe I just told you that."

His hand curved over her shoulder. The comforting weight of it barely registered before he turned her back around.

"Which part?"

"About Curt's…"

"Inability to father a child?" he asked when her voice drifted off.

She gave a nod, not at all sure how she felt having divulged something that, until moments ago, had been only between her, her husband and their fertility doctor. She felt just as uncertain about the odd sense of loss that came as Erik's hand slid away. "And about how his parents felt about me."

He didn't seem terribly interested in that. "Curt was a lawyer?"

Of all the questions he could have asked, he'd gone straight for what had been so hugely important to the Linfield family status. "Corporate. His father's a litigator."

"His mother?"

"She's into charities."

"What about brothers, sisters?"

"A brother. He took after their dad. His life is the firm and his wife is from money. She and Audrey adore each other."

"So they had a problem with you not being equal, or whatever the hell it was?"

Among other things, she thought, though she wasn't

about to get into everything she'd overheard in that bathroom stall before she'd opened the door and watched Audrey's friends go pale.

She'd said more than enough already.

"Seems so," came her embarrassed agreement.

Quick, assessing, his glance swept her face. As if looking for where the problem might lie, apparently finding nothing in what he knew of her, utter certainty entered the low tones of his voice.

"Then this is their loss. Not yours." Lifting his hand as she lowered her head, he caught her chin with one finger, tipped her head back up. "And for what it's worth, everything you've said stays right here." He brushed the back of his finger along the curve of her cheek, only to catch himself and still the motion scant seconds later. Drawing back, he settled both hands on his hips. "All of it."

At the gentleness in his touch, her shoulders had risen with her indrawn breath. They now fell with a soft "Thank you" that had as much to do with his unexpected defense of her as his assurance that her secrets were safe with him.

She couldn't deny how good his support felt. She was also rather horrified by how badly she wished he would stop looking at her as if he wanted to touch her again, and just do it. She felt terrible for her child. Totally powerless to give him the family he'd once had, imperfect as parts of it had been. Knowing what she knew now, she didn't want him around the Linfields anyway. Yet what made her ache the most just then was what Erik had so inadvertently done.

Simply by touching her, he'd reminded her again of how long it had been since she'd been held. There had been brief hugs at Curt's funeral, many of them awkward, most of them part of the blur that awful time had become. She couldn't remember the last time she'd felt any measure of comfort from a man's touch. She couldn't even remember the last time she'd been in Curt's arms. Or the last time they'd made love. She could easily recall the last kiss Curt had given her, though. She'd played it over a thousand times in her head. As rushed and preoccupied with work as he'd been in the mornings, it had been little more than his customary peck on her cheek on his way out the door.

After what she'd overheard, she couldn't think of that kiss without wondering if it hadn't been tolerance more than preoccupation underlying those absentminded good-byes. But the awful possibility that the man she'd adored had merely endured living with her had existed since the day she'd buried him.

She shoved back the memories, fought the threatening ache.

"This is so not what you signed on for, Erik." She shook her head again, tried to smile. "Thank you for listening. And for your help. And for the shelves. I still can't believe you did that. Just tell me what I owe you." She'd add it to what she owed him for the oil. "And thank you for having dinner with my son," she hurried on, because that had been huge. "I'm sure you'll think twice about sticking around for a meal in the future, but if you do happen to stay, I'll make a point of not burdening you with my baggage."

Despite her attempt to brush off the pain of what she'd shared, she looked as fragile to Erik as the thin silver chain resting below the hollow of her throat. He didn't want her thanks or her money. What he wanted was more detail, not less. He especially wanted to know what she felt about the man whose privacy she still protected. He didn't question why that mattered to him, or ask anything about Curt now. He was too busy hating how the man's family had rejected her and the child she clearly cherished.

He'd never have guessed Tyler was not biologically her own. He'd just figured the boy had come by his fairer coloring from his father.

"What I signed on for was to make sure you can make

a success of the business. I'll do what I have to do to make that happen. I'm not taking your money, Rory. The shelves are just part of the service."

He could see her protest forming even as he lifted his hand to her cheek once more. It was as apparent as her disquiet that she didn't want to feel more obligated to him than she already did. Yet that protest died as he curved his fingers beneath her jaw and touched his thumb to the corner of her mouth.

"As for your son, he doesn't need people in his life who don't appreciate him." Having made her go still, he drew his fingers toward her chin. "And you have too much else to do to waste any more energy on people who don't appreciate you, either. Got that?"

She swallowed, gave him a small nod. Other than that questionable agreement she simply stood there, looking very much as if she was afraid to move for fear that he would.

He'd been physically aware of her since the moment they'd met. Knowing she wanted his touch made that awareness tug hard. She looked very much as if she needed to be held. Needed to be kissed. It was that stark vulnerability that drew him as his hand cupped the side of her face.

Lowering his head, he brushed his lips over the soft part of her mouth.

He heard her breath catch, felt it ease out, the warmth of it trembling against his cheek.

Rory wanted to believe it was just anxiety catching up with her as she slowly leaned toward him. Longing curled through her, a subtle yearning to simply sink into the incredible gentleness in his touch and let it take away the ache in her chest.

But that ache only grew.

So did the need for him to make it go away.

She leaned closer, drawn by that need, by him. As she

did, his fingers eased through her hair, tipping her head and causing her to cling a little more tightly, to kiss him back a little more deeply.

It was kissing him back that turned the ache to something less definable. Shattering sweetness gave way to confusion. She craved the feel of this man's arms, his strength, his self-possession. She just hated how needy she felt, and how badly she wanted him to make all the hurts and the doubts go away.

The pressure of her nails pressing into her palm suddenly registered. So did the realization that all that kept them from cutting into her flesh was the fabric wadded in her fists.

Beneath his own hands, Erik felt tension tightening the slender muscles of her entire enticing body. Before he could ease back himself, she'd released her death grip on his sweater and ducked her head.

Her quiet "I'm sorry" sounded like an apology for everything from the desperation he'd felt building in her to the way she'd bunched the front of his pullover. To remove any possible wrinkle she might have left, she hurriedly smoothed the fabric with the palm of her hand.

As if suddenly conscious of her palm on his chest, or possibly the heavy beat of his heart, she jerked back her hand and stepped away.

Erik moved with her, canceling that negligible distance. There wasn't a doubt in his mind that he'd just added to the chaos of all she was struggling with. That hadn't been his intent at all. Not totally sure what his intention had been, feeling a little conflicted himself, he lifted her face to his.

"Hey. It was just a kiss," he murmured, attempting to absolve them both. Just a kiss that had done a number on his nervous system, he qualified, but her decidedly physical effect on him was beside the point. "No apology necessary. Okay?"

Unlike her unease, her nod was barely perceptible.

"I'll call you in a couple of days." Aware of how she barely met his eyes, he consciously lowered his hand. He shouldn't be touching her at all. "Can you finish the inventory by Friday afternoon?"

As segues went, he knew his was positively graceless. All he wanted at the moment, though, was to get past the awkwardness that had her protectively crossing her arms as she pulled composure into place.

"I'll have it finished."

A wisp of her shiny bangs had fallen near the corner of one eye. Instincts that still wanted physical contact with her had him starting to nudge it aside. More prudent senses had him dropping his hand an instant before the small voice coming from the top of the stairs would have had him dropping it anyway.

"I'm ready to tuck in, Mom."

She took another step away. "I'll be there in a minute," she called toward the stairs. Brushing at the taunting wisp, she looked back with an uncomfortable smile. "He has to be up early in the morning."

"Then I'll get out of your way so you can take care of him. I'll let myself out," he said, stopping her as she started for the door. "Just say good-night to him for me."

His jacket lay on the stool behind her. Reaching around her, careful not to touch, he snagged it and backed up. "Thanks for dinner," he added, and walked out the mudroom door, wondering what in the hell he thought he'd been doing when he'd reached for her in the first place.

He had no one but himself to blame for the tension that had his entire body feeling as tight as a trip wire. He was messing where he had no business going. Even if she wasn't so obviously not the sort of woman a man could have a brief, casual affair with, she was just now moving on from a loss that had affected her in ways that went far beyond anything she'd shared with him.

He couldn't even pretend to understand how she felt, or to know what she needed. Whatever it was, he couldn't give it to her anyway. He didn't know how. Even if he did, he suspected she wouldn't let him close enough to try. She didn't want to rely on anyone she didn't absolutely have to. He could appreciate that. He'd been there himself. As it was there were only a handful of people he truly trusted— and not one of them was a female he wasn't related to or who wasn't in his employ. He suspected, though, that her walls weren't nearly as thick as those he'd erected around his heart. There was no denying how vulnerable she was right now.

He wasn't about to take advantage of that, either. He also wasn't going to do anything else to potentially screw up his relationship with her as her mentor and jeopardize his agreement with Cornelia.

That was why he'd told his lovely protégée that he'd call in a couple of days instead of meeting with her. If he wasn't near her, he wouldn't be tempted to touch.

That didn't stop him from being touched by her, though. Or by the little boy who'd strung Christmas tinsel on his toy boat.

He knew Rory wanted her son to have traditions. Knowing how tight her money was, and how badly she wanted this season to be special for the child, he decided there was no reason he couldn't give them one of the traditions that had long belonged there anyway.

Chapter Six

She never should have said she'd have the inventory finished by Friday. She should have asked for another day at least. As much as she required his expertise, she'd just made it a point to accommodate Erik's schedule any way she could.

Had she been thinking, she would have realized how impossible that deadline was. But she'd been too rattled by the needs she'd felt in his arms and the kiss he'd dismissed as inconsequential to consider everything else she'd committed to do before Friday—which happened to be Tyler's last day at his current school.

Given the occasion, guilt over not having kept her word to Erik would have to wait. Her little boy was not taking this latest transition well at all.

The familiar faces and routines at Pine Ridge Day School were the last constants in the life they were leaving behind. As a child, she'd had considerable practice dealing with such separations. Her parents' nomadic lifestyle had made a new school or two every year her norm, and they'd tried to ease those transitions. But her little boy had never known that sort of instability. Even after his father had died, she'd managed to protect him from the biggest upheavals and keep his routine as consistent as possible. Until they'd had to move, anyway.

As she'd feared he would, he started missing his playmates the minute he'd fastened himself into his car seat in the back of their car and they'd pulled out from the portico.

A quick glance in her rearview mirror caught his pensive expression. He looked the way he had driving away from their old house a couple of weeks ago. Solemn and a little uncertain.

"We can always come back for a visit, Ty," she assured him, heading for the freeway and the ferry. "Just because you'll be going to a new school doesn't mean you won't ever see your old teachers or classmates again."

"They'll still be there?"

"They'll still be there," she promised. It wouldn't be like when he'd lost his dad. There wasn't that sort of finality to this parting. She needed him to understand that. "We can come back after the holiday to say hi, if you want."

"Will the tree be there, too?"

The tree. Ten feet of pine studded with a thousand white lights and draped with paper chains and cutouts of students' handprints. It graced the main building's foyer.

"The tree won't be there, honey. Everyone takes Christmas trees down after the holiday. But everything else will be the same."

"Nuh-uh," he replied, picking at the knee of his khaki uniform pants. "I won't be there anymore."

No, she thought with a sigh. He wouldn't be, and the silence that followed hinted at how very much that new change disturbed him.

Thinking the Christmas carols playing on the radio

might distract him, she turned the volume up over the hum of the heater and encouraged him to sing along.

That didn't work. Neither did any of her other attempts to console, cajole or otherwise ease away his dispirited expression.

Fighting discouragement herself, she finally conceded that she had no idea just then how to make everything better for her little boy.

That disheartening fact had just registered when her eyes widened on what should have been nothing more than the dusk-gray shapes of the road, the woods and the distant rectangle of Harbor Market & Sporting Goods.

Peering past the headlights, she heard Tyler's sudden "Oh. Wow!"

Wow, indeed.

The market stood glittery bright in the encroaching dark. Every pillar, post and eave, its roofline, even the chimney had been outlined with twinkling white lights. The bare branches of the apple tree at the near end had been wrapped in peppermint stripes of white lights and red. It was the snowman beyond it, though, that had her attention. Glowing blue-white, his top hat cocked at an angle, the tall, grinning Frosty stood as bold and impressive as the only person she knew who would have put it there.

The light on her answering machine was blinking when she finally coaxed Tyler out of the cold and into the kitchen. Hitting Play, she heard Erik's recorded voice say he was checking to see if she'd finished the inventory and ask when she'd be available to discuss the business plan. He mentioned nothing about the dazzling Christmas lights that hadn't been there when she'd left that morning.

She hit Redial. Apparently taking his cue from the number on his caller ID, he answered with an easy, "You're home."

"We just got here. Erik," she said, her tone half laugh, half hesitation, "I can't believe what you've done."

"Is that good or bad?"

"I don't know." She honestly had no idea how to weigh her son's reaction against her next electric bill.

"Does Tyler like it?" he asked while she figured it out.

"Like it?" *This is* ours, *Mom?* he'd asked, his eyes huge. "He hasn't stopped grinning since we got here. He's practically stuck to the window right now watching the icicle lights."

The sequential lights strung along the overhangs looked like dripping ice. Even the back of the house had been decorated. They'd noticed the lights wrapped around the side of the building the moment they'd driven up the rise. "He loves the snowman."

"You said he would have liked the one my grandparents had," he reminded her over the drone of what sounded like an electric saw. "My grandfather always put theirs facing the sound, but I had it put farther back on the lot, thinking Tyler could see it from the window."

Truly torn by what he'd done, she dropped her scarf on the phone desk and unbuttoned her coat. When they'd talked about his grandparents' traditions with the store, he'd seemed to see maintaining them mostly as a good approach to business. Yet her mentor's gift clearly had less to do with marketing than with the little boy pressing his nose to the glass.

She didn't want his thoughtfulness to mean so much. She just wasn't able to help it. Not with her little boy so totally captivated.

"How did you get it done so fast?"

The drone beyond him grew quieter. Nearer, voices rose, then faded.

"This close to Christmas, lighting companies are usually finished putting up decorations and are just waiting to take them down. I called a company a client uses, told them what I wanted, gave them the building measurements and they did their thing."

Just like that. With one phone call, he'd managed to do what she hadn't been able to do no matter how hard she'd tried and totally distracted her son from his dejection.

"It's just lights, Rory."

The man had a serious gift for understatement. He'd used the same think-no-more-of-it tone right after he'd proved that the shell of control she fought to maintain around her life was about as thin as paper.

It was just a kiss, he'd said.

He was only being kind when he'd reached for her. Just as he was only being kind when he'd overlooked how she'd practically crawled inside his shirt when she'd kissed him back—shortly before he'd pointedly minimized the moment of comfort, security and whatever else she'd felt in his arms.

He, on the other hand, apparently hadn't felt much of anything at all, other than anxious to get out of there.

But this wasn't about them. Not that there *was* a them, she insisted to herself. This was about what he'd done for her child.

"It's more than lights, Erik. To us, anyway." He had to know that. "And Tyler loves them." That was all that she would let matter at the moment. For her son's sake, she wasn't even going to panic over the electric bill. Yet. "So thank you. From both of us."

"You're welcome. Listen," he continued over the thud of heavy boots on metal stairs, "I have to get back to the payroll right now, but we need to discuss your business plan and address inventory. I have to be in Tacoma before noon tomorrow, so let's do it over the phone. Are you okay for an eight-thirty call? That'll give us a couple of hours.

"You there?" he asked when she hesitated.

"Can we make it Sunday?"

"Sunday's not good for me."

"Actually," she began, wondering if Sunday involved the woman he'd taken out last week, "I'm not quite finished with the inventory." She hated telling him that. "I'd have finished last night, but we had to bake cookies."

With the bang of a door, the noise and conversations beyond him died.

"*Had* to?"

"I told Tyler's teacher I'd bring treats for his class today. And I'd promised him he could help. So, yes," she insisted. "I had to."

She'd also brought cookies for the staff—which meant she'd spent the past two afternoons and evenings baking and filling tins and decorating twenty-two gingerbread girls and boys. With Tyler's help, the project had taken twice as long as it might have, but she'd wanted something for him that she'd never had as a child, holiday memories of flour on noses, sugar sprinkles, the air scented with vanilla and spice. Her mom's idea of baking had been heating a muffin in the microwave.

"What about tomorrow? Will you have it finished by then?"

Juggling guilt and priorities, she rubbed the ache brewing beneath her forehead. "I told Tyler we'd get our tree tomorrow. I'm going to work in the store tonight after he goes to bed," she explained, hoping to minimize the delay to Erik's schedule. "After we get the tree decorated, I'll finish whatever I haven't done in the store. I've been working out there after he goes to sleep, but I ran out of hours in the past couple of days.

"Since Sunday isn't good for you," she hurried on, easily

able to imagine a scowl etched in his too-handsome face, "I'll be ready Monday for sure." That would also give her time to read the business plan she'd tried without much luck to study on the ferry and after Tyler had gone to bed. Having to look up terms like *gross margin, inventory turns* and *marketing mix* had also slowed her down considerably. So did being so tired her eyes blurred.

She hated the plea that entered her quiet "Okay?"

Leaning against the edge of his desk, Erik stared past the schematics on his drafting table to the black-framed photos of Merrick & Sullivan racing sloops lining the pearl-gray wall. To his left, the windows of his office, like those of the other offices lining the catwalk, over-looked the production floor a story below. Those on his right exposed the lights of other industrial buildings lin-ing the night-darkened waterway.

The pleasure he'd felt knowing the snowman had been a hit with Tyler had rapidly faded to something far less definable.

When he'd left her place the other night, his only thoughts had been about doing what he could to make the kid's Christmas a little better, and his need for physi-cal distance from the boy's mom. He'd wanted to focus on his work and his world and to get her out of his head for a while. He was good at that. Focusing his thoughts, his energies.

He usually was, anyway. His days were crowded enough to prevent more than a fleeting thought of her undeniably feminine shape, or the way her bottom lip curved when she smiled. But she was messing with his nights, too, driv-ing him from his bed to pace the floor or exhaust him-self with his weights before sleep would finally drive her from his mind.

He never should have kissed her. If he hadn't, he

wouldn't know the sweetness of her mouth, the feel of her satin-soft skin, how perfectly her body fit against his.

Now, frustrated on a number of levels, he pushed from his desk, jammed his fingers through his hair.

"Forget Monday," he muttered. Just because he would have preferred she keep her focus on his schedule didn't mean she could make it her priority.

In roughly two weeks she'd lost her job, sold her home and was settling into a place that hadn't even been on her radar until his amazingly generous neighbor had decided to help them both out. In between, she seemed to be doing everything she could to ease the transition for her son while dealing with the former in-laws from hell and getting a business she knew nothing about back up and running.

No way could he justify pushing her just because he wanted his obligations there over and done with.

"The store can wait for now. We'll pick up after Christmas."

Pure skepticism shaded her quiet "Seriously?"

"Seriously," he echoed. "You and Tyler have a good time picking out your tree. There's a great tree lot on Sydney Road. It's only a few miles from you. Old family operation. Tell them you bought John and Dotty Sullivan's store. I imagine they'll give you a good price on a little one."

"I'll do that. And thank you. Thank you," she repeated, sounding relieved beyond belief by the reprieve he'd offered. "But the tree can't be little. Tyler has his heart set on the tallest one we can fit into the room."

Erik's voice went flat. "The ceilings in there are nine feet high."

"Then I guess we're getting an eight-foot tree. That'll leave room for the angel."

"And you're hauling it how?"

"The only way I can," she replied, ever so reasonably. "On my car."

The thought of eight feet of freshly cut conifer atop twelve feet of rounded, lime-green Bug drew his quick frown.

"Have you ever driven with a tree strapped to your roof?"

"Not exactly. No," she finally admitted, leaving him to assume that her husband had been behind the wheel. He also figured that the guy had transported prior trees on something considerably larger than what she drove now. Or they'd had it delivered, given what she'd said about the sort of family she'd just shed.

"Then you need to know that the weight affects the way a car handles. Especially if it's windy, and we have a wind advisory for the weekend. Make sure they net it for you. It'll be easier to manage that way. And take a blanket to protect your roof. Have someone help you secure it, too. You want it tied tight so it doesn't slip."

She hadn't thought about the weather. Rain at least part of the day was a given. It was the Northwest. She didn't like wind, though. It made inclement weather that much more miserable.

"Did you *promise* Tyler you'd have it up tomorrow?"

"It was the only thing I could think of to take his mind off having to change schools."

"Did it work?"

Her little boy hadn't budged from the window. He hadn't even taken off his jacket.

"Not as well as your lights did."

The admission would have made him smile, had he not just caught the hint of defeat in her voice. Or maybe what he heard was simply fatigue.

"Tell you what." Totally sabotaging his plan to stay away, he did a quick reschedule. "I'll only be a half an hour away from you tomorrow. What time will you be at the lot?"

"About the same time you said you have to be in Tacoma."

"I'm just picking up parts from a machinist. I'll leave earlier and be at the lot about twelve-thirty." It would take an hour to pick up the tree, an hour plus to get back. That left him plenty of time to drop off the parts at the boatworks, get home, shower, change and get to yet another client's holiday party. At least this time he didn't have to pick up a date. He didn't have one.

"You don't have to do that, Erik. You've done enough," she insisted, obviously referring to the lights. "We'll manage."

"We? You mean you and Tyler?"

"We're the only we here."

"Look." He was really getting tired of the I-don't-want-to-be-obligated-to-you tone that had slipped into her voice, but he had neither the time nor the inclination to argue with her. "You've said you want this Christmas to be good for your son. I assume that means you don't want him to have memories of his mom having a meltdown because his tree fell off the car and the car behind her hit it and turned it into kindling. Or because the thing weighs a ton and she can't get it into the house. Or into the tree stand, for that matter. You have a tree stand, don't you?"

"Of course I do. And I don't have meltdowns," she replied. "Especially in front of my son."

"No. You probably don't," he conceded, not at all sure whom he was annoyed with. Her. Or himself. "You just suck it up and try to deal with everything on your own. It's fine if you want to be independent, Rory. I'm sure you have your reasons for being that way. But this isn't about creating an obligation, or you owing me if I help you. It's about Tyler. All I want to do is help with the tree. For him. Okay?"

Silence.

About the time he thought she might simply hang up, she said, "Okay. For Tyler."

"Good. I'll be at the lot tomorrow with my truck." With a glance at his watch, he winced. "Right now I've got to get to this payroll. I'll call you when I'm on my way."

He should probably apologize.

The thought crossed Erik's mind every time he noticed the wary way Rory watched him the next afternoon. He just wasn't sure exactly what he should apologize for. He hadn't said a word to her that wasn't absolutely true. And she'd definitely needed the help.

The rain came in fits and starts. The weather was cold, the temperature dropping, the wind blowing, and the tree Tyler had selected after carefully checking out the small forest under the huge canvas tent was not only the eight-foot maximum she'd given him, but rather wide. Even tied up to make it more manageable and tarped to keep it dry, with the heavy wind gusts, getting it to her place on the rounded roof of her car would have presented a definite challenge. So would the task of her and Tyler unloading the thing and carrying it into the store to get it into its heavy iron stand, a task that involved sawing off a couple of lower limbs and trimming the thick trunk to make it fit before tightening the screws into place.

Mother and son wrestling it into the house on their own would have presented its own set of frustrations. Especially since carrying it into the house through the store—which had been easier than putting it in the stand in the garage and carrying it through the mudroom—involved hoisting the stand end of the eighty-plus pounds of bushy branches, trunk and iron to his shoulder while she brought up the rear with the top end and Tyler ran ahead of them to open the door.

He said nothing about any of that, though. It wasn't necessary. The process proceeded far easier with his truck and his help, and that was all he'd wanted: to make something a little easier for her and her son—and to offset his guilt over having pushed her about the store to the point where she'd given up sleep.

"Where do you want it?" he asked.

"In the corner by the fireplace. On the towel so the stand doesn't stain the carpet."

"Can I help?" called Tyler.

"Just stay back for a minute, sport. I've got it." He told Rory, "You can let go."

Behind him, Rory stepped back as the weight lifted from her shoulder. With a quiet whoosh of branches and the thud of heavy metal on towel-covered broadloom, the stand hit the floor and the tree popped upright.

The whole room suddenly smelled like a pine forest.

Beside her, her little boy grinned. "It's really big, huh?"

Not just big. For the space, it was huge, definitely larger than what they would have wound up with had Erik not been with them. Fuller, anyway.

She'd realized within minutes of arriving at the tree lot that what she'd promised her son would have been a nightmare to manage on her own. On their own, they also would have wound up with something more in the five-foot range.

"Thank you," she said to Erik's back.

He turned, pushing his windblown hair back from his forehead.

"No problem. This is the fourth tree I've hauled this month." He wanted her to know that what he'd done wasn't a big deal. Not to him, anyway. Certainly nothing she needed to feel obligated to him for. "The one at work, a neighbor's and one of Pax's cousins'."

"Do you have a tree?" Tyler wanted to know.

"I don't usually put one up."

"How come?"

"Because I'm not home in the evenings much this time of year and I go to my folks' for Christmas."

Her little boy's brow pinched. Before he could voice whatever had him looking so concerned, Erik motioned to the single green bin sitting near the fireplace.

"You want the rest of those?" he asked her, referring to the others still stacked in the store.

She started to tell him she could bring them in herself. Thinking it wiser to accept his help than risk resurrecting the tension that had ended their phone call last night, she said, "Please," and hurried after him to help.

Tyler wanted to help, too, so she had him carry in their new two-foot-high, red-velvet-clad Santa with its price tag still attached while they brought in the bins filled with the lights and ornaments she'd need for the tree.

The only other thing she needed, other than for the heavy caution between them to ease, was to start a fire in the fireplace to take the deepening chill off the room. While Erik went back for the last bin, she crumpled newspaper under some of the kindling she and Tyler had found by a cord of split logs in the lean-to behind the garage.

Erik had barely walked back in when he shot a narrowed glance at the parka she still wore. Tyler hadn't taken his off yet, either.

"Did you turn off the heat?" he asked, hoping she hadn't gone that far in her efforts to conserve.

"I turn it down when we leave, but it's always colder when the wind blows. It just hasn't been this windy. Or this cold. It's freezing out there."

The house had always been drafty. As his grandmother had done on especially cold days, Rory had closed her heavy drapes over the big expanses of glass to insulate from the chill. With the wind that blew the rain against the windows stirring the fabric, he figured he should probably check the weather stripping.

Just not now. For now, all he'd do was make sure she had enough firewood and get out of there.

"There's plenty," she assured him when he said he'd bring some in. "Tyler and I carried a load into the mudroom this morning."

"Can we decorate now?" Tyler asked. "If you don't have a tree," he said to the man checking his watch, "you can help decorate ours. Mom said she'd show me her magic ornaments. You want to see 'em?"

"Magic ornaments?"

"Uh-huh. They're in here." With his arms still wrapped around the Santa, he bumped his little boot against a bin she'd brought in that morning. "She showed me a heart and a bell. I get to see the rest when we put them on the tree."

He looked eager and hopeful and was still running on a sugar high from the hot cider and big candy cane he'd been given at the tree lot.

"We've kept Erik long enough, honey." She hated to burst his little bubble, but with Erik frowning at the time, it seemed apparent he was anxious to go. She felt anxious for him to go now, too. Every time she met his glance she had the uncomfortable feeling he was wondering how she would ever manage there on her own. Or thinking about how much longer the project had taken than he'd probably planned. "He said he had to leave by four," she reminded him. "Remember?"

"But he doesn't have his own tree, Mom. We're s'posed to share."

They were indeed, which left Rory at a loss for a reasonable rebuttal. She didn't doubt her child's disappointment. Yet that disappointment didn't seem to be only for himself. It was as much for the man she sincerely doubted needed anything from them at all.

"I suppose I could stay a little longer," he said to Tyler,

touched by the child's concern, ignoring her. "How much do you think we can do in thirty minutes?"

"We have to put the lights on before we can do anything," she pointed out to them both. Thirty minutes would barely get them going.

"Then I guess that's where we start." He looked to where she suddenly stared back at him. "Unless you hadn't planned on doing this right now."

He had accomplished his mission: delivering the tree. It hadn't occurred to him that he'd even want to stick around and decorate the thing. Especially with Rory stuck somewhere between grateful for his help, not wanting to have needed it and uncomfortable with his presence. Her little boy's excitement with the process, though, and his innocent desire to share that experience with him held far more appeal just then than heading home to get ready for yet another evening of schmoozing and champagne. Even if he didn't leave for another half hour, he'd barely be late. He just wouldn't stop by the boatworks.

Both males expectantly waited for her reply. That Erik seemed to want to stay caught her totally off guard. Considering how he'd practically bolted out the back door the last time he'd been there and how annoyed he'd sounded with her on the phone yesterday, she'd thought for sure that he'd be on his way as soon as he'd delivered Tyler's tree.

Not about to deliberately disappoint her son, and determined to not upset the precarious equilibrium between her and her mentor, she lifted both hands in surrender. "If we're doing lights, we need a chair," was all she had to say before Tyler started pulling off his coat and Erik started heading toward the dining room table.

On his way, he pulled his cell phone from the front pocket of his jeans.

"I need to tell Pax I won't be in today," he told her, punching numbers. They didn't need the parts until Monday, but his partner would be expecting him. "Just give me a minute."

Taking her animated little boy's jacket, she slipped off her own and headed into the mudroom to hang them up. As she passed Erik, she heard his easy "Hey, buddy" before he relayed his message, told him where he was and added that he'd see him "later at the party."

Marveling at the man's social life, and unsettled to find herself wondering yet again about the woman he'd taken out last week, she walked back into the kitchen moments later to see him still on the phone.

"No, I'm not 'seriously preoccupied,'" he good-naturedly defended. "I've just been getting a tree into a stand. What are you talking about?

"You're kidding," he muttered, and headed for the dining room window.

The moment he pulled back the closed drape, she heard a soft ticking against the glass. Little was visible in the gray light beyond. Blowing rain obscured the view.

His brow furrowed. "Turn on the TV, will you?" he asked her.

"What's going on?"

"Everything's closing down," was all he said before she grabbed the TV's remote.

With Erik joining her on her left, still listening to Pax, and Tyler smashed against her right leg, hugging Santa, the three of them watched the churning weather map on the screen while the authoritative voice of the weatherman warned everyone to stay off the roads. The ticker on the bottom of the screen listed temperatures in various degrees of freezing in Seattle and surrounding areas as the voice went on about predicted accumulations of freezing rain or sleet. Another voice took over as the picture switched to a weather cam with a blurry image of a multicar pileup on I-5.

A viewer video showed the sleet-shrouded image of a ferry rocking at its landing.

"What about the Narrows Bridge?" she heard Erik ask Pax.

The furrows went deeper. "Got it. Sure. You, too, man," he concluded, and ended his call.

Sensing the adults' concern, Tyler pressed closer as he looked up. "Is this a bad thing, Mommy?"

It wasn't good. "It's okay, honey. The weather is just causing a few problems," she explained even as more personal complications dawned.

"Nothing you need to worry about, sport."

Peering around his mom, Tyler looked to the man smiling over at him.

"All you need to worry about is finding a place to put that big guy." Erik nodded to the Santa that was nearly half Tyler's size. "Then we can start on the lights."

His concerns appeased, Tyler plopped his Santa on the floor beside him. Suggesting he put the decoration somewhere a little more out of the way, Erik turned to Rory.

"Pax said they're closing the airport, bridges, ferries and freeways. The roads are all iced." His partner had gone over to their client office. The one by Cornelia's. Now he was stuck there.

Given that the bridge he himself needed to take to get back was closed and that the ferry would be down, he seemed to be stuck where he was, too.

He could usually roll with anything. He just wasn't quite sure how the woman who'd just drawn a deep breath and turned away felt about having him there for a little longer then she'd expected. She didn't say a word as she knelt beside one of the bins and popped off the lid to reveal dozens of neatly wrapped strings of lights.

"We're having soup and sandwiches for dinner," she finally said.

Lifting out two strings, she stood up, turned to face him. "Since it seems you're here for the night, you can stay in my room."

His left eyebrow arched.

Mirroring his expression, determined to prove she could hold her ground with him, Rory added, "I'll sleep with Tyler."

Chapter Seven

Rory left the door to Tyler's room halfway open and paused at the top of the stairs. Her little boy had fallen asleep within seconds of his head hitting the pillow. No surprise considering how exciting the day had been for him and how hard he'd fought to stay awake after supper to finish the tree.

From downstairs, the television's barely audible volume told her Erik had switched from *How the Grinch Stole Christmas* to the news.

She hated the ambivalence creeping back as the low tones mingled with the beat of the sleet on the roof, the muffled sound of it pinging against the upstairs windows. The thought of riding out the ice storm in a still unfamiliar house would have had her anxious on a number of levels, had it not been for Erik.

She felt safe with him there. Physically, anyway. And there wasn't a single part of her being that didn't want exactly what he had just helped her provide for Tyler: an afternoon and evening of moments he might always remember as special.

That, in a nutshell, was her problem. His presence provided as much comfort as it did disquiet. Tyler had turned to her every time he'd had a question about where an ornament should go, but it had been Erik's assistance or advice he'd sought if he couldn't get it on a branch, and his approval he'd wanted with nearly every accomplishment.

She didn't want him being so drawn to the man.

She didn't want to be so drawn to him herself.

Wishing she still had her chatty little boy as a buffer, she headed down the steps, stopping when she reached the foyer.

Erik stood with his back to her, his heavy charcoal pullover stretched across his broad shoulders, his hands casually tucked into the front pockets of his jeans as he faced the talking head on the television. The size of the blaze in the fireplace indicated that he'd added another log. Strewn around him were empty bins and ornament boxes. In front of the sofa, the large, square coffee table held a red candle in a beribboned glass hurricane and the last of the crystal icicles waiting to be hung on the brightly lit tree.

As if sensing her presence, Erik turned toward her. She immediately turned her attention to cleaning up the mess.

"Is he asleep?" he asked.

"We barely got through brushing his teeth."

"I'm surprised he made it that far." Seeing what she was doing, and how deliberately she avoided his eyes, he picked up a bin that had held the faux evergreen boughs now draped over the stone fireplace mantel, set it in the entry and put another on the coffee table for her to fill with what she collected.

"Thanks," she said quietly.

"Sure," he replied, and finally found himself faced with what he'd managed to avoid the past few hours.

It had felt strange decorating her tree. Partly because he'd never helped decorate one with a small child buzzing around his knees, partly because the feel of the room with her understated touches in it was completely different from what it had been years ago. What he'd felt most, though, was the need to get past her guardedness with him. That caution still tempered her smiles, and made him more conscious of little things like how her animation had died when she'd opened a bin to see a Christmas stocking embroidered with *Dad*. Her wariness with him wasn't anything overt. It wasn't even anything someone else might notice. Probably something even he wouldn't notice, if he hadn't known he was responsible for it.

He never should have kissed her. The thought had crossed his mind a thousand times in the past few days, usually right behind the memory of how she'd practically melted in his arms. He'd yet to forget the sweet taste of her, the perfect way she'd fit his body. It was as if the feel of her had burned itself into his brain, leaving nerves taut, distracting him even now.

He shouldn't have gotten so annoyed with her on the phone last night, either, though he was pretty sure that same sort of frustration had been at least partially to blame. But the storm wasn't letting up anytime soon, the thickening ice made escape next to impossible and he didn't want this evening to be any more difficult than it needed to be. Short of apologizing to her, which he had the feeling would only make matters worse, especially for the kiss part, he'd do his best to put her at ease with him some other way.

She'd just reached up to hang a fallen ornament high on the tree. As it had every other time she'd reached that high, the motion exposed a thin strip of pale skin between the hem of her short white turtleneck, shorter green vest and the dark denims hugging her sweetly rounded backside.

"So," he said, forcing his focus to something he wanted

to know, anyway. "What's with the 'magic' ornaments?" He nodded toward the empty shoe box on the end table. "You told Tyler all those you took out of that box appeared out of nowhere."

The tiny crystal ice skates, the little Eiffel Tower stamped *Paris, Texas,* the miniature pink-and-white cupcake—all the ornaments in her "magic" collection looked much like the other decorations sparkling on the tree. Yet she'd even handled them differently, more carefully, he supposed.

"That's because they did," she replied, lowering her arms to pack up more empty boxes. "It didn't matter where my parents and I were, every Christmas morning I'd open the door and there would be a package with a gold box tied with a red bow. Inside would be an ornament that had something to do with where we were staying. Or something I was into at the time."

"Did your parents leave them there?"

"They had no idea who sent them. There was never a return address."

"So that's why you call them magic," he concluded.

"It was more than that." Conscious of him watching her, she packed the boxes into the bin he'd set on the coffee table. "It was what I felt when one of those little packages appeared. That's what made them magic. At that moment, no matter what town we were in, with Mom and Dad mine for the day and that gift in my hands, I had the feeling that everything was right in my little world." That was the feeling she wanted Tyler to know. He deserved that. Every child did. "I wound up with fourteen of them."

"It sounds like you moved around a lot."

"We did. Mom and Dad still do." Their mailing address was their agent's. "They're musicians."

His brow furrowed. "So what's wrong with that?"

The question brought a quick frown of her own. "I didn't say anything was wrong with it."

"I didn't mean you. You said the other day that Curt's parents had a problem with you being his secretary instead of a lawyer. That things got worse when they found out your 'people,'" he repeated, making air quotes, "weren't the right pedigree. What's wrong with being a musician?"

Her instinctive defense eased with his mystified tone. Marginally.

Apparently he had her a little edgier than she'd realized.

"There wouldn't have been anything wrong with it if they'd played the violin or French horn in a symphony, but Dad plays bass guitar and Mom is a singer in a rock band. That was not the image Audrey wanted their friends to have of their son's wife." She closed the lid on the now full bin and moved to fill another. "On the rare occasion mention of my family came up, she said they were in the music industry and changed the subject."

Unlike nearly everything else she'd exposed about herself the last time Erik had been there, she'd forgotten she'd even alluded to her parents. She'd be the first to admit that their decidedly bohemian lifestyle hadn't provided the most stable environment, but it wasn't as if they'd tattooed her forehead and named her Moonbeam or Thistleweed. They were good people who just happened to be creative, extroverted free spirits who'd never figured out which of them possessed the recessive "conventional" gene each accused the other of passing on to her. They were her mom and dad. She loved them. She didn't understand them, but she loved them.

"Are they any good?"

"They're very good."

"Where do they play?"

"Sometimes they get a gig doing backup for tours," she told him, grateful for the ease of his questions as they worked. Relieved, too, that he wasn't letting her dwell on her former in-laws' biases.

Trying to appear as comfortable with their present situation as he did, she looked around for anything she'd missed. "Mostly they're on a circuit where they play small venues for a few weeks at a time."

"That had to make for an interesting childhood," he muttered, and handed her the stack of boxes from the sofa.

"I suppose it was." After adding what he'd given her to the last bin, she snapped on its lid. "I just never knew where we'd be next, or how long we would be there." *Fluid,* her mom liked to call their lives.

"But a little gold box showed up everywhere you went." The container now filled, Erik picked it up to stack with the others. "Just trying to get the rest of the story," he explained, and waited for her to move so he could carry it to the door.

She stepped aside, pretty sure he would have moved her himself if she hadn't.

With him carrying away the last bin, she scooped up a few of the crystal icicles and snowflakes still on the coffee table, started hanging them on the tree. "They showed up every year until I stopped traveling with my parents," she told him. "Mom and Dad had been playing in Seattle and I didn't want to move around anymore. I'd just turned eighteen, so I stayed here when they left for their next engagement. That was the first Christmas a package didn't show up. We finally figured out it was their booking agent's wife who'd been sending them. Apparently, he represented a few other artists who traveled with their kids and she did it for all of them."

"Nice lady." Erik came up beside her, pulled one of the icicles from her hand. "So where will your parents be this Christmas?"

"Colorado. They're booked through New Year's."

He glanced at her profile as she lifted another bit of crystal above her head to hang on a high branch. She wouldn't have family around, he realized. Not liking that thought, not questioning why, he took the icicle from her and hung it below the white angel on top. As he did, he caught the clean scent of something herbal mingling with pine. Her shampoo.

The fragrance was subtle. Its effect on him was not.

Intent on ignoring both, he took one of the snowflakes. "So what will you and Tyler do? Go to a friend's house? Have friends over?"

He was just making conversation. Rory felt certain of that. And the question seemed casual enough. It was his nearness, and the answer, that gave her pause.

"We'll just stay here. My girlfriends from Tyler's school will both be out of town."

"What about other friends?"

"Except for work and Tyler's school, I wasn't involved in much the past year. Most of the other people I socialized with were in Curt's circle. Members of the firm and their spouses," she explained. "I don't belong in that group anymore."

For a moment Erik said nothing. Beyond them, the low voice of the weatherman droned on, the fire snapped and crackled. He could let it go, move on to something less personal. His mention before of the man she'd married—his relatives, anyway—had dented the calm facade she'd worn for her son the past few hours. But her guard with him had finally slipped, and his curiosity tugged hard.

"You said Curt had a different area of practice," he reminded her, "but was he in the same firm as his father and brother?"

With a faint frown, she handed him the last two ornaments she held and turned to pick up more for herself.

"Different firms. Both firms belong to the same country club, though. It's where the guys play racquetball and squash and wine and dine their clients. For the most part," she qualified, moving back to the tree. "Curt liked us to entertain at home." He'd seemed proud of her skills as a hostess, too, she thought, only to banish the memory before others could take hold. The moment she'd seen his stocking a while ago, the old doubts had rushed back, adding a different sort of disquiet to an already challenging day.

"You lived in the same circles as his parents?"

"It's not like we saw them all the time," she replied, hearing the frown in his voice. "But the wives of some of the partners in Curt's firm were on the same committees as Audrey and her friends. The ones who don't work outside their homes, anyway. Symphony. Heart Ball. That sort of thing."

"And you?"

"I was on them, too. For a while." She'd done her best to help Curt's career any way she could. They'd been a team that way, a more intimate extension of the partnership they'd developed when he'd been her boss and she his secretary. Or so she'd thought. "Our personal friends were more into getting together for dinners, or taking the kids out for lunch after T-ball."

"What about them?"

"What do you mean?"

"Why don't you ask them over? I bet Tyler'd be up for it."

She was sure he would. It just wasn't that simple. And what Erik was asking was really quite sweet. Surprising. Unexpected. But sweet—if such a word could be applied to the six feet plus of disturbing male quietly messing with her peace of mind.

It seemed he didn't want her and her son spending Christmas Day alone.

"That's the group I don't belong to anymore." The other one, the country club set, she'd never really had. "I was part of a couple with Curt," she explained, wondering how long it had taken the man beside her to think of himself as an *I* rather than a *we* after his wife had gone. "After he died, the guys didn't have their colleague and I was a reminder to the wives of how their lives would change without their husbands. Or how their lives might not even be what they'd thought they were," she concluded, only to find herself in the one place she hadn't wanted to go.

The place where so many questions begged for answers that would never come because the only person who could provide them was no longer there.

She wasn't at all sure how their conversation had taken such a swerve.

"What part wasn't what you thought it was?"

Her eyes met his, old pain quickly masked as she glanced away.

"All of it." She gave a brave little laugh, tried to smile. "So any advice you have about how to move beyond something I can't do a thing about would be greatly appreciated. Something more immediate than a five-year plan would be nice."

Perspective. That was what she needed. Since she couldn't imagine how she'd ever have it where her marriage had been concerned, the least she could do was maintain some about the too-attractive man who'd kissed her senseless four days ago and now acted as if nothing had happened at all—which she would be eternally grateful for, if she could somehow forget it herself. He was her mentor. Granted, he was her business mentor, but maybe the more she reminded herself of his place in her life, the less she'd be affected by things like the swift concern lowering his brow. Since his place in her life was to provide advice, she might as well take advantage of his counsel.

"Do you want to be a little more specific?" he asked.

Pretty certain the tensions of the day had just caught up with her, she dropped her glance to the slender ornament between her fingers. What she wanted had nothing to do with the store. But Erik did have a certain amount of experience in this particular area. He'd lost someone who'd once been important to him, too.

"I overheard some things at Curt's funeral that I can't seem to forget. About our marriage," she explained, her voice quietly matter-of-fact. "Since he's not here for me to ask about them, I think what I really want is to know how long it will take before the answers don't matter so much."

Erik watched her blink at the ornament, her eyebrows knitted as she stared down at what she held.

She'd never told him what had happened to her husband. Neither Phil nor Cornelia had mentioned it, either. And he hadn't wanted to ask. It had seemed to him that the less he knew about her, the easier it would be to keep her pigeonholed as a project, a duty. Something with a start and end date that required nothing of him in between but a little business advice and elbow grease.

It would have helped enormously if her little boy had been a brat.

It would have helped even more had she not been trying so hard to move on.

"What happened to your husband, Rory?"

Her focus remained on the light reflecting off the crystal. "He was on his way home from work. It was late and a drunk ran a red light." The twin slashes between her eyebrows deepened. "He was dead at the scene."

The unnatural calm in her voice belied how totally her world had shattered at that moment. That same stillness held her there, motionless except for the movement of her finger along the spiral facets.

"And what had you heard that you couldn't ask him about?"

She barely blinked. "That he'd married me to spite his parents.

"It was after Curt's funeral," she added quietly. "At the reception." His parents had wanted the reception after the service at the club. She hadn't cared where it had been held, had been fine with going in whichever direction she'd been pointed. Other than Tyler, she hadn't cared about anything at all.

"I was in the restroom when some other women came in. They didn't know I was there because I overheard one of them ask how long Curt and I had been married. One of Audrey's friends told her, then said I was nothing like the women he'd usually gone out with. Refined women, she'd called them. I heard someone else say that everyone knew he'd married me just to spite his parents. Apparently, not long after Audrey heard we were dating, she started setting him up with women she thought more appropriate. The more polite consensus was that he'd married me to get her off his back."

That was the only clear memory she had of that entire day. So much of it had been a fog of hugs, sympathetic murmurings and just wanting to find the friends watching Tyler and get her son out of there.

She absently hooked the icicle she held onto the nearest branch. "He'd never told me his mother was doing that. But it could certainly explain why he'd wanted to elope." She'd thought at the time that his idea to run off to Lake Tahoe had sounded wonderfully romantic. But at barely twenty-one, what had she known?

"I'd been happy. I'd thought he was, too." Her hand fell, her voice along with it. "He'd always put in long hours. But that last year he'd put in even more. He'd been trying to make partner," she said, though she had no idea why the detail even mattered now. "After hearing those women, I couldn't help wondering if he was really away so much because of work. Or because he just didn't want to be there with me and I'd been too naive to realize it."

Her throat felt oddly tight. It had been well over a year since she'd verbalized that fear. She'd found out later that some of their friends had heard the rumors that day, too. Audrey, grieving herself, and in an apparent effort to save face for both of them, had even called her the next day to apologize for her friends' "lack of sensitivity at such a time." She had not, however, denied their conclusions.

Rory swallowed. Hard.

Feeling nearly as bewildered and betrayed as she had that awful afternoon, she pushed her fingers through her hair, trying desperately to force a smile. "I think now would be a really good time for you to give me the estimate I'm looking for. Six more months? A year? Please just don't say 'never.'"

For long seconds, Erik said nothing. He remained an arm's length away, his thoughts about the women's thoughtlessness anything but charitable, and fought the instinct to pull her into his arms.

He'd had closure when his marriage had fallen apart. He'd had answers to his questions. After he'd divorced, there had been no doubt in his mind that his marriage had been irreparably broken. The way this woman's had ended, she was left with questions that could never be answered.

Not by the man she'd married.

He seriously questioned Curt having had any ulterior motive when he'd married her. There was far too much about her to be attracted to, too much to truly care about.

Since the guy wasn't around to tell her what all those things were, he'd just have to enlighten her himself.

"Come here."

Taking her by the hand, he led her toward the wing chair by the sofa, muting the television on the way, and nudged her to the cushion. With his side to the fire, he hitched at the knees of his jeans and sat down on the heavy hassock in front of her.

Resting his forearms on his thighs, he clasped his hands loosely between them. "You want my take on this?"

Her arms crossed protectively at her waist, she murmured a soft, "Please."

"For starters," he began, being as objective as possible, "it's far more logical to conclude that he married you not to spite his parents, but *in* spite of them. You're beautiful, smart and easy to be with. For the most part," he qualified when she blinked at him in disbelief. "You can be pretty unreasonable at times," he pointed out, mostly so he wouldn't have to consider how unwillingly drawn he was to her himself. "But, trust me, he was attracted to you. He had to be." Especially if she'd showed up at the office looking the way she had the other night in that suit and heels.

"As for what those big mouths in the bathroom said about you being different," he continued, "you probably were. If he'd been going out with society types or old money or whatever his mother considered 'refined,' you'd have been a breath of fresh air."

A few years out from leaving the mobile nest of her fairly unconventional parents, there probably hadn't been an ounce of pretension about her. Even now, the polish he suspected she'd acquired in her husband's circles seemed as understated as her quiet sensuality. There was something about her that defied definition. It was almost as if her desire for permanence had forced her from her parents' artistic, nomadic lifestyle to seek stability in the urbane and conservative and she'd yet to find where she was comfortable in between. What truly impressed him, though, was the strength that pushed her past what many would see as totally daunting obstacles, along with a seemingly innate ability to nurture, to ease and to make a man feel as if every word he uttered mattered.

The way she made him feel just then.

"He might not have even realized how constrained he

felt until you came along." Thinking of the emotionally vacant relationships he personally limited himself to, he cleared his throat, glanced from the quiet way she watched him. "You went to work as his secretary. Right?"

Looking a little doubtful about his assessment, she gave a small nod. "He'd been there four years."

"So even before you came along, his career choices made it pretty clear he had a mind of his own. It sounds like he was willing to follow the family profession, but on his own terms. When he did meet you, I doubt he gave a second's thought to what his mom and dad would think. By the time he realized he wanted you in his life, their opinion might have mattered to him, but not as much as you did."

He knew for a fact that the physical pull between a man and a woman tended to lead the way where the sexes were concerned. If Curt had been half the man Erik suspected he was, he'd have had as hard a time as he was at that moment keeping his hands to himself. On the parental objection front, he couldn't imagine his own folks finding any fault with her at all.

"As for eloping," he continued, not at all sure where that last thought had come from, "he probably knew his parents wouldn't be willing participants, so it just made sense to avoid the problem. Most guys I know prefer to duck all the big wedding plans, anyway. Unless that's what his fiancée really wants," he qualified, because he'd given in on that one himself.

A bit of red glitter clung to one knee of her jeans. With the tip of her index finger, she gave it a nudge. "I didn't care about anything big, Erik. I just wanted to marry him."

He had no idea why that didn't surprise him. What did was how a while ago, he'd wanted details. Now, he did not.

"A little more insider info here," he offered, despite a stab of what felt suspiciously like envy. "Men aren't that complicated. If Curt was like most of us, if he was working longer hours, he was just doing what he needed to do to get ahead in his field and provide the kind of life he wanted for his family. It's what a guy does," he said simply. "Our egos tend to be tied to what we do for a living. But our work is also how we take care of the people we care about."

As if he'd just touched on something familiar, her glance lifted, then promptly fell.

She'd forgotten how often Curt had told her that he wouldn't be putting in those hours forever. That soon he'd be a partner and they could afford a bigger house, better cars, the kinds of vacations he wanted them to take. So many times he'd told her he was doing what he was doing for them.

She'd loved him for that. But she also remembered telling him she couldn't imagine living in a house larger than the one they had. She'd been fine—more than fine—with everything they'd already possessed.

"I think he needed bigger and better more than I did."

"That's entirely possible." Erik watched her nudge again at the bit of sparkle, the rest of her fingers curled into her palm. "A lot of people measure their success by their acquisitions. Especially if the people around them do the same thing." He wouldn't be in business himself if there weren't people who wanted to own the exclusive sailing sloops he loved to build. "That doesn't mean he wasn't thinking of you. And Tyler. And don't forget, he also cared enough about what you had together to work through the…ah… baby problem you two had," he decided to call it, "and adopt that great little guy upstairs."

What she had recalled moments ago had put a microscopic tear in the doubts that had caused her to question nearly every memory. Erik's conclusions had just ripped that hole wide.

She had no secrets from this man, she realized. There was nothing of any import about her he didn't know and, in some inexplicable way, seem to understand. Because of that he had just reminded her of a time when she had known without a doubt that her husband loved her. Curt had been so worried about losing her, of her thinking less of him because he couldn't give her the child they'd both wanted so much. Yet the struggles, disappointments and finally the joy of Tyler had only brought them closer.

So many details of her married life had faded in the past months. So much had been lost or skewed by second-guessing and uncertainties. But that much she remembered with crystal clarity, and while the memory was a bittersweet reminder of what she had lost, it also felt mercifully…healing.

"As for the rest of it," he said quietly, "if you were happy and if he seemed happy with you and Tyler, that's all that matters." Without thinking, he reached over, traced his finger over hers. "If you'd stop looking for ways to explain what you heard, I think you'd probably know that."

The tip of his finger moved over her knuckles, his touch gentle, reassuring. His strong hand looked huge next to hers, and she wanted badly to absorb his certainty as he uncurled her fingers and rested his palm on the back of her hand.

"Do you think you can do that?" he asked.

Watching his fingers curve around hers, she gave another little nod.

"That's a start, then," he murmured.

He had no idea how far beyond a start he'd led her.

At that moment, with Erik doing nothing but holding her hand, she couldn't help but think of how Curt would have really liked this man. She could have hugged him herself for defending Curt the way he had—had she not already been wishing he would hold her.

He tipped up her chin, curved his hand to the side of her face. "Are you okay?" he asked.

Her heart gave an odd little bump. "Sure."

"You're a really lousy liar."

She had no idea what he saw in her expression. She just knew her throat felt suspiciously tight as his dark eyes narrowed on hers.

"You'll be all right, Rory. I don't know how long it will take for you," he admitted, surprising empathy in the deep tones of his voice. "It was a couple of years before I realized I was having a good time again. But you'll get better before you even realize it's happening."

Her head unconsciously moved toward his palm. The heat of his hand felt good against her cheek, warm, comforting. Grounding. At that moment, she just didn't know if it was that anchoring touch or his confident assurance that she needed most. She felt relieved by that contact. It was as if he was letting her know she wasn't as alone as she so often felt. She craved that security as much as she did his disarming gentleness when his thumb brushed the curve of her jaw and edged to the corner of her mouth.

His eyes followed the slow movement, his carved features going taut as he carried that mesmerizing motion to her bottom lip.

Her breath caught. When she felt his thumb give a little tug, her heart bumped hard against her ribs.

An instant later, his jaw tightened and his hand fell.

At his abrupt withdrawal, disappointment shot through her. Swift and unsettling. She wouldn't have pulled away, wouldn't have done a thing to stop him had he moved closer. Knowing that, embarrassingly certain he did, too, Rory rose before he could and reached for an empty mug on the end table.

"Sorry," she murmured. "I said I wouldn't do that again. Dump on you like that, I mean."

When she turned back, Erik had pushed himself to his feet.

Beyond his broad shoulders, a log broke in the fireplace, embers spraying upward. The tick of ice blowing hard against the window grew more audible with another gust of wind.

The storm added yet another layer of unease.

"I asked," he reminded her.

"That's true." Hoping to shake how he unsettled her, she tried for a smile. "So it's your fault."

She was talking about his uncanny ability to uncork her most private concerns. From the way his glance dropped to her mouth, he seemed to be thinking more of the seductive pull snaking across the six feet of tension separating them.

Or maybe it was just her own tension she felt.

"Just part of the service."

He'd only been doing his job.

The reminder had her ducking her head as she turned away. It didn't matter that she'd wanted his kiss, or how badly she'd wanted him to hold her. It didn't even matter that she didn't trust what she'd felt when she'd been in his arms before, that almost desperate need to hide in his strength.

He'd offered her his help, a little comfort and his experience. What he wasn't offering was a refuge, and she had no business thinking of him as one.

"If you don't mind, I think I'll just say good-night now," she murmured. "You're welcome to stay down here and watch TV if you want. My bedroom is the one—"

"I know where your bedroom is, Rory."

Of course he did.

"The sheets are clean and I put clean towels in the master bathroom." Her bathroom wasn't very big, but he already knew that, too. "I set out a new toothbrush for you."

"I'll figure it out," he assured her. "Is there anything you want me to do down here?"

"Just bank the fire."

The rest could wait until morning.

The telltale muscle in his jaw jerked. "Consider it banked. I'll take care of that," he said, taking the mug from her. "You go on up. I'll catch the news for a while and turn off the lights."

He obviously felt the need for a little space, too.

More than willing to give it to him, she started for the stairs.

The silence behind her and the faint ticking of ice against glass had her turning right back.

"Is the roof up there okay? It can handle the weight of the ice, can't it?"

"The roof should be fine."

She lifted her chin, turned back again.

Another step and she turned right back. "Is there anything I can get you before I go up?"

He'd barely met her eyes again before he shook his head and turned away himself. "I don't need a thing," he assured her. "Just go to bed. I'll see you in the morning."

Chapter Eight

For Rory, sleep rarely came easily. When it did, it was usually fitful, an often futile exercise where the loneliness she could sometimes mask with activity during the day reared its ugly head at night to haunt her. But she must have been asleep. Something had just wakened her, a distant, cracking sound followed by an odd, heavy silence.

With Tyler's back tucked against her, she blinked into the dark. Realizing that it shouldn't be that dark since his night-light should have been on, she reached for her robe at the foot of the twin bed.

She had no idea what time it had been when she'd heard Erik come up the stairs and close the door at the end of the hall. She'd lain there listening to the sound of water in the bathroom pipes and the heavy creak of floorboards as he'd moved around her room. When silence seemed to indicate that he'd gone to bed, she'd attempted to block further thought in that direction by listening to her son's deep, even breathing and the wind gusting like muffled cannon blasts against his bedroom wall beside her.

The ice pelting the window had no longer sounded as sharp, as if the buildup had muffled it. The only thing that had allowed her to not feel as anxious as she might have about the fury outside had been thinking about the man down the hall being so near.

Now she heard nothing at all.

There was no clock in Tyler's room. Quietly, so as not to wake her sleeping child, she pulled on her robe and found her way to the door.

The moment she opened it, she realized the electricity had gone out. The night-light in Tyler's bathroom across the hall wasn't on. Neither was the one in the outlet down by her room. The hall was as black as pitch.

She kept a flashlight in her nightstand, another in a drawer in the kitchen. Without questioning why she didn't head for her room, she edged toward the stairs, her hand sliding along the wall to guide her to the handrail.

"Rory?"

Her hand flattened over the jolt behind her breastbone. "Erik," she whispered, turning toward his hushed voice. "Where are you?"

"By your bedroom door. Where are you?"

"By the stairs," she whispered. "What was that noise?"

"It sounded like a tree went down. My guess is that it took out a power line." Across twenty feet of dark came the soft, metallic rasp of a zipper. "Do you have a flashlight up here?"

It seemed he'd just zipped up his jeans. Thinking he could well be standing there shirtless, she murmured, "The nightstand on the left. In the drawer."

She heard him move inside, and his mild oath when he bumped into something, the end of the bed, probably. Moments later, shadows bounced around the room and a flash of bright light arched low into the hall. Following that blue-white beam, he walked up to her, his undershirt and sweater in his free hand, and handed her the light.

She kept the beam angled down, the pool of it at his feet. Still, there was more than enough illumination to define every superbly sculpted muscle of his chest.

Deliberately, she moved her glance to the heavy sports watch on his wrist. "Do you know what time it is?" she asked.

"Almost seven."

It would be getting light in less than an hour.

He dropped the sweater. In two quick motions he shoved his beautifully muscled arms into his long-sleeved undershirt.

"When you did the walk-through with the building inspector, did he say anything about the generator? It should only have taken seconds for it to take over."

The generator? "He said it was set to come on for a few minutes once a week," she told him, scrambling to remember as she watched him pull his shirt over his head. "To make sure it'll be available when I really need it," she added.

Erik's dark head popped out, rearranging his already sleep-mussed hair. His jaw was shadowed, hard and angular in the dim light. "Has it been working?"

"I don't know." The gray metal generator on the slab at the back of the building hadn't been on her priority list. It hadn't been on her list at all. Until now. "I think he said it's set for either Tuesday or Wednesday mornings. We haven't been here then."

He swiped the sweater from where it had landed near her beam-lit, glittery-red toenails. Rising, his glance skimmed the length of her pale robe, only to jerk away before he met her eyes.

She'd barely realized he looked nearly as tense as he

had when she'd left him last night before he dragged the sweater over his head and tugged it down. "I'll check the transfer switch. Then I'll get a fire going.

"I just need this." He took the flashlight from her. "Give me a minute and you'll have enough light to do whatever you need to do up here. The hall light won't work, but the bathroom lights will. Did he explain how the standby works?"

A transfer switch sounded familiar. The guy who'd inspected the building a couple of weeks ago had pointed it out. It was in one of the electrical panel boxes in the basement.

"I think so. I don't remember everything he told me," she admitted. "We looked at a lot around here that day." There'd also been Tyler to calm. He hadn't liked the huge, shadowy space. "There was a lot to take in."

Something shifted in Erik's expression. She knew he'd been aware of how overwhelmed she'd been by Cornelia's intervention, and by how suddenly she'd found herself in a place she'd known nothing about at all. It stood to reason there were a few things she might have missed, or had forgotten. As it was, she could have managed on her own to start a fire to keep Tyler warm. She just had no idea what to do about the generator—which meant, right now, she couldn't fix this particular problem without him.

She didn't doubt that he knew that, too, as he followed the beam of light down the stairs, pulled on the heavy boots he'd left at the bottom and disappeared into the dark.

Feeling at a distinct disadvantage where he was concerned, and hating it, she turned in the dark herself, working her way first to Tyler's bathroom, then back to his room. She'd just started to put on the clothes she'd left on his play table last night when she heard his bedclothes rustle.

"Mom? I'm a-scared."

"It's okay, honey. I'm right here. The power went out," she explained, her voice soft, "but it'll be back on in a minute." Leaving her robe on, she found her way to him, hugged his warm little body to hers. "You don't need to be afraid." Forcing a smile into her voice, she murmured, "You know what?"

His response was the negative shake of his head against her neck.

"I have a big surprise for you."

"Is the tree all done?"

"It is. But that's not the surprise."

She felt him pull back. "Is he here?"

He. Erik.

The man's presence was not at all the news she'd hoped would get his morning off to a better start.

"He's downstairs," she told him, and felt certain he'd have scooted off the bed that very moment had he been able to see where he was going.

She'd thought to tell him her surprise was the big adventure the day might be, since making an adventure of uncertainties, for the most part, had taken his mind off his fears and insecurities before. Since Erik had unknowingly just accomplished that for her, she told him they'd just wait right where they were while his idol turned the lights back on.

Instead of electric lights, however, it was the beam of the flashlight that illuminated the hall outside the open door.

The beam swung inward, causing Tyler to bury his head in her chest at the momentary brightness and her to block the sudden flash with her hand.

"Sorry," Erik muttered. He aimed the beam at the rumpled bedding on the trundle. "It's not the switch. I'll have to wait until it's light out to see what the problem is."

The circle of light bouncing off the cerulean sheets

filled the room with shades of pale blue. Along the far wall, he watched Rory cuddling her son on the higher bed, her hair tousled, her hand slowly soothing the child's flannel-covered back as Tyler turned to smile at him.

It hit him then, as they sat huddled in the semi-dark, that all they really had was each other. He'd realized that on some level last night when he'd prodded her about where they'd spend Christmas. But seeing them now, realizing how much she'd lost and how vulnerable she could easily feel being that alone here, drove that reality home.

The troubling protectiveness he felt for her slid back into place. That same protectiveness had been there last night, protecting her from him.

He'd had no business touching her last night. All he'd wanted when he'd met them at the tree lot yesterday was to make sure she could give her little boy the Christmas she wanted for him.

All he'd wanted last night was her.

There hadn't been a trace of defense in her pretty face when he'd touched her. Nothing that even remotely suggested she would have stopped him if he'd pulled her to him. He'd known when he'd left there a few days ago that distance was his best defense against complications with her. Especially since the not-so-subtle needs she aroused in him simply by her presence had a definite tendency to sabotage objectivity where she was concerned.

Having sabotaged the distance angle himself simply by showing up, it seemed like some perverted form of justice that distance was going to be deprived him for a while.

"Do you have another flashlight up here?" Objectivity now appeared to be his only defense. And objectively, she truly needed far more help from him than a little tutoring with the store. "Something stronger than this?"

"The only other I have is just like that one. It's in the kitchen in the phone desk drawer."

"You need something brighter. I'll get one of the camp lamps from the store and bring it back for you to use up here."

She didn't know she had camp lamps. But then, she hadn't finished her inventory, either.

"We'll wait," she told him, then watched him leave them, literally, in the dark.

There was something he wasn't telling her. She would have bet her silk long underwear on that, had she not needed to wear it under her favorite gray fleece sweats to keep warm.

She couldn't believe how quickly the house had cooled. She turned the thermostat down every night, but without the furnace running at all, the temperature inside had dropped ten degrees within the hour.

She'd compensated by bundling Tyler in long johns, fleece pants, heavy socks, slippers, an undershirt, thermal shirt and sweatshirt and parking him under a blanket in front of the blaze Erik had built in the fireplace.

The only layer Erik had added was his jacket when he'd gone out a few minutes ago. He'd already left it in the mudroom when the thud of his heavy-treaded work boots announced his return.

"This is the last of the wood you brought in yesterday. I'll get more from the shed in a while."

The drapes were still closed, but the edges of the room were no longer dark. The fire had grown to throw flickering light into the room. The camp light that now occupied the dining table illuminated from that direction much like a table lamp.

Tyler smiled up at him.

"Can we turn on the tree?" he wanted to know.

He hadn't been talking to her. "We don't have electricity yet," she reminded him anyway. "Why don't you read

Frosty?" With the suggestion, she handed him his new favorite picture book. "And I'll get you something to eat."

Concern suddenly swept his little face. Dropping the book, he shoved off the blanket and headed for the wall of drape-covered windows.

"Is there a problem with the furnace, too?" she asked Erik, wondering what her little boy was up to. Wondering, too, if a problem with the furnace was what the larger male wasn't sharing. "It's oil. Not electric. Shouldn't it be working?"

Tyler pulled back the living room drapes. Dawn lightened the window, but the coating of frost and ice on the glass made it impossible to make out anything beyond it.

The logs landed with quiet thuds at the far end of the hearth. "The furnace is oil, but the fan and pump are electric. You need power to pump the oil and push out the hot air."

Great, she thought. "Oh," she said.

Tyler let go of the drape. The heavy fabric still swung slightly as he ran to the dining room window next to it and pulled back the drape there.

"How come I can't see it?" he asked.

"See what, honey?"

"The snowman. He has lights."

"Hey, Tyler. I heard your mom say she'd get your breakfast. How about we get that out of the way before we tackle anything else?"

At the obvious change of subject, Rory's glance darted to Erik. It was met with the quick shake of his head and the pinch of his brow.

He moved to her side, his voice low. "I don't think you'll want him to see it yet. Give me time to fix it first. I haven't been all the way around the building, but some of those gusts last night were pretty strong. You might want to take a look from the store porch.

"So," he continued, brushing off his hands as he walked over to the child smiling up at him. "Why don't you show me what kind of cereal we're having?"

Totally distracted by his friend's attention, Tyler dutifully led the way to the pantry while Rory grabbed a flashlight and headed for the door into the store. On the way, she could hear Erik asking questions about flakes versus puffs and Tyler answering like an expert before she closed the inner door and hurried by flashlight beam to the outer one.

She'd barely opened the store's front door and screen and crossed her arms against the freezing air when she froze herself.

The world outside had been transformed into a wonderland as disheartening as it was beautiful. In the pale twilight, the stubbles of her lawn appeared to be a blanket of clear marbles. Across the ice-glazed street, every bough on every tall pine, every branch of every winter-bare tree, every leaf on every bush had been encased in a robe of ice.

In between, the ice-coated electric line sagged heavily from pole to pole—except for where it dangled loose a few feet from the tangle of branches of an oak tree now uprooted from her yard and lying across the road, blocking it completely.

Near the entrance to her driveway, half of the maple tree that would shade it in summer lay squarely in it.

Clouds filtered the cold sunrise, but the sky to the east was lightening enough to add hints of color to the gray when she carefully edged her way over the icy boards to the end of the porch and looked toward the meadow. It was there that she saw the snowman that now rested in parts not far from the still upright and remarkably unbroken apple tree. The white chicken-wire, light-encrusted balls had separated when they'd blown over and were now frozen in place with boughs that had flown in from the grove of pines beyond.

Erik had suspected that seeing the dismembered decoration would have upset her little boy. He was right. And
though what she saw distressed her, too—especially when
she thought of what had to be an identical mess of toppled
debris on the other side of the building—she wouldn't let
herself think about how she was going to clean it all up
right now. Mother Nature froze it, and she'd thaw it, too.
She'd worry then about taking care of the scattered and
broken boughs, branches and trees. Right now she couldn't
let herself think about anything beyond going back inside,
making sure the guys were fed and figuring out how to
make coffee without any power.

The rest of it was just too daunting.

"Thank you," she said softly on her way past Erik the
moment she walked back in.

He stood at the island, Tyler a few feet away at the
silverware drawer. "No problem." He searched her face
quickly, looking to see how she was taking what she had
seen.

Not sure what to make of the deceptive calm she diligently maintained around her child, he turned with two
boxes in his hands. "Cereal?"

"Sure." Doing her best to ignore the knot of anxiety in
her stomach, she reached for bowls and bananas. "What
kind are you having, Ty?"

"Both," her son announced.

"We're mixing 'em," Erik explained.

The camp light now stood on the kitchen counter. In
that relative brightness, Tyler's eyes fairly danced.

The dark slash of Erik's eyebrow arched. "Is that a problem?"

For a moment she thought the suggestion must have
been Erik's, until she considered that Tyler could have
come up with the idea and Erik had decided to let him
think the notion a good one. Looking between the two of

them, she decided it could go either way. And either way, as protective as Erik had been of her son's feelings moments ago, and sensing that what that mountain of muscle really needed was to be outside and moving, she couldn't think of a thing to say but, "Of course not."

Being deprived of his usual five-mile morning run did nothing to help Erik escape the restiveness nagging like a toothache as he headed into the early morning light. The bracing air felt good, though. He didn't even mind that the ground felt like a skating rink beneath his boots. His balance on it was as sure as on a yawing sailboat—managing that shift and roll was second nature to him.

Where he was out of his element was figuring out how to stay objective about the woman inside when he'd been kept awake half the night by her scent on her sheets and thoughts of her tantalizing little body playing havoc with his own.

When he had first agreed to help her, he hadn't considered how much her education would require beyond a business plan and inventory. But the scope of his responsibility had finally hit him. It had taken both of his grandparents to maintain their store and their home. For her to make it here, she'd need to be as self-reliant as they had been.

What he also hadn't considered until a while ago was how much more difficult her tasks might be because part of her focus would almost always be on her child.

Ten minutes and another trip to the basement later, she had power—which was one less thing he needed to be concerned about before he headed back upstairs to see her by the light switch in the dining room.

"You fixed it." Relief lit her guarded smile as she pushed the toggle. "I heard the refrigerator come on. And the furnace."

From where he'd stopped in the entryway, he watched her glance up at the still dark fixture above the long table.

"That light is off circuit right now," he told her. "The only overhead light you have up here is in the kitchen. Besides the bathroom lights upstairs, you have one live outlet in each bedroom. All the appliances up here have power. So does the water heater in the basement, but the washer and dryer don't."

The minor inconveniences barely fazed her. "What was wrong with the generator?"

"The fuel line valve from the propane tank had been left in the off position. It could have been turned when the servicing company filled it, or by the inspector when he checked it out. Either way," he said, conscious of her concentration, "it would be a good idea for you to check it the next time it's filled. I'll show you later how to thaw the valve in case it ever freezes in place again. Right now there are a few things I want to show you in the basement."

"I wanna go to the basement," Tyler announced.

Rory looked to where he had just jumped to his feet. "I thought you didn't like the basement."

With a small shrug, he walked up to Erik.

"It's okay," was all Tyler said, but it was infinitely more obvious than Erik's faint smile that it was only okay because of the big guy.

With more immediate concerns to deal with, she knew she couldn't afford to worry about that growing attachment now. His new hero had the vaguely impatient look of a man on a mission as he led them down the steep stairs and across the concrete floor.

Because Tyler wanted to see what he was talking about, he scooped him up, catching his small hand to keep him from touching anything, and proceeded to describe how the transfer of the power between the generator and the grid took place and how this system had a double-pole, double-throw transfer switch gear as a safety feature because it was the best way to prevent shock or electrocution.

Her son looked fascinated by what the big man holding him so easily was saying about currents, shutoffs and sensors. And while she grasped the basics of what she needed to know, much of the detail escaped her just then. She had no problem, however, recognizing when something could be dangerous. As the day wore on, she even found herself wondering if there was any double sort of safety feature a woman could use to protect herself from the effects of a man who had the disturbing ability to draw her to him even as he pushed her away.

"I just want to know how to use a regular saw. Okay? The one you used to trim the trunk on the Christmas tree would work fine."

"It would work on the smaller branches," Erik agreed, the icy breeze carrying away the fog of his breath, "but not for those you need to cut to get something this size moved. If you're serious about this, a chain saw is faster and a lot less work."

Concern clearly battled her determination.

"If I'm using that, I won't be able to hear Tyler if he needs me. And I can't have him right with me, because I don't want him anywhere near that thing."

"I'll show you how to use the handsaw." He didn't hesitate to offer the assurance, aware himself of the child on the porch, breaking ice off the fir boughs she'd collected for a wreath. "But you should know how to use this, too. We'll be where you can keep an eye on him."

He watched Rory look from the wicked-looking chain saw blade to the long tangle of ice-coated limbs that had split away from the maple on the far side of the drive. A slash of exposed, raw wood on the heavy trunk mirrored the ragged tear on the thick branch where it had fallen from the tree's side.

He'd already cut up the branch that had fallen atop it with the now-silent saw he'd borrowed from her neighbor. He'd heard the saw's droning buzz when he'd come outside a couple of hours ago to fix Frosty and put a little physical distance between himself and his charge. Being near her in the confines of the house had left him too edgy, too restless. Outdoors, he at least had the buffer of space.

His glance slid from her burgundy fleece headband and jacket to the hem of her jeans. Since she'd kept herself occupied away from him for the better part of the morning, he suspected she'd been after a little distance, too.

Apparently having reassessed her options, and with her immediate concern addressed, she anchored the toe of her black boot in the loop of the saw's handle. "So," she gamely began, "I start it by putting my foot here?" she asked. "And pulling on this?"

Catching her arm as she reached for the starter pull, he turned her in the churned-up gravel to face him. "You start by putting on these."

He tugged off his heavy leather gloves, then slipped the clear safety goggles Ed Shumway also loaned him from around his neck.

Teaching her how to use a saw hadn't been on the agenda he'd outlined for himself that morning, but she'd wanted to know how to use one to clear the property after it thawed. Since he didn't much care for the thought of her outside sawing and hauling limbs by herself, he'd already planned to have the mess cleared for her. This wasn't the only storm she'd likely ever encounter, though. And he wouldn't be around once she was on her financial feet. If she was going to be self-sufficient, it was his job to give her the tools she'd need to make that happen.

Reaching toward her, he looped the goggles' wide elas-

tic strap around the back of her head. Not giving her time
to take off her gloves to adjust the bright orange band, he
did it himself and settled the clear skilike goggles in place.

"Keep in mind that the barter system still works for
a few things around here, too," he informed her, tuck-
ing back a strand of the dark hair he'd dislodged from the
fleece covering her ears. "Someone should be willing to
take care of all these trees for you in exchange for a load
or two they can sell or use for firewood."

Far too conscious of the softness of her skin, the silk of
her hair, he deliberately dropped his hand.

Pulling his gloves from where he'd tucked them under
his arm, he jerked them back on and nodded to the saw.
"Now you can start it."

Rory braced herself. Not so much for what she was
about to do, but because everything about this man had
her feeling so off balance.

He'd given her his jacket a while ago. He stood there
now in his heavy charcoal pullover and jeans, seeming
totally unfazed by the cold and the almost familiar ease
with which he'd touched her.

"Hold the blade straighter," he called over the din of the
idling motor. With his broad chest pressed to her back, he
reached his arms around her, placed his gloved hands over
hers and adjusted her angle.

"Ready?" he asked, his breath warm through the soft
knit covering her ear.

Conscious of his body enclosing hers, she gave a tense
little nod.

She wasn't sure which disconcerted her more, the thir-
teen pounds of suddenly screaming machine, or the man
surrounding her, making sure she didn't hurt herself with
it. With the blade engaged, metal teeth spinning, the chain
bit ice. A quick spray of what looked like snow and wood
chips flew.

"Keep your grip steady." He spoke near her cheek now, his body still at her back as he eased his hands to her shoulders. "You need to keep it from bucking back if you hit a knot. Keep it under control."

Control, she thought. She hadn't felt "in control" in ages.

"Like this?" she called, handles in a death grip, her eyes glued to the blade sinking into the wood.

"Just like that," he called back and, just like that, the weight of the free end of the limb cracked it downward and the blade went through.

A second of disbelief was replaced with a grin as she swung toward him.

"Don't!" His hand shot forward, the side of his face bumping the corner of her goggles an instant before his hand caught hers to hold the saw in place. Bent against her, he'd turned his head to hers, his lips inches from the startled part of her own.

"The brake," he said. With a small movement of his hand, the throttle dropped back to idle. "You need to set it as soon as you finish your cut. It's safer that way."

She realized now why he'd stayed behind her. Had she swung around, she could have caught him with the blade in his thigh.

Taking the idling machine from her, he shut off the motor, set the saw on the ground.

In the sudden silence, she could hear her heart hammering in her ears. Shaken from the start he'd given her, horrified by what she could have done to him, she dropped her glance to the short placket on his pullover as he rose and turned to her.

"Erik, I'm so sorry."

His forehead furrowed as he pulled her hand from her mouth and lifted the orange band at her temples. Removing the goggles, he looped them over the fabric covering his forearm.

"Hey. It's okay." Hating how he'd killed her quick smile, he touched his gloved finger to her high cheekbone. It was there that the goggles would have bumped. "We hadn't gotten to that part." Another second and they would have, he thought, searching her pale features. He just hadn't expected her to get excited about felling a limb. "Next time you'll remember."

He couldn't feel the smoothness of her skin through the thick suede. He could imagine it, though. Just as he could too easily imagine so many other things he knew he shouldn't be thinking about her.

Detachment wasn't an option at the moment. Not with her looking so frightened by what she could have done. "Right?"

Beneath his hand, he felt her faint nod. What he noticed most, though, was how her head turned toward his hand, as if somewhere in her subconscious she craved that unfettered contact, too.

She'd done the same thing last night, right about the time he'd been thinking about reacquainting himself with the feel of her mouth. Heaven knew how tempted he'd been to do just that. But he acknowledged now what he hadn't then. It hadn't just been complications with her he wanted to avoid. He hadn't wanted her thinking of anyone but him when he kissed her. And last night had been far more about easing the doubts that had haunted her for so long than whatever it was that kept him from caring about how easy she was to touch.

Rory watched his glance shift over her face. She had no idea what he was thinking, what it was vying with the concern so evident there, but from the way his eyes narrowed on her cheek, he seemed to be looking for a bruise.

"It didn't hurt," she told him, praying she hadn't caused him one as she unconsciously lifted her hand to his temple.

"I don't see a mark," he murmured. "But that doesn't mean you won't have a bruise later. You should get some ice on it." He gave her an encouraging smile. "There's plenty of it."

She felt far too concerned to smile back. "I don't see one on you, either," she told him, tipping her head to get a better look. "Not yet, anyway."

Erik's smile faded. He couldn't remember the last time a woman had touched him simply to make sure he was okay. There was caring in that touch, a hint of worry, a little gentleness. As complex as it seemed, it was really such a simple thing. Something basic. Yet her unveiled concern pulled hard at something deep inside him. Something he hadn't been sure still existed, and which would have felt decidedly threatening had he had time to consider what it was.

"Mom? Come help me?"

At her son's request, Rory's hand fell. Only now aware of how she'd reached to be sure Erik was all right, and of how they must look standing there checking each other out, her glance darted to where Tyler stood by a stack of pine on the porch.

He wanted help with the wreath.

Taking a step back, she called that she'd be right there.

Erik met her lingering disquiet.

"Stop worrying. You're quick. You'll get the hang of this," he insisted. "We'll give it another try later. In the meantime, you did fine. Really."

"Except for the part where I nearly disabled you," she muttered, half under her breath.

"I had you covered, Rory. You were a long way from anything like that."

A split second was hardly a long way. She'd have

pointed that out had his assessment of her capabilities not just registered. It was like last night, she thought, when he'd talked her through the doubts and turmoil of the past year. It seemed he didn't want her doubting her abilities, or herself, about anything.

He clearly expected her to challenge his last claim. The quick part, probably. She couldn't. Last night he had called her beautiful, smart and stubborn. The stubbornness she would concede. That he thought her beautiful and smart still left her a little stunned. But what mattered to her most was that for him to feel so certain about her meant he might actually believe in her himself.

Until that moment, she hadn't realized how badly she wanted that sort of faith—that trust—from him.

"I'm going to go help Tyler now."

His eyes narrowed on hers. "You're good, then?"

He wanted to know if she believed what he'd said.

I had you covered, Rory.

"I'm good," she said, and with him already turning to his task, she headed for the porch to rescue the boughs and her rosy-cheeked child.

He had her back. He wasn't going to let anything bad happen as long as he was there.

He couldn't begin to know how much that assurance mattered to her.

Chapter Nine

Erik had told her not to worry.

Rory wasn't sure she knew how to do that. The un-welcomed trait had become second nature. Yet what concerned her far more than her lack of skill with gas-fueled equipment was how she found herself wishing Erik's solid presence could be part of the community that encouraged her with its potential.

Ed Shumway, the neighbor who'd loaned Erik the saw, was married to Edie, the loquacious neighbor who'd first welcomed her to the neighborhood. He had come to repay Erik for his assist moving a limb from his garage that morning. Having heard on the news that it would be at least two days before crews could get in to restore power, he'd brought his bigger saw to help him clear the uprooted oak from the road that was their main access to town.

Even for her neighbors who didn't have access to TV news, word traveled fast by cell phone. Crystal Murphy, her laugh infectious and her carrot-red hair clashing wildly with her purple earmuffs, brought her four-year-old son to play with Tyler while her husband, Tony the roofer, joined the men. Her mom was at their house a quarter of a mile away with their two-year-old. They didn't have power but that seemed just fine with them. They had a woodstove and kerosene lamps and Crystal confessed to liking the throwback lifestyle. She turned out to be the candle maker Edie had told Rory about.

Jeremy Ott came for the same reason as Tony and Ed. Talia, his wife, who taught riding lessons at the stables a mile farther up, had braved the cold with her five-year-old twins because Edie had mentioned that Rory had a son their age.

Edie herself showed up with her two children, twelve and six, and a half gallon of milk. With all the children, hot cocoa went fast.

Even with all the activity, Rory found her attention straying to the man who stood just a little taller than the rest.

It was nearing four o'clock when the women stepped out onto the porch to see how much longer the men would be. The kids were warming up in front of the TV, under Edie's preteen's supervision, and it would be dark soon. There were suppers to prepare.

Rory doubted that Erik had taken a real break since lunch. All she'd noticed him stop for was to stretch his back or absently rub his neck before tossing aside another log or attacking another limb on the downed oak.

She was standing by the railing between Crystal and Edie when he made a V of his arm and hitched his shoulder before putting his back into hefting another chunk of tree. He and Tony were hauling cut sections of limbs to the side of the road while the other two men continued decreasing the size of what had blocked it.

Seeing who had Rory's attention, Edie flipped her braid

over her shoulder and tipped her dark blond head toward her. A navy Seattle Seahawks headband warmed her ears.

"He's an attractive man, isn't he?"

"Who?" asked Talia, leaning past Crystal.

"Erik," the older woman replied.

Rory gave a noncommittal shrug. "I suppose." *If you like the tall, dark, unattainable type,* she thought. Suspecting her neighbor was fishing, she glanced to Edie's nearly empty mug. "More coffee?"

"I'm good. Thanks." The loquacious woman with the too-keen radar kept her focus on the men methodically dismantling the tree.

"He and his business partner have done quite well for themselves, you know."

"I'd say they've done extremely well," Crystal emphasized. "Pax—his business partner," she explained helpfully to Rory, "is from here, too. I've heard they're both millionaires."

"I've met Pax. Nice guy," Rory admitted. What she didn't mention was that she already knew that Erik had means—that he even had friends among the very rich and famous.

She had been surrounded by the well-to-do, and those intent on joining their ranks, from the moment she'd married until she'd moved mere weeks ago. The understated way Erik used his wealth and the way he didn't balk at getting his own hands dirty just made her forget that at times.

Edie gave her a curious glance. "Would you mind a personal question? I didn't want to ask when I first met you," she explained. "I mean, I did, but it didn't seem appropriate at the time."

Rory smiled, a little surprised by the request for permission. "Ask what?"

"How long you've been widowed."

"A year and two months."

"That's too bad."

"It really is," Crystal agreed. "I'm sorry, Rory."

"That has to be so hard." Talia placed her gloved hand over her heart. "I don't know what I'd do without Jeremy."

Edie shook her head. "I meant it's too bad it hasn't been longer. I was just thinking how nice it would be if you two hit it off. I'm sorry for your loss, too," she sincerely assured Rory. "But I imagine you need a little more time before you start thinking in that direction."

"I don't know about that," Talia piped in. "My uncle remarried six months after my aunt passed."

"I think men do that because they don't know how to take care of themselves," claimed Edie.

Crystal frowned. "I thought that the men who married fast like that were the ones who'd had good marriages, so they weren't afraid to jump back in."

"If that's true," Talia said, leaping ahead, "then the opposite could explain why Erik hasn't remarried. I've never heard what happened with him and…what was her name?"

"Shauna," the other two women simultaneously supplied.

"Right. She wasn't from here," she explained to Rory. "They met one summer and she moved here after they married, but they left for Seattle after a year or so. My point, though," she claimed, getting to it, "is that maybe his experience has put him off women."

"Oh, I wouldn't say he's off women," Rory admitted. "We've had a couple of meetings where he had to leave because he had a date."

Talia shrugged. "Well, there goes that theory."

"That doesn't mean he's not gun-shy," Crystal supplied supportively.

"True. But Rory's not looking right now," Edie reminded them. "Anyway, I was just thinking it would be nice if Erik would come back. I can't imagine that he ever would," she insisted, certainty in her conclusion. "Not with his business so well established over in Seattle. But he still seems to fit in so perfectly here."

The woman who'd brought up the subject of her potential availability had just as abruptly concluded it. Relieved to have escaped matchmaking efforts, for a while at least, and not sure how she felt having reminded herself of her mentor's social life, Rory found herself silently agreeing with her well-intentioned neighbor.

Erik did seem to fit in. But then, he'd been raised there. Without letting herself wonder why, she'd also wondered if there was ever anything about this place that he missed. Or if his emotional barriers kept him from even noticing.

It hadn't sounded to Rory as if the women knew the other, more personal reasons why he wouldn't be coming back. The dreams he'd buried there. Still, Edie was right. Everything Erik cared about was in Seattle.

And everything she now cared about was here, she thought, and went back to looking a little concerned about him again.

"Why didn't you stop?"

"Because we were almost finished."

"You were out there another two hours, Erik."

"That's close enough to almost. I'll be fine after a hot shower. How did it go with the neighbors?"

The man was hopeless.

"It was nice." *You escaped the part where Edie wanted to make us a couple,* she thought, *but other than that...* "Crystal is going to bring me samples of her candles to see if I'd be interested in selling them. And Talia's twins go to the school I enrolled Tyler in. We're going to carpool."

She frowned at the way he cupped his neck as he sat down at the island. He'd said he'd be fine, though. The man had a scar as wide as Tyler's tired smile on the inside of his forearm. It was visible now where he'd pushed up his sleeves. He knew how much discomfort he could handle.

"What are you grinning about, bud?" he asked, tired but smiling himself.

Tyler took a deep breath, gave a decisive nod. "This was the best day ever."

"Wow. That's pretty cool." Forearms resting on either side of his heaped and steaming bowl of stew, he looked over at the little guy who'd mimicked his position. "What made it so good?"

Tyler looked over his shoulder at the white lights softly illuminating the room behind them. The fire in the stone fireplace crackled and glowed.

"My tree. And the ice on everything. And my new friends." He wrinkled his little brow, thinking. "And Mom, 'cause I got cocoa two times. And you."

"Me?" Erik exhaled a little laugh. "What did I do?"

"Well," he began, pondering. "You fixed things. And you made Mom laugh."

Erik's glance cut to where she sat at the end of the island, back to the child between them. "I did?"

"Uh-huh," Tyler insisted, his nod vigorous. "When you dropped your coat on her."

Though Erik looked a little puzzled, Rory knew exactly what Tyler was talking about. The two of them had just gathered boughs for the wreath. She'd been sorting them on the porch, her head bent over their project, when Erik had walked up behind her and asked if she'd take his jacket. With her back to him and him in work mode, she'd no sooner said she'd be glad to when he'd unceremoniously dropped it over her head.

He'd meant it to land on her shoulders. But she'd looked up just then. Heavy and huge on her, she'd practically disappeared under the soft black leather.

She'd already been smiling at what he'd done and gone

still at the unexpectedness of it when he'd lifted the back of the collar and peeked around at her.

"You okay in there?" he'd asked, and the smile in his eyes had turned her smile into something that had sounded very much like a giggle.

She hadn't giggled since she was sixteen.

Erik apparently remembered now, too.

Looking over at Tyler, he gave his little buddy a knowing nod. He remembered the bright sound of that laugh, of hearing a hint of lightness in it he suspected she hadn't felt in a very long time.

"She needs to do that more often," he decided, and after arching his eyebrow at her, suggested Tyler finish his stew before he went after it himself.

Rory glanced away, stabbed a piece of carrot. She wished he wouldn't do that—arch his eyebrow at her that way. Something about the expression seemed teasing, playful and challenging all at once. Except for the challenging part, it also tended to disarm her and she'd been having a hard enough time remembering why she needed to keep her emotional guard in place with him pretty much since he'd strong-armed her into trying Ed's saw. Or maybe the problem had started last night, when she'd unloaded on him. Again. Or yesterday, when he'd sided with Tyler about the size of the tree.

There were reasons. Compelling ones, she was sure. She just couldn't remember them as she gave him her most charming smile and told him there was more stew if he wanted it.

He had seconds, told her it was great, then finished the bit in the pot before she carried his and Tyler's bowls to the sink.

"What Tyler said about it being a good day," he murmured, handing her his milk glass when she came back for it. "It was." He kept his focus on the glass and her hand, his tone thoughtful, as if he was a little surprised by that perception. Or perhaps by the admission.

"Now," he continued, moving past whatever had prompted it, "if you don't mind, I'm going to get that shower. You wouldn't have a spare razor, would you?"

She told him she did. A small package of them was in the drawer below where she'd left the toothbrush on the counter for him last night. She didn't bother telling him they were hot pink.

It did Rory's heart good to know her little boy had had such a good time that day. It did something less definable to it to know Erik had somehow appreciated it, too. Something that fed an unfamiliar bubble of hope that common sense told her was best to ignore. But with Tyler pretty much worn out and in need of a bath, she gave it no further thought. By the time she'd helped him with his bath and his prayers, it was all he could do to keep his eyes open.

Erik seemed to have had the same problem. When she finally came back down the dimly lit stairs, the fire was nearly out and Erik had fallen asleep in front of the television.

He lay stretched out on the sofa in his jeans and pullover, one leg angled with his bare foot on the cushion, the other foot on the floor. With his dark head propped on the curved arm of the sofa, one arm thrown over his eyes, his other hand splayed on his stomach, it looked as if he'd intended to catch something more entertaining than the weather report before turning in for the night.

The volume on the detective series had been muted, though.

They hadn't talked about it, but there had been no question that he would stay again that night. The negligible melt that afternoon had started refreezing the lower the sun had sunk and, last they'd heard, it was taking forever to get anywhere on the roads. Those that were open, anyway.

That was why he'd followed the Otts home in his monster of a truck, because they'd made the drive on balding tires, and dropped off the Shumways since it was dark by then and they'd all walked earlier.

His breathing was deep and even as she picked up the television's remote and turned off the set.

As exhausted as she suspected he was, she didn't want to wake him. She shouldn't stand there thinking about what a beautiful man he was, either. Or how kind and generous he truly seemed to be even when he didn't want her getting too close. There was something terribly intimate about watching him sleep. Something that might almost have felt intrusive had she allowed herself to remain there any longer.

She lifted the soft throw blanket from the arm of the chair, moved back to lift it over him. Smiling a little at his freshly shaved face, she eased the covering over him. When he didn't move, she let out the breath she hadn't even realized she'd been holding and carefully lifted her hand to his head.

Her fingers had just skimmed the barely damp hair he'd combed back from his forehead when she went still. She hadn't been thinking. She'd simply started to do what she always did with Tyler when she tucked him in and brushed back his hair. The gesture was one of simple affection, of taking care.

As oblivious as he remained to her presence, she let her fingers slip over the soft strands, then curled her fingers into her palm as she stepped away and quietly headed for Tyler's room. Since she felt pretty certain Erik would wake up at some point and head for bed himself, she left the tree lights on so he'd be able to see.

It was to that soft light that he awoke a little after midnight, along with a cramp in his neck and an ache in his back that, he realized an hour later, made sleep impossible.

* * *

Rory heard the faint tap on the door, blinked into the shadows. It had been raining for a while now. She'd lain there, listening to the steady sound of it, imagining the drops taking all the ice away, before the new additions to her usual anxieties about what she'd taken on ruined the little exercise. Everything always felt so much more overwhelming alone at night. With Erik there, she'd at least been able to manage the more restful thoughts for a while.

Hearing the tap again, she slipped from the trundle by the night-light she'd moved to the only working outlet in the room and opened the door.

Her glance collided with Erik's solid, shadowed and bare chest. Down the hall, light from her bathroom filtered through her bedroom door, too dim to reveal more than curves and angles and the shadow of his forearm as he gripped his neck.

He stepped back as she stepped out and pulled the door closed behind her.

She hadn't grabbed her robe. Shivering a little, she crossed her arms over the sleep shirt that barely hit her knees. "Are you just now coming up to bed?"

"I came up a while ago. Do you have anything I can rub on my shoulder?"

He still hurt. Pretty badly, she assumed, to have come seeking help. Feeling guilty that he'd hurt himself helping her, feeling worse because his discomfort was bad enough to keep him from sleep when she knew how tired he must be, she headed for her bedroom door and the bathroom right inside.

The light above the vanity cut a swath across the near edge of the queen-size bed that had once occupied her guest room. If the rumpled purple comforter and sheets were any indication, whatever sleep he had managed had been as fitful as hers tended to be. As she turned into the bathroom, she noticed his nearly dry socks, his long-sleeved undershirt and a pair of gray jersey briefs on the towel rack above the heater vent. With the washer and dryer off circuit, he'd had to improvise.

Realizing what he wasn't wearing under his jeans, she quickly opened the medicine cabinet, pulled out a tube and turned to hand it to him.

He'd stopped in the doorway beside her.

The light was infinitely better here. There were no shadows to hide the broad expanse of his beautifully formed chest, the flare of dark hair, the impressive six-pack of his abdomen or the fact that while he'd zipped his pants, he hadn't bothered with the button.

Her glance jerked up. His hand still clasped his shoulder, his fingers kneading the tight muscles there. But it was his cleanly shaven jaw that held her attention. The hard line of it looked tight enough to shatter teeth. The way he arched his back and promptly winced made it evident his shoulder wasn't the only problem.

His frown of discomfort shifted to the pastel tube he took from her.

"What is this?"

"Herbal cream. I bought it when I pulled a hamstring."

"When?"

"It wasn't anything I did here," she assured him, since she had been known to acquire a bump, bruise or strain herself during her move. "It was in a yoga class. It'll help," she insisted, pretty sure he'd had something more industrial strength in mind.

The skepticism carving deep lines in his face remained as he held up the tube and backed into the bedroom to let her pass. A gravelly edge of fatigue roughened his voice. "I appreciate this. Sorry to wake you."

She didn't bother telling him that he hadn't. Or that she

was actually grateful for the reprieve from her sleepless-
ness. All that concerned her now was that he was in pain.

"Where do you need that?"

He'd moved to the foot of her bed, away from the narrow shaft of light spilling across the bedding at the corner. Her bare feet soundless on the carpet, she stopped
three feet away.

"By my right shoulder blade."

He wouldn't be able to reach there. Not very well, anyway, as stiff as he appeared to be.

"Do you want me to do it?"

He didn't look as if he thought that a very good idea.
"I'll manage."

"You're sure?"

"Yeah. I've got it," he insisted, only to wince again the
instant he moved his hand in that direction.

Not allowing herself to overthink the situation, she took
back the tube. Twisting off the cap, she squeezed a hefty
dab of the white cream onto her fingertips and handed the
tube back to him.

"You have no business calling me stubborn, you know
that?" With him filling the space in front of her, she added,
"Turn around," and after a second's hesitation on his part
found herself faced with his broad and sculpted back.

In the filtered light, the view of him half naked was no
less unnerving, but at least he couldn't see how hard she
swallowed before she reached up and spread the cream between his shoulder blade and the long indentation of his
spine. His skin felt as smooth and hard as granite when
her fingers slipped upward.

Traces of rosemary and mint mingled with the scents
of soap, shampoo and warm, disturbing male.

Silence didn't seem like a good idea.

"Why is it that when I came literally a split second from
wounding you, you said I wasn't even close? You actually

did hurt yourself," she pointed out, rubbing the cream over a knot the size of an egg, "and your 'almost' is two hours."

He lowered his head, gave a small groan with the movement.

"It had to do with circumstances."

She was about to tell him he'd have to do better than that when he sucked in a breath.

She went still. "Did I push too hard?" she asked instead.

His breath leaked out, the tightness in his back audible in his voice. "In a good way."

She'd smoothed her fingers alongside the wide curve of his shoulder blade, the long muscle there as unyielding as the bone beside it. Repeating the motion, keeping the same pressure, she felt his broad back rise as he drew another deep breath, then slowly released it.

What she was doing felt good to him. So she did it again, slower this time. It felt good to her, too, she realized, easing her motions even more. Though she'd tended to fight his efforts, he had been taking care of her in one form or another since the day they'd met. As little as there seemed to be for her to do for him in return, as little as he seemed to want from her beyond what centered on their professional relationship, the least she could do was take care of him now.

"What about the other side? Is it sore?"

"Not as bad."

Meaning it hurt there, too.

Reaching around him, she held out her hand. "I need more cream."

"You don't have to do this," he told her, but even as he spoke, he uncapped the tube and squeezed the analgesic onto her fingers.

"You hurt yourself helping me," she pointed out. "So, yeah, I do." As tall as he was, her elbows were even with her eyes as she raised her arms to work on the other side.

He seemed to realize how far she had to reach.

The bed was right there. "So it's guilt motivating you," he concluded, and sank to the nearest corner. He straddled it, his legs planted wide.

She sat down a little behind him. With one leg tucked under her, the other dangling over the foot of the mattress, she rested her hands on his shoulders to knead the knots with her thumbs.

"Must be," she conceded as he lowered his head again. "Especially since I know this isn't how you'd planned to spend your weekend."

She'd thought before that there were reasons she needed to keep her guard in place with this man. She just hadn't bothered recalling them at the time. With the feel of his big body relaxing beneath her hands, her palms tingling as much from the feel of him as from friction and herbs, it seemed wise to recall those points now.

Reminding herself of the subtle but definite distance he'd put between them last night helped her remember why that need was there. Recalling her comment to the girls about his dates helped, too. There were other reasons, she knew. Even more compelling ones. But for the moment, the last one served her purpose perfectly.

"I'm sorry you missed your party."

"Everybody missed it."

That would be true, she thought, now working her fingers up the cords at the back of his neck. "I'm sure your date was disappointed."

For a moment Erik said nothing. Her fingers were making slow little circles at the base of his skull, reversing their motion to follow the rigid cords to where they met the equally taut muscles in his shoulders.

"I didn't have a date," he finally muttered.

She kept moving down, past the sore spot on the right,

but before he could wish she'd stayed there, she'd continued lower, working her magic along the sides of his spine.

What she was doing felt like pure paradise. She had wonderful hands. Soft. Surprisingly strong. Yet incredibly gentle as she lightened her touch to soothe away the worst of the soreness, then gradually increased the pressure again.

He'd felt a different sort of gentleness in her touch before. He'd thought he'd been dreaming, that he'd only imagined her touching him with even more tenderness—until he'd opened his eyes to see her turning away. The brush of her fingers over his forehead had brought something he couldn't remember ever experiencing from a woman's touch. A feeling of ease, of comfort.

There had been a disturbing contentment to the feeling that didn't coincide at all with the direction his thoughts headed now, but something in him craved that kind of caring. Something undeniable and essential and that should have felt far more threatening than it did with the feel of her small hands unhurriedly working over his back.

The ache running from his neck to the bottom of his ribs had started to ease, the tightness there no longer threatening another spasm. An entirely different sort of tension replaced it as her fingers methodically moved over his skin, massaging toward the base of his spine.

His breath slithered out when she stopped well above the waistband of his jeans. Still, the thought of her dipping her hand lower had every other muscle in his body going taut.

"I thought you might be taking the woman you'd gone out with before," she said into the quiet. "Is she someone you've been with a long time?"

There was nothing deliberately sensual about her touch as she worked her way back up. Nothing provocative in the quiet tones of her voice. Yet the question added a certain strain to his own.

"I haven't been with anyone in a long time, Rory."

Her hands had reached his shoulders. Feeling her go still at the status of his sex life, or maybe the fact that he'd so frankly admitted it, he turned as he spoke, catching her wrist as her hand fell.

"Why the questions?"

Beneath his grip, her pulse jumped.

Rory wasn't sure how to answer. She hadn't expected him to tell her how long it had been since he'd slept with a woman. That hadn't been what she was asking. Or maybe it had been and she just hadn't let herself acknowledge her need to know. The queries had started out simply as a defense against the undeniable emotional pull she felt toward him. She hadn't allowed herself to consider why his being in a relationship with someone should even matter to her. But it had. And he wasn't. And all she could do now was scramble for an explanation that wouldn't betray how very much he already mattered to her. And he did, in ways she was only beginning to comprehend.

"I guess I wanted to know if you were involved with anyone." She lifted her shoulder in a shrug. "Just curious, you know?"

In the pale light, she looked impossibly young to him. Incredibly tempting. Mostly, she looked much as she had last night. Far more vulnerable than she wanted to be, and trying hard for a little bravado.

He saw weariness in her guileless features. He'd heard that same drained quality in her admission. It was almost as if as late as it was, as long as the day had been, she was simply too tired to keep the bravado in place.

"I'm not," he assured her. "I haven't been involved with anyone in years." Involvement implied an attachment he'd avoided for the better part of a decade. A need to be there for someone. A need to let that someone count on him to be there for her. A need to know she'd be there for him.

He'd had absolutely no interest in that sort of commitment. Until now.

"Just curious, huh?"

"A little."

If she'd been trying for nonchalance, she failed miserably.

"You know, Rory," he murmured, self-preservation fighting the need to tug her toward him. "Now would probably be a good time for me to let you get back to bed."

"Probably," she agreed softly. "But I think I'll just go downstairs and read for a while. Seems like a good night to tackle the business plan." She lifted her chin, gave him a tiny smile. "I tried, but I can't sleep."

The simple admission pulled at him, the helplessness in it, the weary frustration of trying to escape what kept a person from rest. What got him, though, was the loneliness she tried to hide with the quick duck of her head.

She'd made no attempt to reclaim her hand, and he couldn't quite make himself let go. Unable to shake the thought of how alone she'd seemed cuddling her son on the boy's bed that morning, realizing how she undoubtedly spent many of her nights, he put self-preservation on hold.

"So what kept you awake? Old worries?" he asked, because he knew how long she'd struggled with them. "Or new ones?"

"Both."

"Today probably didn't help."

He probably hadn't helped. He just wasn't sure how else he could have accomplished what they'd both needed for her to know. Yet while he'd been busy making sure she was aware of everything that needed to be done around the place to keep it up and how to take care of the problems she could expect, the weight of even more responsibility had piled on her shoulders.

"Today was actually a good day." He and Tyler weren't

the only ones who'd thought so. "The worry part is just always there. It's okay during the day when I'm busy, but at night…"

"You can't shut it off," he concluded for her.

"I managed for a few minutes tonight. But then it all came right back."

"What was it about tonight that helped?"

She lifted her glance.

"You," Rory said quietly. Of everything he had done for her in the past two days, everything he'd done in the weeks before, what he had done since yesterday had mattered to her the most. "You being here."

Especially tonight, she thought. Tonight, for a while, anyway, because of him she'd been able to shut everything out and concentrate on nothing but the soothing sounds of the rain still pattering on the roof. Because he was there, because he had her back, because he had everything under control, for the first time in well over a year she'd had a day when she hadn't had to make every decision on her own. She hadn't had to worry about how she would get a tree home for her son, or get one out of her driveway. Or remove the one that had blocked the street. Because of him, they had heat and lights. And for that day, anyway, she hadn't had to handle everything thrown at her alone.

Erik brushed the back of her hand with his thumb, conscious of the small weight of it where he held it on his thigh. The thought that he had somehow given her some measure of relief had just made it that much harder to let her go. Not until she was ready, anyway.

"Do you want to go downstairs?" he asked.

She met his eyes, looked away with a small shake of her head. "Not really."

"Do you want to go back to Tyler's room?"

Another small shake. "Not yet."

"Are you cold?"

"A little."

He knew what she needed even before he asked. He asked anyway. "Could you use a pair of arms?"

That was all he was offering. Just to hold her. This wasn't about wanting her between her sheets. Heaven knew it wasn't about self-protection. It was about giving her a break.

She didn't have to say a word for him to know that his arms were exactly what she needed. But her quiet "Please" was all it took for him to rise and turn out the bathroom light. The night-light now filtering through the doorway cast the room in shadows.

"Come here," he said, and tugged her to her feet.

Leading her to the side of the bed, he pulled the comforter over the sheets and propped both pillows against the headboard. He didn't want her in the bed, just on it.

The distinction seemed just as clear to her as she snagged the wadded throw blanket from the foot of the bed and sat against the far pillow, hugging her arms around her knees when the mattress sank beneath his weight. With his back against his pillow he drew the throw over them both and pulled her knees toward him, his arm low around her back, his hand at the curve of her waist.

"How's this?" he asked, coaxing her head to his shoulder.

He felt her sigh, the long, quiet leak of air leaving her nearly limp against the side of his body.

For a moment, Rory couldn't say a word. She could barely believe she was actually where she had so badly wanted to be. It didn't matter that his jeans felt rough against her bare calf, or that the contrast of his heat and the cool air against the back of her neck made her shiver. She could hear the heavy beat of his heart beneath her ear, could feel it where her hand rested on his hard, bare chest. It didn't even matter that for some strange reason her throat had suddenly gone raw, making her quiet "Good" sound a little tight.

His chin brushed the top of her head as he settled himself more comfortably.

"Good," he echoed, slowly skimming his hand over her upper arm.

She swallowed, then made herself take a deep, even breath. "Erik?" she finally said.

"Yeah?"

"Thank you."

A tired smile entered his voice. "For holding you?" It was hardly a hardship, he thought. She felt wonderful curled up against him. Small, feminine, trusting. The only difficult part was trying not to think of how curvy she truly was with his hand at the dip of her waist, inches from the curve of her hip.

Wanting distraction, he smoothed his hand back up her arm. The herbal scent of her hair teased him, filling his lungs every time he breathed.

"For all of it. But yes." Her tone grew muffled. "For this, too."

He wasn't sure what all she meant. It could have been anything. He just forgot to wonder what might have meant so much to her when he caught the hitch in her voice.

He started to tip up her chin.

She wouldn't let him. Instead, he cupped his hand to the side of her face, brushed it with his thumb and caught the moisture gathered at the corner of her eye.

His heart gave a strange little squeeze. "Hey." *Don't do that,* he thought. He could handle anything but tears. "What's wrong?"

"Nothing. Honest," she insisted, keeping her head right where it was. "Absolutely nothing is wrong." She tried to draw a deep breath, made it halfway before it caught. Swallowing, she tried again. "For the first time in…forever," she said, because that was how it felt, "right now there really isn't a thing wrong."

Which was what had brought the sting behind her eyelids, she realized. Not because of sadness, fear or grief. But because of an amazing, unfamiliar and totally unexpected sense of relief. She knew it wouldn't last long. That it couldn't. It was just for now. While he held her. So just for now, relief was what she felt.

"Then why tears?"

Because of what you let me feel, she thought. "Because I'm tired," was easier to admit to him.

She felt his lips against the top of her head. "Then go to sleep."

"I don't want to."

The slow shake of her head brushed her hair against his chest. Letting his fingers sift through that dark silk, he gave a small chuckle. "Why not?"

"Because I don't want to miss you holding me."

It had to be the hour, the lateness of it, the need for sleep himself. Or maybe it was his need to let her know he'd be there for her in the morning if she'd just let herself rest, but he didn't question what he did as he slipped down, bringing her with him.

His lips grazed the spot on her cheek where they'd literally bumped heads that morning. "You shouldn't say things like that."

Turning her face to him, she whispered, "Why not?"

He'd been about to tell her to go to sleep, that he wasn't going anywhere. But with her sweet breath filling his lungs, the feel of her supple little body playing pure havoc with his intention, he leaned closer.

"Because you'll make me forget why I shouldn't do this," he murmured, and brushed his mouth over hers.

Once.

Again.

"Or this." He carried that gentle caress between her eyebrows, to the space where the twin lines formed when she was worried.

He cupped his hand at the side of her face.

"Or this."

The admission vibrated against her mouth a faint second before he increased the pressure ever so slightly. His lips were firm, cool and far softer than anything that looked so hard had a right to be, but it was the feel of him tipping her head to gain the access he wanted that had her reaching for him herself.

Relief gave way to something infinitely less soothing. It barely occurred to her that this was exactly what she *hadn't* wanted when she found herself opening to him, flowing toward him, kissing him back. She'd known what she would feel if she ever got this close to him again. And she'd been right. She felt everything she had when he'd kissed her before: that deep, awful longing, the yearning to simply sink into his compelling strength, his incredible gentleness, and have him take away the ache in her chest. To relieve the void, the emptiness. Only now with her fingers curling around his biceps and his hand slipping to the small of her back, pulling her closer, the hollowness inside her seemed to be receding, and the emptiness felt more like…need.

When he lifted his head long moments later, his features had gone as dark as his voice. "I think you'd better remind me."

Her own voice came as a thready whisper. "About what?"

He touched the first of the short line of buttons on her nightshirt. His fingers trailed down, found her soft breasts unrestrained beneath thermal cotton.

His lips hovered over hers. "Why we should stop."

Surrounded by his heat, that warmth gathering low in her belly, her voice went thin. "I don't remember."

She didn't know what he saw in her shadowed face when he lifted his head. Whatever it was caused his body to go beautifully taut before his hand slipped over her hip.

"Me, either. But if you do," he warned, the low tones of his voice sounding half serious, half teasing, "stop me."

She was about to tell him that wasn't going to happen, but he lowered his mouth to hers just then and she almost forgot to breathe.

There was no demand in his kiss. Just an invitation to a heady exploration that was deep, deliberate and debilitatingly thorough.

Winding her arms around his neck, she kissed him back just a little more urgently. With him, because of him, she finally felt something other than alone and uncertain, or the need to be strong.

She'd been so frightened by her doubts, so afraid that what she'd thought had been real in her marriage hadn't been at all. If she'd been so wrong about all of it, that meant she couldn't trust her judgment about anything, or anyone, else. But he'd helped her see that she hadn't been wrong about what had mattered most. And more important than anything else he'd taught her, he was teaching her to trust in herself.

She could love him for that alone.

The thought had her clinging a little more tightly, kissing him a little more fiercely. It hurt to know how much of herself she'd let others take away from her. But he was taking that pain away, too, allowing parts of her to come back, allowing feelings she hadn't realized she still possessed to finally surface. For the life of her she had no idea why those thoughts made the back of her eyelids start to burn again. She just knew that at that moment, nothing mattered to her so much as the sense of reprieve she was only now beginning to feel. And the fact that it was he who had finally allowed it.

Erik caught her small moan as she pressed closer. Or maybe the needy little sound had been his own. There wasn't a cell in his body that wasn't aware of how beautifully female she was, and of how badly he wanted her beneath him. To him, she was perfect. Small, supple and infinitely softer than his harder, rougher angles and planes.

He would have just held her if that had been what she'd wanted. It would have about killed him, but he'd have done it. Yet, incredibly, she seemed to hunger for the feel of him as much as he ached for her.

Stretched out beside her, he drew his hand over the nightshirt covering her belly, letting it drift upward, pulling soft cotton away with it. He kissed her slowly, tracing her soft curves, allowing himself the sweet torture of finally knowing the silken feel of her body, the honeyed taste of her skin. He didn't know what to make of the tears he tasted again at the corners of her eyes when he kissed her there, or the almost desperate way she whispered, "No," when he started to pull back to make sure she was all right. Slipping her fingers through his hair, she drew him back to her, meeting him in a kiss that nearly rocked him to his core.

Gritting his teeth against the need she created, he skimmed the bit of silk she wore down her long legs. It landed somewhere beside the bed, along with his jeans.

He'd left his billfold on her nightstand. Some miracle of common sense made him drag himself from her long enough to fumble for the small packet inside. He'd barely rolled their protection over himself when she curled into him, seeking him as he sought her.

The intimacy of gentle exploration had created its own tormenting heat. What they created as they moved together now, his name a whisper on her lips, had him thinking he'd never be able to get enough of her before that heat turned white-hot and he was barely thinking at all.

Chapter Ten

Rory burrowed deeper under her comforter. A delicious lethargy pulled at her, coaxing her back toward sleep. But she heard voices. Male ones. One sweet, the other deep.

Sleep was suddenly the last thing on her mind.

Tyler was awake. Erik was with him. Through the two-inch-wide gap he'd left between the door and the jamb, she could see the light from Tyler's bathroom faintly illuminating the hall. The gap in the curtains next to the bed revealed a thin sliver of gray.

It was daylight. That meant it was somewhere after seven-thirty. She couldn't remember the last time she'd slept that late.

She threw off the covers. Nearly tripping over her night-shirt, she snatched it up and moved to the door. They were just disappearing down the stairs, Tyler in his pj's, Erik in his undershirt and jeans. From the conversation, it sounded as though they were discussing breakfast. Specifically, which one of them got to slice the bananas.

Minutes later, thoughts of how she'd practically fallen apart in Erik's arms adding to the anxiety of wanting to hurry, she'd pulled herself together enough—in the physical sense, anyway—to head into the hall herself.

Slipping a blue corduroy shirt over a cotton turtleneck and yoga pants, she could hear her little guy as she reached the first step.

"Can I help you work today?" he asked. "An' can you help put my train around the tree?"

The low tones of Erik's voice drifted up the stairway. "I think all I'm going to do out there this morning is check the gutters. It's too dangerous for you to help."

"Why?"

"Because it's a long way up there."

"How come you need to check 'em?"

"Because I need to see if the weight of the ice pulled them from their brackets."

"Why?"

She heard a deep, indulgent chuckle. "Because if they're not lined up right, the rain will pour straight off the roof instead of draining to the downspouts and get you and your mom all wet."

Her foot hit the bottom step just as she heard a pondered little "Oh."

Tyler hesitated. "Can we do the train after, then?"

Across the entry, she could see Tyler sitting in front of the lit tree, the blanket she'd covered Erik with last night wrapped around his shoulders. Expectation beamed from his little profile.

Erik sat on the edge of the hearth, his gray undershirt stretched across his broad shoulders as he closed the glass doors on the growing fire.

"I'll have to see how it goes, but I don't know that I'll have time for that, Ty." He picked a stray bit of bark from the stone beside him, tossed it onto the logs in the curved wood basket. "Now that the rain's melted the ice, I need to finish here, then get to my own place."

"You're going home?"

There was no mistaking her son's disappointment at that bit of news. She heard it in his small voice, could practically feel it in him as she watched Erik look up at her an instant before Tyler turned and looked up himself.

Shoving her fingers through her hair, partially undoing what she'd managed to arrange with a few random strokes of a brush, she found it infinitely easier to meet Tyler's sad little face.

"Good morning, sweetie," she murmured, bending to give him a hug. "How did you sleep?"

"Good," came his usual, though decidedly disheartened, reply.

She nudged back his hair, wanting to ease away his sudden seriousness. What Erik had done hadn't been deliberate. There had been nothing but kindness in his voice as he'd explained why he wouldn't be staying. But the painful proof of how her little boy could come to rely on him, could even come to love him, only added to the confusion of wants and uncertainties tearing at her as she kissed the soft, tousled hair at the crown of his head.

"I'll help you with your train later, okay?"

"'Kay," he reluctantly replied.

"So, what's up down here?" she asked him and, as casually as she could, straightened to meet the caution in Erik's smile.

He rose himself, all six feet plus of him, and came to a stop in front of her.

His gray gaze skimmed her face. Slowly assessing. Unapologetically intimate. "The plan so far was to turn on the tree, then build a fire." His eyes held hers. "Then what, Ty?" he asked, since the child hadn't answered his mom.

"Breakfast," came the slightly more enthused reply. "And cartoons?" he added hopefully from below them.

"And coffee?" Erik asked with that disarming arch of his eyebrow.

"Definitely coffee," she agreed.

Grabbing the remote, she punched in the channel she usually only let Tyler watch as a treat. With him on his way to the sofa with his blanket, she headed for the kitchen, Erik's footfalls behind her matching every heavy thud of her heart.

She pulled the carafe from the coffeemaker, turned to see him watching her from beside the sink.

Holding the carafe under the faucet, she turned the water on.

"Why didn't you wake me?" she asked, her hushed voice muffled further by the sound of running water.

"Because I was already awake. When I heard him in the bathroom, I figured he'd come looking for you, so I intercepted him before he could. I thought you might not want him to find us in bed together.

"Besides," he added quietly, "you were out. You barely moved when I pulled my arm from under you."

The reminder of how she'd fallen asleep tucked against his side, their bare limbs tangled, had heat rising in her cheeks.

"I can't believe I didn't hear him." It was so unlike her not to hear her son. "I never sleep that hard." Except with this man beside her, she obviously had.

"Thank you for the rescue," she all but whispered.

He turned off the water for her. With Tyler hidden by the sofa, he lifted his hand, curved his fingers at the side of her neck.

"I'm going to leave in a while," he told her, brushing his thumb over the lobe of her ear. "Pax said everything was okay at the boatworks yesterday, but I have some things I need to do. There's something here I want to check first, though. Is there anything you can think of that you need me to do before I go?"

In the past eight hours, his touch had become as exciting to her as it was calming, as disturbing as it was comforting. He had reawakened her heart and her senses and she'd never felt as confused as she did now, standing there desperately wanting him to pull her to him and hoping he wouldn't.

He'd said he needed to leave, that he had things he needed to do. He'd already talked with Pax, asked about the condition of their properties, their business. She'd heard him tell Tyler that he needed to check on his own place. She knew his entire life was on the other side of the sound. In her need for the temporary escape he'd offered, she'd forgotten that for a few critical hours last night.

"You don't need to check my gutters, Erik."

"Yeah, I do," he said, thinking of her lovely, long limbs and how perfect they'd felt wrapped around him. He'd really prefer that none of them got broken. "It'll save you having to do it yourself."

"I'd have to do it if you weren't here."

The hint of defensiveness in her tone sounded all too familiar.

"But I'm here now," he pointed out, looking a little more closely to see the unease he'd missed in her moments ago.

"You can just tell me what I'm supposed to look for. I'll need to know, anyway."

Caution curled through him. "It's raining out there."

"So I'll wait until it stops."

"That could be June."

He had a point. She just wasn't prepared to concede it. "Is there a particular bracket you noticed?"

There was. The one at the front of the garage that would keep water from pouring over her and Tyler when they came and went from the car. He'd noticed it yesterday and had meant to walk around the garage and the main building to see if any other gaps were visible. But this wasn't about a bracket. It wasn't about a gutter. From the uncertainty underlying her quiet defensiveness, he'd bet his business this wasn't about anything but what had happened between them last night.

Not totally sure what he felt about it himself, not sure what to do about any of it with Tyler wandering over in search of cereal, Erik decided it best to just go do what he'd planned to do anyway.

"I'm going to get the ladder from the basement. I'll be back when the coffee's ready."

It took eight minutes to brew a full pot of coffee. It was another ten before she heard the rattle of the ladder being propped against the wall in the mudroom and the faint squeak of the door to the kitchen when it opened.

Tyler had just handed her his empty bowl and was on his way past the island to go get dressed when she heard him tell Erik he'd be right back.

"Take your time, sport." Ruffling the boy's hair as he passed, Erik looked to where she again stood at the sink.

Still holding the bowl, she watched his easy smile fade to something less definable as he pushed back the navy Merrick & Sullivan ball cap he'd taken from his truck. It looked as if he'd shaken the rain from his cap and swiped what he could from his leather jacket. Beneath it, the charcoal pullover he'd pulled on before he'd gone out was dry, but the darker spots on the thighs of his jeans and the hems looked damp.

"You have two broken brackets," he told her, conscious of Tyler still moving up the stairs. "I'll pick up new ones and be back with them in the morning. I leave for my folks' house in San Diego tomorrow afternoon, so that's the only chance I'll have."

She set the bowl in the sink, picked up the mug she'd taken out for him and poured him his coffee.

Tomorrow was Christmas Eve.

She held the heavy mug out to him.

"You know, Erik," she said as he took it, "you really don't need to come all the way over here to fix those brackets."

The mug settled on the counter beside her.

"I know I don't. And I don't need you telling me that," he insisted, and skimmed her cheek with his knuckles.

The small contact compounded the anxiety knotting behind her breastbone.

Taking a small step back, needing to break his touch as much as the hold he'd gained on her heart, her voice dropped to an agonized whisper. "I can't do this."

Even as his hand fell, his shoulders rose with a slow, deep breath. His hard, handsome features were suddenly impossible to read.

"By 'this' you mean the sex."

"No. Yes." Shaking her head, she shoved her fingers through her hair. "I mean, it's not just that. Making love with you was amazing," she admitted, because it had been. "It's that I can't let myself feel what I'm starting to feel for you." What she already did feel, she thought, and which totally terrified her. "I can't let myself count on you to do things for me. Or for you to be around to talk to. Or for you to be here. If I do, it would be too easy to rely on you even more."

Apparently nothing she'd said explained why she was withdrawing from him. If anything, Erik just looked a little mystified. She figured that was because of what she'd admitted about the sex part. But then, she always had had a problem filtering what she said to him.

His eyes narrowed on hers. "Why not?"

Crossing her arms over the knot in her stomach, her voice dropped another notch. "Because I'm not going to set myself up to lose something I don't even have. It doesn't make sense to do that," she admitted, not sure she was making sense to him. "I can't do that to myself. And I definitely can't do it to my son. It will only hurt Tyler if I let him grow any more attached to you than he already is, Erik. I know people will come and go from his life. People already have, but I've never seen him take to anyone the way he has to you." She'd done a lousy job of protecting herself. That failing would not keep her from protecting her son. "Since the arrangement between us is temporary anyway, it just seems best to back away and keep business…business."

Her heart hurt. Rubbing the awful ache with her fingertips, she watched his jaw tighten as he stepped back.

Erik wasn't at all sure what he felt at that moment. He wasn't even sure what he felt for this woman, beyond an undeniable physical need and a sense of protectiveness he wasn't familiar with at all. All he knew for certain was that they had stepped over a line she clearly had not been prepared to cross.

Recriminations piled up like cars in a train wreck. He'd known all along that it would be a mistake to get involved with her. He'd known from the moment he'd met her that she was dealing with far more than he'd gone through when his marriage had ended. What he didn't understand was how he could have forgotten that his sole goal in agreeing to help her was to have no reason to return to this place once his obligation to Cornelia had been satisfied.

The fact that he hadn't considered any of that last night had his own defenses slamming into place. Having done enough damage already, he wasn't about to complicate their relationship any further. Or let her push him any farther away.

"Just answer one question for me."

"If I can."

"Last night. The tears. Were they because you were thinking of Curt?"

He figured he had to be some sort of masochist for wanting to know if that was what really had been going on with her while they'd been making love. No man wanted to think a woman had another man on her mind while he had her in his arms. Still, for some reason he couldn't begin to explain, he needed to know.

For a moment, Rory said nothing. Partly because the question caught her so off guard. Partly because it was only now that she realized her only thought last night about the man she'd married was how Erik had lessened the void he'd left.

She couldn't begin to explain everything she'd felt last night. Or what she felt now because of his question.

It seemed easiest to just go to the heart of what he really wanted to know.

"The only person in that bed with me was you, Erik."

He heard something a little raw in her quiet reply, something that made her look as if he'd just totally exposed how absorbed she'd been in only him—which was no doubt why she stood there with her arms crossed so protectively and her eyes begging him to go.

He could hear Tyler racing down the stairs.

"We're supposed to meet with Phil after the first of the year." He spoke the reminder quietly, as conscious of the child coming toward them as he was of the definite need for distance. "I don't remember the date, but I'll get it from her. We can figure out our work schedule from there."

"Can we do the train now?"

Tyler had stopped at the end of the island, his expectant glance darting from one adult to the other. He'd pulled on pants and a green thermal shirt and held a red flannel shirt in his fist.

"I have to go now," Erik told the grinning little boy. "But I heard your mom say she'd help you."

His smile fell. "You have to go?"

"Yeah, bud. I do." Unprepared for how the child's disappointment affected him, not sure what to make of the strange hollow in his chest, he tousled his sandy hair one last time, gave him a smile and let himself out through the store.

"Erik! I was just going to call you!"

Erik turned from where he was locking the front door of Merrick & Sullivan's client office. Phil had just emerged from the silver Mercedes parked behind the construction Dumpster in front of the building next door. The tails of her white scarf flew in the breeze as she hurried around to the sidewalk. "Do you have a minute?"

He didn't feel particularly sociable. What he did feel was defensive, edgy and impatient to be on his way. Still, he made himself smile. "Sure," he called back, pocketing his keys. Hunching his shoulders against the chill, he headed to where she'd stopped by Cornelia's building's front door. "What's up?"

"Let's get out of the cold. I'll make us some coffee."

"A minute is really all I have, Phil. I'm leaving to see my folks in a couple of hours."

"Oh. Well, then." Hitching her bag higher on her shoulder, she crossed her arms over her furry white coat. Beneath her matching hat, her eyes smiled through the lenses of her bookish, horn-rimmed glasses. "Rory said you were there when I called the other day. The power being out everywhere had us concerned about her and her son," she explained, "but some neighbors were visiting so I knew we didn't have to worry. We didn't have a chance to really talk, though. Is everything all right with the property?"

Realizing she was checking up on Cornelia's investment

threatened to turn his mood even more restive. "There are a few downed trees and a loose gutter, but no structural damage," he told her, thinking that was about all she'd be interested in. "I heard the power was restored a while ago."

He'd learned that from Ed, who'd done as Erik had asked him to do and called when the area had gone back on the grid. Since he'd told his old friend about Rory's unfamiliarity with the generator when he'd borrowed his saw, Ed hadn't questioned his concern about wanting to make sure there were no other glitches.

Erik hadn't let himself question his concern, either. He'd tried hard to keep thoughts of her and Tyler to a minimum.

"That's good to know. Just one other thing, then, and I'll let you go." She flashed him a smile as she crossed her arms tighter, anxious to get out of the wind. "I take it the two of you were working when the storm hit," she said quickly, making it apparent that Rory hadn't mentioned his insistence about helping with their Christmas tree. "So, how do you think she'll do? Or is it too soon to tell?"

He wanted to say she'd do just fine. She certainly didn't lack for aptitude or the determination to succeed. She even had the incentive of keeping a roof over her son's head pushing her. It would be a challenge doing it on her own, but she'd make a living there. With the connections she was establishing, she'd probably even make a life.

He brushed past the thought that she'd be making that life without him. He had a life of his own right where he was. He had work he loved, a great business, good friends. He had money and the freedom to come and go pretty much as he pleased. His obligation to the woman messing with his carefully constructed status quo ended once they had the business established. Once it was, he could walk away and never go back there again.

"Is there a problem, Erik?"

"No. No," he repeated, waiting for the quick shutdown

of feeling that normally reinforced his last thought. "I'll make it work."

I will. Not *we*.

Phil apparently heard the distinction.

"Isn't she cooperating?"

Not when she was giving him grief about helping her, he thought.

"She just needs a break right now," he decided to say. "With her little boy and the holidays, it just seemed like a good thing to do."

"Was that your idea?"

Initially, it had been. For the business part, anyway.

"The decision was mutual."

"So when do you meet again?"

"Whenever we're scheduled to be here."

"That will be the fifth."

"That soon?"

"At two," she added, and cocked her head. "Do we need to meet before then? We certainly can, if there's ever a problem," she hurried on, having caught his lack of enthusiasm for the meeting. "Part of what we do for our ladies and their mentors is help them work through challenges. Differences of opinion can arise over anything from creative priorities to scheduling—"

"It's nothing like that."

"May I ask what it is?"

It was clearly too late to deny a problem even existed. But all he would admit was, "It's complicated."

"I see." Adjusting the frame of her glasses, she peered at him with interest. "Do you have a solution to the problem?"

He wasn't sure there was one. Not for the two of them. "Not yet."

"Can you work together?"

"Yeah. Sure. There's always email and the telephone." He'd given his word. He'd hold up his end of the deal. For his grandparents. For her. "She wants the business to work. That's what I want, too."

She considered him for a moment, her head tipped thoughtfully, the fine fibers of her white hat fluttering. "You know, Erik, when I gave Rory the address of your grandparents' property, I suggested she look for the possibilities. We knew what she would see when she got there, and that it would be nothing she could have imagined she would want.

"What she'd been looking for was a small home for herself and her son," she confided, "but her needs changed when she lost her job. To see the potential in that property, she had to let go of a mind-set that focused on what she had been looking for and what she now needed. To find the solution to your problem, maybe you should look at the possibilities, too."

She smiled then, gave a little wave of her white-gloved hand. Crystals shimmered on its cuff. "I've kept you long enough," she said. "You have a plane to catch. And I need to get inside before I freeze. Have a safe trip. And merry Christmas."

He thanked her. Added a quick "You, too" and started to turn away.

As he did, his glance caught on the gold plaque engraved with three letters above their doorbell. He'd been curious about it ever since it had gone up last week.

"Hey, Phil," he called, catching her unlocking the door. "What does FGI stand for?"

"It's who we are," she called back. "Fairy Godmothers, Incorporated."

His forehead furrowed. As near as he'd been able to figure out, he'd thought they were in some sort of mortgage business. "Fairy Godmothers? Don't they have something to do with pumpkins?"

"And helping dreams come true." With a charming smile, she disappeared inside.

Mentally shaking his head, he strode toward his truck at the curb in front of his office. He had no idea how anyone over the age of ten could possibly believe in fairy tales, happily ever afters or that other impossibility that Rory had once imagined, Christmas magic. As for dreams, they died by the thousands every day. Reality simply wore them down, if it didn't kill them outright. He knew. He'd spent years in the emotional limbo that remained after his vision of his future had turned to ash. But he'd glimpsed those dreams again, and what Phil had said about possibilities now gave him pause.

She'd said Rory had to let go of a mind-set that focused on what she had been looking for and what she needed now. She'd had to be open-minded enough to see what would be possible living in a place she'd have never considered, rather than writing it off as not what she'd had in mind.

He certainly hadn't considered any sort of personal relationship with her when they'd first met. But one had evolved in spite of him. To see the possibilities in it, he'd need to get past the defenses he'd spent years honing before he could be open to what those possibilities were.

Part of the problem there was that he had no desire to give her a chance to push him any farther away.

The other part would be getting Rory to see past whatever it was holding her back from him to see their potential, too.

Rory had hoped for snow. For Tyler's sake, because that was what he'd said he wanted for Christmas. But Christmas morning had dawned with a gray sky that promised little beyond more rain.

Until a week ago, every other time she'd asked him what he wanted Santa to bring, all he'd wanted was a big tree.

The day after Erik had left, he'd told her he'd changed his mind. Since he already had the tree, what he wanted Santa to bring was Erik.

She'd explained that Erik would be with his parents for Christmas, so Santa wouldn't be able to bring him. Though decidedly let down by that bit of news, he'd decided later that he wanted snow.

All he seemed to want as far as a gift was concerned were things beyond her power to give him.

Without any sort of hint for something that Santa could bring down the chimney, she, being Santa's helper, had left him a mini kick scooter that he could ride between the counters in the store while she worked to get it ready. He'd been excited when he'd come downstairs a couple of hours ago to see it by the tree. He'd been tickled to see that Santa had eaten all but a few crumbs of the cookies they'd left out for him, and awed and delighted by the small tuft of faux-fur trim that appeared to have snagged on one of the fireplace stones when the jolly old guy had departed.

What had truly thrilled him, though, had been discovering the present from Erik among the others from her and her parents beneath the lit and glittering branches. It had been delivered yesterday with a note asking her to please put it under the tree for him to find Christmas morning. Except for the "Thanks" he'd scrawled at the bottom, that was all the note had said.

Tyler had declared the huge pop-up book about sailboats his "very favorite" and gone through every page with her while they sat on the sofa.

It had been only two days since Erik had left her standing in the kitchen feeling as if the world was falling out from under her all over again. Two long nights of missing him more than she'd thought humanly possible. The man was a rock. A truly decent guy. And while she suspected he was fiercely loyal to those he cared about, he held back from needing anyone himself—from needing her, anyway—in the way she now knew she needed him. It wasn't about survival. She could survive on her own. It was about the need to share, and he had worked his way into her life and into her heart as if he was simply meant to be there.

That had only happened with one other man.

Too unsettled to stay still any longer, she left Tyler with his book and cleaned up the bright paper wrappings and ribbons from the carpet.

She had no idea how to repair the damage done to their relationship. He was her mentor. He'd become her confidant. His voice had been one of experience and his advice had been invaluable where other situations were concerned. She just didn't know how to ask what she could possibly do to make things right between them when he was part of the problem, even though she'd picked up the phone a dozen times to try. He had no responsibility to her beyond the agreement he'd made with her benefactor, and now even that part of their relationship had been jeopardized.

The two-tone chime of a bell startled her from her painful thoughts. She'd only heard the chime ring twice before: the first morning she'd met Edie, when the woman had stopped by to welcome her to the neighborhood, and two days ago when Talia had brought the twins over to play. Erik had explained that the service bell was used for after-hours deliveries. A few of the locals obviously used it as a doorbell to save themselves from having to walk around back.

Thinking it might be one of the neighbors she and Tyler had delivered Christmas cookies to yesterday, she headed through the store and opened its front door.

No one was there.

Stepping out, the cold breeze tugging at her hair, her

glance caught on a small package on the weathered plank boards.

The little gold box was tied with a red bow.

Now conscious of the dark truck in the parking lot, her heart beating a little too fast, she picked it up.

The neat print on the back of the gold tag read "I want you to find it again."

She knew exactly what *it* was. It meant the inexplicable feeling of magic she'd told Erik she'd once known every Christmas. The feeling of everything being right in her world. He knew it was the feeling she'd wanted her son to know and something she'd given up hope of ever experiencing again herself.

Yet that sense was what she felt now as she lifted the lid on the box to find a glittery little life preserver on a thin gold cord.

She had the feeling he was only letting her know he'd help her stay afloat with the business. And that was huge. But the way he'd done it had her closing the box and holding it with both hands to her heart.

It was only then that she looked to where Erik unfolded his arms and stepped away from his driver's side door.

Gravel crunched beneath his hiking boots as he moved past the bits of storm debris still strewn over the wet grass. Dark plaid flannel hung open over a navy Henley shirt, his broad shoulders looking impossibly wide as he climbed the steps and stopped in front of her.

He hadn't been at all sure what to expect when he'd left the box for her. He'd just wanted her to discover it the way she had the others she'd told him about. They seemed to have appeared out of nowhere, she'd said, so that sense was part of what he'd wanted to give her, even if only for a moment.

He knew he could have just left it for her. But that would have defeated another part of his purpose. He'd needed to see her reaction to his gift so he'd have some idea of what to do next. It was so unlike him not to have a clear plan, but he felt much as he suspected he would setting sail without a compass or preparation. He wasn't totally sure how to get where he wanted to go, or if the waters he'd face would be calm, rough or totally unpredictable.

Encouraged by the way she held his gift, he quietly said, "Merry Christmas."

"Merry Christmas," she echoed, still clutching the little ornament. Caution merged with disbelief. "What are you doing here? I thought you were in San Diego."

"I was. I spent Christmas Eve with my family and caught the first flight out this morning. I don't want to keep you from Tyler. I just wanted you to have that."

Rory watched him nod toward her clutched hands. She could have hugged him for his gift. The reserve carved in his expression held her right where she stood.

Considering the bated relief she felt at his presence, her "Thank you" seemed terribly inadequate. "Do you want to come in? Tyler loves his—"

Erik was already shaking his head. "There's one other thing." More than one, actually, but he wanted them alone right now. "The other day, you said you didn't want to set yourself up to lose something you don't even have. You said it would be a mistake for you to count on me. I understand the need to protect yourself," he insisted. He'd mastered that one in spades himself. "And I get the reasons you don't want Tyler to start believing I'll be around for him. But I'm not all those other people who've let you down, Rory.

"You seem so certain the only way you can create stability for yourself is to keep anyone who could rock your boat at arm's length. But you've rocked mine, too. You already have me," he admitted. "I figure the least we owe each other is a little time to reconsider our positions before we totally blow something that could have a lot of potential."

She looked at him warily, a betraying glint of a smile in her eyes. "You think we have potential?"

"Yeah," he said. "I do."

She'd rocked his boat. The thought made relief harder to suppress. His admission that she already had him made it nearly impossible.

She took a step closer. "If I let myself count on you," she began, already wanting that more than he could possibly know, "what are you offering to reconsider?"

"Are we negotiating?"

"Apparently," she replied, holding his gift even tighter.

She couldn't begin to identify what she felt as the tension left his handsome features. Reprieve, for certain. But something that felt suspiciously like hope had risen right behind it. He didn't want them to close any doors.

Lifting his hand toward her, he curved it to the side of her face.

"In that case," he said, more relieved than he could have imagined when she tipped her cheek toward his palm, "you should know I've already considered how much my hang-ups were getting in the way of possibilities where we were concerned. I've spent years thinking I just wanted to be away from here. But once I moved past thinking about what I'd wanted and considered what I might need, I realized that what I needed was another chance with you.

"You made me realize how much I still want a family. And a home here. It's not just the place," he assured her. It was how she made it feel. Comfortable. Familiar. As if he belonged there. "It's you. And Tyler."

He knew he already had a good life. Until he'd met her, he'd just refused to let it matter that he didn't have anyone to share it with. He'd work or play late so that he was too tired to care that he had no one to come home to who actually cared that he'd had a great day or a bad one, or whom he could care about in return.

"We're good together. If we want to make this work between us, we can. I'm in love with you," he confessed, finally acknowledging what he'd denied to his partner well over a week ago. Pax had somehow known that she was the woman he'd been waiting for, though he hadn't realized he'd been waiting for her at all. "All I'm asking is if you're willing to try."

Rory knew his walls had existed far longer than hers. Yet he'd just put his heart on the line for her. Her own heart feeling full enough to burst, she went up on tiptoe, curved her arms around his neck and hugged him hard.

Folding her to his chest, his hold just as tight, he chuckled against the top of her head. "That's a yes, then?"

"Absolutely."

"Are you okay?"

She nodded against his shoulder. "I'm falling in love with you, too, Erik. I think that's what scared me. I knew the day we met that it could happen, but I wasn't ready for it. It happened so fast."

Drawing a deep breath, she lowered herself to her heels and let her hands slide to his chest. Still holding the little box, she met his eyes. "I think I panicked," she explained.

He brushed back the hair the breeze fluttered across her cheek.

"I know you did." She'd been no more prepared than he'd been to put a name or label on what had seemed to be growing more complicated by the moment. A little apprehension on her part hadn't been surprising at all. He hadn't dealt with it all that fearlessly himself. "We'll take it slow now. Okay? No pressure. No rush. We'll just take our time and stay open to possibilities."

"Possibilities," Rory repeated. "That's what Phil told me I should look for here." She'd only been thinking about the property, though. As Erik smiled into her eyes and drew his hand to the back of her neck, Rory remembered that the woman had also warned her to keep an open mind about him.

"She told me that, too," he told her, and lowered his mouth to hers before she could say another word.

There was relief in his kiss as he pulled her closer, and promise, hunger, possessiveness and need. It was the need she felt most. His, definitely, but her own, too, in the long moments before he lifted his head and eased back far enough to release her hands from where they'd been trapped against his chest.

"What?" he asked, seeing the question in her flushed features.

She looked at the little gold box, lifted off its lid. Suddenly she felt certain the little life preserver didn't represent what she'd thought.

Erik's voice was quiet. "You said there was a time when you could always count on something like that being there for you Christmas morning."

Her smile came easily at the reminder. "I thought this had something to do with the store. Something about keeping it afloat. But it's a lifeline, isn't it?"

"It is," he murmured, touching his lips to her forehead. "I'm just not sure which one of us I thought needed rescuing."

"Erik!"

In a flash of maroon fleece and gray denim, Tyler bolted through the door onto the porch.

"Hey, buddy!"

"You're here!"

"I'm here," Erik agreed, and pulled him between them for a hug.

It was then that Rory felt what Erik had wanted her to glimpse again.

At that moment, all felt truly, completely and utterly right in their little world. That was the magic, and it was the most wonderful gift of all.

As they headed in from the cold, it started to snow.

Epilogue

"Why are we waiting in here, Erik?" Confusion shadowed Rory's smile. "We've said hi to Phil and Cornelia," she pointed out, their purpose at the FGI office accomplished. Or so she'd assumed.

"We'll go in a couple of minutes. This is just some of that year-end stuff I need to take care of."

He'd been busy with work off and on for the past week. That afternoon, though, he was going to show her and Tyler where he built boats.

As if anxious to get business behind him, he tugged her closer to where he stood by a gold filigree chair. "Do you want to spend tomorrow night on my houseboat? Tyler might get a kick out of the fireworks."

Tomorrow was New Year's Eve. "He'd love that. I'd love it," she stressed.

She hadn't seen his place yet, though he had warned her it was small. By land-standards, anyway.

"Then that's what we'll do."

Looking more preoccupied than impatient, he glanced to the open door of the room the elegant older woman presently used as her private office. The space off the lovely conference room wasn't much bigger than a closet, but it apparently served her purpose until the major construction behind the sheets of heavy plastic in the entryway would be completed.

Beyond them, Phil and a petite, honey-gold blonde sat beneath the crystal chandelier at the mahogany table. On its surface, hundreds of letters from the mailbags mounded by the delicate French writing desk teetered in stacks. Others had been sorted into piles as the women carefully read each one.

Cornelia had introduced the pretty woman with Phil as Shea Weatherby. She was the reporter who'd written the article that had resulted in the continuing deluge of mail from prospective Cinderellas, or "Cindies," as Rory had just learned her fairy godmothers called the ladies they sponsored. She'd also just learned she'd been their second success.

As focused as Shea appeared to be on her reading, she seemed even more intent on ignoring Pax. Erik's business partner had come over with them after Erik had showed her and Tyler around their client office next door. Pax had used the excuse of needing a decent cup of coffee, something he apparently mooched off the women with some regularity. Yet it was as obvious as the charmingly devilish smile that clearly wasn't working on Shea that she was the reason he was hanging around with Tyler by the pretty little Christmas tree, checking out the boats beyond the window.

"Do you mind if I ask what we're waiting for?" Rory ventured.

"Not at all," came Erik's easy reply. "I just need to give Cornelia a check and pick up a deed from her. I'm paying off the mortgage on your property so you can stop worrying about it."

He was paying off her mortgage? "I never said I was worried."

The look he gave her said she couldn't possibly be serious. "Honey." Brushing back her bangs, he planted a kiss on the furrows between her eyes. "You've never had to tell me when you were concerned about something. I can see it. This way, the pressure's off."

"You're giving me the place?"

"Consider it a pre-engagement present."

She opened her mouth, closed it again.

"Pre-engagement?" she finally asked.

"Yeah. You know. It comes before an official engagement. If you want, I can hold off titling it to you until then. Either way, the property is yours to do with as you please."

He'd figured they could eventually live together there or he could have a bigger house built back by the woods. Whichever she wanted. With the boatworks here, he'd commute by plane most of the time. If she decided to sell or lease the place, that was her call, too. He just wanted them together. But he'd already gotten way ahead of where he figured she mentally was with their relationship.

Seeing that he'd left her a little speechless, he figured it best to change the subject. He'd told her they wouldn't rush. That they could take their time.

"Hey. Ignore me. I was just in business mode," he explained. "I hadn't intended to bring that part up until you got used to me being around." He hitched his head toward the open door. "I'm going to see what's holding up Cornelia."

He gave her a kiss, quick and hard, and turned away.

Catching his arm, she turned him right back. "I'm getting used to you," she assured him. "How long an engagement are you talking about?"

"However long you need."

Christmas morning, he'd given back to her a feeling she'd thought she'd never know again. Now he was ready to offer himself, along with the gift of time, to accept what, in her heart, she already knew.

"Then, I have no problem discussing it now." Some things, simply felt, simply were...right. "All you have to do is ask."

His eyebrow arched. "Seriously?"

"Seriously," she echoed.

With now familiar ease, he slipped his arms around her, drew her close. "In that case, I'm ready if you are."

The teasing in her expression met the smile in his. Narrowing her eyes, she tipped her head as her hands flattened on his chest. "That's a proposal?"

"It's due diligence. I don't want you to shoot me down."

"Never," she murmured. "I love you too much."

"I love you back, Rory." There'd been a time when he couldn't imagine ever saying anything like that again. Or, ever feeling what he felt with her. "And just for the record," he said, glancing toward Tyler before lowering his head to hers, "you made me believe in the magic, too."

* * * * *

A ROYAL TEMPTATION

CHARLENE SANDS

To Allyson Pearlman, Robin Rose, Mary Hernandez and Pam Frendian. You're my crew, my Best Friends Forever. Your friendship puts lightness in my heart and a smile on my face every day. I am surrounded by the best and I love you dearly.

One

Juan Carlos Salazar II stood at the altar in Saint Lucia's Cathedral, holding his head high as he accepted the responsibility and honor of being crowned King Montoro of Alma. In a dreamlike state he went through the motions that would bring the monarchy back to what it had once been decades ago. He'd been orphaned at a young age and taken in by his uncle. Since then, he'd lived a life filled with determination and dignity. He'd always known great things would come to him if he worked hard and kept his focus. But king? Never in his life would he have guessed his own true destiny.

With the golden orb and blessed scepter in his hands, he saw the austere ceremony in the cathedral was coming to a close. Prime Minister Rivera had given a speech full of renewed hope for the country, the small set of islands off the coast of Spain that had been ravaged by the now overthrown dictatorship of the Tantaberras. Seventy years of oppression overturned by loyal citizens, who looked to Juan Carlos for the reinstatement of a monarchy that would capture their hearts and minds.

Archbishop Santiago placed the royal robe over Juan Carlos's shoulders. As he took his seat on the throne, the archbishop set the jeweled crown of Alma upon his head. All of the tradition, ritual and protocol of the coronation had been observed, and he was now King Montoro of

Alma, the true heir to the throne. He spoke an oath and vowed to be much more than a figurehead as he promised to restore order and hope to the country.

It was a monumental time in Alma's history and he was happy to have the support of his cousins, Gabriel, Rafe and Bella. They were smiling and nodding their approval from their seats, Bella with tears in her eyes. They'd all lived and thrived in the United States before this, and forgive him, but heaven knew Rafe and Gabriel, who were once thought to be first in line to the throne but had been disqualified for separate and unique reasons, were not cut out for the rigors and sacrifice of royal life. They were only too glad to see Juan Carlos accept the position of sovereign.

A woman seated several rows behind his cousins caught his attention. Deep cerulean-blue eyes, clear and large, stood out against her porcelain face and white-blond hair. She reminded him of a snow queen from a fairy tale in his youth. And as he was ushered down the aisle after the coronation their gazes locked for an instant and her one eyelid closed in a wink. Was it for him? His lips immediately quirked up at the notion and he forced the smile from his expression. Still, his heart did a little tumble as it had been doing all day, but this time it was the woman, and not the ceremony, that had caused the commotion.

The next hour passed, again in dreamlike wonder, as he was escorted out of the cathedral by Alma's finest royal guards, to be met with unrestrained jubilation all along the parade route. He sat atop a convertible car and waved with gloved hands, as they made their way toward the palace. And there, on the top steps of Alma's regal old-world palace, Juan Carlos began his first speech as king.

"Citizens of Alma, as your new king, I promise to honor the sovereignty of our nation, to always put the country first and to work alongside our parliament to restore our democracy. It is a vow I take with an open but steady heart and a determination to see that our freedoms are never threatened again."

Cheers went up. "Viva Juan Carlos!"

Juan Carlos waited until the crowd calmed to finish a speech that was interrupted three more times by applause.

He left the palace steps energized, instilled with the very same hope he saw in the eyes of his fellow countrymen. He was a foreigner, by all rights, an American, and yet, they'd accepted him and looked to him to help establish a newer, brighter Alma.

He would not let them down.

As austere as his day was, he took a moment to reflect on the coronation and picture the beautiful woman in the light blue chiffon gown, her eyes as vibrant as deep ocean waters. He'd searched for her during the procession, the parade and the speech that followed, only to be disappointed.

She'd been a diversion from the gravity of the day.

Winking at him had brought a smile to his lips.

Who was she?

And would she have his children?

"Do I need to call you Your Highness?" his cousin Rafe asked as he pumped Juan Carlos's hand. They stood off to the side in the palace's grand ballroom. The coronation gala was well underway and the orchestra played lively tunes. An array of fresh flowers decorated the arched entryways, aisles and tables.

"You mean, as opposed to Squirt, Idiot and Bonehead like when we were kids?"

"Hey, I wasn't that bad."

"You were a year older and that gave you bullying rights."

"Okay, guilty as charged. But now you can have me hung by the neck until dead."

"I could've done that to you back then, too."

"Ha, funny."

"Call me Juan Carlos or cuz, just like you do now. Your Highness comes into play only on formal occasions or royal business."

All amusement on his cousin's face disappeared. "Seriously, Juan Carlos, congratulations. The family is proud of you. You're the only one of the lot who was cut out for this. You are honoring our aunt Isabella's final wishes by restoring the monarchy."

Juan Carlos came to the throne quite by accident, after Bella discovered a secret cache of letters that revealed Rafe, Gabriel and Bella's late grandfather, Raphael Montoro II, was illegitimate and not the true heir to the throne. As such, neither of Juan Carlos's cousins would have been the rightful king. The former queen's indiscretion had been kept hidden all these years until her great-grandchildren had uncovered it.

"Thank you, cousin. I've thought about my grandmother these past few weeks and I think she would approve. It means a great deal to me." He sighed. "I hope to make a diff—" He caught a glimpse of a woman in blue and craned his neck to get a better look.

It was her. She was attending the gala. Only dignitaries, friends and family members along with the royal photographers and journalists had been invited to the party, two hundred strong.

"Hey," Rafe asked. "What are you stretching your neck to see?"

"She's here," he muttered, without shifting his gaze. She was standing near an archway leading to the foyer, looking to make an escape.

"Juan Carlos?"

"Oh, uh, I saw a woman at the coronation and I haven't stopped thinking about her."

"This I've got to see. Any woman who can take your

mind off a day as big as this has got to be something special. Where is she?"

"I'm not going to point. Just look for the most beautiful woman in the room and you'll find her."

"Emily is right there, talking to Bella."

"Spoken like a besotted newlywed. Okay, yes, Emily is gorgeous, now find a woman in blue who is not your wife."

"If you'd agreed to a formal receiving line, you'd have met her already."

He hadn't wanted a stiff, awkward line of people congratulating him. He'd make his way over to his guests and speak with them during the course of the evening. He'd vowed to be a king *of* the people and *for* the people and that started right now. "Do you see her?"

"Ah, I do see her now. Very blonde, nice body, great eyes."

"That's her. Do you know who she is?"

"No, but apparently she knows Alex and Maria Ramon. They just walked up to her and they appear friendly."

"Well, then, I think it's time I spoke with Alma's deputy prime minister of commerce and his wife, don't you?"

Juan Carlos moved swiftly across the ballroom and as he approached, Alex spotted him and smiled. "Your Highness." Juan Carlos nodded. It would take some time getting used to that greeting.

Maria, not one to stand on ceremony, hugged his neck. She and Alex had just married and postponed their honeymoon to attend the coronation. "I'm happy to see this day, Your Highness. You are just what Alma needs."

"Thank you, Maria."

As he made eye contact with the blonde woman, it felt as if something quick and sharp had pierced his body. Her eyes were large, shaped like perfect twin almonds, the sparkle in them as bright as any star. Mesmerized, he couldn't look away.

"And please, let me introduce you to Portia Lindstrom, Princess of Samforstand."

Princess?

She *could* have his children.

Juan Carlos offered her his hand and at the touch of her delicate palm, he once again felt that quick, sharp sensation. "Nice to meet you, Princess. I'm glad you could make the coronation. It's a good day for Alma, I hope."

"I'm sure it will be, Your Majesty. And please, call me Portia."

"I will," he said. "If you call me Juan Carlos."

A pink cast tinged her porcelain skin. "I couldn't."

"Why not?"

"Because, you're the king."

"I'll let you in on a secret. Up until a few months ago, I was living in Miami and running a rather large business conglomerate. I'm afraid I still have American ties and king is not in their vocabulary, unless we're talking about Elvis."

She smiled. "I live in America, too. I'm on the west coast right now. My family was from a tiny country near Scandinavia."

"Well, then, we have a lot in common. As you can see, Alma is not a large country, either."

Maria and Alex exchanged looks and excused themselves. He'd forgotten they were there. It was rude of him. But now, he was alone with Portia.

"You are a curiosity. You won't call me Juan Carlos, but yet you wink at me just as I am crowned king."

Portia froze. Surely the king didn't believe she'd actually winked at him. It was that darn nervous twitch of hers. It would have to happen at the exact moment she'd first made eye contact with him. She should be immune to royalty—she'd met enough princes and princesses in her twenty-eight years—but Juan Carlos Salazar seemed different, strikingly handsome and down to earth. Before she could explain about the wink, the orchestra began playing a lovely Latin waltz.

He bowed in old world fashion. "Princess Portia, I'd be honored if you danced with me."

"I'm afraid I don't waltz."

"Neither do I," he replied. "We can wing it and set a new trend."

She chuckled. He didn't act like the stuffed-shirt royals she'd met in the past, and when he took her hand and led her to the unoccupied dance floor, she didn't protest. He was a better dancer than he let on, and she glided across the floor with him, fully aware every set of eyes in the room were on them.

"We're the only ones out here," she whispered.

He grinned, flashing white teeth against golden-brown skin. He was tall and dashing and at the moment, charming her silly by staring into her eyes as if she was the only person who existed in the world. It was quite flattering.

"Don't worry. Other guests will join in after the king's first dance. It's tradition."

"Then I should be honored you picked me."

"After that wink, how could I not pick you?" He held her possessively and spoke with authority, as if he'd been king all of his life.

"It was a twitch. I had something in my eye."

"I choose to believe it was a wink."

"Yes, Your Highness."

He smiled again and moved her across the dance floor as if she were light as air.

When the dance ended, he didn't release her hand. "Will you take a walk with me?"

"You want to leave your own gala?"

He shrugged and didn't appear worried. "It's been a long, monumental day. I could use a little break."

Portia couldn't very well say no. And getting some fresh air did sound good. Because of her title, she'd been invited to the gala, and to refuse such a high honor would've been unheard of. Her mother and father's greatest wish, as her grandmother told it, was for her to remain true to her royal bloodlines, even while having a career and life of her own. So she juggled her time accordingly, to honor her deceased parents' wishes. She hadn't had enough time with them, but she'd hoped to make them proud. "Well, then, yes. I'll walk with you."

They strode off the dance floor in silence. His hand pressed to her back, he guided her toward a small back door and they ducked out to a deserted foyer. "There are private gardens just outside where we can sit."

He opened a door she was sure only royals were privy to, and a gust of cool autumn air hit her. Without a second's hesitation, Juan Carlos removed his tuxedo jacket and placed it around her shoulders. "Better?"

"Yes, thank you." She tugged the lapels closed and kept her hands there, away from the king's tempting grasp. His dark eyes were on her every move, and when he touched her, her pulse raced in a way it hadn't in a very long time.

He led her to grounds surrounded by lattices covered with vines. "Would you like to sit down?"

"Okay."

She sat on a delicately woven rattan love seat and he lowered down beside her, his six-foot presence looming large next to her. Aware of the solid breadth of his shoulders and the scent of his skin, she found the new king of Alma a little too appealing. "It's nice here. Quiet," she said. "You must be exhausted."

"Yes, but invigorated, too. If that makes any sense to you."

"It does. When I'm researching a piece of art for a client, I might work sixteen-hour days, but I always get excited when I locate it." His brows came together as if he were puzzled. "I'm an art advisor," she explained. "I help collectors build their collections."

"Impressive. And do you work in your country?"

"I'm based out of Los Angeles and New York. I don't spend any time in Samforstand."

"That's how it was for me. I worked out of Miami and New York, but now, Alma will be my permanent home. My duty is here and I will adjust. The country is beautiful, so it won't be a hardship."

"Excuse me, Your Highness," said a voice from behind the bench.

"Yes?" Juan Carlos turned around.

"I'm sorry to interrupt, but Chancellor Benoit has been called away and insists on saying his farewells to you personally. He is waiting in the antechamber."

"All right, thank you. Please tell the chancellor I will be in to see him shortly."

The man gave a curt nod and walked off.

"Well, looks like duty calls. I'm sorry." He rose and extended his hand. "Please save another dance for me tonight, Portia. There's more I want to learn about...*art advising*." He smiled.

Her heart hammered. She didn't know what to make of the cocoon-like hold he had on her. She'd only just met him and already he was wrapping himself around her thoughts with his silent compliments and easy ways. "I will."

She rose and he walked her back to the ballroom, depositing her exactly where he'd found her, beside Maria and Alex.

"I will be back," he said.

Portia's throat hitched and she nodded.

"Looks like the king is smitten." Maria kept her voice

low enough for only Portia's ears. She was sure Maria, a public relations expert and friend, had been instrumental in her receiving an invitation to the coronation and gala.

"He's being gracious, Maria."

Maria seemed to ignore her comment. "He's a good man."

"Perfect for Alma. But not for me." She was attracted to Juan Carlos. Any woman with blood running through her veins would be, but talk about high profile. You couldn't get much higher, and that's the last thing Portia needed in her life. It had taken her three years to climb out of the hole she'd dug for herself by getting involved with the Duke of Discourse, Travis Miles, LA's favorite talk show host.

Charming, debonair and controversial, he'd dragged her into his limelight from the start of their love affair to the bitter, heartbreaking end. Her career had suffered as the details of his neglect and wandering eye came into play. She'd almost lost all credibility with her clients. Luckily, she'd managed her way out of that situation, vowing to keep a low profile, stay in the small circle of the art world and not allow another high-profile charmer to get to her. And that included the king of Alma.

"I don't know about that," Maria said, matter-of-factly.

"I do," she said, convincing herself of that very thing. "I have an important meeting in Los Angeles with a client in a few days."

"A lot could happen in a few days, Portia."

But the conversation ended when a nice-looking gentleman approached, introduced himself as Alma's secretary of defense, and asked her to dance.

Portia accepted, and as she was being led to the dance floor, shot an over-the-shoulder glance at Maria.

Only to find Juan Carlos standing there, his gaze following her every movement.

He had indeed come back for her.

* * *

Gnashing his teeth, Juan Carlos ran a hand down his face to cover the tightness in his jaw. Princess Portia had danced nonstop with three men since he'd returned from seeing Chancellor Benoit off. Every time Juan Carlos thought to approach, he was interrupted or summoned into a conversation with a group of dignitaries. He couldn't fall short of his duties on his coronation day, yet the beautiful snow queen consumed his thoughts, and as he spoke with others, he kept one eye on Portia.

Finally free from conversations, he had an aide approach the orchestra and suggest that they take a five-minute break. The music died instantly and Juan Carlos strode over to the table where Portia had just taken a seat. "Hello again."

Those startling blue eyes lifted to him. "Hello."

"I'm happy to see you having a good time."

"I am," she said. "Would you like to sit down?"

"I have a better idea."

Her eyes twinkled. "Really? What would that be?"

He offered his hand again, hoping she'd take it. "Come with me and find out."

Her hesitation rattled his nerves. "Where?"

"Trust me and I'll show you."

She rose then, and as they walked out of the ballroom again with her hand in his, she watched him carefully. She had no reason not to trust him. He would never steer her wrong.

"In here," he said.

He tugged her into a spacious office and shut the door. It was black as coal at first, but the light of the full moon streamed in and his eyes adjusted so that he could make out Portia's silhouette. He took her gently into his arms and overwhelming sensations rushed through his body. Silently, with a look, she questioned his actions, but with his eyes he assured her she had nothing to fear. Then the orchestra began playing and as music piped into the room through the air ducts, he began to move her along to the beat. She tossed her head back and laughed. "You aren't serious."

He grinned. "It's the only way I can assure us not being interrupted again."

"You are resourceful, Your Highness. We have an entire dance floor all to ourselves."

"What would make it perfect would be if you'd call me Juan Carlos."

"But you've earned the right to be called king."

"Tonight, for now, think of me as a man, and not a king."

"I'll try, but you have to understand, after all the adoration, the photos and parades and galas in your honor, it's not easy for me."

He did understand, but pressed his reasoning a little further. "Think of it this way. How would you like it if everyone you knew called you Princess Portia?"

She gave it some thought and nodded. "I see your point."

He drew her inches closer, so that her sweet breaths touched his face, but he didn't dare do more. Though he wanted to crush her against him, feel her body sway with his, he couldn't rush her or scare her off. These feelings pulsed through him with near desperation. He'd never been so…besotted. Such an old-world word, but that's exactly how he felt.

"How long will you be in Alma?" he asked.

"I leave for the States in two days. I'm due back at work."

News he didn't want to hear. "Are you working with a client?"

"Yes, he's someone very influential and I'm thrilled to have the chance to meet with him for the first time. He's new to collecting, and I have an interview with him to see where his tastes lie."

"I see. It's a good opportunity for you. I would imagine being Princess Portia of Samforstand carries some weight in your line of work."

"I'll admit, using my royal heritage has helped me attain clients, but it's my expertise that has earned their trust."

"Trust is important," he said.

"You have the trust of the entire country right now."

"Yes," he said, sighing. "It's a big responsibility. I'm sure you take your responsibility seriously."

"I do. My reputation earns me that trust and I guard it like a mother would her child."

He smiled at the image gathering in his mind, of Portia, mother of his child.

Dios. He was in deep. How was it possible? He had known her less than a day.

And already, he was naming their first-born child.

Two

Stately and grand, Portia's hotel in Del Sol was just a short distance from the palace. The big bed in her room was cushy and comfy. The morning sunlight streamed in to warm her and the air was sweetened by a bouquet of roses, compliments of the hotel manager. It was all fit for a princess. Yet she hadn't slept well.

Last night, as Juan Carlos bid her farewell, he'd almost kissed her. She was sure he would have if they hadn't been surrounded by his guests. She'd thought about that non-kiss during the night. How would his lips feel against hers? Heavens, she hadn't had so much as a date with a man in almost a year, and it had been even longer since she was ravaged by a kiss. Which, she was sure, would have happened had they been alone.

She was thankful that he hadn't locked lips with her in front of the attendees at the gala. Yet, lightbulbs had flashed and pictures had been snapped of the two of them. It was last thing she needed and she'd dashed out as rapidly as Cinderella racing against the midnight hour.

When he'd asked her to join him for brunch this morning, she'd quickly agreed, despite her tingling nerves and fuzzy brain.

Her brunch "date" with the King of Montoro would happen precisely at ten o'clock and he'd promised they wouldn't be interrupted.

She heard the familiar Bruno Mars ringtone of her cell phone and grabbed it from the nightstand. Her assistant's name popped up on the screen and she smiled. From the very beginning, her assistant had been her closest friend. "Hello, Jasmine."

"Hi, Portia. I hope I didn't wake you?"

"No, not at all. I'm getting ready to have brunch. It's good to hear your voice."

"Did you survive the coronation?" Jasmine Farr never minced words. "I know you weren't thrilled about attending."

"Actually, it wasn't so bad." The newly named king was quite a man. "And it's my lot in life to attend these functions every so often."

"That's what you get for being a princess." She chuckled. "I saw some of the coronation on YouTube."

"That was fast."

"It always is. Anyway, I'm calling to tell you that Mr. Greenboro had to cancel your meeting this week. He's flying out of the country and won't be back for three months. He sends his apologies, of course, and he did reschedule. I hope it's okay that I took the liberty of making that appointment. I didn't think you'd want to let him get away."

"Oh, I'm disappointed. I'd set the entire week aside to work with him, but I'm glad you're on the ball and rescheduled with him. Text me that date and I'll mark it on my calendar."

"Will do. So, now you don't have to rush back. There's really nothing else going on this week."

"Right."

"You've worked hard these past few months and you've been meaning to pencil in a vacation. Seems like a perfect opportunity."

"It is beautiful here."

"From the pictures I'm seeing, the beaches are to die for. I wish I could join you. I'd come in an instant."

"Why don't you come? We could have spa days together."

"I can't. I'm flying to Maryland for my cousin's wedding at the end of the week. "

"I'd forgotten about that. Darn."

"But that doesn't mean you can't stay on. I can book you a villa suite in Playa del Onda. The beach resort is top notch. You'll get lots of R&R."

"Let me think about it. I'll get back to you later on today."

After she ended the call, she stripped off her pajamas and entered the shower. The pounding water rained down and woke her up to the possibility of an actual vacation: away from phones, away from the hectic pace of gallery openings, away from the pressures of making art selections for her obscenely rich or drastically eccentric clients. Her schedule was a busy one, and this did seem like a perfect opportunity to unwind.

When she was finished with her shower, she slipped into a white dress with red polka dots that belted at the waist, slid on navy patent leather shoes and tossed her hair up into a ponytail. She applied light makeup, including eyeliner and soft pink lip gloss.

The jewelry she chose was delicate: a thin strand of pearls around her neck and wrist. She fastened her watch on her left arm and noted the time. Juan Carlos was sending a car for her in ten minutes. She grabbed her purse and left the hotel room.

In the lobby, she was greeted by a uniformed driver who escorted her to an ink-black limousine. She played the role of princess well, but she would rather be wearing a pair of jeans and going to the local café for a bite of breakfast.

"Your Highness," the driver said, as he opened the door for her, "allow me."

She slid into the backseat and bumped legs with Juan Carlos. Her breath hitched in her throat. He took in her wide-eyed surprise and grinned. "Good morning, Portia."

"Excuse me, but I didn't expect you to come to pick me up."

Should she worry about the implications? This wasn't a date. At least, not in any real sense.

"It's a nice morning for a drive. After yesterday's events, I thought you might like to join me to see some of the city. I hope you don't mind, but I've changed our brunch plans for today."

He wore dark slacks and a casual white silk shirt, opened slightly at the collar. She glimpsed his tanned chest and gulped for air.

"Of course not."

"Great. You look very pretty this morning."

"Thank you." *And you look dynamic, powerful and gorgeous.*

He issued directions to the driver and they took off.

"How were your first twenty-four hours as king?" she asked.

He rubbed his chin, thinking for a second. "It's strange that I don't feel any different. I keep expecting a big transformation, but I'm just me."

She smiled at his earnest answer. "I thought it would be an adjustment for you. Every move you make now will be documented somehow." She glanced out the window, expecting to see photographers following the limo, snapping pictures. She'd had experience with her ex-boyfriend's fame and it had gotten old very fast. No one should be followed and photographed at every turn for entertainment's sake. "How did you escape the palace?"

He chuckled. "You make it seem like prison."

"No, no. I'm sorry. That's not what I meant."

"I know what you meant, Portia." Her name slid effortlessly from his lips. "There are some advantages to being king."

"Such as?" she probed.

"Such as, I didn't make my intentions known. No one expected me to take a drive this morning. No one questioned me. I had the car ready to pick you up, and then I merely slipped into the backseat before anyone at the palace got wind of it."

"You snuck out."

He laughed again and she joined in. "Okay, yes. I snuck out."

Speaking to him put her at ease and she settled back in her seat. "Do you have bodyguards?"

"Yes, they are following behind somewhere."

"You're not worried?"

He shook his head. "No. I'm not worried. And neither should you be."

"Okay, I'll trust you." She'd never traveled with bodyguards, but her situation was quite different. As an exiled princess, she'd grown up in America and never had what Juan Carlos now had: a citizenry eager to reinstate their monarchy. "But you must have dozens of dignitaries and family members waiting to speak with you at the palace."

"Which I will do later. But for now," he said, reaching for her hand, "I find being with you more important."

Juan Carlos held her hand during the tour of the city. He showed her sites of great historical significance and some trendy new hot spots that were cropping up. The rise of democracy was good for enterprise, he explained.

As he spoke, the tone of his deep and sincere voice brought a smile to her lips more times than she could count. It was intimate in a way, hearing the love he had for a country that was almost as new to him as it was to her. He kept her hand locked in his as if it was precious. As if he needed the connection. To hear him say that being with her was important did wonders for her ego.

Yet she only indulged him because nothing could possibly come of it. And because it had been a long time since she'd enjoyed a man's company so much.

Tomorrow, she would leave Del Sol.

The limo stopped at a tiny café off the main street of town. "I hear Matteo's is fantastic."

"You've never eaten here before?" she asked.

"No, I haven't. We'll experience it together. Do you mind?"

"I love adventure."

He nodded, a satisfied glimmer in his eyes. "I thought you might."

They exited the limo, which looked out of place on the backstreets of the royal city. Once inside, they were escorted to their table by the owner. He was sweating, nervous and fidgety. Juan Carlos clapped him on the back gently to reassure him. "Bring us your specials, Matteo. I hear they are the best in all of Del Sol."

"*Si, si.* I will be glad to serve you myself, Your Majesty."

Juan Carlos nodded. "Thank you."

Though the café walls showed signs of age, it was a clean, modest place. "Are you sure the food is good here?" she asked.

His brows gathered. "It comes highly recommended. Why?"

"We're the only ones seated."

Juan Carlos looked around the empty café. "My bodyguards. They called ahead to announce my arrival. I'll make it up to Matteo. I can't have him losing business on my account."

"I'm sure he'll be boasting that King Montoro of Alma dined in his café. His business will double by next week."

Juan Carlos sharpened his gaze on her. "I hadn't thought of that."

"You're new to this royal thing."

"Yes, I guess I am."

Just wait, she wanted to say. He was an intelligent man, from all she'd read about him. He managed the sizable personal accounts of the Montoros and had helped build a fortune for the family. He had wits and smarts, but nothing would prepare him for the limelight he'd just entered. He'd have to experience it himself, the good, the bad, the ugly. His life would be under a microscope now.

And she didn't want to be the amoeba next to him.

Coffee was served, along with fresh handmade tortillas, butter and a bowl of cut fruit. "Looks delicious," Juan Carlos said to Matteo.

"Please, is there anything else I can bring you while the meal is cooking?"

"This is perfect. Don't you agree, Portia?"

She nodded and smiled at the owner.

When Matteo left the room she continued to smile. "You're kind. He will always remember this day because you put him at ease."

Travis Miles had been kind, too, in the beginning.

"Now who is being kind?" he asked.

"I'm just speaking the truth. You'll impact a great many lives."

"In a positive way, I hope and pray."

"Kind," she repeated. "You care about the people in the country."

"Thank you." His incredibly warm brown eyes softened and her stomach did a little flip.

She buttered a tortilla, rolled it up and took a few bites. She sipped coffee and asked Juan Carlos a few pointed questions about his life to keep the conversation flowing and her mind off the fact that King Montoro was a hunk.

The meal was delivered with fanfare. Matteo and his staff put out the dishes in sweeping motions and finally left them to dine privately. The food was delicious. The main dish consisted of bits of sautéed pork topped with eggs and lathered with a creamy, mildly spicy sauce. There was also some type of sweet corn soufflé served inside the husks, as well as caramelized plantains. Every bite she took rewarded her taste buds. "Mmm…this is heavenly."

Juan Carlos nodded, his mouth full.

As he chewed, his gaze remained on her. He had warm, luxurious, intense eyes that didn't stray. Goose bumps rode up and down her arms. As far as men went, Juan Carlos had it all, except for one thing. His fatal flaw. He was king. And that meant after today, she couldn't see him again.

"So what are your plans for the rest of the day?" he asked.

"Oh, I'm, uh, going to…" She really didn't have any plans. Maybe do a little shopping. Check out the only art museum in the city. "I'll be packing."

"That can't take all day."

"I wouldn't think so."

"Would you consider having dinner with me?"

No. No. No. "I really shouldn't."

Juan Carlos leaned back in his seat, studying her. "Do you have a man in your life, Portia?"

Slowly, she shook her head. She felt a trap coming.

"No one? I find that hard to believe. Do you date?"

"Rarely. My career is demanding. And it's very important to me. I've worked hard to get where I am."

"Admirable. Are you working tonight?"

"No, but I…"

He grinned. "I'm only asking for a dinner date, Portia." Her shoulders sagged an inch. A barely noticeable move, but she felt the defeat all the way down to her toes. She couldn't insult the king. "Then, yes, I'll have dinner with you."

After the meal, Juan Carlos escorted her to the limo. She took a seat at the far window and he climbed in after her. To his credit, he didn't crowd her, leaving a modest amount of space between them. But as the car took off, he placed his hand over hers on the empty seat, and wild pings of awareness shot through her body.

Don't let him get to you, Portia.

He's not the man for you.

As the limo pulled up to the hotel, Juan Carlos spoke to the driver. "Give us a minute please, Roberto."

The driver's door opened and closed quietly. Silence filled the air and suddenly she did feel crowded, though Juan Carlos hadn't made a move toward her. "I cannot walk you to your door, Princess."

"I understand."

"Do you? Do you know how much I want to?" His eyes were down, gazing at her hand as his thumb worked circles over her fingers. Her nerves jumped, like kernels of corn popping in a fry pan, one right after the other. "I don't want to cause you any inconvenience."

"I…know."

He tugged her hand gently and she fell forward, closing the gap between them. His dark-fringed eyelids lifted; she was struck by all-consuming heat. He wasn't moving a muscle, but leaving it up to her. As if she had a choice now. As if she could deny him. His mesmerizing hunger was contagious; years of abstinence made her hungry, as well. Her gaze lowered to his mouth. Lord in heaven, she wanted his kiss.

She moistened her lips and his eyes drew down immediately. "You leave me no choice, Princess."

He used a finger to tilt her chin, and then bent his head

toward her. Anticipation pulsed through her veins. Every single second was an unnerving kind of torture. And finally, his mouth was on hers, his hand coming to wrap more firmly around her jaw, as if he couldn't get enough, as if he would devour her.

Long live the king!

Her tummy ached from goodness and she indulged like a miser finding a hidden supply of cash. She touched his face, his jaw steel under her fingertips, and a groan erupted from his throat.

A whimpering mewling sound came from hers. Mortification would have set in, if the king wasn't equally as needy. But there was no shame, just honesty, and it was, after all, the kiss to end all kisses. Juan Carlos didn't let up, not for a moment. His lips worked hers hard, then soft, then hard again. Under her dress, her nipples ached. She was pretty sure the king was experiencing the same agony, but farther south on his body.

She didn't know whose mouth opened first, or whether it was at the exact same instant, but suddenly she was being swept up and hollowed out, his tongue doing a thorough job of ravaging her. Any second now, she'd be out of her head with lust. But Juan Carlos placed his hands on her shoulders and, she sensed, with great reluctance, moved her away from him.

He leaned back against the seat, breathing hard. "I've never made love to a woman in a limo before, Princess. It wouldn't take much to change that," he said. He tried for amusement, tried to chuckle, but a serious tone had given away his innermost thoughts.

"It would be a first for me, too," she said, coming up for air.

A rumpled mess, she tried her best to straighten herself out before she exited the limo.

He pressed a button and the window rolled down. Roberto appeared by the car door. "See Princess Portia to her hotel room," Juan Carlos said calmly. He'd gotten his emotions in check already, while she was still a ravaged jumble of nerves.

Again, those warm brown eyes lit upon her. "I'll send a car to pick you up for dinner at seven."

She swallowed. "Maybe…we shouldn't," she squeaked.

"Are you afraid of me?" he asked, though his confident tone indicated that it wasn't even a concern.

She shook her head. "I'm leaving in the morning."

"And you love your job. Your career means a lot to you. Yes, that's clear."

He'd made her refusal seem silly. And it was. Nothing would happen unless she wanted it to happen. She already knew Juan Carlos was that type of man.

"I'll see you tonight," she said finally. When the driver opened the car door, she rushed out.

She hadn't exactly lied to him, had she?

She said she'd be gone, and he thought she meant back to the States. But she'd made up her mind to vacation on the shores of Alma, at least until the end of the week.

But he didn't need to know that.

After a late lunch, Juan Carlos had a meeting in the city with the prime minister and few of Alma's most trusted and prominent business leaders. He struggled to keep his mind on the topics at hand. The restoration of the entire country was a tall order. But every so often, his mind traveled to that place where Portia was in his arms. The image of her lips locked on his, their bodies pulsing to the same lusty rhythms, knocked him for a loop and sent his brain waves scrambling. She was, in his estimation, perfect. For him. For the country.

Wow. Where had that come from? Why was he thinking of her in terms of permanence? As a queen for Alma, for goodness' sake.

Because aside from the fact that his sensual response was like the national flag being hoisted to full mast every time he looked at her, there was no doubt in his mind that she could take a place by his side at the throne.

As a public figure, he was never alone much anymore, but that didn't mean he wasn't lonely. He hadn't had a serious relationship for years. His ambition had gotten in the way and sure, he'd had a few women in his life, but nothing serious. No one who'd made him feel like this.

Portia's face flashed in his mind, that porcelain skin, those ice-blue eyes, that haughty chin, that mouth that tasted like sweet sin. The snow queen had become important to him in a short time, and…

"Your Majesty? Juan Carlos, are you all right?"

"Huh? Oh, yeah, I'm fine." Prime Minister Rivera was giving him a strange look. "Just deep in thought."

They'd been talking about how to bring new enterprise to Alma and how the rise of the monarchy would bring in tourism. They needed to brand themselves as a free country and show the world that democracy reigned, that new visitors and new businesses were welcome to their stunning Atlantic shores.

"Actually, I have an idea as to how to draw more tourists," Juan Carlos said.

"Really?"

Alex Ramon's ears perked up. As the deputy prime minister of commerce, he was fully immersed in the issue. "Tell us your thoughts."

"It's been rumored in our family for years that our ancestors had stashed a considerable amount of artwork, sculptures and paintings on land that had fallen to ruin. Land that Tantaberra overlooked. Right before the family was deposed, they'd thought to hide the art so it wouldn't fall into the dictator's greedy hands."

Juan Carlos's mind was clicking fast. He didn't know how true those rumors were. He'd only heard the tales while growing up; Uncle Rafael had spoken of hidden treasures the way a master storyteller would about a pirate's bounty. It had all been exciting, the sort of thing that captured a little boy's imagination. But the rumors had held fast and true during his adulthood, and only recently, his cousin Bella had found a hidden cache of letters at one of the family's abandoned farms, letters that proved that he, a Salazar and not a Montoro, was the rightful heir to the throne.

"I have plans to visit the area myself and see what I can find. If it's true, and artwork is indeed on the property, think of the story. The art could be restored, and we could have a special showing or a series of showings to bring awareness to Alma."

"It's genius, Your Highness," Prime Minister Rivera said. Others around the board table agreed.

The meeting ran long and Juan Carlos didn't get back to the palace until six. He had just enough time to shower and dress for dinner. His pulse sped up as he thought of Portia again, of her sweetly exotic scent and the way she'd filled his body with pleasure when he was near her. She caused him to gasp and sweat and breathe hard. It wasn't ideal. She was a hard case. She didn't seem interested in him. And that worried him, because as far as he was concerned, she was The One.

He came down at precisely six forty-five and bumped into his new secretary at the base of the winding staircase, nearly knocking the clipboard out of her hands. "Oh, sorry, Your Highness." She was out of breath, as if she'd been running a marathon.

"My apologies," he said. "I've been preoccupied and didn't see you."

Alicia was redheaded, shapely and quite efficient. She wore glasses, but under those glasses were pretty, light green eyes. She'd taken on a lot, being a first hire, as there was much ground to cover. "Your seven o'clock appointment is here."

Warmth spread through his body at the mention of his dinner date. "Princess Portia?"

"Oh, uh. No, Your Highness. I'm sorry. I don't see Princess Portia on the books." She studied her clipboard, going over the names. "No, you have appointments every half hour for the next few hours. I penciled in a dinner break for you at nine."

"I thought those were on tomorrow night's schedule." Surely, he hadn't been mistaken, had he? Yet he had to take Alicia at her word. He'd already come to find that she rarely if ever made mistakes. He, on the other hand, had been hypnotized by a pair of deep ocean-blue eyes and was more than distracted.

"I can't possibly make all of those appointments." High-ranking officials and the heads of businesses along with their wives or husbands wanted to meet the new king. It was as simple as that. It was good for commerce to know the pillars of trade in Alma, so he'd agreed to a few evening appointments. Under normal circumstances, he'd rather cut off his right arm than cancel them, but he couldn't break a date with Portia. "See what you can do about cancelling them. Who was first on the schedule?"

"Mr. and Mrs. Rubino. The Rubinos are in the royal study. And your next appointment after that is already here, I'm afraid. They are notoriously early for every occasion, I'm told. They are waiting in the throne room."

He ran his hands through his hair. "Fine. I'll see them. But see what you can do about cancelling the rest."

"Yes, Your Highness. I'll do my best." She bit her lower lip, her eyes downcast. "Sorry for the confusion."

"Alicia?"

"Yes?"

"It's not your doing. I forgot about these appointments. We're all learning here. It's new to all of us."

She had ten years of experience running a duke's household in London, coordinating parties and events with dignitaries and the royal family. She hadn't much to learn. He was the one who had screwed up.

"Yes, Your Highness. I'll get on those cancellations right away."

Juan Carlos rubbed the back of his neck and headed to the study.

With luck, he could salvage the evening.

Portia had been stood up. She'd been delivered to the palace minutes before seven, only to be informed that the king had visitors and to please be patient and wait. She was shown to the dining room and shortly after, the palace chef himself had set dishes of appetizers on the table before her.

Candles were lit and soft music filtered into the room.

The only problem? Her date wasn't here. And she wasn't about to eat a thing until he showed. Call her stubborn.

It was after eight. She knew because her stomach refused to stop growling and finally, she'd glanced at her watch.

She'd already taken in the paintings on the walls, assessing them and noting that they weren't up to par with usual palatial art. Oh, they were lovely pieces, but from contemporary artists. Many of them were replicas of the real thing. It was a curiosity. The monarchy stretched way beyond the years of the dictatorship. There should be older, more authentic works on the walls. But this was only one room. Maybe for security reasons, the gallery held the most valuable pieces.

After wandering the dining hall, she picked a particular patch of space near the fireplace and began pacing.

She couldn't fault Juan Carlos. His secretary had taken the blame, explaining that she'd failed to remind the king of his visitors. She'd tried her best to cancel the meetings, but she was afraid she wasn't as successful as she'd hoped.

But the more Portia thought about it, the more pangs of anger replaced her patience.

How long would he keep her waiting?

Travis is in a meeting. He won't be available for hours. He'd like you to wait, though.

This isn't the same thing, she reminded herself. Her ex-boyfriend wasn't a king. Well, maybe the king of late-night television. And she'd fallen for him. He was funny and charming and kind. It was like a regular Cinderella story, the poor broke comedian hooks up with a real live princess. Travis was far from poor now, although he'd come from humble beginnings and the press loved their story and ate it up.

A new American fairy tale, they'd called it.

Travis had been on top of the world when they were together. Everyone loved him and thought he was worthy of a princess from an obscure little country. Only dating a supermodel would have given him more credibility.

And here she was, doing the same thing. Another American fairy tale, only this time with a real king.

Stupid of her.

Her nerves were jumpy and by the time eight-thirty rolled around, she was royally pissed.

Juan Carlos had twisted her arm to accept this dinner date, the way charming men did. He'd trapped her and then kissed her until every brain cell was lulled into capitulation. God, she'd been looking forward to being alone with him again. That kiss was good. Better than good. It was the best kiss she'd ever had. Not even Travis could kiss like that, and he'd been plenty experienced in that department.

"Sorry, so sorry, Portia."

She jumped. "Oh!" Juan Carlos entered the room, looking dashing in a dark buttoned-up suit but no tie. Another growl emitted from her stomach, this time not due to hunger.

"Did Alicia explain what happened? It was my fault. This is the first chance I've had to—"

"It's been over ninety minutes," was all she could think to say.

"I would've cancelled with you and sent you home, but this is your last night in Alma. Selfishly, I wanted to see you again."

Guilt rose like bile in her throat. She remained silent.

He glanced at the feast of food that had been put before her. "You didn't touch anything Chef prepared. You must be famished."

"I'm not hungry anymore, Your Majesty."

His lips pursed in disapproval.

She still couldn't bring herself to call him by his given name.

"You've been so patient. There's just one more meeting I have to get through. Will you wait?"

She shook her head. "Actually, I think I'd like to go."

"You're angry."

"No, I'm tired and, and…"

"Angry."

She didn't respond. "Will you have your driver take me back to the hotel?"

Juan Carlos closed his eyes briefly. "Yes, of course. I just assumed after we kissed, you'd… Never mind. You're right. I shouldn't have made you wait."

A man who admitted when he was wrong? How rare.

"Duty called. I'm afraid it always will."

That's how it had worked with Travis. The difference? Travis had been building his own personal dynasty, while Juan Carlos was trying to build one for his country. But that still left Portia with the same end result. She'd never be a top priority and while she liked Juan Carlos, she had vowed, after many disappointments with Travis, to never get herself in that situation again.

With that, she wished Juan Carlos a good evening, assured him she wasn't angry and put enough distance between them that he couldn't touch her, couldn't plant his delicious lips on hers again and make her change her mind.

Three

The beach at Playa del Onda was one of the most stunning Portia had ever visited. Warm sand squeezed between her toes as she sat on a lounge chair, reading a book. This morning she'd gotten up early and taken a long jog along the shoreline, the October sun warming her through and through. She'd met a lovely family of tourists and had breakfast with them at a terrace café that overlooked the Atlantic. But their two little children, aged five and three, reminded her that it would probably be a long time before she was blessed with motherhood.

Often, she thought of having a family. She'd been orphaned at a young age. Aside from her great-aunt Margreta, she had no other family. Her grandmother Joanna had died during Portia's sophomore year in college. But she had her work and it fulfilled her, and she had good friends. She wasn't complaining. Yet being here on this beautiful beach was not only relaxing, it was…lonely.

Face it, Portia. How many books can you read this week? How many hot stone spa treatments can you indulge in? How many solo dinners in your room can you enjoy?

It had been three days of torturous relaxation. And it didn't compute. How odd for her to realize while on a vacation in a beautiful locale that she wasn't made for inactivity. She liked to keep active, to busy herself with things that mattered. Yesterday, she'd given herself a mental slap.

You deserve this vacation, so shut up, sit back and enjoy yourself.

Today, the mental slaps weren't working. Her relaxation was even more forced. She fidgeted in her chair; the book in her hands no longer held her interest. Sunglasses shading her eyes, she watched others frolicking on the sand, tossing a Frisbee, their laughter drifting over to her, reminding her how lonely she was. How bored.

She wished Jasmine was here. They would've had a good time with shopping, spa dates and maybe a nightclub or two.

The Frisbee landed at her feet and a teenage boy trotted over and stopped abruptly, blasting sand onto her legs. "Excuse me," he said. He reached for the Frisbee slowly, eyeing her legs, then her bikini-clad body. "Want to play with us?" he asked.

He had Spanish good looks, dark hair, bronzed skin and a charming smile. He was sixteen tops, and she would've actually considered tossing the Frisbee around with him, if he hadn't been so blatant about ogling her breasts.

She was saved from refusing, when the concierge from the Villa Delgado approached. "Excuse me, Princess."

The boy blinked at her title, turned a lovely shade of cherry-blossom pink and bowed, before dashing off. She chuckled under her breath. Her royal status did have some advantages. "Yes," she said to the concierge, removing her sunglasses.

"You have a phone call at the desk. A woman named Jasmine. She says she works for you. Apparently, she hasn't been able to reach you on your cell phone."

"I left my cell in my room," she replied. She didn't want to be interrupted in her state of lonely boredom. Now she realized how silly that seemed. "Sorry you had to track me down."

"Not a problem, Princess Portia."

"Will you tell her that I'll call her as soon as I get to my room?"

"My pleasure," he said.

When he walked off, she gathered up her beach bag, hat and sunglasses and promptly made her way toward the villa. Her suite with its second-floor terrace came into view. It was really quite picturesque, the columns and archways suggesting old-world grace and style. Why couldn't she like being here more? Why wasn't she okay with being idle? Maybe things had changed with Jasmine. Maybe her friend would come join her, after all. Her hope in her throat, Portia hiked a little faster to reach her suite of rooms.

Once inside, she set her things down on the dining table and headed for the bedroom, where she was sure she'd left her phone. It was charging on her nightstand. She unhooked the charger, just as she heard a knock at the door.

She belted her cover-up a little tighter and moved to the door. With a gentle tug on the knob, the door opened and she came face to face with Juan Carlos Salazar. The king.

She blinked and a rush of heat rose up her neck. She trembled at the sight of him, *the gorgeous, unexpected, surprising* sight of him. The phone slipped slightly in her hand and she grabbed at it before it crashed onto the floor.

His eyes were on her, and those dark raised brows made her flush even hotter. With guilt. Piercing disappointment flickered in his eyes. She hadn't told him the absolute truth when she'd left Del Sol.

"Princess," he said.

"Your Majesty," she responded.

His lips twitched. "I see you've decided to stay on in Alma, after all."

"I, uh, yes." She didn't owe him an explanation. One heart-robbing kiss didn't give him that right. "My plans changed."

"Quite unexpectedly, I assume."

"Yes, that's right." The movement of two bodyguards caught her attention. They stayed back, at least five feet away, but she was certain they could hear every word. "Would you like to come in?"

His gaze dipped down to her bikini-clad body, covered only by a soft robe of silk that reached her thighs. "Yes."

She backed up a few steps and he nodded to his bodyguards and then entered. They stood face-to-face again, alone in her suite.

Despite her guilt and a sense of being caught red-handed, this was the most exciting thing that had happened to her in three days. But how did he find out where she was and what did he want from her?

Her cell phone buzzed and she looked down at the screen. A text was coming through from Jasmine. She hadn't had time to call her back yet. Quickly, she scanned the message.

Heads up. I might've made a mistake by giving King Montoro your location. He was charming and said it was a business thing. Apologizing in advance. Love you!

She lifted her lids to him. Okay, so he wasn't psychic. But he was thorough.

"It's good to see you again," he said.

Warmth swelled inside her like an overflowing river. He had too much of an effect on her.

"It's nice to see you, but I do admit, it's quite a surprise."

On this warm day, he was wearing dark trousers and a tan shirt, sleeves rolled up with his hands in his pockets, looking as casual and delicious as any man she'd ever met. Man, *not king*. But she couldn't forget who he was. "I have to admit, I was also surprised to learn you hadn't left the country."

"You were looking for me?"

"Yes, I spoke with your assistant. She's very nice, by the way, and she's loyal to you. But the fact is, I have something of a business venture for you. And after I told her a little about it, she was willing to let me get in touch with you."

His eyes skimmed over Portia's body. Another wave of heat shimmied down to her belly and she turned away from his hot, assessing stare. Man or king, he was dangerous. "Would you like to sit down?" She waved him over to a latte-colored leather chair by the window that faced the Atlantic. "Please give me a minute to change my clothes."

"Only if you have to."

There was a wicked twinkle in his eyes that tweaked something lusty and recently unleashed in her body. It made her run, not walk toward her bedroom. "I'll be a minute, Your Majesty," she called over her shoulder.

His chuckle followed her into her room.

She scrubbed her face clean of sunscreen and removed her hair fastener, combing the tangles away and then gathering the strands back up into a long ponytail. She put on a pair of white capris and an off-the-shoulder cornflower-blue blouse.

A hint of lip gloss, some shading to her eyelids and she was ready. And more than mildly curious as to what was so important that King Juan Carlos had come all the way here to seek her out. She gave a last glance in the mirror and nodded. She felt a little less vulnerable to the king's hungry eyes now.

Juan Carlos stood when Portia entered the room. His heart hammered in his chest at the sight of her. She didn't know it yet, but he was determined to possess her. Aside from his newfound reign over Alma and his duties here, she'd become the most important thing in his life.

In such a short time.

It wasn't rational. He had no explanation for it. He'd never experienced anything quite like this. When she'd left the palace the other night, remorse had plagued him and lingered for days. Was he pathetic? Or simply a man who knows what he wants.

She was perfect, his ideal woman. She was royal, beautiful, smart, but at the moment…quite unattainable.

"Princess," he said.

"Would you like something cold to drink?" she asked.

"No, thank you."

"Okay, then maybe we should sit down and you can tell me what this is all about."

She took a seat, her eyes widening as she waited for him to explain.

"It seems I might have need for your services."

"My services? As an art advisor?"

"Well, yes. In a way. It would be something quite adventurous. You did say you liked adventure, didn't you?"

"I do."

"Well, then, let me explain. I don't know how much you know about the history of Alma, but it's been rumored that right before my family fled the country, they hid artwork dating back before World War II on the grounds of their abandoned farm. It's very run-down and Tantaberra never went there, so it was the perfect hiding place. Now that I'm king, I want to find those treasured pieces belonging to the royal family. It would go a long way in helping the country heal and bring new hope to our people. Imagine what a find that would be."

"It would be monumental," she agreed. Fireworks lit in her eyes at the mention of hidden art.

Good. He had her attention.

"But I see that you're vacationing here, so maybe you'd be too busy to help me locate the treasure."

"You want my help in locating the artwork?"

"Yes, I would need someone to help me hunt for it, and then assess its value. You'd be able to look at something and determine if it's authentic, I would imagine."

"Yes, for the most part. It's what I do. But you plan on doing this by yourself?"

"I can donate a few days of my time, yes. I wouldn't want word to leak out about what I was doing. If I come up empty, or if there are other issues regarding the artwork we find, I would rather it not become public knowledge immediately. Bella and her husband had already begun renovations on the property but given the site's historical significance, they've agreed to allow me to take over and devote the full resources of the crown to the project. As we speak, there is a team working on the grounds, getting it ready for my arrival. So Princess Portia, would you consider helping me? Of course, you'd be paid for your time."

"So, this is a job offer?"

"Yes, I'm offering you a job and an adventure."

She smiled, leaning forward and placing her hands on her crossed knee. "Who else will be there?"

He gathered his brows. "No one but my bodyguards. As I said, I plan to do this discreetly."

"It's intriguing, Your Majesty. But the two us alone, all that time?"

"Is that a problem for you?" God only knew, it was a problem for him. How could he keep his hands off her? It would be a living hell, but not worse than having her living a continent away. A few days was all he was asking of her.

"Maybe. Answer one thing for me, please."

He extended his arms, palms up. "Anything."

"Do you have an ulterior motive in offering me this opportunity? And please don't make me spell it out."

He smiled. She'd made her point and he wouldn't do her a disservice by lying to her. "If you mean, do I value a few more days in your company, then yes. I suppose. But I do honestly have good reason to be asking this of you. You are an expert, are you not?"

"I am."

The sparkle in her eyes evaporated.

"What is it?"

She rose from her seat, and good manners had him rising, too. She walked behind the chair, putting distance between them, and leaned her elbows on the back, a battle raging in her eyes, on her face. "I'm not presuming anything here, but I do have to tell you where I stand. It's… it's complicated. Because I do like you."

Encouraging. He nodded.

"And that kiss we shared…well, it bordered on amazing."

He nodded again. She had something to say and he wanted to hear it.

Or maybe not.

"But the truth is, you're King Montoro of Alma. You're new to this king thing, but you'll find out how demanding a job it will be. And you'll be in the spotlight. All. The. Time."

"Does that worry you?"

"Yes. You see, I'm not one to share heartbreak stories, but in this case, I should probably share with you, why I've been—"

"Playing hard to get?" He couldn't hold back a smile.

"Yes. Only I'm not playing. I'm seriously not interested in getting involved with a man with so much…glitter."

"Glitter?" He laughed. "What's that?"

"You're always going to shine. No matter what." His smile faded. She was dead serious. "And any woman who gets involved with you, will be giving up her identity, her dreams, her heart, to someone who has pledged his life to his country."

"Who was he, Portia? Surely, someone has broken your heart."

"Yes, my heart was broken. I don't like talking about it, but since it's important to our conversation, I'll tell you about Travis Miles. He's like a king in America, a big time Hollywood celebrity."

Juan Carlos nodded. "Of course I know of him. I don't go in much for entertainment news, but he sure has quite a résumé."

"Travis knows everyone of substance in the country from sports figures and superstars to high-ranking politicians. We ran hot for a short time, and then...I became old news to him. He didn't have time for me and we began seeing less and less of each other. Shortly after, I found out he'd been cheating on me with a woman on the staff of his TV show for a long time. Seems that everyone knew about it but poor little gullible me. He'd made me out to be a fool and my career and credibility suffered. It's taken me three years to get my reputation back. Princess or not, I wasn't immune to the blonde-bimbo stigma and so now, I'm cautious. Which is why your royal status isn't a plus in my book."

He stood with hands on hips, silent, taking it all in. He understood her caution. The pain in her eyes, the tremor in her voice were telling, and his heart hurt hearing her confession. He should leave and let her resume her vacation. He shouldn't press her. But his feet were planted and they weren't moving. He couldn't face not seeing her again.

"If things were different, would you accept my offer?"

"Yes," she said, her eyes clear now. "I wouldn't hesitate. It sounds far too exciting to pass up."

"Then let's pretend that we've just met. There was no amazing kiss from before. We haven't danced and spent time together. This is a business meeting. And I promise to keep things completely professional between us."

"Why is it so important to you?" she asked.

"Because, I...I see how much you want to say yes. I see that you'd love to locate the secret artworks."

"And you promise that after we discover this wonderful treasure, we'll just be friends?"

He let a split second go by. He was a man of his word.

If he promised, he'd have to adhere to his vow, regardless of how much he wanted things to be different.

"I promise, Princess."

She nodded. "I know you mean what you say. So yes, I accept your offer."

The next morning, Portia informed the concierge that she'd be checking out earlier than expected from Villa Delgado and offered her thanks for his accommodations. He'd questioned her, hoping she hadn't been disappointed in her stay, and she assured him that was not the case. She'd been called away unexpectedly, she explained. And his brows arched as if he'd suspected King Montoro had something to do with her sudden departure.

And so, her adventure was beginning. Dressed for the search, wearing a pair of Gucci jeans and a red plaid shirt tucked in and belted at the waist, she swopped out her Bruno Magli shoes for tall leather boots and stood outside the villa at precisely eight o'clock. Sunglasses shielding her eyes, her bags packed and ready to go, she gave one last glance to the Atlantic shoreline and the clear azure waters lapping the sands. There would be no five-star accommodations where she was going. She was told to expect rustic and that was fine with her. She'd gone camping before; she knew how to rough it.

Sort of. Jasmine had convinced her once to rent a motor home and they'd trekked as far as Pismo Beach, California. They'd parked the giant thing facing the ocean, and then had gone out for lunch and dinner every night. They'd hit a few clubs, too, dancing until dawn. So maybe that wasn't roughing it per se.

But they had cooked their own breakfasts and hiked the beach in the mornings. Did that count?

One of Juan Carlos's bodyguards drove up in a black SUV, right on time. Poker-faced, he promptly opened the door for her and she got into the backseat as he hoisted her luggage into the cargo space.

As they drove off, she sat quietly in the car, enjoying the sounds of morning, excitement flowing through her veins.

She'd taken Juan Carlos at his word. He would treat her as a professional and so she had nothing to fear and everything to look forward to. Her little heartfelt speech seemed to convince him that she wasn't looking for romantic involvement. Surprisingly, it hadn't been hard admitting her failings to him. He'd put her at ease and that was saying something, since she didn't go around revealing her innermost feelings to anyone but her best friend.

They drove away from the shore, through the streets of Playa del Onda and onto a highway that led inland. "Excuse me. When will we be picking up King Montoro?" she asked Eduardo, the driver-slash-bodyguard.

"His Majesty will be meeting you there," he said.

Ah...discretion.

"Is it a long drive?"

"Not overly so. We should arrive in less than an hour. Is there anything you need, Princess?"

"No, no. I'm perfectly comfortable."

She gazed out the window taking in the scenery, where residential streets were soon replaced by more rural-looking spaces. As the minutes ticked by, the groomed vegetation bordering the road gave way to untamed brush and wildflowers. There was a certain neglected beauty to the land that inspired her. The road though was becoming less and less car friendly. The tires spit broken gravel as they traveled along a bumpy country road.

"Sorry, Princess," Eduardo said. "The road is washed out from here on."

"Is it much longer?"

"No, just another mile or two."

And shortly, he turned onto a path and drove through

wrought-iron gates clawed by fingers of dead branches and vines. Weeds and overgrown scrub led to a two-story house in desperate need of a good solid paint job. Banging sounds reached her ears and she searched for the source as the car came to a stop in front of the house. Juan Carlos appeared on the porch holding a hammer, his shirt slung open and sweat glistening on his beautiful bronzed chest. His dark hair gleaming under the October sunshine, he gave her a wide welcoming smile.

She sucked oxygen in. If she could slither away in a trembling mass, she would. She could order Eduardo to turn the car around, drive and keep on driving until she forgot the exact chestnut color of Juan Carlos's eyes, the deep dark shine of his hair and the powerful rock-solid muscle of his body.

She bit her lower lip until it pained her.

As he made his approach, she bucked up and remembered why she was here, and the promise Juan Carlos had made to her. Now, if she could get her heart to stop racing…

"Welcome," he said, opening the door wide for her. He offered her his hand and helped her out of the car. Eyes shining, his smile broadened. "I hope your trip wasn't too uncomfortable."

"No, no. It was fine," she said, looking beyond him to the house.

"Sorry about my appearance."

She nearly choked on her own saliva. Was he kidding?

"I found some loose planks on the porch. They could be dangerous."

"You're handy with a hammer?"

"You sound surprised. Actually, I had a lot of odd jobs in my younger days. My uncle believed in hard work and I was always employed during my college years."

"Doing?"

"All sorts of things. Remind me to tell you about the time I worked at a strip club in Miami."

"You were a stripper?"

The image of him shedding his clothes made her mouth water.

"I didn't say that. But I sure got a quick education." Her eye fluttered and he squeezed her hand. "There's that wink again. I'm very happy you're here, Portia."

"It's not a wink," she assured him.

He smiled again and released her hand. Breath quietly swooshed out of her mouth.

"Let me assure you, the inside of the house is in better shape than the outside. Bella and James had two bedrooms renovated upstairs and my crew made sure the kitchen and living space are clean and functioning."

She flinched at the mention of the bedrooms and slid a glimpse at Eduardo, who was removing her luggage, appearing stoic as ever. "That's...fine."

She only wished that Juan Carlos would button his shirt so that she could breathe freely again.

Eduardo stopped at the steps with her two suitcases. "Just leave them. I'll take it from here," Juan Carlos said. "Thanks, Eduardo."

The man nodded, but it looked more like a bow. "Your Highness."

Juan Carlos rolled his eyes.

She chuckled. It would take him a while to get used to being royalty.

"Stop laughing," he whispered out of earshot of his bodyguard.

"I'll try," she whispered back. "Not promising anything."

He shook his head but grinned like a schoolboy.

She was up against massive charm and a killer body.

"Let me show you around." Juan Carlos took her arm and guided her inside.

The living room was cozy with a large brick fireplace and old wood floors that looked as though they'd been scoured and polished. A new patterned rug was laid down between two sofas covered with floral tapestry pillows. The smell of fresh drying paint filled the room.

"Come see the kitchen," he said, taking her hand. "It's rustic, but I didn't have the heart to replace everything. I'm assured the oven is in working order." The oven was indeed, quaint and lovely. She could tell it, too, had been scoured to a new brilliance, but it must date back to the 1940s. The refrigerator had been replaced, and the counters were chipped in places but the sink had passed the test of time. A kitchen table sat in front of windows overlooking the backyard grounds. Someone had recently plowed the area and planted a garden of fresh flowers and herbs so the immediate view was quite picturesque.

"It's charming the way it is."

"The refrigerator is stocked. Would you like a cold drink?"

"Sure."

He opened the door and peeked inside. "Lemonade, soda, orange juice and sparkling water."

"Lemonade sounds good. I'll get the glasses." She flipped open a few cupboards and found them. It was obvious the dinnerware and glassware were all new, or imported from the palace. "Here we go." She set two glasses in front of him on the counter and he filled them.

A cool, refreshing swallow quenched her thirst and as she sipped, she strolled through the kitchen, exploring. She passed a utility room and then entered a large bathroom. Juan Carlos was just steps behind her and prickles of awareness climbed up her spine. She felt his eyes on her and as she turned slowly, he didn't even try to look away. He was in the doorway, his arms braced on the doorjamb, his shirt hanging open loosely from his shoulders. All that pure masculinity in one man didn't seem fair.

He stared at her for long seconds, until regret seemed to dull the gleam in his eyes. She had the same regret. If only she was just a woman and he was just a man and they were here together, sharing a grand adventure.

She swiveled around, pretending interest in a claw-foot tub, running a finger along the porcelain edge. "Makes you wonder about what life was like here when the farm was active." She turned to him again. "Do you know if there were animals?"

"Hmm. I think so. There are many outer buildings on the acreage. Supply sheds, barns and feed shacks. They owned livestock. Probably sheep, maybe cattle, but definitely horses. Do you ride?"

"Horses? Yes, I do. I'm no expert but I know how to plant my butt in the saddle."

He smiled.

"Will we be riding?"

"Possibly. There's five thousand acres here to investigate. Between the Jeep and the horses, we should be able to scour the entire grounds. The horses will be here this afternoon."

"Did your family ever live here?"

"I don't think a Salazar ever lived here. But a Montoro must have at some point. This land is all part of the Montoro holdings."

"Do you have any idea where to start looking?"

"I'm thinking we should stick close to the house today and if we come up empty, we can venture out tomorrow."

"Sounds good. I have to admit, I'm eager to start."

"Okay, then I'll get your luggage. Your room is upstairs at the end of the hallway. It's been painted and furniture was brought in yesterday. Take some time to relax. I think you'll like the room, but if there's anything you need, just let me know."

"I'm sure it's fine." She'd roughed it with Jasmine, after

all. She really could handle her own luggage, but His Majesty would never allow that. His sense of gentlemanly duty would become tarnished. And darn, if she didn't find that amazingly appealing. "Thank you."

As she headed upstairs, a sigh escaped from her lips.

Juan Carlos was a big juicy ripe apple, dangling his unabashed charm and beautiful body in front of her.

And the wicked serpent in her head was daring her to take a bite.

Four

Portia's room was more than adequate. A queen-size bed, adorned with Egyptian cotton sheets, a snowy comforter and pale pink pillows took up most of the space. Southern light streamed into the room through twin windows with ruffled curtains and an exquisitely crafted armoire made of inlaid mahogany and cherrywood held the bulk of her clothes.

She glanced out one window to the unkempt grounds below. The Montoros owned all the land as far as her eyes could see. Would they find the hidden artwork somewhere out there? Her belly warmed to the idea. She was grateful for the opportunity to search for it.

And ready.

As she headed for the stairs, movement caught her eye from a room at the opposite end of the landing. Juan Carlos was in his bedroom, changing his shirt. Twenty feet separated them, and she immediately glanced away, but not before she caught sight of bare broad shoulders tapering down to a trim waist. She gulped and scurried down the stairs before she got caught ogling him.

She wandered outside into the yard. Birds flitted between tree branches and flew away. She knew the bodyguards were out here somewhere, watching over the place, but she'd yet to see anyone else since Eduardo had deposited her here this morning.

She heard the door open and close behind her and foot-steps crunching the fallen leaves as Juan Carlos approached. "Where are they? I know they are out there somewhere," she said.

He chuckled. "Luis and Eduardo have orders not to disturb us unless there's danger. They're here, trust me."

"I'm not worried." She put on a pair of sunglasses.

"That's good. How do you like your room?" He sidled up next to her. Dressed in jeans and a chambray shirt, with a black felt hat shading his eyes, he looked like a modern-day Spanish vaquero.

"It's better than I imagined, considering the state of the grounds around us. I'm sure you had a hand in making it comfortable for me."

He shrugged. "If you're comfortable, that's all that matters. Let's check out what we can on foot. There's a stable and a few broken-down buildings nearby." He reached into his back pocket and came up with a pair of work gloves. "Here, put these on."

She slipped them on. "I'm ready." And off they went.

The stable was in ruins, like pretty much everything else on the property. As they entered, she spied a wagon wheel, some rusted harnesses and a stack of rotted grain bags. It didn't seem as though anything could be hidden in here, but Juan Carlos touched every wall, kicked clean every stall and scoured the entire area with assessing eyes.

She took his cue, and searched the outside perimeter of the building, looking for anything that could be used as a hiding place.

He met her outside. "Nothing here. I didn't think we'd find anything this close to the house, but we need to be thorough."

"Okay, where next?"

"There's some feed shacks farther out we should check. Are you up for a long walk?"

She stared into his eyes. "You know that pea under my mattress didn't ruin my sleep last night."

He gave her a look of mock concern. "There was a pea under your mattress, Princess? Twenty lashes for the chambermaid who made up your bed last night."

She grinned. "More like fifty lashes for the king who thinks I can't keep up with him."

"Okay, I get your point. You're not frail."

"Not one little bit. But I think your concern is sweet."

"And antiquated."

"That, too. But what woman doesn't dream of a knight in shining armor once in a while?"

He peered directly into her eyes. "Do you?"

"I'm…not going to tell."

With that, she dashed ahead of him and hoped she was heading in the right direction.

Juan Carlos's laughter reached her ears, but he hung back a little, watching her.

She came upon three outer buildings, each one fifty feet or so from the others. She was just about to enter one when Juan Carlos called out, "Portia, wait!"

She whirled around. He came marching toward her, making up their distance in long strides. "Let's do this together."

He was being overprotective again. "I don't see why I can't—"

"Humor me," he said, sweeping up her hand and tugging her inside with him.

The small shed was in better shape than the stable had been. Juan Carlos remarked on how it was a newer building, perhaps added on later as the farm prospered. The open door allowed a sliver of light inside the windowless and otherwise dark space. Juan Carlos released her hand and the tingles streaming down her arm finally eased.

He got down on his knees and scoured the floorboards, looking for a trap door while she tapped at the walls. She tugged at a splintered hoe leaning against the far wall, moving it out of her way. A deafening hiss broke the silence. She looked down and saw a snake coiling around her boot. Panicking, she gasped quietly.

Juan Carlos jumped up. "Don't move!"

She froze. Oh, God, no. "What should I do? What should I do?" The thing was moving up her leg.

"Hold still, sweetheart. Trust me."

Juan Carlos reached into his boot and a glint of silver caught her eye. A knife?

There was a flash of movement as he lunged forward, and she squeezed her eyes shut. He ripped the thing off her in seconds flat. When she opened her eyes, she saw that he'd slashed the snake's neck all the way through. Juan Carlos tossed the dead reptile, head and all, across the shed. It landed with a smack and her stomach recoiled.

She shook uncontrollably and Juan Carlos took her into his arms. "You're okay, Portia. You're okay, sweetheart."

Tears spilled from her eyes and she nodded.

"Let's get outside," he said softly.

"I don't know if I can move."

"You can. I'll help you."

She nodded. "Okay." She clung to him as he guided her into the daylight. Fresh air filled her lungs and helped with her shaking.

"I'm sorry," he said, over and over, kissing her forehead.

She held his neck tight. She'd never been so frightened in her life. It all happened so fast, but the thought of that thing crawling up her body would surely give her nightmares for days to come.

"No, she'll be fine. I've got this," he was saying to someone, shaking his head. Then he turned his attention back to her. "Sweetheart, we'll go back to the house now."

"Who were you talking to?" She glanced past his shoulders and caught Eduardo gazing at her for a second before he lowered his eyes.

"We can walk, unless you want Eduardo to drive us back to the house?"

"No." She clung to Juan Carlos tighter, still shocked. She wasn't ready to let go. "No, we have more to do."

He ran his hand over her ponytail, like a father would a child. "But not today, Portia." His voice was gentle. "Not if you're not up to it."

She glanced to where Eduardo had been standing. He'd disappeared.

"Just hold me a little longer, please."

"Of course." One hand ran comforting circles on her back.

"I...I guess you have your answer." She spoke into his shirt, still too freaked out to back away.

"What do you mean?"

"You're my knight in shining armor today."

"Just today?" There was amusement in his voice and Portia couldn't deny how safe she felt being in his protective arms.

"Hmm." To say more would be too revealing. She was vulnerable right now and had let her guard down with him. She didn't want to let go of him. She needed his strength. He bolstered her courage.

"I guess, I'll settle for that," he said.

She tipped her chin up and gazed into his eyes. It would be so easy to kiss him now, to thank him for saving her from that creature.

"Portia," he whispered. His gaze tumbled down to her lips and the longing in his voice tortured her.

Debating with herself, she closed her eyes.

She heard him sigh deeply as one hand gripped her shoulders. He gave a little shove and she stumbled back and then blinked. He'd set her away deliberately. She focused on the blade he still held in his other hand and the image of that snake's split body flashed again in her mind.

A tick worked at his jaw, beating an erratic rhythm. "You test my honor, Portia. I made you a promise."

"I...know."

He put his head down, not meeting her eyes, and then bent to wipe the blade clean on the grass. One, two, three slashes were all that he needed. Then he stood and sheathed the knife, placing it in his waistband. "Come," he said, reaching for her gloved hand. "We should go."

"Yes. I can make it to the other shacks now."

He nodded and led the way.

"Here." Juan Carlos set a glass of whiskey into her hand. "Take a few sips and drink slowly." She sat on the sofa near the fireplace and kept her eyes focused on the jumping blue-orange flames. They sizzled and popped and brought warmth to the cool evening. "You'll need it to calm down."

"I'm calm." She wasn't really. Her body still quaked inside even as she sipped the numbing whiskey. The thought of that snake wrapped around her made her stomach curl. Yuck, it was disgusting. And frightening. Juan Carlos had been wonderful. He'd stayed by her side and comforted her, and hadn't balked when she'd insisted on continuing on their search. Though he'd made a thorough check of the next two buildings for creatures before he allowed her to step foot inside. He'd told her he was proud of her. It hadn't been courage on her part, but rather sheer stubborn determination that made her put one foot in front of the other and kept her from running back to the house for refuge. They hadn't found a thing in those other sheds, not one clue as to the whereabouts of the treasure, and she'd been ridiculously happy to return to the house after they'd exhausted their foot search.

"How's that going down?" he asked.

"Smooth. I'm not usually a hard drinker."

"But you needed something tonight."

"I'm not usually such a wimp, either," she said, smiling awkwardly. She'd felt like an idiot for panicking after Juan Carlos explained that the snake probably wasn't poisonous or deadly, but her fear was real, and he'd understood that. Rather than take a chance, he'd done the manly thing. He'd killed the culprit. Her knight.

"You were very brave. You kept your cool."

"You mean I froze in panic?"

He stared at her from his perch atop the sofa arm. "I'm sorry you had to go through that. I promise nothing like that will ever happen to you again. I'm very cautious. I'll take care to secure the site before you go pouncing."

"I don't *pounce*," she said.

"Don't you?" He smiled over his glass and sipped whiskey. "I had to stop you from going inside by yourself."

"I didn't know there would be snakes."

He arched his brows. "All the more reason for us to stick closer together."

"Can't get much closer than this," she said, chuckling. Oh, but yes, they could, and Juan Carlos's arched brow, the amusement in his eyes, said he was thinking the same thing. The thought of sleeping just down the hall from him tonight killed her laughter. The alcohol was already affecting her brain, and her rational thinking. She set her glass down, looking into the amber liquid that remained. She needed her wits about her. It would be too easy to fall into lust with the king. "I think I'll be okay now. What's the plan for tomorrow?"

He thought about it a few seconds. "Tomorrow, we go out on horseback. There's some terrain I want to explore that we can't get to with the Jeep."

"Are the horses here?"

He nodded. "They arrived this afternoon. Eduardo and Luis have stabled them."

"You've thought of everything, Your Highness."

"Juan Carlos."

She grinned. "I'm sorry. Still can't get there."

He shrugged, and it dawned on her that she needed that wall of separation in order to remind herself who he was. She'd do better to think of him as a monarch, rather than a man.

"Are you getting hungry?" he asked, and she was glad he didn't press the issue.

"A little." It was after six and up until now, she hadn't thought about food.

"Wait here, I'll be right back."

He rose and entered the kitchen. She heard him rustling around in there, opening the refrigerator door and banging shut the cupboards. The dance of lights in the fireplace mesmerized her for the few minutes he was gone.

Juan Carlos returned with a plate of delicacy cheeses, a bunch of deep red grapes and a loaf of bread. "I hope this will satisfy your hunger. If not, I can cook a few steaks and bake some potatoes."

"No, this is perfect. I don't think I could eat much more."

"Want to sit in front of the fire?"

"Sure." She grabbed a fringy knit throw blanket hanging over the sofa and fanned it out in front of the fireplace. Juan Carlos waited for her to sit, and then handed her the plates before taking his seat facing her.

"This is nice, thank you." She arranged the plates in front of them.

The flickering flames cocooned them in a warm halo of light. She nibbled on the cheese and bread. Miles away from the city, she was at peace in this farmhouse.

She reached for a grape, and met with Juan Carlos's hand as he did the same. Their fingers touched and she lifted her eyes to him. He was staring at her, as if memorizing the way she looked right now. Her heart began to beat faster. Their gazes remained locked for a second, and then she tore a bunch of grapes off and popped one into her mouth.

Outside, breezes blew, making the windows rattle. The distant sound of horses whinnying carried on the wind and she pictured them in their stalls. How long had it been since there was life in those stalls? She hoped the winds wouldn't frighten the animals.

"What is it?" he asked.

"I'm just wondering if the horses are okay out there. The stable walls aren't solid anymore."

"I was going to check on them after you went to bed."

"I'd like to see them."

He pulled air into his lungs and nodded, as if convincing himself of his suggestion. "Then you'll join me."

Juan Carlos held a battery-powered lantern in one hand and Portia's hand in the other. He hadn't planned on spending more time with her tonight. Holding her shaking body and consoling her after the snake incident had stirred a possessive streak in him. He'd wanted to protect her from harm and keep her safe, but having her melt into him, her heartbreaking tears soaking his shirt, had sliced him up inside. He could have held her for hours and not tired of it, yet they'd continued on their search and he'd cursed that damn promise he'd made to her. He'd been desperate to get her to stay on in Alma. And he'd had to agree to her terms with a promise he hoped like hell he could uphold.

Tonight, he'd thought to escape her. Maybe he would have had a drink with Eduardo and Luis or taken a late-night ride, or simply waited until Portia was safely ensconced in her bedroom before making it up to his room. Yet he couldn't refuse Portia her request to join him in the stables.

So here he was, gritting his teeth as she walked beside him under the stars. The stables weren't far and he'd given the bodyguards strict orders to watch without being seen. They were out there somewhere.

The night air had grown cooler, and Portia wrapped both of her arms around herself despite her coat. She might've shivered once or twice.

"Cold?"

"Yes, but I'm okay. I have Scandinavian blood flowing through my veins. Cold weather doesn't bother me."

Juan Carlos hunkered down into his jacket. He'd lived in Miami most of his life. Neither Florida nor Alma got down into freezing temperatures very often. He could tolerate cold weather, but it wasn't his favorite thing. "This is about as cold as it gets here," he said. "At least that's what I'm told."

"It's mostly the wind I don't like."

Right on cue, a howling gust blew from the north. She shivered again and on impulse, he wrapped his free arm over her shoulder and drew her close.

She looked up at him.

"Thanks for keeping me warm," he said.

"Yes, Your Majesty. Anything for the king." A teasing smile played at her lips.

He laughed.

Before long they reached the stables.

"Want me to go in and check for snakes?"

She drew a breath and glanced around the property completely encased in darkness. "I have a feeling it's safer inside than out."

She had a point. There could be all manner of animals roaming the land. Wolves, wild boars and lynx were indigenous to the area. "Okay, then stick close to me."

"You still have your knife?"

"Of course."

"Then you won't be able to shake me."

"I wouldn't even try," he said, quite honestly.

A hum ran through her body. His subtle compliments did crazy things for her ego. After what she'd been through with Miles, that part of her brain had needed nourishment and was now being fed day in and day out by His Hunkiness the King.

She gasped.

"What is it?"

"Oh, nothing. I was just thinking." Jasmine would have a good laugh over this one. Portia was resorting to using terms from a romance novel to describe the handsome, honorable Juan Carlos Salazar II, King of Montoro.

He gripped her hand and led her into the stables. The protective way he held her was another turn-on.

The lantern lit up about five feet of the path in front of them. The place was dank and colder than she'd hoped for the animals. Juan Carlos lifted the lantern to his shoulder and illuminated the stalls. There were shuffling sounds, whinnies and snorts as all four horses came into view. Beauties.

They were curious enough to approach their individual gates. Though she'd been here earlier, Portia could see hints of work done today to make the stable more secure for the horses. The stalls had been shored up, and beds of straw had been laid down. Holes in the walls letting in cold air had been hastily boarded up. Juan Carlos knew how to get things done.

Her eyes darted to the animals' backs. "They're wearing blankets."

"To keep warm. I put Luis on it tonight. They seem comfortable enough, don't they?"

She smiled, relieved. "Yes, I feel better now. They are amazing creatures. Are they yours? I mean do they belong to the palace?"

"We haven't had time to build a remuda of horses for the palace. The transition takes time, but we will have a royal guard on horseback one day soon. These horses belong to me personally, as of two days ago. I have it on good authority they are gentle and trustworthy. I've yet to ride any of them. Tomorrow will be a good test."

"For them or for you?"

His brow arched. "Maybe for all of us."

"Maybe," she agreed. "I've never claimed to be an expert, but I do love animals. What are their names?"

"Come. Let me introduce you." Straw crunched underfoot as they made their way to the first stall. "This is Julio. He's a two-year-old gelding," Juan Carlos said. The sleek charcoal-colored horse had a thick black mane and tail. "He's an Andalusian."

"The horse of kings," she said.

"Yes, I've heard them referred to that way."

"Because they're powerful and sturdy?"

"Because they're intelligent and docile."

She eyed the commanding animal in front of her. He was gorgeous. "Docile?"

"Not as hot-blooded as a thoroughbred. He'll be my mount."

Julio was tall and grand. His curious ink-black eyes watched her. She lifted her hand to him cautiously and he edged closer. She took that as an invitation to stroke the side of his face. "That's it, boy. You and I are going to be good friends," she crooned. Back in Los Angeles, she volunteered at an animal rescue when she wasn't working. Her lifestyle and schedule didn't allow having a pet of her own and she enjoyed donating her time to animals in need.

"You're good with him."

She touched her cheek to Julio's cold nose and he nuzzled her throat eagerly. The force pushed her back a step and she righted herself and giggled. "Oh, he is sweet."

Juan Carlos's gaze touched upon her. Something flickered in his eyes. He swallowed and stroked his hand over his chin. He hadn't shaved today, and his stubble only added to his good looks.

With an inward sigh, she focused back on Julio, giving his mane a solid but loving stroke. She sensed that she had indeed made a new friend today.

Juan Carlos tugged her along to the next stall. "This is Sugar. She's an Arabian. Quick, sharp and good-natured. You'll ride her tomorrow."

"Hello, Sugar. You're a pretty one."

Sugar wasn't as tall or commanding as Julio, but was equally as stately. She had sensitive eyes and seemed friendly. Her chestnut coat glistened under the lantern light. "I'll see you in the morning, girl."

Juan Carlos showed her the other two horses, Arabians named Estrella and Manzana, who were presumably for Eduardo and Luis. Were the king's bodyguards good riders? Was that part of their job description?

New feedbags hung from nails in the walls, replacing the shredded ones from this morning, and a bag of carrots sat on a splintered bench. "Can we give them a treat?"

"Good idea." Juan Carlos went to retrieve the carrots. He dipped his hand inside the bag and came up with four. "One for each."

"Only one?"

"We don't want to spoil them."

"I bet you'd be a tough disciplinarian with your children."

At the mention of children his eyes twinkled and somehow the mischief seemed aimed directly at her. "I'm ready to find out."

Her blood warmed. She hadn't thought along those lines for herself. Parenthood was a long way off for her. But Juan Carlos seemed to know exactly what he wanted. He was resolute, an action taker and at times, he intimated her with his decisiveness. "You want a family one day?"

"Of course…I've lived my life without my parents. I have

no brothers or sisters, although I have my cousins and we have been on good terms. But to have a child of my own, to share that bond with someone I love…it's a dream of mine."

He handed her all four carrots and she walked the stalls, allowing Sugar to nibble at hers first.

"I would think being king would be your dream."

"It's my duty and a role I'm proud to uphold. But a man can have more than one dream, can't he?"

His eyes darkened, his gaze boring into her like a nail being hammered into the wall. He was too close, his expression telling her too much. She couldn't look at him and not see his life all planned out…with her beside him. Were the limited lighting and her silly imagination playing tricks on her?

She turned away from him, taking interest in the horses again. "I suppose." Three beggars were vying for her attention, shuffling their feet, bobbing their heads back and forth. She walked over to Julio next. "Here you go, boy."

Juan Carlos shadowed her to the next two stalls and watched her feed the other Arabians. "Do I make you nervous, Princess?"

Her eyes crinkled as she squeezed them closed. Why did he have to ask her that? She took a breath to steady her nerves and pivoted around. Her back to the stall door, the lie was ready to fall from her lips. Her one eye fluttered, like a wink, but certainly *not* a wink. Oh, boy. She wanted to sink into a black hole. "Y-yes." Damn her honesty. So much for pretending disinterest in him.

Juan Carlos gave her an approving smile as if he'd expected her answer. As if he was pleased with her honesty. "I promised not to pursue you, Portia. But I didn't say I would back off if you came to me. If you decided you wanted me, craved my body as I do yours, I would claim you in an instant and not feel I'd betrayed my vow to you."

He took her hand then, and led her out of the stable. "Come, it's time for bed."

Five

Sugar kept an even pace with Julio as they ambled farther out onto the property. The horse was gentle, took commands well and her sure-footed gait put Portia at ease. She gazed at the cloudless blue sky above. The warmth of the rising sun removed the bite of coolness in the morning air and made the ride pleasant.

Juan Carlos's felt hat shaded his eyes. Portia had put her hat on, too, one that Juan Carlos, who planned for everything, had given her to wear.

"How are you doing?" Juan Carlos asked after five minutes of silence.

"I have no complaints, Your Highness."

He paused. Gosh, why did she goad him? Oh, yeah, to put distance between them. "We've been riding a while now. Is your rear end sore?"

She chuckled. "A little, but I'll survive."

"You just let me know when you want to take a break."

Things had been a little weird between them since last night. Juan Carlos had put a bug in her ear. He'd given her an out. Up until then, her idea to keep their relationship strictly platonic had rested solely on Juan Carlos's shoulders. She'd made him promise to keep his distance. But now he'd tossed the ball into her court. And it had gotten her thinking. But it wasn't a good thing for a woman desperately attracted to a man who was all wrong for her to be given those options.

If you decided you wanted me, craved my body as I do yours...

Those hot words had thrown her. She'd thought of them, of him, all through the night. What would it be like to have Juan Carlos make love to her? What if, here, in this remote, private place, she gave in to temptation and spent the night touching him and being touched. Kissing his perfect mouth, running her cheek along that sexy stubble and nibbling on his throat? What would it be like to have him inside her, the steely velvet of his erection impaling her body?

She squirmed in the saddle, suddenly uncomfortable. Mentally, she forbade Juan Carlos to look over, to see her struggling with thoughts he'd planted inside her head. *Don't look at me. Don't see the expression on my face. Don't see me...wanting you.*

"Portia?"

Darn it. "I'm fine." She stared straight ahead. "Everything's good and dandy."

She sensed him studying her as they rode the length of five football fields until they came upon a graveyard surrounded by a run-down picket fence. The square of ground was full of weeds, unkempt. The neglect was almost sacrilegious. It was out in the middle of nowhere, a place long forgotten.

Juan Carlos slowed his gelding and she did the same. "We'll stop here," he said.

Her rear end rejoiced. She spotted trees that offered perfect shade just yards away. The horses moved toward an oak, massive in size, its roots splayed in all directions.

Juan Carlos dismounted quickly and strode to her. Sugar wasn't as tall as Julio, but Portia still needed help with her dismount. Either that, or run the risk of breaking an ankle when she tried to slide down the horse's left flank.

Juan Carlos's arms were up, reaching for her. She swung her leg over the saddle and his hands found her waist, securing her with a firm grip and guiding her down until her boots hit the ground. He held her for a few beats of time, with her back to his chest, his nose tickling her neck, breathing in her hair. "You smell delicious," he whispered, and then released her.

She sighed. If only she didn't miss his hold on her. Didn't enjoy having him touch her.

I would claim you in an instant and not feel I'd betrayed my vow to you.

He stood beside Julio, gazing at the graveyard as he unlatched a saddlebag and came up with a bottle of water. He walked over to her. "Here," he said. "Take a drink, you must be thirsty."

The water, cool and refreshing, slid down her throat. "That's good." She handed it back to him. His mouth clamped around the lip of the bottle and he tipped it back. He swallowed a big gulp, then another. A trickle of sweat ran down his forehead and he wiped it away.

Simple gestures. Yet her heart raced being near him, sharing water, doing natural things that seemed to bind them together.

"I'd like to check out the graveyard. You can stay here and rest. I'll put a blanket down. You'll be in the shade."

She shook her head. She was curious about the graveyard, too. "I'll come with you."

He nodded and began walking. She followed behind. Wind kicked up and almost blew her hat off. She grabbed it just in time and held it to her head as she approached a wooden gate. Overhead, tree branches made a makeshift archway, and scrolled in wood a sign read: Montoro Family Cemetery.

"So this is where the farm families ended up," she said.

Juan Carlos nodded. "They were probably distant cousins, relatives of my uncles. I'd bet Tantaberra made sure no one has ever come to honor their graves."

They walked through the battered gate. There were many headstones, maybe twenty-five in all. Portia stopped beside Juan Carlos as he bent his head in prayer over one after another. She sent up her own prayers for the lives forgotten here, stepping from one grave site to the next. "Do you know any of these names?" she asked.

"Some sound familiar," he said. The first and middle initials were etched on the headstones along with the last names. "Montoro, of course, and Olivio I've heard mentioned, but many I don't know. I will have this cemetery restored to honor their graves."

Juan Carlos insisted on clearing away the larger of the weeds that had overgrown the area. She bent to help him. "No, please. Your hands will be cut," he said.

"I'll be careful. I want to help." Her chin up, she was ready to do him battle.

He stared at her. "I forgot to bring you gloves." And then he warned, "See that you are careful, Princess."

She smiled and something tugged at her heart. He was angry with himself for the oversight. "I promise to be careful."

He began to pull away tumbleweeds clustered around the graves, staring at the names embedded on the stones as if embedding them into his brain. She, too, had little family. She could see the sadness and the loss in the contoured planes of his face, in the shadows of his dark eyes. The dictatorship had taken so much from his family.

"Let me see your hands," he said when they were all through. They'd cleared away as much as they possibly could. The wind was howling; breezes that had cooled the day's heat were swirling more rapidly now.

She turned her palms up.

Juan Carlos inspected her hands carefully, turning them one way then another.

"See. I'm not a wimpy princess."

He laughed, the shine returning to his eyes. "I'd never describe you that way. I'm grateful for your help."

"You're welcome. But there's one more thing to do."

His right eyebrow shot up. "What would that be?"

"I'll be right back. Don't follow me. I'll only be ten minutes."

She left him in the graveyard. This was something she wanted to do by herself. For his family. He leaned against the post outside the cemetery and watched her march into the fields. Every time she turned, his gaze was glued to her. He wouldn't let her out of his sight. She got that. He was a protector by nature. Gallant. He didn't interfere with her independence though and she appreciated that.

Ten minutes later, she returned to the Montoro family cemetery. Juan Carlos smiled broadly as he gazed at the large bunch of wildflowers she'd gathered in her hands. Some were probably classified as weeds, but they were indisputably pretty anyway. Bluebonnet blues, pale yellows, creamy whites and carnation pinks.

"Would you like to help me lay these down?"

He nodded, a play of deep emotion on his face.

They walked through the cemetery one last time, offering up the flowers to grave sites and headstones to tell the deceased that someone remembered them. Someone cared.

They left the place quietly, Juan Carlos taking her hand. It was a solemn moment, but a sweet one, too. Portia was moved by the care he'd taken with his distant relatives, the honor he'd bestowed upon them.

How many would have just ridden past? How many wouldn't have bothered to stop and clear up the neglect and mess?

This feeling she had for Juan Carlos wasn't going away. It grew stronger each moment she spent in his company.

The horses whinnied upon their return, huffing breaths and stomping hooves. Juan Carlos dipped into the saddlebag again, this time to offer the animals a handful of oats to keep them satisfied. "There, now. You two be quiet. No more complaining." He stroked Julio's head a few times and then turned to Portia. "Let's sit a minute. Take a rest."

"All right."

He grabbed a blanket and spread it out under the tree. The shade was no longer an issue; the weather had cooled and gray clouds were gathering in the skies. She shivered and walked to her saddlebag, picking out a jacket from the things she'd brought along.

"Cold?"

"A little bit."

"We can head back."

It was too early to return to the house. They had more ground to cover and she didn't want to delay their mission because of a little cold weather. Her family hailed from Scandinavia, where food was put out on windowsills to freeze quickly, where the elderly lived over one hundred years because germs couldn't survive the environment. She refused to slow Juan Carlos down.

"Ten minutes is all I need," she said.

She put on the jacket and sat down. He sat next to her and roped his arm around her. It seemed only natural to put her head on his shoulder.

"There is a giant rock formation about half an hour from here. The terrain is rough but these horses can make it up there. I found it on a GPS map of the area." His voice soothed her even as he spoke of a tough task. She closed her eyes. "I think it's a good hiding place for the artwork. I suspect caves have formed between the interlocking rocks. At least, that's what I'm hoping."

"Sounds reasonable. We'll check it out."

"Are you up for it? We can return tomorrow if you're not."

"I'm up for it," she said. "We're already halfway there, aren't we?"

"Yes, but the weather might be a problem."

"It won't be, Juan Carlos. I'm not a wimpy princess, remember?"

Laughter rumbled from his chest. "How can I forget? You keep reminding me."

"Good," she said, snuggling deeper into his arms.

The solid beats of his heart were like the revving of a powerful engine. It was dangerous and thrilling and though she hated to move, it was time to break this cozy moment with him. She slid away from his grip and rose to her feet. "I'm ready when you are."

He bounded up, regret in his eyes, as if she'd taken something precious from him.

From both of them.

The rocks were adobe-red, huge and intimidating. They were also beautiful against the landscape of gray skies and brown earth. The horses treaded with agility through the gravelly terrain, their sure-footed gait assuring her she would not fall to her death as they climbed a plateau that led to the face of the mountain. "This is amazing. It reminds me of Sedona back in the States. Have you ever been there?"

"In Arizona?" Juan Carlos gave his head a shake. "No, but I've seen pictures. It's an artist colony, isn't it?"

"Yes, among other things. There are some wonderful galleries and art exhibits in the area. I studied there one summer."

"Did you ever climb the rocks?"

She nibbled her lower lip. "I'd been tempted a few times, but no, I didn't climb the rocks. I was there for the art. Are we climbing rocks today?" she asked pointedly.

Juan Carlos spread his gaze over the entire mountainside, studying the terrain. "Just like back then, you came here for the art. So no. We don't have to climb the rocks.

The openings seem to be on the lower levels. We can reach them without climbing."

She released a tight breath. She didn't like heights and they didn't like her, so no rock climbing was a good thing. "I'm excited. I have a good feeling about this," she said. "I'm imagining the artwork tucked inside the mountain somewhere, deep inside a cave."

"Then let's go find it," he said.

He dismounted and strode over, lifting his hands to her waist again. Dust kicked up by the strong wind mingled with the potent scent of horseflesh and earth. More threatening clouds gathered above, and a shiver shook her shoulders as she slid into his arms. His hands steadied her until her boots hit the ground. Then he took the reins of both horses and they began walking toward a row of rocks, stacked neatly like building blocks five stories high.

He stopped at the base of a formation where two giant boulders separated and an opening appeared. It wasn't much wider than a double-door refrigerator, but large enough to allow a man to enter. "Wait here," he said. "Stay with the horses. I'll go inside and see if it goes anywhere. It might be a dead end. I'll be back in a minute." He pulled out a flashlight and turned to her. "Okay?"

She took the reins with one hand and stroked Sugar's nose with the other. Eyeing him, Portia confessed, "I'm not very patient."

A grin crossed his features, that gorgeous mouth of his lifting crookedly. "Good to know."

For real? The man had a one-track mind. "Come and get me, if you find anything."

"Will do. We're in this together," he said, and then disappeared into the gap.

Just then, the wind knocked her back against the rocks. It was fierce today. She huddled behind the horses, allowing them to block the sharp bite of cold. Her teeth chattered anyway. Goodness, it seemed as if Juan Carlos had already been gone for hours but it was more like a minute or two.

Then she heard his approach, his footfalls scraping the ground of the cave. Thank God. A thrill shimmied through her belly. She really wasn't patient, not when it came to this. If only they could find the artwork today.

When he emerged from the opening, she took one look at Juan Carlos's expression and her shoulders slumped. "You didn't find it?"

He shook his head. "Not in there." His eyes were solemn as they toured over her face and body. "You're freezing."

"I'm…not."

His lips twisted at her denial. Then he turned away from her and grappled with both of their saddlebags, freeing them from their fasteners and tossing them over his shoulder. "Come," he said, handing her their blankets. "It's warmer inside. Besides, there is something I want to show you."

"Really? What is it?"

"You'll see." He took her frigid hand and immediately the blood began pulsing more warmly through her veins. One would think he was a flaming hot furnace with how easily his touch could heat her up through and through.

He led her into the darkness. The flashlight illuminated the way and she squinted as her eyes adjusted. Around her, stone walls made up a cavelike space, tall enough for them to stand in and wide enough for an entire hunting party to take refuge. The air inside was cool, but without the outside wind gusts it was warmer by a dozen degrees. "You're right, it is warmer in here."

"Take a look at this," he said, aiming his flashlight at a far corner.

Eyes appeared first, round and frightened, and then the light followed the length of the animal, stretched out on the ground nursing her young. "Kittens!"

Five tiny bodies fought for a place at mama's table, eager for their meal. The mother cat, striped in reds, browns and grays, eyed both Juan Carlos and Portia warily. "She's scared," Portia said. "Poor mama." She'd had lots of experience with birthing pups and kittens at the rescue where she volunteered. "She might be feral, though I doubt it. She would've been hissing and scratching her way out of here by now. The babies look to be only a few weeks old."

"You think she's domestic?" he asked.

Portia crouched down, studying the cat from five feet away. "I think she's somewhere in between. She might've been abandoned. She's doing what comes natural and found this place to have her kittens. Cats like dark cool isolated places to give birth."

"Well, she found that," Juan Carlos said, keeping his voice soft. Both of them whispered now, so as not to startle the wary cat.

"I wonder if she's hungry. She looks pretty scrawny."

"About all we've got is water and sandwiches."

"Water, for sure. She'll need that. And we can pull out cheese and bits of meat from our sandwiches. If she's hungry enough, she'll eat it."

"Good idea. I'm getting hungry. Maybe we should stay inside and eat, too."

Portia kept her eyes fixed on the new little family. "I'd like that."

Outside the wind howled. The refuge they'd found would do for now until the weather let up. Portia worked with Juan Carlos to fix the mama cat a meal of beef and cheese, and laid it out on a cloth napkin. She was at a loss as to where to put the water. They had narrow-necked bottles and not much else that would work for a bowl.

"Here," Juan Carlos said, handing her his hat, tipped upside down in his palm. "She needs it more than I do."

Under the dim flashlight rays, his eyes were full of

compassion. He was a problem solver, but it was more than that. He was doing this as much for Portia's sake as he was for the sweet cat family. "You'll freeze your head off when we go back out there."

"Not if we stay here overnight."

Her heart skipped. To be alone with Juan Carlos all night? She couldn't possibly. He didn't mean it. It was hard enough knowing he was sleeping down the hallway at the farmhouse. "Surely, we can't."

His eyes twinkled. "It was a nice thought, though. Being trapped in here with you all night…*to watch over the kittens*."

Blood rushed to her cheeks. Suddenly, the cold dank cave sizzled with heat. She coughed, to cover errant thoughts of spending the night with Juan Carlos, of wearing nothing but a blanket to keep each other warm. His arms would wrap around her, and then their bare bodies would conform, mesh and he would nudge himself inside her.

"Are you okay, sweetheart?"

He knew. The sparkle in his eyes lit up even brighter.

"I'm fine."

"Are you sure?"

"Perfectly," she snapped. Goodness, she sounded like a witch.

He shrugged a shoulder, a smile teasing his lips as he handed her the cat's meal. "Do you want to take it to her?"

She nodded, recovering from the image that had sprung up in her head. "I'll try. I hope she doesn't run."

Portia took pained steps toward the cat, catching her eye and hoping her slow movements would show her she wasn't a threat. The cat's tail tensed and arched, her head came up and those tigerlike eyes watched her every move. Then she meowed.

"It's okay, sweet mama. I don't want to hurt you. Look, I have food. I hope you'll eat it."

The cat hissed, but she was just protecting her young. "This is as far as I'll go," Portia said softly. "See." She set down the napkin two feet from her and as soon as she backed away, the cat sniffed at it. "Put the hat down carefully," she said to Juan Carlos. He was only half a step behind and he set the water down next to the food. Then his hand clamped over her arm as he guided her several feet back, the beam of light dimming on the mama cat.

"Chances are, she won't eat or drink anything until she gives everything a complete smell test."

"We've done what we could for them," Juan Carlos said. "They are cute."

"Adorable," Portia said. The fuzzy fur babies were nestled against mama cat's underside, many of them satisfied and ready to nap.

Juan Carlos spread the blanket out and they began eating their sandwiches. Nibbling on her sliced steak sandwich sitting cross-legged, her eyes kept darting over to the cats.

"She'll eat eventually," Juan Carlos said.

"She's starving, but she won't make a move until we leave."

"Then we'll go as soon as we finish up here."

She nodded and within a few minutes, Portia was back atop Sugar, waiting for Juan Carlos to take his mount. She was torn about leaving the kittens in there, hoping the mama would survive the cold and be able to care for her young babes. How would she feed herself after the food they left behind was gone?

"Where to next?" Portia asked, blinking away tears, trying to distract herself from the sick feeling in her gut. She was a softie when it came to animals.

He stared into her eyes and smiled. "They'll survive. Don't worry."

He'd read her mind, but unlike most people, Portia didn't believe cats had nine lives. Sometimes, they couldn't beat the odds. If only this wasn't one of those times. She mustered a smile, but her heart wasn't in it.

"Since the wind has died down, I'd like to check out two of the nearby dwellings while we're here. If you stay put, I'll go in and be out quickly." He pointed north. "They aren't far. We'll get home before we lose light."

"I'm fine with that." She really was, though part of her wanted to stay behind and nurture the kittens. But that was impossible. Mama cat wanted no part of them right now. "I like the plan."

He nodded. "Let's go."

After showering and getting dressed, Portia marched downstairs in new jeans and a beige ribbed sweater to start dinner. She wasn't going to have Juan Carlos waiting on her. She planned to do her part. As she reached the bottom stair, she saw the fire crackling in the hearth and warmth settled around her. It was after seven; the darkened sky was lit with a scant few stars tonight. Her stomach grumbled, protesting over only having a light afternoon lunch. Thank God Juan Carlos wasn't around to hear the commotion her belly made.

The blaze in the front room beckoned. She could just as easily plop in a chair and watch the flickering fire, but she moved on and headed for the kitchen.

She found fresh tomatoes, whole garlic cloves, cans of tomato paste and packaged pasta in the cupboard. "Spaghetti it is." She wasn't a bad cook. She could crush tomatoes with the best of them.

Inside the fridge, she also found a covered dish of already cooked meatballs.

It seemed as though Juan Carlos had kitchen minions. She wasn't complaining.

She turned the stove on, grabbed a cast-iron pan, peeled and mashed two garlic cloves with a butcher knife and poured a little oil in the pan. Garlicky steam billowed up and pungent scents filled the room.

The back door opened and Juan Carlos walked in. "Mmm. Smells great in here."

"I hope you like spaghetti and meatballs."

"Who doesn't?" he said, coming to stand beside her.

"Hand me those tomatoes," she said, fully aware of his freshly groomed presence beside her.

Instead of walking to get them, he grabbed her waist with one hand from behind and stretched the other hand out as far as he could, snapping up three ripe tomatoes from the counter without leaving her side. "Here you go."

His touch sent heat spiraling through her body. "Into the pot with them, please."

"Like this?" He lowered them down gently, his face brushing against her hair.

He was a tease.

"Thank you."

"Don't you have to peel them?"

She shook her head. "The skin will peel off easily later from the heat. And then, you'll get to crush them."

"Me?"

"Yes, you. They need a manly crush."

"Well then, I'm your man."

She stopped and gazed into his eyes. Those words. They could be true. If she allowed it. Juan Carlos had owned up to his deal. He hadn't really come on to her, but every single second of every single minute of the day, he told her in his own silent, heart-melting way that he wanted her.

"Yes, well, uh…just let me get the meatballs."

How was that for a change of subject?

"I can crush those, too," he said.

She laughed. "I'm sure you can."

Dinner was half an hour later. They decided to eat in the kitchen this time, at a wooden table with inlaid painted tiles. One of the nearby windows faced the backyard garden, now bathed in starlight, and if she squinted she could see the plants. It was cozy and nice, and she'd put out a mason jar candle that cast a pretty glow over the room. Juan Carlos kept glancing at his watch as they forked spaghetti into their mouths and spoke of easy simple things. She refused to think any more about the snake with the severed head lying in that shack. Or the cemetery with so many families who'd lived here before.

After his eyes shifted to his watch once again, her curiosity got the better of her. "Am I keeping you from something?"

There was no television in the house. No important soccer games to watch. No distractions. Maybe he couldn't wait to get upstairs to finish the book he'd been reading.

He shook his head. "There's no place I'd rather be than right here."

Oh, she'd stepped into that one.

"The meal is delicious," he said.

"It was all that manly crushing," she remarked, and he put his fork down to grin at her.

She jingled in places that normally jangled. He turned her life upside down. She'd miss him when this adventure was over and she went back to LA.

She rose and grabbed up their empty plates. "Would you like another helping?"

He patted his flat, washboard stomach. "No, I'd better stop here."

"Then no cherry cobbler? It seems the kitchen minions made a trip to the bakery."

"Maybe later, Princess."

She washed dishes and he dried. It was all so domestic. Well, as domestic as she'd seen on the Hallmark Channel. Her life was hardly a typical American tale. What did one do after the dishes were cleaned and the night loomed ahead?

Her gaze slid to Juan Carlos, wiping his hands on a kitchen towel. He folded the towel neatly, set it on the counter and smoothed it out. With a slight tilt of his head, he sought her out, a question on his lips.

Before he could voice his thoughts, the purr of an engine reached her ears. Juan Carlos strode to the kitchen window that faced the side yard. "It's Eduardo. He ran an errand for me. Wait here, I'll be right back."

"Why?"

But he dashed out the door before giving her an answer.

She heard their voices and strained to hear what they were saying, but she couldn't make it out.

The back door opened with the slight kick of Juan Carlos's boot and he strode in holding a wire cage in both hands.

Meeeow.

The cats! Juan Carlos had the mama cat and her kittens.

Eduardo followed behind him, his hair rumpled, drops of blood staining his scratched hands. He looked almost as frazzled as the cat.

"Eduardo, you're bleeding!"

"Hazard of the job," he mumbled.

It took only a second for her to figure out what he'd done. What they'd both done. Juan Carlos had sent Eduardo on a mission to rescue mama cat and her babies.

"He wouldn't let me go," Juan Carlos was saying.

"My job is to protect you, Your Majesty."

"Not from cats." The king appeared annoyed at himself for allowing Eduardo to do the job he'd wanted to do. "I should've gone. Now look at you."

"Better me than you. They're nothing but a few scrapes. She put up a good fight." Eduardo grinned. "She is a feisty one."

Juan Carlos gritted his teeth. "Those injuries should've been on my hands."

"Stop arguing, you two," Portia said. "What you both did was very kind. Juan Carlos, take the cats in the living area. The room is dark and cozy. It might put mama at ease. Eduardo, come with me. I'll take care of your hands." She marched into the bathroom and heard footsteps behind her. Grateful that Eduardo had obeyed her order, she grabbed a washrag, filled a bowl of warm water and pointed for him to sit on the edge of the bathtub.

Goodness.

She sat, too, and took his big hands in hers, scouring over half a dozen scratch marks. "She must've been very frightened."

"That made two of us."

"Oh, Eduardo." She began dabbing at the wounds. He flinched, but took the pain. She dabbed a little more gently, cleansing and dressing his wounds. "There."

"The king is very angry with me. Luis and I both, we convinced him not to go. He wanted to do this thing... for you."

Portia closed her eyes. "I...know."

Her chest tightened. It was the sweetest gesture anyone had ever done for her. Or tried to do.

"He is a proud man. But don't worry, he won't be angry for long."

"He won't?"

"No. I think not. And thank you, Eduardo, for rescuing the animals."

She placed a chaste kiss on his cheek. He was large, built like a block of stone, but his expression softened and as he rose, he bowed to her with his eyes twinkling.

And she felt as though she'd made a new friend.

Six

"Do you think she'll try to escape if we open the cage?" Portia asked as she sat facing Juan Carlos on the floor beside the fire. The cage was between them. The leery mama cat's eyes were guarded and wide. Portia made a move to get a better look at the babies, and a mewling hiss, one born of fear more than anything else, pressed through the feline's tight lips.

Juan Carlos shrugged. "She has nowhere to go. The house is locked up and the doors to this room are closed. Right now, I think she needs to see us and know we won't harm her."

"I think you're right." Portia tilted her head to one side. "You're intuitive when it comes to animals."

While she had been bandaging up Eduardo, Juan Carlos had set out a bowl of water and a plate of leftover cheese bits for when they let the cat out later.

"At least she won't starve tonight," he said.

Outside the wind was howling again, even pushing through the flue of the fireplace. The flames scattered momentarily in the hearth, blazing wildly before returning to a normal easy burn again. "No, she won't starve and the kittens will thrive. Thanks to you."

He kept his eyes on the fire, not commenting, refusing to take any credit for the deed. It didn't matter. He couldn't hide his intentions from her.

"They're the cutest little things," she said, her voice squeaking. She couldn't help it. Babies in all forms brought her voice to a higher pitch. Who in the world didn't love furry new kittens? "I'm glad they're here."

She had a view of his profile, so sharp and defined. Firelight played across his face and when he turned to her, his expression softened. "Me, too."

"Why didn't you tell me your plan to rescue her?" It was what all his watch-glancing had been about. It made sense to her now and she was incredibly relieved to learn the reason for his impatience. "Was it a surprise?"

He nodded. "I didn't want you to be disappointed if Eduardo couldn't bring her back."

And there it was. On his face. Concern. Caring. Almost love.

Something shifted inside her. It wasn't a blunt move, but something that had been tilting and leaning gradually, like dominoes toppling in super slow motion. She could feel each one fall, until every shred of her defenses was being taken down by this good, kind, *sexy* man.

"It's late," he said.

No, it wasn't.

"We should unlatch the cage now and leave her, so she can eat."

"Okay," Portia said, sorely disappointed. She knew that meant saying good night to Juan Carlos and parting ways at the top of the stairs once again.

He sighed as he rose to his feet and strode to the fireplace to take up a metal poker. He slashed at the logs, until only simmering embers heated the brick floor inside.

Portia carefully unlatched the hook on the cage and flipped it away. The wire door swung open but the cat stayed put. "Here you go, Duchess. You're free now."

"Duchess?" Juan Carlos turned to her.

"She needs a name." She shrugged. "It seems fitting somehow."

He smiled, but his eyes remained hooded. "Duchess it is. What's one more royal around here, anyway? Well, I'll say good-night now. We have an early call tomorrow."

They did. They were going even farther out on the grounds in the Jeep.

"Are you coming up?" he asked. He had almost reached the hallway door.

She rose to her feet and stared at him from across the room. Words wouldn't come. Her heart was thumping, drowning out everything else in her world.

"Portia?"

"What if…?" A swallow stole her next words.

He waited, his face in the shadows so she couldn't see his expression.

"What if I said I was a w-wimpy princess, after all?"

He paused. "Would you rather not go out in the Jeep tomorrow?"

"No." She shook her head, her hair falling like a sheet around her shoulders. "Juan Carlos, it means I don't want you to go to bed…"

He stepped out of the shadows, his eyes dark, intense. Waiting.

She froze. Oh, God, she was breaking every rule she'd ever committed to.

"Say it."

The force of his command sent thrills careening through her body.

"Say it, Portia."

He wouldn't break his vow to her. She had to do it. He'd told her as much just the other day. His honor meant that much to him and he wouldn't have it any other way.

"Without me." She nodded, convincing herself. "I don't want you to go to bed without—"

And suddenly, he was there in front her, gazing into her eyes, cupping her head in his hands and brushing his lips over hers. Once. Twice. His hungry mouth devoured her over and over again. His arms wrapped around her, his hand brushing away her hair tenderly, his body trembling as he took her in kiss after kiss.

She was lost in the goodness of him, the thrill of his hands finally on her. The scent of his skin. The power of his body. Tears spilled down her cheeks at the clarity of this moment. She was his. He was hers. It was so easy, so simple. How had she managed to keep this amazing man at bay? How had she not realized earlier how perfect they would be for each other?

"Portia, don't cry," he was murmuring between kisses.

"I'm…happy, Juan Carlos."

"Oh, God. How I've waited for this. For *you*. Say my name again."

"Juan Carlos. Juan Carlos. Juan Carlos."

He grinned, a flash of white teeth in a broad happy smile that branded her heart. His gaze roved over her face and traveled the length of her body, his smile fading into something delicious. Something dangerous. And something she no longer feared. His eyes burned with want, the heat in them back full force. The man knew how to smolder.

"Portia." He breathed her name as if his life depended on it. "I need you."

"I need you, too," she admitted softly. She reached for the hem of his shirt, pushing the material up his torso.

"No," he said, taking her hands in his. "We'll do this right."

And in the next instant, he swooped her up into his arms. She wound her arms around his neck and as he headed upstairs, she pressed her lips to his, kissing him until they reached the threshold to his room.

"Here we are," he said, his voice reverent, as if the next step he took would be monumental. He carried her over the threshold with great ceremony and smiled at her. "I've wanted you since the moment I laid eyes on you."

"You have me," she said softly.

"God. I cannot wait much longer, but I will not rush with you." He lowered her down onto the bed. The mattress cushioned her body and then his hands were there, removing her sweater and unbuttoning her blouse, spreading it out so he could see her breasts. "You are beautiful," he said, planting both hands on the mattress beside her head, trapping her. She may never want to escape. His kiss was rough and hungry, and when she looked up, the sharp lines of his face tightened, a passionate preamble of what was to come. Her skin prickled in anticipation.

His fingertips grazed over her breasts lightly, hovering, teasing the sensitive tips. Hot liquid warmth pooled between her thighs. Then he wound his hands behind her back and she lifted herself up enough for him to unfasten her bra. With his help, she shrugged out of it and then lay back down.

"Fair is fair," he said, rising to grab the hem of his shirt. He pulled it up and over his head. Her mouth gaped open and she took a hard swallow, gazing at the tempting sculpted bronze chest.

"That is totally *unfair*," she whispered.

A smile spread across his face as he bent on his knees to remove her boots, her belt and then slowly, achingly moved the zipper of her pants down. Cool air hit her thighs, but she was too swamped already, too raggedly consumed by heat for that to have any lasting effect. He tugged at one pant leg and then the other, until she was free of them. All that was left on her body was a pair of teeny hot pink panties. "I like your style, Princess," he murmured, sliding up her thighs to hook the hem with his fingers.

"I like yours." She gulped.

He smiled again and dragged her panties down her legs.

Then the mattress dipped as he lowered down next to her. Immediately, his scent wafted to her nose: fresh soap and a hint of lime. She squeezed her eyes closed, breathing him in. He cupped her head and kissed her lips, her chin, her throat. "Let me explore you, Portia," he whispered.

She nodded. "If I can explore you."

"Be my guest," he said, his tone once again reverent. He fell back against the bed.

She rose up part of the way to lay a hand on his chest. Heat sizzled under her palm as she slid her fingers over tight skin and muscle. His chest was a work of art and as she continued to explore, he took sharp gasps of breath. Empowered now, she moved more confidently, her fingers flat over his nipples, weaving them through tiny chest hairs and reaching his broad shoulders. She nibbled on him there, nipping his hot skin and breathing the scent of raw sex emanating from his pores. "You are amazing, Juan Carlos," she said. And suddenly she was eager for him to explore her, to touch her in ways she'd secretly dreamed about. "Your turn."

She lay back on the bed and he rose over her to take a leisurely tour of her naked body, his eyes a beacon of light flowing over every inch of her. Then his hands began to trace the contours of her body, caressing her curves and moving effortlessly over her skin. He was thorough, leaving no part of her untouched. Goose bumps rose on her arms and legs, his precision and utmost sensitivity leaving her trembling in his wake.

Next, he covered her trembling body with his, wrapping her in his heat and claiming her with his presence. She bore his weight and peered up at him. He was amazing, so handsome, so incredibly virile. His hands cushioned her breasts, massaging them until the peaks were two sensitive tips. The pads of his thumbs flicked at them gently, and something powerful began to build and throb below her waist.

She had not been with a man in a long time. It felt so good. So right. Being with him.

He pressed her a little harder and she cried out. "Juan Carlos."

It seemed to satisfy him. He took her in an earth-shattering kiss, pressing her mouth open and sweeping into her. She moved under him, arching her hips, that feeling below her waist becoming stronger and stronger the longer the kiss went on.

His hand was moving again, leaving her full breasts and moving down her torso, past her navel and below her waist, where she ached and ached for him. "Trust me," he said.

All she could do was nod.

And his hands and mouth worked magic on her, shredding her into tiny pieces, squeezing tortured moans from her lips and making her squirm until she finally reached a fantastic, bone-melting orgasm.

"Juan Carlos," she breathed, lifting her head to find his eyes on her as he unbuckled his belt. He shucked out of his clothes quickly and sheathed himself, in all his naked glory, with a condom.

He touched her where she was most sensitive, lending her comfort and warmth in the aftermath of her pulsing release. She relaxed and eased back slowly, as another fire began to build. "I've waited for you all of my life, Portia. And now, you're mine."

She was ready for him when he entered her, wanting him this way, taking his weight and watching a fiery veil of passion burn in his eyes. He began to rock back and forth, each thrust a love note, a daring caress and sugary candy for her hungry body. "You are all I will ever need," he murmured.

She smiled as he pressed farther and farther inside her body. She was his. *He* was all she would ever need and as she met his driving rhythm, arching up and down, her breaths heavy, her body primed, she found solace and peace in his arms and lust and desire in his bed.

Juan Carlos drew a deep breath into his lungs. He'd often dreamed of waking up next to Portia, and now his very fantasy had come true. He turned his head and watched her chest rise and fall slowly. Her hair fanned across the pillow. He ached to touch it and sift the strands through his fingers. He wanted to kiss her awake and then make love to her again. But the sun had barely risen and the day would prove a long one. She needed her sleep. He'd worn her out last night. He shook his head at the thoughts running through his mind. He couldn't touch her again this morning and have her think he was lecherous, waking her with only one thing on his mind.

He smiled. He would come to her again sometime today. It would be hard to keep to the task at hand, but they were on a mission. Though a wicked part of him wanted to play hooky today. Why couldn't they just stay in bed all day? The States had snow days. Why couldn't he declare a Royal Day?

A little noise pressed through her lips, a moan that he'd come to know. Last night, she'd moaned plenty and turned his world on end.

She shifted toward him and one hand—warm, delicate and soft—flopped onto his cheek. He moved his head enough to press his lips there and kiss her.

"Hi," she said, smiling, though her eyes were still closed.

"Good morning, sweetheart."

"Is it time to get up?"

"You can stay in bed as long as you'd like."

"With you?"

"Yes, only with me."

Her eyes opened and he gazed into their sleep-hooded amazing blue depths. He could fall into those eyes and never want to return.

"Juan Carlos," she said, "last night was…"

"I know."

"I didn't know it could be that good."

He leaned in and kissed her tenderly. "I'm humbled to hear you say that."

"Humbled? Not over-the-moon, cocky and feeling proud of yourself?"

He chuckled. "Maybe that, too."

"I had…uh, you know. Three times. That's never happened before."

"Keep telling me things like that and we'll never get out of this bed."

She grinned and reached over to move a tendril of hair off his forehead, her delicate fingertips sliding down his cheek. He loved it when she touched him. "You know, that doesn't sound like a bad idea."

He caught her wrist and kissed her pulse point. "We can make that happen, sweetheart."

"If only," she said, sighing, her head falling back against the pillow. "But we need to finish what we started."

She would be leaving soon. She didn't have to say the words. He had only a few more days with her, before she would head back to the States. How quickly reality reared its ugly head. "We will finish it, one way or another."

"I hope we find something today," she said.

"We'll give it a good shot."

"I should get dressed. I'm anxious to see how our little family is doing."

She meant the cats. Juan Carlos had almost forgotten about them. "Right. Let's go check on them together."

She rose from the bed and turned away. As she fitted

her arms through the sleeves of his shirt, he glimpsed her lush blond hair falling down her back, the creamy texture of her skin, her rounded backside and the coltlike legs that had wrapped around him last night.

He sighed, enjoying the view and ignoring his body's immediate reaction to her. He threw on a pair of jeans and a T-shirt. Hand in hand, they strolled out of the bedroom and into the living area.

"Shhh," she said, spying the cat nursing her kittens outside the cage on a loop rug in front of the fireplace. "We don't want to startle her."

Duchess was resting with her head down, her eyes closed, allowing her five offspring to take their morning meal. Juan Carlos was moved by the sweet look on Portia's face as she silently watched mama and babies. He wrapped his arm around her shoulder and drew her closer, kissing the top of her head. How could he ever let this woman go? The answer was simple: he couldn't. It wouldn't be easy but he would convince her to stay. And marry him.

"Do you think Duchess will eat eggs?" she asked Juan Carlos as she scrambled four eggs in a cast-iron skillet. Morning sunshine brightened the kitchen, filling it with warmth. Bacon sizzled on the griddle and toast was cooking under the broiler. "I'll put a little cheese on them."

"You can try," he said, pouring two mugs of coffee. "She'll eat when she gets hungry enough. I'll send Eduardo out this morning for cat food."

She'd managed to get fresh water over to the cat without her running for cover. Duchess was still wary, but the kittens slowed her down or else she probably would've bolted when Portia set the bowl down. In time, Duchess would come to trust her. Sadly, she wouldn't be around long enough to see it.

She had work waiting for her in Los Angeles.

It was for the best that she leave Alma. She couldn't fall in love with Juan Carlos. He didn't fit into her plans for a quiet, unassuming life. Yet spending time with him had been magnificent.

He came up behind her, kissed the side of her throat and ran a hand up her thigh. She tensed in all the good places. He'd asked her not to dress yet, and now she knew why. She was only wearing his shirt, which gave him easy access to her body. Not that she minded. Heavens, no. She loved him touching her. "I'll be right back," he said. "Coffee's ready and on the table."

"Where are you going?" she asked.

"Don't be so nosy. I'll be back before you know it."

She smiled and turned, and his arms automatically wound around her. "See that you are. Breakfast is almost ready."

"Bossy, Princess," he said, staring at her mouth.

Her heart skipped a beat and a moment passed between them before he kissed the tip of her nose.

She shrugged a shoulder. "Kings."

He laughed and exited the back door.

Juan Carlos may have originally been a reluctant king, but there was no doubt in her mind that he was good for Alma and that he would put the country's welfare above all else. As it should be. Alma had been through tough times under a ruthless dictatorship. The country needed a strong man.

So do you.

No, she couldn't go there. The map was already drawn up for both of them, and after this little interlude, their paths wouldn't cross again.

After she set the table, Juan Carlos returned holding a bouquet of tall azure flowers. "For you," he said, handing her all but one stem. "Scilla hispanica."

"They're beautiful." She lifted them to her nose. "Are these from the garden?"

He nodded. "Spanish bluebells. They're almost a perfect match to your eyes, sweetheart." He pinched off the end of the one he still held and fitted it behind her right ear. "There. Now you're perfect."

"Hardly," she said.

"I think so."

"You think I'm bossy."

"Dressed like that, cooking my breakfast and wearing flowers in your hair? I can deal with a little bossiness."

She shook her head. "You're wicked." And so very thoughtful.

"So I'm told."

He took the flowers from her hands, snapped off the tips of the stems and arranged the bouquet in an old thick green glass bottle. After he filled it with water, he placed it on the table. "Have a seat, Princess," he said, pulling out a chair. "I'll serve you."

She had a protest on her lips, but Juan Carlos's expression wouldn't allow arguing. "Yes, Your Highness."

He smiled. "Good. I'm glad you know who the real boss is around here."

Portia's heart swelled. And as they sat down and ate, easy conversation flowed between them. Juan Carlos touched her hand often, as if needing the connection. She leaned over to brush hair from his forehead and he'd steal a kiss or two. They were in sync with each other; nothing had ever been as perfect as it was now, with the two of them doing ordinary everyday things, like cooking breakfast, sharing a meal and worrying over the cat family.

"So what will happen to Duchess and her babies when we have to leave here?" she asked.

"She'll become the official palace cat, of course."

"And the kittens?"

"We'll find them good homes, Portia. Don't worry."

Her eye twitched. "I know you're doing this for me." She covered his hand with hers. "Thank you."

The feelings between them were getting too heavy, too fast. She had no way of stopping it, short of leaving him right here and now. But she couldn't do that. Not only did she not want to, but she'd promised to spend a few days here helping with the search, and with the exception of a snake decapitation, she was having a wonderful time.

"You're welcome. Now, if you'll excuse me, I have to speak with Luis about a few matters."

Juan Carlos rose and began clearing the dishes. What a guy. She bounded up quickly and took the plates from his hands. "I'll take care of that," she said with enough authority to keep prison inmates in line.

"Okay," he said. "Thanks."

He bent his head and took her in a long amazing kiss. When their lips parted and he was through, her head spun. "That was…promising."

He grinned, shaking his head at her understatement. "Get ready. We'll be leaving in a little while. Unless you've changed your mind and want to play hooky today."

He was reaching inside her shirt. She slapped his hand away and pointed. "Go."

He went.

And Portia cleared the dishes and cleaned up the kitchen. She checked on Duchess and her brood; they were all sleeping. What a pretty serene picture they made, a mass of calico colors and balls of fluff all nestled together. She was grateful they'd have a home after they left the farmhouse. Her heart had never been so full.

Thirty minutes later, Portia climbed into the passenger side of the Jeep and Juan Carlos got behind the wheel. They said goodbye to Luis, though that didn't mean anything. He was sure to follow. Eduardo had gone into the local town on a cat food mission.

"All set?" Juan Carlos said, gunning the motor. "Strapped in?"

She nodded. The weather was glorious, the temperature in the mid-seventies with clear blue skies. She wore a lightweight white jacket that billowed in the breeze as Juan Carlos drove off and picked up speed.

"We're going out about five miles," he shouted over the engine's roar.

She sat back and relaxed, enjoying the scenery, excitement stirring her bones. Maybe today they'd find the art treasures.

For four hours they traveled at a snail's pace over lush lands, where wildflowers and lantana grew in abundance, the vista opening up to a prairie as they scoured the grounds looking for possible hiding places. They came upon another shack but after a thorough inspection, with Juan Carlos insisting on going inside first, they found absolutely nothing. Not even a snake.

"We have a little more land to cover before we head back," Juan Carlos said, and she heard the disappointment in his voice. She, too, was disappointed.

"Let's stop for lunch by that little lake we passed a few minutes ago." Maybe regrouping would give them a fresh perspective.

"It wasn't much of a lake," Juan Carlos said. "More like an oversize pond."

She entwined their fingers. "But it's pretty there and I'm getting hungry."

He smiled and gave her hand a squeeze. That was all it took for her heart to do a little flip. "Okay, we'll have a picnic." And he maneuvered the Jeep around, heading for the lake.

Warm breezes ruffled her hair and sweat beaded her

forehead as the sun climbed high overhead. She loved being outdoors. Much of her time in the States was spent indoors at art exhibits, galleries or simply poring over books and surfing the internet. She took a full breath of Alma air and vowed not to let disappointment ruin their day.

They'd packed a lunch and had a blanket. That was all they would need.

Juan Carlos braked the Jeep several yards from the water's edge. There were no shade trees so they used the vehicle to provide a bit of cover. From Luis. They were always being watched, but Portia was starting to get used to the idea and it wasn't as creepy as she'd once thought. Juan Carlos jumped down first as she gathered up the blanket. Then he reached for her and helped her down, crushing her body against his and taking her in a long, slow, deliberate kiss.

When he released her, her breathing sped up, coming in short clips. The blanket between them was her only salvation from being ravaged on the spot. She clung to it and backed away. "I should spread this out."

He backed off, too. "You do that," he said, his voice tight. "I'll get the cooler."

Once everything was in place, they sat down facing the water, their backs propped against the side of the Jeep. "The kitchen minions make great sandwiches," she said, taking a bite of chicken salad.

"I'll remember to thank them."

At some point during the day, either Luis or Eduardo would fill the refrigerator and cupboards with food, much of it readymade. She wasn't entirely sure it didn't come from the palace itself. The King of Montoro had a wonderful cook staff. But she decided the mystery was exciting and she didn't want to know how it magically appeared. She liked that it just did.

"What do we do now?" she asked, taking another bite.

Juan Carlos's throat worked, as he tipped a water bottle back and took a sip. He wiped the back of his hand across his mouth and turned to her, his eyes dark and searching. "I don't know. I think we've exhausted all possibilities. Where else is there to look?"

She had to agree. They'd searched the entire grounds—the prairies, the hills, the outer buildings—and found nothing. "The art could be anywhere and we'd never know it. There are no clues and sadly those secrets have been buried along with your family members."

He nodded. "At least the artwork didn't fall into the hands of the dictator, which was their main intent. I can't say I'm not disappointed. I thought we'd find something, a clue, some hint that would lead us to it. I can only hope it is found one day."

"I'm sorry, Juan Carlos." She set her sandwich down and brought her lips to his mouth. It was a chaste kiss, one of commiseration.

Instantly, his arms wound around her shoulders and he tugged, pulling her practically on top of him, deepening the kiss. "You're the only woman who can make me feel better," he murmured.

A pulse throbbed in her neck. She loved hearing his sweet words, even though they might be some of the last she'd hear from him. Soon, when the search was finally concluded, she'd have to say goodbye to him and all that they'd meant to each other in this short span of time. Yet, right now, she wanted to make him feel better—but she couldn't do it here. Out in the open. "We should go," she said. "Luis is watching."

He kissed her again, and then lifted himself up, pulling his phone out of his pocket. He spent a few seconds texting someone and then returned to her. "He's not watching anymore."

"Juan Carlos! What did you say to him?"

His lips twitched. "I told him to retreat one hundred yards and turn his head away from the Jeep for twenty minutes."

"You didn't!" Her face instantly burned. Her pride was stung. "He's going to know."

Juan Carlos touched her face gently, his fingertips on her cheeks, calming her. "Sweetheart, any man who sees how I look at you *knows*. Luis won't say a word."

"But I'll know he knows."

"It's beautiful here, Portia. And I need you. Do you not need me, too?"

His words worked magic on her. Yes, she needed him, too. She nodded. "But—"

He kissed away her doubts and then lowered her onto the blanket. His mouth was brutally tender, claiming her with each stroke of the tongue as soul-wrenching groans escaped his throat.

Thrills ran up and down her body as he exposed her to the sun's rays. The scent of fresh water and clear skies combined made her forget her inhibitions. She'd never made love outdoors and she only wanted to experience it with this one exciting man.

Firelight created jumping shadows across the living room walls. Juan Carlos sat with Portia beside him on the sofa as they watched Duchess bathe a kitten, her tongue taking long swipes across its furry body. The kitten took a playful swing or two at mama cat, but Duchess didn't relent. She used one paw to hold her charge down, determined to finish the job and lick away the grime of the day before moving on to her next one. She cleansed and fed her young diligently. Duchess, for all her wildness, was a good mama cat.

"You're quiet tonight," Portia said. "Still thinking about the missing art treasure?"

That was part of it. His failure to find it bothered him. He'd been so certain that there were clues here on the property and yet, he felt as if he was missing something important. He couldn't say what, but deep down in his bones he still believed the answers were here.

Yet most of his thoughts concerned Portia. They'd exhausted their search and there was nothing to keep them on the farm any longer. Tomorrow they would head back to Del Sol and then Portia would return to the States. Eventually. Unless he could convince her to stay.

"I'm thinking about us," he answered honestly.

Portia put her head on his shoulder. "What about us?" she asked, her smooth-as-velvet voice tapping into his heart. At least she didn't say, *there is no us*. She recognized that they were edging toward a precarious cliff.

Three sharp raps at the door interrupted their conversation. He gave it a glance and waited for the next two knocks, which would signal him that all was well. Those two knocks came and Juan Carlos rose, striding to the door. "It's either Luis or Eduardo," he said over his shoulder to reassure Portia, and then opened the door. "Eduardo. I trust everything is all right?"

"Yes. But I have something of interest I thought you would want to hear right now."

Eduardo glanced at Portia, who was now sitting on the edge of the sofa, her eyes round with curiosity. "Regarding?"

"Your search, Your Majesty."

Juan Carlos swung the door open wider. "Come in."

"Your Highness," he said to Portia as he made his way inside the room.

"Eduardo." She granted him a beautiful smile, most likely grateful it wasn't his counterpart, Luis, seeking them out. He could see the relief in her eyes. This afternoon, making love under blue skies behind the Jeep, Portia had let go her inhibitions and made a memory that would live forever in his mind. But afterward his Portia had gone on and on about Luis, asking how she could ever face him again.

Juan Carlos had succeeded in kissing away her worries.

"Would you like to sit down?" Portia asked.

"No, thank you. I didn't mean to interrupt." Eduardo regarded the kittens, his expression softening.

"Duchess is coming around," Portia said, her eyes glittering.

One look at Eduardo and the cat's back arched, and a low mewling hiss sprang from her mouth.

Portia rolled her eyes. "*Slowly* she's coming along. She should know better than to bite the hand that feeds her. Sorry, Eduardo. And how are your hands?"

He waved them in the air. "They are fine, Princess. No need to worry."

"What did you find out of interest, Eduardo?" he asked. "Something about the search?"

"Yes, Your Highness. You gave me the list of names on the graves at the Montoro family cemetery."

"Yes, I committed many of them to memory." He'd tasked Eduardo with contacting his uncle Rafe and alerting him about the cemetery. Juan Carlos wanted those family plots cleaned up and the headstones that were damaged beyond repair to be replaced as soon as possible.

"Yes, well, I spoke with your uncle, as you asked. He has no knowledge of those family members or that there even was a Montoro cemetery on the grounds. Not one name seemed to jar his memory."

"We didn't have first names. We only found initials on the headstones. It doesn't matter if he remembered the names or not. We will have that cemetery restored."

"There's more."

Juan Carlos nodded. "I'm listening."

"Your uncle claims that as a rite of passage, every Montoro had the privilege of being buried in the family mausoleum in Alma, whether rich or poor. If they were related to Montoro and had bloodlines, it was an honor to be buried there."

"Yes, I know that. But surely during Tantaberra's reign, that wouldn't hold true anymore. After the war, everything changed. I assumed those graves were there because Tantaberra controlled even where a person would lay to rest."

Portia walked up to take his hand. "But Juan Carlos, think about some of the dates on the headstones. Many were pre-Tantaberra."

He gave it a moment of thought, his mind clicking back to the headstones. "You're right. There were at least four that I remember that dated back to the 1920s and '30s. Before the war, before Tantaberra."

"Yes," Portia said, her voice reaching a higher pitch. "And those initials might've been used to throw people off. They'd have no real way of investigating who was laid to rest there."

"Hold on a second," Juan Carlos said, pulling out his phone. He clicked over to the list he'd brought with him of the known art pieces missing from the palace. His heart racing, he located the titles.

"*Joven Amelia.* J.A. were the initials on one of the headstones," he said. "It means Young Amelia. *Almas Iguales.* A.I. was another set of initials. The sculpture is called *Equal Souls* in English. And then there is *Dos Rios.*"

"D.R. I remember that one," Portia said. "I thought he was a doctor."

"There's a painting called *Dos Rios* that's missing," he said. "Portia, you said it yourself this afternoon, the secrets have been buried along with my family members.

But I don't think there are any family members buried in the cemetery."

"You think the artwork is buried there." Portia's voice was breathless and eager.

"It's a long shot, Princess. I think the cemetery is bogus. It was the family's way of protecting the art from Tantaberra. We have to find out. Eduardo, get in touch with Luis. We'll need a bulldozer, but for now, round up shovels and some high-powered lights. I'm going tonight."

"Oh, Juan Carlos, do you really think you've found it?"

"*We* found it, Portia. You're as much a part of this as I am."

Portia nodded, an excited smile teasing her lips. "I'll go change my clothes."

"Portia," he said, "are you sure you want to go? If I'm wrong, it will be pretty gruesome."

"If you really want to see *gruesome* try and stop me, Your Highness."

He grinned. "That's right. You're not a wimpy princess."

He was glad. It wouldn't feel right going on this search without her by his side.

Whatever they found.

Seven

"I really know how to show a lady a good time, don't I?" With shovel in hand, Juan Carlos dug at the foot of a grave alongside Eduardo and Luis as the high beams of two cars cast the cemetery in an unearthly glow.

Dirt flew through the air and landed at the toes of her boots. If she weren't so excited, she'd be totally creeped out. "I can't think of anywhere else I'd rather be," she countered honestly.

Even her embarrassment with Luis had been forgotten.

"I can help out," she said, "when anyone wants to take a break."

Eduardo covered his laughter with a grunt.

Juan Carlos slanted her a be-serious look. "I'll keep that in mind, Princess."

Luis was too busy digging to look up.

She wrapped her arms around her sides as the night air became chillier. She'd refused Juan Carlos's suggestion to sit it out in the car and so she stood watching, waiting.

They were digging up the grave of J. A. Molina. The headstone dated the death to 1938.

After ten minutes of silent digging, she heard a thump. Eduardo's shovel smacked against something solid. Thump, thump. "I hit something, Your Highness," Eduardo said.

"Let's keep digging," Juan Carlos said. There was a

boyish tone to his excitement. "It shouldn't be long now before we know."

The men worked twice as fast now, focusing their efforts. The scraping sounds of shovels against wood filled the quiet night.

"Portia, will you get the flashlight and shine it down here."

The men were five feet below ground level now and working furiously.

She grabbed the biggest flashlight she could find and stood as close as possible over the grave site, sending beams of light down. Portia's heart sank. "It's a coffin, isn't it?"

"Maybe," Juan Carlos said. Under her flashlight, his eager eyes had lost some of their gleam. A layer of dirt remained on top of the box, and he used his gloved hands to swipe it off, searching for any hint of what lay inside. He found nothing written. "Let's bring it up."

It took some doing, but the three men hoisted the box up and set it on a patch of flat ground.

"Hand me the ax," Juan Carlos ordered. He made the sign of the cross over his chest. "And may God forgive us."

Luis handed Juan Carlos the tool and he carefully began to hack at the very edges of the coffin. Each blow of the ax brought the mystery closer and closer to an end. Eduardo used his shovel to help pry the lid of the box open.

It was time. Their work was nearly over. Juan Carlos hesitated a moment, drew breath into his lungs and then glanced at her. "Ready?"

She nodded.

"You might want to look away," he said.

"No, I will be fine with whatever we find." Her eye twitched, closing in a wink.

Juan Carlos stared at her. Perhaps he was equally as nervous as she was. With his gloved hands, he lifted the hacked lid. She beamed the flashlight on the contents, her heart thumping hard.

"There's no corpse." His voice elevated, he continued, "But there's something in here."

She held her breath, her pulse jumping in her veins. He unfolded a sheath, and found another box, no more than two by three feet, this one carved and quite ornate. He lifted it out and she shined the flashlight on it. *Joven Amelia* was etched in golden lettering on top.

Juan Carlos's hand shook. "It's here. Thank God," he said. Setting the box down on the ground, he kneeled, and she took a place beside him. He took great care to remove his filthy gloves and then opened the latch and lifted the lid.

Inside, surrounded by lush black velvet, there was a painting of a little girl, no more than ten years old, playing near the seashore with a much younger sister. The canvas was secured, not rolled up as one might expect, but mounted to a frame as if taken from the palace in a hurry. Portia would have to inspect it thoroughly and do some research, but she was almost certain that it was genuine, given the great pains the royal family had taken to hide the painting decades ago.

"It's beautiful," she said. "She is Young Amelia."

Tears welled in Juan Carlos's eyes. "We did it, Portia. We found the missing treasures."

"Yes," she breathed, her heart swelling. "Yes."

"Eduardo, Luis, come see."

Taking her hand, Juan Carlos rose and tugged her up with him. Once standing, he wrapped his arms around her waist and drew her close, so they were hip to hip. Joy beamed in her heart. It was a monumental occasion and she found no reason for pretense. As Juan Carlos had said, the way he looked at her left little room for doubt of his feelings, anyway. They were lovers. It was hard to disguise.

The bodyguards peered at the painting in its casing. Both seemed awed and a little surprised to be looking at a royal masterpiece lost for generations.

"Congratulations, Your Majesty," Eduardo said.

"Alma's precious treasures have been restored," Luis said.

The two men shook the king's hand. There was pride and resolve in all of their eyes.

Eduardo turned to her. "Princess Portia, congratulations to you, as well. It is a great find."

"Thank you, Eduardo. That's very kind of you to say." She stepped forward and placed a kiss on his cheek. "I'm thrilled to have helped in a small way."

Eduardo blushed, but gave no indication he was alarmed by her affectionate display. A smile tugged at his lips, bringing her a rush of friendly warmth inside.

Juan Carlos got right down to business again. "I would like you to secure the grounds tonight. When the bulldozers arrive, we will resume digging in the morning. Assemble a team. I would like to have all the art secured by the end of the day tomorrow, if possible."

"Yes, Your Highness," Luis said. "It will be done."

The men turned to do their tasks, and Juan Carlos took her hand and began dragging her away from the stream of lights. "Come with me, sweetheart," he said.

"Where are we going?"

"To bed, as soon as I can arrange it," he said. "But for now, this will have to do."

He pulled her behind the cars, out into the darkness under the stars. And the next thing she knew, Juan Carlos's hands were about her and she was flying, sailing through the air, spinning around and around. "We did it, Princess. We did it."

"Yes, yes, we did." Laughter spilled from her lips and a lightness of spirit filled her.

"This is an amazing moment. I'm glad to be sharing it with you," he said.

Her smile broadened. "I feel the same way, Juan Carlos. I'm bursting inside."

He brought her down to earth gently, her boots gracing the sacred grounds. And his lips sought hers instantly, kissing her mouth, chin, cheeks and forehead. His hands sifted through her hair and his dark, luscious eyes bored into her. "Do you have any idea how much I love you, Portia? I do. I love you, Princess. With all my heart."

"Oh, Juan Carlos, I love you, too." And there it was. Her truth. Her honest feelings poured out of her in this instant of happiness and joy. She could no longer hide away from the sensations rocking her from head to toe. The words she spoke were not damning, but blissful and joyous. She loved Juan Carlos Salazar II, King Montoro of Alma.

"You do? You love me?" His grin spoke to her heart in a language all its own. His was the sweetest of tones, as if he was in total awe of her love.

She nodded eagerly. "I love you."

He lifted her up and twirled her around once more before he set her down. His kiss this time made her dizzier than a dozen spins in his arms. His mouth claimed her, his lips demanding, his tongue penetrating through to sweep in and conquer. Her knees wobbled and she sought his sturdy shoulders for balance, her monumental declaration swaying both of them.

"Oh, Portia, my love. I cannot think of a life without you. Marry me. Be my wife. Be with me forever."

The words rang in her ears. It wasn't as if she hadn't expected them to come, but the surprise came only in her answer. "Yes, Juan Carlos. I will marry you."

The next morning, Portia woke in Juan Carlos's arms, opening her eyes to a face she had come to love. Handsome, breathtaking and dynamic. He was a man who got things done. He'd certainly pursued her to the point of her complete compliance. How could she not fall in love with this man?

"Good morning, fiancée," he said, kissing the tip of her nose.

"Hello, my love," she said.

They'd celebrated in this very bed well into the night. There was champagne and candles and bone-melting caresses.

As she plopped her head against the pillow, the sheets pulled away, exposing her bare shoulders. Her eyes lifted to the ceiling, focusing on tiles that were chipping away. The farmhouse, old and neglected as it was, had undeniable charm. She sighed. "Is this real?"

"So real," Juan Carlos said. "Here, feel my heart."

He grasped her hand and placed it on his chest. Under her fingertips, life-sustaining beats pulsed through his veins. "I am real. A man who loves a woman."

"But you are the king of Alma."

"And you are the princess of Samforstand…we are meant to be, sweetheart. Can you not see how perfect this is? Fate has stepped in and brought the two of us together. I can only marry a woman of royal blood. And that's you." He brought her hand to his lips and tenderly kissed one finger, then another and another. "When I became king, marrying was the last thing on my mind. But then I saw you at the coronation and all bets were off."

"And what if I weren't a princess? Then what would you have done?"

"I would have…" He hesitated and sighed, bringing her up and over his body so that she straddled his thighs. He nipped at her lips and wove his fingers through her hair, eyeing the locks as if they were made of gold. "Luckily, I don't have that burden."

"No, you don't," she said, taking his hand and placing it on her chest. The heat of his palm warmed her breast and she squeezed her hand over his. "Feel my heart."

His eyes filled with hunger and every cell in her body reacted to his sensual touch. "You are wicked, Princess."

She chuckled. "You bring it out in me."

"You see, we *are* a perfect match."

"Are we?" She nibbled on her lip. She'd disobeyed her hard and fast rule of not falling for a high-profile man. You couldn't get much higher than king. Was she destined to fame through association even though it's the last thing she wanted?

"Let me show you again, so that you will never doubt it."

His hands on her hips, he gently guided her over him and they welcomed the dawn with their bodies and hearts joined as one.

But her doubts remained, locked and hidden away, even as she agreed to marry him. Even as she claimed her love for him. Half an hour later, she was showered and dressed. She and Juan Carlos ate a quick breakfast of cereal and fruit, both anxious to get back to the cemetery site this morning. But Portia couldn't forget her six charges. She walked into the living area with bowls of water and cat food in her hands and set them down by the fireplace hearth, where Duchess had taken up residence. "Here you go, girl."

Duchess no longer looked at her with frightened eyes. She had at one time been domesticated, and she was beginning to remember her life before hunger and fear had changed her. Portia kneeled and watched the cat rise, stretch her neck and shake out her limbs, and then walk over to the water. She lapped furiously as five balls of fluff scrambled to be near her, one kitten losing his balance and plopping half his body into the bowl. He jumped back, as if hit by a jolt, and gave himself a few shakes. Tiny drops of water sprinkled Portia's clothes.

She giggled and pressed her hand to the top of the little one's head. Silky fur tickled her palm. "You are a feisty one."

Juan Carlos strode into the room. "Are you ready to go, sweetheart?"

She stood. "Yes. I can't wait to see what else we uncover."

According to Eduardo, two bulldozers and a full crew were working furiously this morning. In the middle of the night, he'd called upon and assembled a team of men he could trust with this secret. Soon, the entire country would know about the hidden artwork. What a story to tell.

Last night, Juan Carlos had shared his hopes of putting many of these treasures on display for Alma citizens as well as tourists who would come to view the find. It would be nothing short of a boon for the country. The restoration of the artwork would instill pride and honor in a country once diminished and downtrodden by a dictator. First, though, Portia, along with a Latin art specialist, would have to verify that the pieces were not fakes.

By the time they reached the site, half the graveyard was dug up. Dust swirled through the air from the many mounds of dirt dotting the cemetery. Ten men with shovels and axes were hoisting boxes up from the graves. Luis, with pen and pad in hand, was making an inventory list. As ordered, none of the boxes had been opened.

Juan Carlos helped her down from the Jeep. He took her hand and they walked to where Luis stood next to a gravestone marked with the initials P.P. Tasked with documenting and photographing each headstone before the box was brought up, Luis lifted his head to greet them.

"Your Highness, Princess," he said. "We have twelve boxes already accounted for. As you can see, we have more to do. We've placed them inside the tent over there," he said, pointing to a room-size tent set up outside the cemetery under guard by two men, "and they are ready for you to open."

"Thank you, Luis," Juan Carlos said. "Your men are working faster than I thought. Now, if you'll come with me, I'll need you to document what we find as I open the boxes."

"I'll take the photos," Portia said.

Luis handed over his digital camera and nodded. "Thank you, Your Highness."

Excitement stirred in her belly. To be a part of this find was a dream come true. How many dreams was one person allowed in a lifetime? All this joy in such a short span of time? She'd found adventure and love where she'd least expected it, in the arms of a king.

Inside the tent, Juan Carlos opened box after box, carefully removing the pieces for documentation. Oil paintings, sculptures, bronzed statues and the famed ancient Alma tiara had been locked away and hidden from the world for decades. Portia photographed everything, carefully making mental notes of the pieces she would research for authentication.

They worked alongside the men, until all the pieces were uncovered and the mock cemetery was emptied out. By late afternoon, they'd unearthed twenty-two boxes in all, the grave sites now nothing but pockmarks in the earth.

Juan Carlos climbed to the top of a pile of dirt in the center of the graveyard, his boots spread out, his voice booming to the loyal men who had labored here. As he spoke, shovels were held still, conversations died down. "The Montoro family cemetery has done its job to preserve what is sovereign to our country. You are all a part of Alma history now and I thank you for your hard work today. Until these items are authenticated, I would ask for your silence. Luis and Eduardo have assured me all of you can be trusted. The next step is to transport these pieces back to the palace in the trucks you arrived in. Again, thank you all for your diligence."

Juan Carlos jumped down from the dirt hill and once again, Portia was reminded of how well he fit the position of king. He was a true diplomat and leader. A man to be admired. Staunch in his beliefs and fair-minded…she was sure if the clocks were turned back in time to when Alma was last ruled by a king, he would have reigned over his people justly.

"What are you staring at?" he asked, approaching her.

She shook off her thoughts and smiled. "How handsome you are with dirt on your face."

He grinned. "I could say the same about you, Princess. The smudges on your face only make you more beautiful." He touched her nose, right cheek and forehead.

Goodness, she'd never considered what the hours of dust and grime had done to her fair complexion. "I must be a mess."

"Nothing a hot bubble bath wouldn't cure, and I'm volunteering to scrub your back," he whispered.

"I'll take you up on that, Your Highness."

And shortly after, they left the graveyard and returned to the farmhouse.

They had one night left to share here. And Portia was sure, Juan Carlos would make it memorable, bubble bath and all.

Portia was too much in love to think about her future and how marrying Juan Carlos would affect her life and her career. She had no details to cling to, only love, and it would have to see her through the tough decisions she would have to make. Now, as she sat at a long dressed table in the palace's elegant dining room, she gazed first at her secret fiancé seated at the helm. Dressed in a charcoal-black suit, he was beaming and full of determination. He appeared ready to make the announcement to his family. Rafe and Emily sat across from her with her friend Maria and Alex Ramon.

Gabriel and his wife, Serafia, sat to her left, along with Bella and James. James's little girl, Maisey, was holding tight to her chest a princess doll dressed in aqua-blue with hair the color of glistening snow.

"It's a lovely doll, Maisey," Portia commented, smiling at the child.

"She looks a lot like you, Portia," Bella commented. "I'm just noticing the likeness."

Maisey's curious eyes shifted to Portia and the girl giggled. It was true that she shared a resemblance with a famous cartoon character that all young girls seemed to love.

Juan Carlos covered Portia's hand, entwining their fingers. "Ah, but Portia is a one-of-a-kind princess."

All those close to Juan Carlos were here. He'd invited them for dinner tonight under the pretense of disclosing the facts around the graveyard find. Only he and Portia knew the truth.

"Before the meal is served, a toast is in order," he said. "We have much to celebrate tonight."

Waiters poured champagne into crystal flutes.

Once all the bubbles settled, Juan Carlos rose. "Thank you, cousins and friends, for joining me tonight. We all have much to be thankful for. As you know, with Portia's help, we have found the missing pieces of art at the Montoro family farm. Yes, it's true, we dug up mock graves to unearth the treasures. The finds are yet to be authenticated, but we are fairly certain our ancestors wouldn't have gone to such extreme measures to hide fake artwork. Portia will do the preliminary research on the items we've found and under her advisement we will also hire an expert to verify each piece.

"But that is not why I've called you here today. I have

something more personal to share with you." He turned to Portia, offering his hand. She took it and rose, warmth traveling up her cheeks. All eyes were on her and the king.

Juan Carlos went down on one knee, and gasps erupted from the diners at the table. She had no idea he would go traditional on her in front of his family. But how silly of her not to think it. Juan Carlos was a man of tradition and so as she gazed into his gleaming dark eyes, she began to tremble.

"Princess Portia, you know I love you with all of my heart. I have since the moment I laid eyes on you."

Tears wet her eyes.

"I have one precious thing left of my childhood and now, I am offering it to you." He reached into his jacket pocket and came up with a diamond ring, the stone so brilliant, it caught the chandelier light and virtually illuminated the room. "This was my mother's wedding ring," he said, his voice tight. "And here before our family and close friends, I ask you to wear it and become my wife. Portia, Princess of Samforstand, will you marry me?"

Not even a breath could be heard in the roomful of people.

Her cheeks were moist with tears as she nodded. "Yes, yes. Of course I'll marry you, Juan Carlos. I am honored to wear your mother's ring."

Her hand shook as he slid the ring that once belonged to his mother onto her finger. He stared at the ring, his eyes deeply reverent, and then grinned wide, looking foolishly happy. With the pads of his thumbs, he wiped at her tears and then took her in a kiss that nearly muffled the screams of delight and applause coming from behind her.

After the kiss, they were both swarmed with handshakes and hugs.

She was beside herself with happiness. The love and acceptance she experienced from his family and friends was more than she'd ever expected. There were no, *Are you sures?* or *This has happened so fasts*, but rather, "Congratulations" and "You two are perfect for each other."

After everyone returned to their seats, Juan Carlos lifted his glass of champagne. "Please join me in welcoming my fiancée, Portia, to our family. Today, she has made me the happiest man on earth."

Glasses clinked and sips were taken.

Portia's heart swelled. All doubts about her future were laid to rest. She and Juan Carlos would work things out. They would find a way to keep each other happy and not lose their own identity. She would be his wife in all ways. She would one day bear his child, an heir to the throne of Alma.

She locked the thought deep inside her heart and it filled her with joy.

"Jasmine, yes. It's true, it's true. I'm engaged to Juan Carlos. I wanted to tell you before news of our engagement reached the States. The king's assistant will be speaking to the media tomorrow to share our engagement news." Portia held the cell phone to her ear as she looked out the window of Juan Carlos's master suite in the palace. The king's room had a view of the gardens below, with its expertly groomed fall flowers.

"Congratulations, Portia. Wow. It's hard to believe. The king moves fast, doesn't he?" Jasmine asked, a little bit in awe.

"Yes, he does," she said softly, focusing on a row of red carnations growing in the garden. They were hardy this time of year. "He's quite persuasive when he wants something. That's why he'll be a great king and not just a figurehead. After news of our find comes out, the country will see how much Alma means to him. They'll rally behind him, and he'll be… Jas, forgive me, I'm rambling, aren't I?"

"Oh, my gosh, Portia. I hear it in your voice. You're really in love, aren't you?"

"He's amazing, Jas. And I resisted him as long as I could, but Juan Carlos…well, when you meet him, you'll see what I mean."

"I'm going to meet him?" She pictured her friend's eyes snapping to attention.

"Of course, silly. At the wedding. Jasmine, I want you by my side. I know it's a lot to ask, since the wedding will be held in Alma, but I'd be thrilled if you'd be my maid of honor."

"Portia…this is… Of course I'll be your maid of honor! I wish you could see me jumping up and down right now."

She chuckled. "I've got the image in my head. Just be careful. The last time you jumped for joy, you crashed into my dining table and nearly broke your leg."

"Okay, I've stopped jumping now," she said, out of breath. "This is all so very exciting."

"I can hardly believe it myself. Juan Carlos wants to be married, like, yesterday, so I think it's going to happen as soon as we can put all the pieces together."

"Count on me to help."

"Thank you. I was hoping you'd say that and I'm glad you're going to be in my wedding. Right now, I'm working on an art authentication project that will take me until the end of the week to finish. I should be home in three days. Then it'll be full steam ahead with wedding plans."

"I can't wait to see you. I have a million questions for you."

"And I don't have a million answers. But it'll work out," Portia said, taking a deep breath. "It has to. Have to run now. Love you, Jas."

"Love you, too," her assistant said, and then hung up.

"What don't you have a million answers to?" Juan Carlos was suddenly beside Portia at the window. His arms around her waist, he took the cell phone from her hand and turned her to face him. She looked into curious, warm dark eyes.

"All of this?" she said. She couldn't lie. The roller coaster was going fast and she was holding on for dear life. "I don't know how this will all work out. I have a career, a life and a job on both US coasts. As it is, I'm not home much."

He lifted her chin and tilted his head. She braced herself for the onslaught of his kiss. When he held her this way and gazed at her, she turned into a puddle of mush. The kiss was long and leisurely. He took his time with her and every bone in her body melted. Yes, her fiancé knew how to devastate.

"As long as we love each other," he said, "the obstacles won't be too great. I don't expect you to give up your work, Princess. I won't demand anything of you but your love."

When he spoke so sincerely, she believed him. She saw her future bright and clear. Nothing was more powerful than their shared love. "You have that, Your Highness."

His fingertips traced the outline of her lips. "I heard you say you'll be going in three days."

"Yes," she said. "When I'm through researching and authenticating what I can of the Montoro art collection, I'll head back to the States. I have appointments to keep."

"And you'll look into wedding protocols from your native Samforstand?"

"Yes, I know that's important to you. It is to me, too."

"Our union should reflect both of our heritages and royal traditions. The wedding must be a melding of both of our countries. The sooner, the better, my love. I can hardly stand the thought of you leaving." He sent her head swirling with another earth-shattering kiss.

"Well," she said, licking her lips. "We do have three

more days together. And nights." She arched her brows and slanted her head, playing coy.

Juan Carlos took the bait. With a growl, he lifted her up and carried her to the bed, unceremoniously dropping her so that she bounced on the mattress. A chuckle ripped from her lips. "Your Highness," she said, staring at the bulge growing in his pants. "It's half past eleven in the morning."

"Princess, I don't see a problem with that, do you?"

She shook her head, giggling. It didn't take much to tempt her new fiancé and she loved that about him.

He climbed onto the bed and Portia spent the next hour making up for the time she and Juan Carlos would be apart.

Eight

"Wow, Portia, you look beautiful in this dress. I think it's the one," Jasmine said, nodding her head in approval. Her friend was having a grand time getting her in and out of wedding dresses, much to the dismay of the shop owner who stood just outside the dressing room, hoping to be called in to aid and assist in the fitting.

Portia stood on a pedestal platform gazing at her reflection in the three-way mirror in the tiny wedding shop in Santa Monica. "You said that about the last three gowns I've tried on."

"I can't help it. They all look amazing on you. But this one with the ivory tulle and Swarovski crystals." Jasmine sighed. "It's heavenly."

"It is lovely," Portia said, admiring the lines of the dress. "It's such a big decision."

"I'll say. It's not every day a friend of mine marries a king. Princess or not."

Portia chuckled.

Once word of the new king of Alma's American fiancée had hit the Los Angeles newsstands, Portia had been inundated with offers of gown fittings, hair and makeup, photographers and wedding planners. She'd had requests for radio and television talk shows. She'd refused them all, trying to scale down the hoopla. She hadn't expected to be crowded at the airport by the paparazzi, or followed home for that matter. Once again, her personal life was under the spotlight.

None of it mattered, though. She was so deeply in love with Juan Carlos, the unwanted attention was manageable. On some level, she understood the public's desire for a fairy-tale love story. Ghastly news reports of wars, poverty and chilling murders needed some balance. The country craved something positive and lovely to grasp onto, and a newly crowned king marrying a princess, both of whom had lived in America, fit the bill.

Portia stepped out of the gown and redressed in her own clothes before letting Amelia of Amelia's Elegance into the dressing room. "Thank you for your time," Portia said to the shop owner. "I will keep this gown in mind. It's certainly beautiful."

Jasmine was careful handing the wedding dress over to Amelia. "This is my favorite, with the chapel length veil."

"I agree. It's certainly fitting for a princess," the shop owner said, nodding her head. "It's from a most talented designer. I shall put it on hold for you, if you'd like?"

Jasmine nodded. "Yes, the princess would like that."

Portia did a mental eye roll. Jasmine loved using the princess card for special favors.

"Your Highness, thank you for considering my shop for your wedding needs."

"You're welcome. I appreciate your time. You do have some stunning things here."

Amelia beamed with pride. "Thank you. We try to accommodate our clients with only the highest quality material and design."

"We have a few other stops to make, but I will personally call you when the princess makes up her mind," Jasmine said.

Amelia thanked them and walked them out the door.

"Did you love the dress?" Jasmine asked. "A bride has

to fall in love with her dress. They say as soon as she puts the right one on, she knows. Did you know?"

"Well, I did like it."

"But you didn't love it?"

Portia got into the front seat of Jasmine's car. "No, I didn't *love* it."

Luckily, no one had followed her to the dress shop. Jasmine got into the driver's seat and glanced around. "Did you hear? Rick Manning just got engaged to the daughter of a United States senator. It's all over the news. They claim to be crazy about each other."

Rick Manning, an A-list movie star, was dubbed the man least likely to ever marry. Handsome and charming and very much a ladies' man. "Yes, it was all over the news this morning. I've met Eliza Bennington. She's a nice person."

"Well, you can thank them both. Luckily, the tabloids have dropped you like a hot potato. At least, until more royal wedding news is announced. The dogs are on a different scent right now."

"I don't envy them. It's no fun having your every move analyzed."

"I hear you," Jasmine said, and pulled out of the parking spot. "Are you hungry?"

"Starving. Let's have lunch."

"Okay, but afterward, the great wedding dress search goes on."

Portia agreed to that plan and looked out the window. Jasmine was taking her maid of honor duties seriously. The truth was, Portia had a hundred loose ends to tie up before the wedding, and she missed Juan Carlos like crazy. They spoke at least twice a day since she'd left him at the airport in Alma.

"You are perfect for me, Princess. Always remember

that," were his last words to her as she boarded his private airplane.

It was after six in the evening when Jasmine dropped her off at home. She climbed the few steps of her one-level Brentwood condo, knowing she had another hunt on her hands. She'd promised Juan Carlos she'd look up royal wedding protocols from Samforstand. She'd been too busy with rescheduling her work appointments and dress shopping to dig into her old files until now.

She dropped her purse on the couch and then strode to the fridge and grabbed a Coke. Sipping from the can, she walked into her bedroom and pulled out the old cedar trunk from the back of her walk-in closet. The trunk held the few remaining things she had left of her parents.

Unlatching the lid, she found a massive amount of papers, deeds, bank account records and folders upon folders of news clippings about her parents when they were a young royal couple in exile. She lifted out an article written about them from the *New York Times*, just days before the tragic car accident that claimed their lives. Her eyes misted as she looked at a picture of the loving couple that accompanied the article. Her father was decked out in royal regalia with her mother by his side. They were young and happy and it hurt her heart still to look at them and think about all they had lost.

Her mother's wedding ring was in its original sapphire-blue velvet box, her father's tie clips and a gold wedding band were stored in a polished walnut case. She assumed most of their other possessions were sold to keep her comfortable and pay for her expenses. She'd been raised by her grandmother Joanna. But now all she had was her great-aunt, Margreta, who was a little senile. Portia paid for her care in a nursing home and visited her whenever she could.

As the evening wore on, she pored over every piece of paper in the trunk. She read every article and viewed every picture taken. Yet nowhere could she find any research that dated back to her great-grandparents' era of rule before they'd migrated to the United States after World War II. Surely, there had to be something? Having lost her parents early in life, she had only a fragmentary account of her heritage from her grandmother. Grandma Joanna hadn't liked to talk about the old days. It was too painful, a past wrought with the loss of her only son. Portia's questions about her parents were met with hushed tones and sadness and she'd never really learned much about them. She did remember her mother's bright smile and her father's light blue eyes. But even now, she wondered if those were true memories, or just recollections of the pictures she'd seen.

Her cell phone rang and a name popped up on the screen. She answered before the second ring. "Juan Carlos." She sighed.

His baritone voice drifted to her over thousands of miles. "Hello, Princess. I had to hear your voice once more before I started my day. I hope I didn't wake you."

She glanced at the clock. It was 8:00 a.m. in Alma. "No, not at all. I'm doing some research right now. I'm glad you called. How are you?"

"Besides missing you, I'm doing well. I'm scheduled to do a television interview later this morning. All of Alma is rejoicing over our art find, sweetheart. But I have a feeling the interviewer is more interested in our engagement. I'm sure I will be barraged with questions about our wedding."

"I'm sure you can handle it, Your Highness."

"What I can't handle is not being with my perfect princess. When will you be returning to me?"

"Give me a week, Juan Carlos," she said. "I need the time to get some things in order."

"Sounds like an eternity."

"For me, too, but I have a lot to accomplish. Jasmine

has been persistent. We are very close to choosing a wedding gown."

"I can't wait to see you in it. No matter which you choose you'll be beautiful. But what have you decided about your work?"

"I've managed to take a three months' leave of absence. I'm thinking of relocating to Europe. There are many American art collectors living abroad who might need my services. I...I don't have it all figured out yet."

"Take your time, sweetheart. I want you to be happy with whatever you choose."

"Okay. Thank you."

"I've been thinking. How does a Christmas wedding sound?"

"A Christmas wedding?" She pictured lush holly wreaths, bright red poinsettias and twinkling lights decorating the palace. "Sounds heavenly. But it's less than two months away."

Her fiancé was eager to make her his wife. She couldn't complain, yet her mind spun. She had so very much to do.

"We can make it work, Portia."

"Yes, yes. Okay," she said, smiling. The idea was too tempting to pass up. "Let's have a Christmas wedding."

There was a pause, and she pictured him smiling. "I love you, Portia."

"I love you, too, Juan Carlos."

The nursing home smelled of lye soap and disinfectant. Yet somehow the word *sterile* didn't come to mind as Portia walked the halls toward her great-aunt Margreta's room. Her aunt had once told her, "The odors of old age are too strong to conceal." Sharp old bird, Aunt Margreta was, back in the day. But Portia never knew what she'd find when she visited. Some days, her great-aunt was lucid, her wits about her. And some days, it was as if she'd fallen into a dark hole and didn't know how to get out.

This kind of aging was a slow, eternally sad process. Yet, as Portia popped her head into her aunt's room, she was greeted with cheery buttercup-colored walls and fresh flowers. Aunt Margreta sat in a chair, reading a crime thriller. A good sign.

"Hello, Auntie," Portia said. "It's me, Portia."

Her aunt looked over her thick eyeglasses and hesitated a moment. "Portia?"

Her voice was weak, her body frail and thin. "Yes, it's me."

The old woman smiled. "Come in, dear." She put the book down on her lap. "Nice of you to visit."

Thank heaven. Her aunt was having a good day. Maybe now, she could gather information about the Lindstrom monarchy that Portia hadn't been able to find anywhere else. She'd used up every one of her massive tools of research, including going through newspaper archives searching for an inkling about her family's rule and traditions carried out in Samforstand. She found nothing, which was very odd, and that lack of information brought her here today. Maybe Aunt Margreta could shed some light. She was her grandmother's sister and had lived in the homeland before the war.

Portia pulled up a chair and sat down beside her. "How are you, Auntie?"

"I can't complain. Well, I could, but it would do no good. I'm old, Portia. And you," she said, gazing over her glasses again. "You are as beautiful as I remember."

Portia took her hand and smiled. Aunt Margreta's hands were always soft, the skin loose and smooth over the aging bones. At ninety-three years old, she was as physically fit as one could expect, but for daily bouts of arthritis. But her mind wasn't holding up as well as her body and that worried Portia. "So are you, Aunt Margreta. You're a beautiful lady."

She'd always been a sweet woman, though as Portia remembered, she'd also been feisty in her day and not always in agreement with her sister, Joanna. The two would argue when they thought Portia couldn't hear. She never knew what they argued about, but as soon as Portia would step into the room, they'd shoot each other a glare and stop arguing, pretending things were all fine and dandy. Which they were, most of the time. Portia missed her parents, but she'd never discount the love Grandma Joanna and Great-Aunt Margreta bestowed upon her. It was the least she could do for her aunt to see to her care here at Somerset Village.

"Auntie, are they treating you well here?"

She nodded. "I'm fine, dear. The food's better now. We have a new chef and he doesn't cut corners. You'll see. You'll stay for lunch?"

"Of course I will. I'm looking forward to it."

"Then I'll get dressed up and we'll go to the dining room later."

"Okay. Auntie, I have good news." She lifted her left hand and wiggled her fingers. "I'm engaged."

Margreta squeezed her eyes closed. "Is it to Johnny Valente? That boy wouldn't leave you alone when you were younger. I never liked him. "

Johnny Valente? Portia used to play with him in grade school, two decades ago. He was a bully who'd called her Polar Bear Portia, because of her light hair and skin tone. "Gosh no, Auntie. I never liked him, either." She hoped her aunt wasn't digressing. "I'm engaged to…" How should she say this? "I met this wonderful man when I was visiting Alma."

"What's Alma?"

"It's this beautiful island country just off the coast of

Spain. I met him at his coronation. Auntie, he was just crowned king. His name is Juan Carlos Salazar, King Montoro of Alma."

Aunt Margreta put her head down. "I see."

Her aunt's odd reaction surprised her. "Do you like my ring?"

She gave Portia's left hand a glance. "It sparkles."

"Yes, it does."

"But it looks old."

"Yes, I suppose it's at least fifty years old. It was his mother's ring. He…lost his family at a young age also."

"In a car accident, just like your mother and father?"

"Yes, the same way. We have a lot in common."

Pain entered her aunt's eyes. "That's terribly sad, isn't it?" Her aunt made a move to get up from the chair. "Is it time for lunch yet, dear?"

Portia's eye twitched. "Not yet, Auntie."

Her aunt relaxed back into her seat.

"Auntie, I have a question to ask you. It's very important to me, so please try to concentrate. I will be marrying a king and, well, since I also have royal bloodlines, my fiancé wants very much for me to carry out the protocols of my homeland during our wedding. Do you know where I might find that information? I can't seem to find anything about our family's rule before World War II."

Aunt Margreta put her head down again.

"Auntie, please. Try to remember."

"There are no protocols from the family," she said stoically.

"But surely…there have to be. Have you forgotten?"

"No, my dear. I have not forgotten. Your grandmother and I never saw eye to eye about this."

"About what, Auntie?"

Margreta stilled. "Tell no one. Tell no one. Tell no one," she repeated.

"Not even me, Auntie? What is it you're not supposed to tell?"

Margreta looked straight ahead, as if Portia wasn't there. As if she was going back in time, remembering. "Don't tell Portia. She must never know the truth."

"What?" Portia absorbed her words, but they didn't make any sense. "What do you mean, I must never know the truth? What truth?" Portia grabbed her aunt's hand, gently squeezing. "Auntie, please. You have to tell me."

Her aunt turned to stare at her. "You are not a princess," she said. Her voice was sorrowful, etched in pain and Portia's heart sunk at her earnest tone. "Our family never ruled in Samforstand. Your mother wasn't royalty and neither was my sister, Joanna. It's all a lie."

Surely, the old woman was having a senile episode. "But, Auntie, of course Grandmother was queen. She raised me. I would know if she wasn't."

Silence.

"Aunt Margreta, please?"

"Yes, you're right, dear. You would know. Never mind."

Her aunt's quick compliance confused her even more. And she started thinking back about her life and how she'd never really seen any official documents regarding the Lindstrom monarchy. They'd been figureheads, holding no great power, yet she'd never known much about her homeland. It wasn't talked about. It seemed from her recent research the monarchy started to take shape in the United States, just after World War II.

"Oh, my God," she murmured. Her body began to tremble as tears stung her eyes. "You're telling the truth, aren't you? I'm not a princess."

Her aunt's eyes softened, dimmed by sorrow. "I'm sorry, Portia dear."

"But how can I believe that? How can that possibly be true?"

Could she take the word of an elderly senile woman who went in and out of coherency?

"There's a diary," her aunt said. "Joanna kept a secret diary."

"Where?" Now Portia would get to the truth. "Where's the diary?"

Aunt Margreta pointed to the bookshelf against the far wall overflowing with books. "Behind Agatha Christie."

Portia strode over to the bookshelf. Her hands were shaking as she parted half a dozen mystery novels. She lifted a weathered, navy blue soft-covered book from the shelf and brought it close to her chest. It had no title on the cover. Her heart racing, she took her seat next to Aunt Margreta and began reading the words that made a lie out of her entire life.

Portia lay quietly on her sofa, a cool towel on her forehead. She'd cried a river full of tears and every cell in her body was now drained. Princess Portia Lindstrom of Samforstand no longer existed. She never had. She was a fraud, a fake. An imposter. How could her family do this to her? How could they have perpetrated a lie that would affect her entire life?

How cruel.

How unjust.

Damn the circumstances behind their decisions right now. Their bold blatant betrayal was all that mattered to her. How dare they mislead her and let her believe in the fairy tale? She wasn't the snow queen. Hell, once the truth got out, she'd be deemed the black witch.

She'd been involved in one scandal already and it had taken years to live that down. But this? This was too much. The press would devour her. They'd make her out to be the villain, a lying deceiving bitch out to ensnare a wealthy king.

The humiliation alone would destroy all the positive good Juan Carlos had done for his country.

She muffled another sob. She didn't have it in her to shed more tears.

Feeling empty, she closed her swollen eyes, unable to rid herself of the thoughts plaguing her. The lies she'd been told, the deceptions perpetrated by her family. What of her career? Most importantly, what would she do about Juan Carlos? He was king, and as king he was pledged to only marry a woman of royal heritage. It was his destiny. It was what the citizens of Alma expected. Juan Carlos was the most dutiful man she'd ever known. This would destroy their relationship.

The towel was removed from her head. "Feeling better yet? Want to get up?" Jasmine asked.

"Nooooo. I don't want to ever get up."

Jas sat down on the floor beside the sofa. "Hey, that doesn't sound like the Portia I know. You've been wallowing for two hours."

"I'm not the Portia you know. I'm not… I don't know who I am. And I have a right to wallow."

"Yes, it sucks. But Portia, you are you, no matter if you have the title of princess or not."

"It's just…it's just so darn humiliating. I feel like a fool. I feel, well, I feel like everything's a lie. My childhood, my upbringing, my friends."

"Hey, watch it there."

"You know I don't mean you."

Jasmine reached for her hand and squeezed. "I know."

"All the doors that have opened for me because of my title, Jas… Those people will think the worst of me. They'll think I deliberately deceived them to get ahead in my career."

"When in truth, we know, they were using you. They

wanted to be associated with a princess. So it was a trade-off. You have nothing to be ashamed of."

"I'm ashamed of everything."

"And angry."

"Yes, of course. I'm spitting mad at my family."

"I'm not justifying what they've done, honey. But they came to the States after the war destitute, and like so many immigrant families, they didn't know how they'd survive here. And, well, pretending to be royalty from a tiny country…"

"It's far-fetched. Yet they got away with it."

"Yes, your grandmother speaks of it in the diary. How scared they were and how confused things were in Europe and Scandinavia after the war. There was a lot of rebuilding and restructuring and things just fell into place for them. Surprisingly, they weren't questioned. After all, we didn't have close ties to the monarchy of Samforstand the way we did England. Your grandmother speaks of Americans having much to deal with after the war. Hundreds of thousands of soldiers were coming home. Work and housing in our country was scarce. Things were chaotic."

"But others found a way to survive without deception. They worked hard and built honest, decent lives for themselves." Portia hinged her body up from her prone position and swiveled to plant her feet on the floor. Sitting upright, her head spun a little. "I don't know what I'd do without you, Jasmine. Honestly, you're the only person I can trust with this."

Jasmine rose from the floor and the sofa cushions dipped as she came to sit next to her. Her friend hung her arm around Portia's shoulder and they sat there like that for long minutes, quiet.

"I'm scared, Jas."

"I know."

"I don't know who I am. I can't expect you to understand fully how I'm feeling, but suddenly, I'm confused about everything. My heart is aching so badly right now."

"That's why I'm here, Portia. You're not alone."

She rested her head on Jasmine's shoulder. "Thank you."

The house telephone rang. "Want me to get it?"

"No," she said to Jasmine. "I can't talk to anyone right now."

Jas nodded.

Shortly after that, her cell phone began ringing and she knew both calls were from Juan Carlos.

They spoke every evening before she went to bed. Never fail.

Until tonight.

She couldn't speak to him and pretend everything was all right. She couldn't pretend that she was still a princess. She had a lot of thinking to do and she couldn't burden Jasmine any further in the decisions she'd have to make about her future.

Thoughts of Juan Carlos always squeezed her heart tight in a loving embrace.

This time, though, it was as if her heart was being strangled.

And the pain of losing Juan Carlos wouldn't go away anytime soon.

Portia sat in the throne room at the palace in Del Sol, her eyes closed, her heart pumping hard. Yesterday, she'd texted and emailed Juan Carlos one excuse after another as to why she wasn't answering his calls until she'd realized the only way to break it off with him was to face him in person. She'd flown half the night to get here. To see him one last time.

His family had been through a great deal to once and for all return the true and rightful heir to the Alma throne.

There'd been one debacle after another with his cousins, as they attempted to reinstate the monarchy, and the entire process had come under great scrutiny. All eyes were on Juan Carlos now and he'd made promises, staunch, determined promises to the citizenry that he would take his role seriously. By royal decree from decades ago, he was obligated to marry a woman of royal stature. The last thing he needed was to be made a fool of by marrying an imposter, a woman who hadn't a drop of royal blood flowing through her veins.

She wasn't his perfect princess any longer.

A tear dripped down her cheek. She wiped it away and steadied her shaky breathing. She glanced down at the engagement ring she wore. It was magnificent and maybe someday would belong to a woman worthy of wearing it and claiming a place beside Juan Carlos.

Her stomach ached at the notion of Juan Carlos living with and loving another woman. But it would happen one day. Rightfully so. She could only hope getting over him wouldn't destroy her.

She heard footsteps approaching along the corridor. She rose from her seat and mustered her courage. She'd never been much of an actress, but today she needed to provide an award-winning performance.

The door opened and there he stood, dressed in a crisp white shirt, sleeves rolled up—as if he'd been busy at work—and tucked into well-fitting black trousers. A lock of his neatly combed hair swept across his forehead and his tanned face showed a hint of stubble. Some days, when he wasn't going out in public, he didn't shave. She preferred him that way…a little rough around the edges. Tall, elegant, gorgeous.

Juan Carlos's gaze lit upon her and her heart tumbled. Oh, how she'd missed him.

"Portia, sweetheart. You're here." His warm winning

smile devastated her as he strode across the room. Genuine love entered his eyes. "I'm so glad to see you. You've come back to me early."

"Yes."

"I was worried when I couldn't reach you. But now I see, you wanted to surprise me."

He took her into his arms and heaven help her, she allowed him to kiss her.

His lips were warm, welcoming, filled with passion and beautifully familiar. She'd never been kissed the way Juan Carlos kissed her. She held her back stiff and didn't partake, but he was too caught up in the moment to notice her reluctance.

"We have much to talk about," he murmured, brushing his lips over hers again.

She stepped back and gazed into his dark gleaming eyes. "Yes, Juan Carlos. It's the reason I've come back to Del Sol so quickly."

He took her hand, covering it with his. "Come, let's sit then and catch up."

He began walking, tugging her along to the king and queen's thrones, two ornate tall chairs of plush red velvet and gilded carvings.

The irony of sitting upon that chair was too much. "I'd rather stand," she said.

"Okay." He looked at her oddly, but then nodded. "Would you like to take a walk? It might feel good to stretch your legs after the long plane ride. We can talk of the progress you've made with our wedding."

"No," she said. "No, Juan Carlos. I didn't come here early to discuss our wedding. I came to say that I can't go through with it."

"With what, sweetheart?" He blinked and appeared totally confused.

"The wedding. I can't marry you, Juan Carlos. I went home and really gave our situation some thought."

"Our situation?" He frowned. "You love me, I love you. That's our situation. We're engaged, Portia."

"No, as of today, we are not."

She inhaled and twisted the diamond ring off her finger. He was shaking his head, baffled. The gleam in his eyes dimmed. He almost appeared frightened. It killed her to wipe the joy from his face. "I'm terribly sorry."

"What is all this, Portia?"

She took his hand, spread open his palm and dropped his mother's wedding ring inside. "It's too much, Juan Carlos. We…we got caught up in the moment. Finding the art treasures put us both on a crazy romantic high and we took the little fling we had too far."

"Little fling?" he repeated, his voice hitching.

Oh, God, she'd hurt him. She knew she would, but she almost couldn't bear seeing that expression on his face. Better a small lie to save him, than the truth, which would make him look the fool in the eyes of his family and country. She loved him enough to suffer his anger and wrath. But the pain she'd inflicted would stay with her a long, long time.

"It happened so fast. You and I, we're different people. I love my job, Juan Carlos."

"You wouldn't have to give it up."

"Please understand," she said softly. "It isn't going to work out. I don't want to live here. I don't want to get married or have children right now."

His eyes snapped to hers. "I never rushed you about children, Portia."

"You'd expect it one day. And…and I'm afraid I'd disappoint you. I—I… It was a mistake to get engaged."

She backed up a step, putting distance between them. God should strike her dead for the lies she was telling. But it had to be done. Her sacrifice would make it easier on Juan Carlos in the long run. Yet her heart burned at the thought of leaving him forever.

"You're having cold feet. I hear it's common before a wedding."

"No, being away from here, from you, made it all clear to me, Juan Carlos. It's not cold feet, it's reality. I hope you'll understand and not make this harder on me than it already is."

He opened his palm to stare at the diamond ring. Then the sound of his deep wobbly sigh reached her ears. He was in pain. God, she hated this. "I love you, Portia," he said, searching her eyes.

Tears blurred her vision. Her throat constricted. She couldn't return his love. For his sake, she said nothing.

He gripped her forearms, gently shaking her. As if the impact would somehow clear her head of this nonsense. "Portia, you told me you loved me. You agreed to be my wife."

"I'm…I'm…" She took a swallow. Could she do this? Could she tell the biggest lie of all? She forced the words out. "I'm fond of you, Juan Carlos."

He dropped her arms. "Fond?"

She nodded.

"Then why are you crying, sweetheart?"

Her tears now were soaking her dress. She hated herself at the moment. "I don't like hurting you."

"Then don't. Stay and we'll talk this over. Give us time, Portia."

"I can't, Juan Carlos. It won't do any good. We're… over." She sobbed now, unable to hold back any longer. "I'm s-sorry."

He didn't reach for her. Thank goodness. If he touched her again, she'd melt into his arms. But he watched her carefully, as if trying to figure her out. Skepticism lingered in his eyes. He didn't believe her, but there was also resignation there and definite injury. She must have baffled him. He didn't know what to say to convince her she was wrong.

There wasn't anything he could say to her to change her mind. This was the hardest thing she'd ever had to do. She had to leave, to muster her strength and walk out the door. "I'll never forget the time I had with you... It was... *amazing*," she whispered.

He closed his eyes, shaking his head.

And that was her way out.

She turned her back on him and dashed away, leaving the palace and Juan Carlos and the love they'd shared behind.

Nine

"If you don't mind me saying so, Your Highness, you could use some sleep. Why not close your eyes while we travel," Eduardo said.

Juan Carlos sat facing his bodyguard in the reclining lounge chair on the palace's private plane. Under normal circumstances, Juan Carlos wouldn't travel so extravagantly; he wanted to be known as the king who flew coach. But it was imperative that this journey be kept secret and away from curious eyes. "Are you saying I look less than kingly, Eduardo?"

His bodyguard straightened in his seat. "No, I, uh, I know how hard this week has been on you, Your Highness."

"Eduardo, I'm in total agreement with you." Juan Carlos sighed. "I know I look like hell. I will fix that before we arrive in Los Angeles. The best I can, that is."

Eduardo's eyes softened. "Yes, Your Majesty."

Eduardo was quickly becoming his good friend and confidant. "Do you have a girl, Eduardo?"

"Yes, I do."

"Is it serious?"

Eduardo shook his head. "No, not really."

"Because of what you do for a living?"

"Yes. I cannot get serious with anyone while I'm away so much of the time. She understands."

"Ah, an understanding woman. It's lucky for me, not so fortunate for your girl."

"*Si*, that is true. But I am twenty-eight and not ready to settle down."

"I used to think that way. But sometimes fate steps in and knocks you over the head when a beautiful snow queen enters your path."

Eduardo chuckled. "Princess Portia."

"Yes, Princess Portia. And now I'm chasing her all over the globe."

"She is worth it, I would say, Your Majesty."

"*Si*, she is worth it."

He lifted the tumbler of bourbon he held in his hand and stared into the golden liquid. "I wish you could share a drink with me, Eduardo. We'll be in the air for five more hours. Surely the effects will have worn off by then."

"Thank you, Your Majesty, but no. I cannot drink while on duty."

Juan Carlos nodded. "Coffee then and a pastry?"

"I'd never refuse a pastry from Chef Andre, Your Highness. He showed me his creations before packing them up for this trip."

Juan Carlos pressed the button on the arm of his chair and ordered up coffee and pastries from his personal flight attendant. Then he rested back in his seat and sipped bourbon. Sleep was elusive lately and eating had become a chore. But he could tolerate a shot or two of bourbon when his mind wouldn't shut down. It helped blur the pain of losing Portia.

It had been one solid week since she'd left Alma and he hadn't heard from her since. What was she doing? Had she gone back to her work routine as if *they* hadn't happened? As if the time they'd shared together was nothing more than a passing fling?

He couldn't believe that. Something was up with her.

He felt it deep down in his soul that something had happened to Portia to make her deny their love and break off their engagement. Juan Carlos had waited patiently all week to hear from her, anticipating a call that had never come, and his patience was at an end. Now he was taking matters into his own hands. He knew enough about relationships to know women liked to be pursued. They liked to have men come after them. Maybe Portia was testing him? Maybe she'd expected him to come running and convince her she'd been wrong?

If only it would be that easy.

But he had to try.

Outside of his bodyguards, he hadn't told a soul of their breakup. He couldn't bring himself to share the news so soon after publicly announcing their happy engagement. He had hopes of winning Portia back, hopes of restoring their love. He'd vowed to bring honor and credibility back to the monarchy of Alma as well as to carry out his grandmother Isabella's dying wishes for the country. He wanted, needed Portia by his side. He and Portia belonged together. She was the love of his life.

Living without her would only be half a life.

Hours later, the plane touched down in Los Angeles, a place Juan Carlos had visited often. But this time, he had more than business to attend to—he had come to retrieve his woman. He'd managed to get a few winks of sleep, shaved and changed his crumpled clothes while they were in the air. Now he felt human again and more like himself, rather than the shell of the man he'd been this past week. Dressed in a slate-gray suit and neatly groomed, he planned on sweeping his princess off her feet again.

Returning home without her wasn't an option.

"Are you ready, Your Highness?" Eduardo asked, rising from his seat.

"Yes, and you have our little surprise all set?" he asked.

"I do. If it doesn't help your cause," Eduardo said, grinning, "nothing will."

Juan Carlos nodded. He couldn't disagree.

A frozen waffle popped up out of the toaster and Portia set it next to the scrambled eggs on her plate. She doused the waffle with maple syrup, grabbed a fork and took the plate over to the kitchen table. Breakfast for dinner was always an option when one didn't have the stomach to really cook. Or eat for that matter. Her belly squeezed tight as she looked at the food. She'd promised Jasmine she would eat something tonight.

Her friend had apologized profusely for breaking their dinner date. Jas had planned to cook a roast prime rib tonight, her specialty. They were going to do it up right with champagne and soufflé, and have a fun girls' night watching Turner Classic Movies on television. It was the only reason Portia had put on a dress, instead of wearing her usual comfy gray sweats. She didn't want to disappoint her friend.

"Poor Jas." She'd come down with a bug. Hopefully it wasn't the flu. Portia felt a little guilty about it, having dominated a lot of her time lately. Jasmine had been the best friend she could ever hope to have. Every day she'd come over to help Portia clean out her closets or rearrange furniture or cook a meal. Jasmine would bring in Mexican food on Taco Tuesdays and play card games with her until very late at night. She understood Portia needed to kill time so she didn't have to think too hard.

Now her friend was sick.

"For you, Jas, I'm going to eat this." She took a bite of her eggs and chewed and chewed. The eggs went down like rubber. She'd overcooked them again.

The waffle wasn't much better. It was still frozen in the center. Two bites later, she figured she'd fulfilled her promise and took her dish to the sink, dumping the contents down the garbage disposal.

Now what? She glanced around the condo. It was spotless. She'd been cleaning all week long. She had no official work to do. She hadn't been back to the office yet—they weren't expecting her anyway since she'd taken a three-month leave to deal with wedding plans and her new life as wife to a king.

She'd truly questioned whether to go back to her job. Could she continue with the pretense? How could she go back, when her friends and associates still believed her to be Princess Portia of Samforstand? Could she go about her life, living the lie? And what if she decided it was impossible to resume her life as usual? What if she revealed all the lies about herself and her family? What would that mean for Juan Carlos? His humiliation would be monumental. He would hate her. And appear a fool, a man easily duped.

She was at a crossroads in her life, and didn't know which way to proceed.

No one could possibly know how she felt right now. She was a phony, a fraud and an imposter. Jasmine kept telling her it wasn't her fault and no one would blame her if the truth got out. But Portia didn't know who she was anymore. Her life had been ripped out from under her. She felt at odds, lonely and bereft. Her emotions were all over the place. Anger took up residence, but sympathy crept in sometimes, as she imagined her family's plight after the war. Still, those emotions didn't come close to the emptiness she felt deep inside her heart. Because of something that had happened decades ago, she had had to give up the man she loved. The price was high, costing her her happiness.

The doorbell chimed and she jumped. "Who could that be?" she whispered. Surely, Jasmine wouldn't come out tonight. She was in bed with a fever.

Portia had a mind not to open the door, but the bell chimed once again and her curiosity had her heading to the front door.

She stuck her face up to the peephole and gazed out.

"Eduardo?" What on earth was he doing here?

"*Si*, Princess, it's me."

She cringed at his reverent greeting. She didn't deserve to be called Princess. The chain lock allowed her to open the door three inches. She peered out and he smiled wide. "Hello."

Eduardo had become her friend. Seeing this solid block of a man on her doorstep was a welcome sight.

"Hi."

"Will you open the door for me?"

"Oh…of course." She undid the chain and opened the door.

Eduardo stood rooted to the spot. "Are you alone, Princess?"

"Yes, I am alone. Why?"

"I had to ask as it is my duty to protect the king. It's good to see you, but I am here on official bus—"

Juan Carlos stepped into her line of vision from a place on the porch that had concealed him. "Thank you, Eduardo. I'll take it from here."

Portia's mouth dropped open. She blinked and started trembling. "Juan Carlos."

He held a cat carrier in his hand. "Before you say anything, I brought you a gift. Well, two gifts. May I come in?"

With a lump in her throat, she looked away from Juan Carlos's face to the two kittens from Duchess's litter she'd appropriately named Mischief and Mallow. The kittens—one black and gray and mostly all trouble and the other almost all white with spots of caramel color here and there looking like a toasted marshmallow—were sleeping, curled up into little balls of fluff. Mallow's head rested on Mischief's body. Their sweetness brought a tear to her eye.

"Juan Carlos, you...you brought them," she said, touched by the thoughtful gesture. Words she wanted to say tightened in her throat and wouldn't come out. Initially, her heart had lurched when she spotted Juan Carlos, though he looked worn out. His eyes were rimmed with red—from sleepless nights? His handsome face looked haggard, as if he'd been through a war and his hair, while combed, needed a cut. She should have known he wouldn't take no very easily. He wasn't a man easily dissuaded. It was one of the qualities she loved most about him. "You didn't need to do that," she said, finally realizing she wasn't up to caring for pets. She'd barely been able to care for herself lately.

"I figured you might like the company. They are yours as much as they are mine."

She gazed into his solemn eyes. "Come in," she said.

She'd been engaged to a man who had never stepped foot into her home. How telling was that? An impetuous engagement, even though love was involved, wasn't an ideal way to start a relationship. She understood that now. During the coronation and then while living at the farmhouse searching for hidden treasures, they'd lived in a fantasy world, untouched by outside influences. It wasn't reality.

Juan Carlos stepped inside and glanced around, taking in the details of her home. "It's as beautiful as you are, Portia. I wouldn't expect any less."

"Thank you," she said. Her heart thumped hard in her chest. Thankfully, Eduardo's presence helped defuse the situation at the moment. She peered over Juan Carlos's shoulder. "Eduardo, would you like to come inside?"

She'd spent enough time with Juan Carlos and his bodyguards to know what Eduardo's answer had to be. He would be securing the premises and standing watch outside. "I wish I could, Your Highness," he said. "Thank you, but I will be right out here."

It was just as she'd suspected. "Okay, I understand." She turned to Juan Carlos and pasted on a false smile. "Surely, you and I both know that bringing me the kittens wasn't the reason you've come."

"But you're glad I did?"

She glanced at the sleeping kittens. "I'm glad to see them. They are sweet and I did…miss them." She cleared her throat. She couldn't admit she'd missed Juan Carlos also. "They've been weaned from Duchess, I'm assuming?"

He nodded. "Early this week. Where shall I put them?"

"A good question. If you'd called and asked me I would've told you not to bring them, Juan Carlos," she said softly. "I'm not equipped to care for them."

"I'll take them back to Alma with me, if you prefer." His back stiffened a little.

"No, no. Now that they're here, I can't turn them away. I… They're special to me."

Juan Carlos set the cat carrier down on the floor of the foyer. When he returned his gaze to hers, his eyes bored into her. "I had hoped you would say the same of me, sweetheart."

Her eyes closed at his hopeful plea. "You shouldn't have come, Juan Carlos."

"I couldn't stay away. It's not finished between us."

She sighed. "It has to be. We're not right for each other."

He approached her and heaven save her, her pulse accelerated as he laid his palm on her cheek. She lifted her eyes to his. His heavy expression softened, as if touching her made all the difference. As if a light inside him was turned back on. "Not true. We're good together. We're meant for each other. I am here. Don't turn me away, Portia. I would hope I am special to you, as well."

His gaze dipped to her mouth. She swallowed. Oh, God, the pull, the magnetic force of his love surrounded her like a protective shield. She didn't know where she found the will to back up a step, and then another. She couldn't hide her emotions or the passion he instilled and as she moved, he moved with her, thrusting his body against hers until her backside met with the wall.

"I've come a long way for you, Portia." His hands braced the wall, trapping her, so that she could only stare into his face and see his truth. "I've waited my entire life."

His sweet, sincere words stymied any defenses she could muster. She put her hands on his chest but instead of shoving him away as she'd planned, her fingertips clung onto his shirt and her palms flattened against him. His breath hitched from her touch, and his immediate reaction to her nearly buckled her knees. How could she not love this man? How could she turn him away now?

"I came here to talk to you, sweetheart."

She whispered, "Is that what you're doing to me? Talking?"

He flashed a charming, inescapable smile. "Maybe showing is better than telling, after all."

Then his mouth swooped over hers and claimed her in a breath-stealing kiss. His lips were rough but not unkind, wild but not crazy, sexy but not demanding. Caught up in the kiss, she couldn't think beyond the pleasure he evoked. The love she'd tried to bury was resurrected and she fell deeper in love with this man, this honorable king who had come for her.

She'd missed him and didn't know how much until this very second.

His tongue played over her lips and she opened for him. Sweeping inside her mouth, he kissed her again and again. A fire was building in her belly. She was past the point of refusal.

She was putty. He could do with her what he liked.

And she would enjoy every second.

She was lifted, floating on air now, held by two strong arms. She wrapped herself around his body, nestling her head into his chest. "Where's your bed, Portia?"

She pointed to the doorway down the hall.

His strides were long and determined and steady.

He continued to kiss her without missing a step.

Juan Carlos set Portia down on a ruffled lavender bedspread. Matching pillows, some big, some small, surrounded her head. He did a quick scan of her room decorated in soft whimsical colors. Wispy white curtains covered the windows and modern pieces of art, mostly pastels and some oils, adorned the walls. It was so Portia: soft, delicate, sweet.

God, he loved her.

And he wasn't going to leave here without her.

She was his prize, his love, the treasure he couldn't live without.

He unbuttoned his shirt, spread it wide across his chest and then gave it a toss. He kicked off his shoes and socks and gazed into her eyes as he unfastened his belt.

Her brows lifted, her lips parted slightly and a sharp breathy gasp escaped her lips. Her hungry expression softened his heart, but made every other part of his body hard. He had one night to change her mind. He wouldn't waste a minute. He took her hand and lifted her to her knees. "Come here, sweetheart," he demanded. "Touch me. Put your hands on my body."

Another gasp ripped from her lips and she moved to him. She wore a simple black dress with thin straps and short hemline. It adorned her breasts with just enough material to tempt him beyond belief. He ached to touch her, to shed her clothes and join their bodies, but first, he had to make her see how much she needed him, too. How perfect he was for her.

Her hands came to his torso and he gritted his teeth. She explored the breadth of him, tracing her fingertips over his chest, and then kissed everywhere her fingers had just touched. His body flamed; it was almost too much to bear. She was proving to him that they belonged together.

"Your touch is like no other, Portia. You know that. See what you do to me."

"We are good here, in bed, Juan Carlos," she whispered.

"We are good everywhere, sweetheart. Why do you fight me on this?"

She turned her face from him and disengaged, and he knew he'd pushed her too far. Something was eating at her. Something was making her hold back from him. "Don't retreat," he whispered. He couldn't let her think. Couldn't let whatever notions she had in her head continue to separate them.

He sank down on the bed beside her and unleashed his love for her, stripping down her defenses, loving her with everything he had inside. Holding her steady with one hand, he eased her dress off with the other, baring her upper body. He cupped her breasts, made love to them with his mouth and tongue and was rewarded with sighs of pleasure, little throaty moans of delight. Her throat, her chin, her lips. He devoured them all while covering her body with his. She arched her hips and they moved in the same unique rhythm, thrusting, aching, groaning until he couldn't take another second. He joined their bodies, pushing through her mental defenses and bringing them skin to skin.

Her eyes closed to the pleasure, her face beautifully masked in satisfaction. He thrust into her deep and long. It was hot and damp and sweaty and when he sensed her readiness, he called her name. "Portia." Her eyes snapped open. He stared into them and announced, "This is our place."

Connected by more than their bodies, she sighed and nodded her head.

Then he brought her home.

* * *

Early dawn broke through the curtains and Juan Carlos smiled in his drowsy state, his eyes still closed as images of making love to Portia flashed in his head. God, how he'd missed her. And now she was where she belonged. With him. After the night they'd shared, he hoped he'd convinced her that she loved him, he loved her and whatever was bothering her could be worked out and put to rest. It wasn't rocket science. Perhaps he'd pushed her too far early in their relationship. They'd only known each other for weeks. Not the months or years some take to cement their connection. She'd gotten cold feet. Any problems that arose could be dealt with. He couldn't see a reason why they shouldn't live their lives together. They'd made love twice during the night, and the second time had been even more thrilling and revelatory than the first. No one could tell him that Portia didn't love him. She'd displayed that in the way she'd taken the initiative, kissed him, touched him and made love to his body.

It was good, so good, between them. In all ways.

Juan Carlos rolled over to cradle her in his arms. They'd welcome the day together. But his hands hit upon cold sheets. He squeezed his eyes open. Portia was gone, her half of the bed empty. Was she always an early riser? He didn't know. They'd spent time together at the farmhouse in Alma on his schedule, not hers. There were still things they needed to learn about each other.

He hinged his body up, eager to see her. Eager to kiss her. Rising from the bed, he dressed in his trousers and shirt, ran a hand through his hair to comb down the spiky ends and then padded out of the room.

Halfway down the hallway of her modest three-bedroom condo, he halted, hearing mewling sounds coming from the living room. Of course, the kittens. Portia must have been anxious to see them this morning and tend to them the way she always had. Their carrier came equipped with kitty food, and water was their drink of choice. He grinned. He could almost picture her playing with them on the carpeted floor. Bringing them here had been a good plan to get his foot in the door and soften Portia's heart, but ultimately he'd done it to bring a smile to her face.

As he approached the sounds grew louder and no, they didn't appear to be coming from the kittens. It was a human sound, the heartbreaking echo of quiet crying. He stood on the threshold of the living room to find Portia, sitting up on the sofa, her arms around her legs, rocking back and forth with tears soaking her face.

The kittens were happily swatting at her feet, but it was as if they weren't there. Her sorrow was so deep she didn't hear him stride into the room. "Portia, sweetheart. What's wrong?"

She wiped her cheeks with the back of her hand, shaking her head. "You shouldn't have come, Juan Carlos," she whispered.

He narrowed his eyes. What on earth? Last night, they'd settled things. Maybe not verbally, but after the night they'd shared she had to recognize what they meant to each other. He'd come to retrieve her and bring her back to her rightful place, beside him on the throne of Alma. But now she was crying, looking so achingly sad. His gut clenched seeing her that way. "I don't understand."

He sat beside her and she unraveled her legs to face him, her eyes swollen from tears. "I can't be with you. I can't…"

"Sweetheart, my perfect princess, of course you belong with me. We don't have to rush into a wedding, if that's your concern. Whatever it is, we'll work it out. Just tell me. It kills me to see you in so much pain."

She rose then, yet her body slumped in defeat, her long hair falling onto her face. "That's just it, Juan Carlos," she said, shoving her hair aside. "I'm not your perfect princess.

I'm nobody's princess. I'm a fraud. I don't have an ounce of royal blood in my body. I cannot marry you. Ever."

Juan Carlos blinked several times, absorbing her words. He rose slowly, his heart pounding, his body shaking. "What you do mean you're not a princess?"

"I'm not. I never was. It's all a lie my family told after they migrated to the United States after World War II."

Portia spent the next few minutes explaining her family's duplicity to him. She gave him very little to hold on to as she presented the cold cruel facts that tore his life into shreds. Everything she told him made sense, yet nothing made sense. This couldn't be happening. Suddenly, he looked at Portia Lindstrom differently. She'd lied to him. Why? "How long have you known this?"

"I found out a little more than a week ago while researching our...my wedding rituals."

Juan Carlos stood ramrod stiff, his shoulders back and his heart breaking. "Yet you came to me and lied about the reasons for breaking it off between us. You told me you weren't ready to marry. You gave me excuses about your career and your love of the States. You knew, and yet you lied. How many other lies have you told me, Portia?"

"I didn't know what to do when I found out. Who to turn to. I'd just found out I'm...I'm an *imposter*." She spit the word out as if saying it stung her tongue. "I had trouble facing it, Juan Carlos."

His voice rose. "You should have trusted me with the truth. Or maybe you didn't want anyone to know the real truth? Maybe you wanted to keep on with the deception? Being of royal blood has its privileges. If I hadn't shown up here, what were you going to do? Live the lie forever?"

Her words from last week rang in his ears. *I'm fond of you. This isn't going to work. I don't want to get married. I don't want children.*

Had the woman he loved been nothing but a gold digger? Had her hard-to-get act been a ploy? All the warmth he had nestled inside evaporated. Last night had meant nothing to her. She'd deceived him over and over during the past few weeks. She'd broken off her engagement to him, but she hadn't revealed the truth to anyone. Of course, her precious career would suffer. She'd hidden the truth because she couldn't afford another scandal. She needed the art world to believe that she was a princess. So, of course, she had to come to him with lies about why she was breaking off their engagement in order to keep her secret.

"I took the bait and you reeled me in, didn't you, Portia? Then what happened? You ran scared when I offered marriage? Did you have a bout of conscience? Or did you finally realize you'd get caught if you didn't break it off with me? You couldn't marry me and risk being found out. Just think what would happen to your career if you were discovered to be a fraud. You'd never survive another scandal. Not professionally. No one in their right mind would hire you so you lied your way out of our engagement."

Her tears gone now, she squeezed her eyes closed for a second. As he waited, her breathing steadied and when she opened her eyes again, they were twin pinpoints of blue, focused on him. "You see things in black-and-white, Juan Carlos. There is no room for grays in your narrow line of vision. You only wanted me when I fit into your plans, but now you know the truth. I'm not royal. I'm flawed and can't be a part of your unblemished world."

His lips tightened. "You should've told me the truth, Portia."

"Another point against me. I'm human. I make mistakes." She folded her arms across her stomach. "Now that you have the truth, what are you going to do with it?"

He stared at her, wondering what had happened to the woman he'd fallen in love with. Thoughts clogged his head. She wasn't a princess. She had no royal blood flowing through her veins. She was an imposter. A fraud, as she put it. His shoulders dropped as he shook his head. He had no answer for her.

"You only loved the idea of me, Juan Carlos. You said it just a little while ago. You think of me as your perfect princess. But now you know I'm not perfect. Hardly that. And how can a man who demands perfection in everything and everyone want me? I was only good to you when I was Princess Portia of Samforstand."

He let that sink in. He loved her, wanted her as his wife. Now, nothing made sense, and blackness from deep in his soul overwhelmed him. His Portia, the woman he'd thought she was, was gone. She wasn't a princess, but a fraud. He couldn't marry Portia Lindstrom. According to royal decree he was obligated to marry royalty. She was once a part of everything good that had happened to him and now there was nothing left between them.

"We had a fling, and it's over," she whispered. "Let's let it go at that. I think you should leave. Go back to Del Sol, be the king you were meant to be. Give me some time, I'll make sure…no blame will come to you about this."

"Portia," he said. He couldn't bring himself to move.

"Go, please." Her quiet plea broke his heart. "You shouldn't have come back. Goodbye, Juan Carlos."

She picked up the kittens playing at her feet, hugged them to her chest and walked out of the room.

She was right. He should leave.

There wasn't anything left for him here.

"Mr. Tanaka, it was a pleasure seeing you again. I'll be in touch once I've found the right prints and antique paneled floor screens to separate your work spaces. You've given me a good idea what you are looking for. I promise you, you'll be happy with the collection I come up with for your magnificent new corporate offices."

"Thank you, Princess. I have faith in your abilities. Your recommendations for my home have worked out nicely. I'm grateful you would take time from your leave of absence to do this for me."

Portia shook hands with her client outside his private office, her belly squeezing tight every time he called her princess. The title she'd grown up with no longer rang true and his respectful use of it during their meeting reminded her constantly that she was a fraud. "Goodbye."

Mr. Tanaka, founder and president of a highly successful Japanese food chain, hadn't wanted to work with anyone else. He'd called her personally to request her expertise, offering a big bonus if she would consider advising him on the artwork for his new offices. She'd agreed without hesitation. Pining for Juan Carlos and what would never be had grown old. She couldn't cry herself to sleep any longer. Three days' worth of tears had exhausted her. But she was glad her secret was out. At least to him. Admitting the truth to Juan Carlos had been difficult, but it had also been liberating. There would be no more lies between them now.

He'd been angry with her when he'd left her condo the other day. She'd seen the pain in his eyes, too, and she'd shivered when he'd looked at her as if she were a stranger. It had been so very hard to hear him berate her. He hadn't believed her, and even thought so little of her that he'd accused her of putting her career above her love for him. His accusations had slashed through her body like a dagger. But ultimately, it was better to allow him to believe the worst about her. It was a clean break.

Still, the love she had for him would never die. It would be hard, if not impossible, to get over him. Even if he had believed her claims, he couldn't marry her. They would have no future. He lived by a stringent set of rules. He did everything by the book. It was a no-win situation. So she'd made the supreme sacrifice for his benefit. She'd dismissed him without defending herself. As if her life wouldn't be forever altered after knowing and loving him.

He would get over her. He had to. He had to go about his life as if they had never met. In the near future, she didn't know exactly when, she would quietly make an announcement that they'd broken off their engagement. Their whirlwind romance was over. And then at some later point, when it had all died down, she would admit to the world, or anyone who cared, that she wasn't of royal heritage.

She would not go on living a lie.

But for now her goal was to protect Juan Carlos from a scandal. She would not have him looked upon as a fool.

As she headed to the parking garage, her eyes clouded with tears. She was broken inside and there was no way to repair her. Taking on Mr. Tanaka's account would be a good distraction. She'd focus on work for the next few weeks and the terrible ache in the pit of her stomach would eventually go away.

She got in her car and glanced in the mirror. She looked a wreck. With the tips of her index fingers, she smoothed away moisture under her eyes. "No more," she whispered. She had to put on a happy face. It was Jasmine's birthday today and she was taking her to dinner to celebrate the big three-oh.

Ten

Juan Carlos ran a hand down his face. He stood at the bar in the study of his living quarters in the palace and poured himself a double whiskey, straight up. "It's impossible." He lifted the glass to his mouth and took a sip.

"What's impossible?"

He turned, a little shocked to find Maria standing beside him. He'd been so deep in thought, he'd almost forgotten about his dinner date with the Ramons tonight. Normally his senses were keen and no one could sneak up on him. Especially not a woman wearing a pretty dress and heels and smelling like something exotic. It served to show him how off he'd been lately.

"Sorry if I startled you. Your staff assured me I was expected."

"No, it's okay. You are." It was good to see a friendly face.

"Alex is running late. He's meeting me here."

Juan Carlos nodded. "That'll give us a chance to talk. Let me get you a drink. What would you like?"

"Just a soda, please."

He dropped two ice cubes into a tall glass and poured her a cola. "Here you go."

She took the offered glass and sipped. "So what were you mumbling about when I came in?"

The corner of his mouth crooked up. It was the best he could do. He didn't have a smile for anyone these days. "My life."

"Your life?" Maria's aqua eyes opened wider. "Your perfect, kingly, marrying-a-beautiful-princess life?"

He lifted his whiskey glass and pointed with his index finger to the bone leather sofa. "Have a seat. I have something to… I need some advice."

Maria arched an eyebrow. "Advice? About your wedding?"

He waited for her to sit and then planted himself on the other end of the sofa. "Maria, uh, there isn't going to be a wedding."

It was hard getting the words out, and seeing Maria's mouth drop open only added to his discomfort. "That's why I asked you here. I haven't told a soul yet. I can hardly believe it myself."

"But you and Portia seemed so perfect together. What happened?"

Perfect. He was beginning to really hate that word. Portia had accused him of demanding that everyone and everything around him be perfect. Was he guilty of that? Did he expect too much?

"We're not perfect. Far from it. We've broken up and I don't know what to think about it."

"Why? What happened, Your Majesty?"

"She came back to Del Sol almost two weeks ago to break it off. She claimed she didn't want to get married and move to Alma. She loved her career and didn't want it to end. She claimed all we had was a fling, and that she, we, were high on romance. Finding the hidden artwork and being on the adventure together made it all seem possible but when she got back home, she was hit with reality."

"Do you think she was running scared?"

He hung his head, staring at the ground. "Initially, that's what I thought. I believed I could convince her that we could work out logistics and that we belonged together."

He met with Maria's eyes. "I was fool enough to go after her. I was in love."

"Was?"

He shrugged. "From the day I met her, something inside me told me she was the one. I pursued her like crazy. She didn't make it easy and now that I'm home, putting the pieces together, I think I know why."

There was a beat of silence. Maria was waiting for him to continue. It was difficult to admit to anyone how wrong he'd been. "When I went to Los Angeles, we...connected again. And it was as it had always been—amazing. I thought I'd relieved her of her cold feet. But in the morning, I found her quietly crying. She said she wished that I hadn't come for her. I was confused and didn't know why she'd had a change of heart."

"Why did she?" Maria asked.

He shrugged and shook his head. "I think she was cornered and didn't see a way out, so she finally told me the truth. Portia is not who she says she is. She's not a princess. She never was. She claims she found out while trying to dig up protocols for our wedding. Her family fled to the United States right after World War II and assumed the role of royalty. They were impoverished and used their phony status to gain a leg up. Supposedly, Portia's great-aunt has a diary that confirms all this."

"Wow, this is...big. Poor Portia. She must've been devastated when she found out. I can only imagine how she feels right now."

He stared at her. "You mean you believe that she didn't know about this all along?"

"Why wouldn't I? More importantly, why wouldn't you?"

"I'll tell you why. When she came back to Del Sol a couple weeks ago she lied about her reasons for breaking it off. She made up one excuse after another and if I hadn't gone to LA, I would still believe those lies she'd told. Only when she couldn't get rid of me any other way, she was forced to reveal the truth."

"Oh, I don't know about that." Maria began shaking her head. "That doesn't sound like Portia. What did you say to her when you found out?"

"In the beginning I was shell-shocked. And then my methodical mind started working and I said some things out of anger. I practically accused her of being a gold digger. Now that I think back on it, she looked so…lost. She kept saying she was an imposter, and I couldn't sympathize with her. I wasn't in the frame of mind. I felt betrayed. She should have come to me with the truth from the beginning."

"It must've been a hard thing for her to admit. To herself, much less to the man she loved. Just think, everything she believed about herself and her life is a lie. If that were me, I wouldn't know what to do, who to turn to. I don't know if I'd have the courage to do what she did. It was a hard day for both of you."

He drew oxygen into his lungs. "I suppose. I still don't know what to think."

"What else did she say? How did you part?"

"She pretty much told me off. She said that I expected perfection in everything and that I only loved the idea of her." He stared into his tumbler at the last gulp of whiskey left. "That's not true."

"No?"

He gave Maria a glance. "No," he assured her. "I loved her."

"You still love her, Your Majesty. You can't shut down those emotions so quickly. And what if she still is that woman you fell in love with, without the title of princess in front of her name? What if Portia Lindstrom is the woman for you?"

"How can I believe that when she doesn't believe it? She

didn't try to defend herself against my accusations. She didn't try to convince me that I'd been wrong about her."

"Well, since you asked me for my advice, I'm going to give it to you. I know Portia a little bit, and I'm a pretty good judge of character. I have seen the way she looks at you. The eyes don't lie. She was deeply in love and happy."

A lump formed in his throat. In the short weeks that he and Portia had been together, they'd gotten to know each other pretty well. They'd shared an adventure or two, but it went deeper than that and he'd felt they were meant for each other from the very beginning. It was a sense he had, a feeling that clamped onto him and never let go. It wasn't an overreaction to her beauty or the fact that she was a princess. But that factored into the equation, at least a little bit, because her status meant he was free to seriously pursue her.

"I thought so, too," he said. "We were good together."

"Did you ever stop to think that she wasn't thinking about herself when she broke up with you? Maybe she loved you so much she didn't want you portrayed in a bad light. A hasty then broken engagement wouldn't instill much faith in the monarchy you are trying to reestablish. After the big splash announcing your engagement, how would King Juan Carlos appear to the country that trusted his honor? Wouldn't it make you seem frivolous? Or duped? Or worse yet, impetuous? Seems to me, if I was in that situation, I would do everything in my power to protect the man I loved from scorn and speculation."

He scrubbed his jaw and sighed. "The last thing she told me was that she would make sure no blame came to rest on my shoulders."

Maria smiled. "There, you see. Only a woman still in love would say that. She was shielding you from harm. I would bet on it."

"You would?"

"Yes, and you should, too, if you still love her."

"To what end? I can't change the future…"

"Who says you can't? You're the king."

"I'm not that kind of king. I don't want to break with tradition."

"No, you'd rather have your heart broken."

Juan Carlos sighed. She was right. He would never love another the way he loved Portia. Right now, he physically ached for her.

Maria continued, "Think of it this way. You'll rule with more clarity and fairness having Portia by your side. You won't be stung by bitterness and regret and live an empty life without her."

"But the people expect—"

"A ruler they can admire and look up to. If you make it clear to them that this is for the best, they will rally behind you, my friend. And as the newly reigning king of a lost monarchy you have the luxury of not needing a parliament to vote on changes you might want to make in your dynasty."

A slow smile spread across his face. "I hadn't thought of that." And just as the notion elevated his hope, another thought brought him down again. "No…it's too late after the way I walked out on Portia, without believing in her. She may not forgive me."

Maria scooted closer to him, the sparkle in her eyes grabbing his attention. "But she may. And I think she will. She sacrificed herself for you. Don't you think you owe your relationship one more chance? If you don't try, you'll always wonder and you'll live to regret it."

Did he still love Portia? Yes, very much, and the more he thought about Maria's argument, the more he began to believe she could be right. He couldn't throw away something so precious to him without giving it one more try.

A light flashed in his head as he began to formulate a

plan. Finally, after these past few days of living in a depressed stupor, he was waking up alert and seeing things much more clearly. He had the power of the throne behind him. He hoped it would be enough.

"Maria, I'm going to need your help."

"I'll give it gladly, Your Highness."

A knot formed in the pit of his stomach. "A lot will be riding on this," he warned.

"I know. But I have enough faith in love for both of us. Alex says I've taught him something about that."

Juan Carlos nodded. If only he had that same faith. He leaned forward to kiss Maria's cheek. "Thank you."

"What is it exactly that you've taught me, sweetheart?" Alex stood at the threshold of the study, catching Juan Carlos's lips leaving Maria's cheek.

"How important *trust* is, Alex," Maria said slowly, straightening her position on the sofa, "when it comes to matters of the heart."

Alex gave them a nod as he entered the room. "It's true…once upon a time my fist might've met with His Majesty's jaw seeing him kiss you. But now, I only see love shining in your eyes for me."

A chuckle rumbled from Juan Carlos's chest. It was a good sound. One he hoped to make more often, after Portia was back where she belonged.

The sound of her Nikes pounding against the treadmill echoed off the gym walls. Sweat beaded up on Portia's forehead as she gazed out the window of the high-rise. She was offered a view of distant mountains and below, a city waking just after dawn. It was a good time of day to work out, before the world came alive. She had about thirty minutes before the gym would crowd with businessmen and women coming for their daily fix. She'd be gone by then, away from any nosy members who'd try to talk to her, get to know her. Many people recognized her, but thankfully she was old news as the other royal couple—the Brits—were in town for a charity event and all eyes had turned to them.

It was a lucky break and she valued the bit of anonymity it afforded her.

"Oh…kay, Portia," Jasmine said, shutting down her machine. "I've had enough."

Portia continued running at a six-mile-per-hour pace. She had one more mile to go. "You've barely broken a sweat."

"You're insane this morning." Jas used her towel to wipe her face as droplets rained down from her eyebrows.

Portia slowed her pace, allowing her body to cool down. "I know. But this is the only time I have to work off my…"

"Sexual frustration."

Portia swiped at her friend's butt with her workout towel. "Shh…no. Stop that! Just frustration in general."

Jasmine reached over and pushed the Off button on Portia's machine. "You're done."

The treadmill's thrumming quieted as it shut down and Portia finally stood stationary facing Jas. "I know I am. So done." She sopped up her face and neck and allowed herself a moment of accomplishment. It had been a hearty workout.

"I meant on the machine, girl. You're being cryptic today. What's really bothering you?"

Aside from her broken heart? It was hard to put into words exactly but she tried to explain. "I'm almost finished with the Tanaka account, Jas. You've helped me so much this past week and we've been working at breakneck speed for long hours. When I'm through… I don't know how it will play out. I'm still officially on leave. I don't know what to do after this. I'm living a lie, but I can't do anything about it at the moment. I feel weird in my own skin right now."

"Wow, Portia, I'm sorry. Juan Carlos doesn't deserve you. You're hurting because of him."

"You got that backward. I don't deserve him."

"Oh, brother. Listen, I know it's going to take time getting over him, but you will, honey. I hate to stand by and see you beat yourself up over something out of your control."

"Thanks, Jas. It means a lot to know you have my back."

"I do."

They left the workout area and headed to the showers. After a quick rinse off, Portia dressed in her casual street clothes and combed her hair.

"Too bad we can't grab breakfast," Jas said, exchanging a look with Portia in the dressing room mirror as she slipped her long mane into a ponytail.

"Wish we could, but we've both got busy mornings. Sorry if I'm overworking you on this account."

"You're not at all. I was only looking for an excuse to have waffles and bacon this morning."

"And you wanted an accomplice, right?"

Jas nodded. "No fun eating alone."

"Another day, I promise."

"Okay, then I'll talk to you later. Oh, and thanks," she said, wrinkling her nose, "for dragging my butt in this morning." She pouted. "I ache all over and my legs feel like Jell-O."

"You'll thank me in twenty years when you're still hot and gorgeous."

"So I guess I'll have to be your friend forever now."

"BFFs. That's us."

"Yeah, that's us," Jas said, waving goodbye.

Portia rode the elevator down to the parking garage. Just as she was getting into her Volvo, her phone beeped. She glanced at the screen. Odd, she'd gotten a text from Maria Ramon.

I'm in town and would love to see you. Can you make time for me today?

"No," she whispered. Any reminder of Juan Carlos right now was hard to take. Seeing Maria would only bring back memories of her time in Alma. She did have a terribly busy day. Hadn't she just turned down a breakfast date with her best friend?

Another text came in. It's important that I see you.

Portia's breath caught in her throat. Her heart began to pound. She couldn't refuse Maria. She was a friend and more than that, Portia was curious as to what she wanted. But that didn't stop her hands from trembling as she typed her answer. Sure, would love to see you. Stop by this morning. She gave her the address and sighed, starting the car. She planned on working from home this morning, anyway.

As it turned out, Portia couldn't concentrate when she returned home. Those phone conversations could wait another day, she decided. She changed into a powder-blue silk blouse and white slacks, and brushed her hair back and clipped it on one side with a gemstone barrette à la Gwen Stefani. She finished with a few flips of mascara to her lashes and some pink lip gloss.

In the kitchen, she prepared coffee, arranged fresh pastries on a plate, and then brought it all to the dining table. Mischief and Mallow played at her feet, swatting none too gently at her toes. Before they destroyed her sandals, she scooped them both up and carried them to the sofa. "Here, let's cuddle," she said, laying them across her chest. They obeyed, burrowing into the warmth of her body. The sound of their purring brought a smile to her face. She stroked the top of their soft downy heads. She loved the two fur balls with all of her heart.

A few minutes later, the doorbell chimed and Portia jerked up straight. The quick move sent the kittens tumbling to the floor. The little guys landed on their feet. Oh, to be a cat.

Portia rose and glanced at herself in the foyer mirror, checking hair and makeup. She approached the door, but her hand shook on the knob. She paused, took a deep breath. *Stay calm, Portia. Maria is a friend.*

She opened the door to find Maria smiling warmly, her pretty aqua eyes bright. A sharp twinge tightened Portia's belly. "Hi, Maria."

"Portia, it's good to see you."

She stepped forward to give Maria a hug. "I'm happy to see you, too. Please come in," she said, retreating as Maria made her way into the foyer.

She glanced around, noting the high-vaulted ceilings and the living and dining rooms. "It's a lovely place, Portia."

She shrugged. "Thanks. It's a rental. I travel back and forth from coast to coast a lot, so I have a small apartment in New York City, too. I haven't really made this place my own yet." She'd never felt settled enough in either place to put too much of herself into them. Aside from her treasured artwork on the walls, the rest of her furniture was simply… there. She had no emotional attachment to it, which had never really dawned on her before now. "It's not a big place. Would you like a tour?"

"Sure." Portia walked her through the condo, showing her the home office, the guest bedroom, her master suite and the kitchen. They stopped in the dining room. "Would you like coffee and a pastry?"

Maria's eyes darted to the dish of fresh pastries. They were impressive. Portia knew the pastry chef at the Beverly Hills Hotel and she'd made a call this morning to have them delivered. "I'd love some. Thank you. It's good seeing you in your own element here. This is very nice."

"Let's have a seat," Portia said. "Everything's ready." Maria sat down across the table and Portia poured them each a cup of coffee. "I was surprised, in a good way, to hear from you this morning. What brings you to California?"

Maria cradled the cup in her hands. "I, uh, I had no real business here, Portia. I came specifically to see you."

"Me?" Portia halted before the cup touched her lips. "Why?"

"Maybe because I'm a hopeless romantic. Maybe because I found the love of my life in Alex and want my friends to find that same kind of happiness. Don't get me wrong, Portia, I'm not here to meddle, but I do think Juan Carlos made a mistake with you."

"He told you?" Portia wasn't sure how she felt about that.

"Yes, I know you've broken the engagement."

"Who else knows?"

"No one. I don't think he's told his cousins yet."

Portia nodded. Her belly began to ache. "Do you know everything?"

Maria's expression softened. "I know you're not a princess, Portia. Juan Carlos told me the entire story. I'm so sorry you were misled all those years. It must have been extremely difficult finding out the way that you did."

Portia's eyes squeezed shut at the truth of those words. "Yes." Oh, God. This was so hard. If only she could blink this entire ordeal away. Too bad life wasn't that easy. Soon everyone would know her dirty little secret and they probably wouldn't be as kind as Maria. "It's been an adjustment. My whole life is a lie."

"Not all of it, Portia."

She snapped her eyes open, just as Maria's hand came to touch hers. She welcomed the warmth of her friend's gentle touch. "I can't possibly know exactly how you feel, but I do know you. Portia Lindstrom is a wonderful, sweet, caring woman. She's smart and funny and she's terribly in love with a good man."

Portia shook her head. "No. Juan Carlos...there's nothing left between us."

"There's love, Portia. Don't discount it. It makes the world go round, you know."

"Well, I'm spinning fast, Maria. And I'm about to fall off."

"No, you don't have to fall off. I know Juan Carlos still loves you. He's made a terrible mistake. He was in shock, I think, hearing the news about your identity, and he regrets how you two left off. He's sorry for how he treated you, Portia."

"I accept his apology. If that's what you came for, you can tell him not to worry about me. I'm...fine."

"That's not why I came. You love him very much, don't you?"

Portia sat silent.

"I know you're protecting him, Portia. I know, because if I were in your shoes, I'd do the same thing."

"You would?"

"Yes. Isn't it why you initially lied about the reason you broke off your engagement?"

"Maybe."

"Maybe yes?"

"Okay, yes. That's why I lied. It was inevitable that we had to break up, so why should both of us go down with the ship? I was to blame. It was my family's illicit behavior that put us in this position. Juan Carlos didn't need to suffer, too."

"I thought so." Maria selected a pastry and eased it onto her plate. "Juan Carlos is very lucky."

Portia scoffed. "Hardly. I'm a fraud."

"No, you're not, Portia. You may not be a princess, but that's not all you are. Juan Carlos believes in your love."

"Then why isn't he here? Never mind. I'm glad he's not. It was hard enough breaking it off with him the first and second time."

Maria chewed her raspberry cheese tart with a thoughtful expression on her face. "The third time's the charm, they say. And he's not here, because well, he wants to see you again. In fact, it's urgent that he see you. But he wants you to come to Alma. What he has to say must be said in Del Sol."

"Me? Go back to Alma? I couldn't possibly."

"I was afraid you'd say that. I'm not to leave here without you, but...I think I have something that will change your mind."

"Nothing much could change my mind."

"Wait right here. I have something in my car. I'll only be thirty seconds," Maria said, rising. "Don't you think about putting those pastries away."

Portia smiled despite the mystery unfolding. What on earth was Maria up to?

Just seconds later, Maria walked back into the dining room holding a large package wrapped in brown paper. The box was the size of a small television or a microwave. Ridiculous.

"What do you have there?"

"Oh, no, I'm not telling. You have to open it. First read the note."

"I don't see a note?"

"It's inside."

Portia stared at Maria and shook her head. Nothing would get her to change her mind. But she had to admit, she was intrigued. Her eye began to twitch. *Damn. Stop it.* Okay, she was nervous.

"Go on," Maria said.

Portia dug her fingers into the wrapping and tore it away. Paper flew in all directions. An envelope with her name on it taped to the box popped into her line of vision. She lifted it off, pulled the note out and read it silently.

Portia, sweetheart,
Give me another chance to prove my love.
This was to be my wedding gift to you.
I hope you will accept it and me back into your life.
It speaks for itself.
Juan Carlos

Tears trickled down her face. The note was short, but held the words that could make all things possible. She loved Juan Carlos. Would always love him. And now, dare she take a chance? What could he have possibly sent that would impact her more than those loving words?

"Open the box, Portia."

"I'm afraid to," she said, eyeing the lid, her body shaking so badly she could hardly move. "What if it isn't…"

"It is. Trust me," Maria said.

Portia pulled open the lid and found yet another box. She lifted it out and set it on the table, staring at the ornate workmanship on the box, the beautiful wood carvings of intricate design.

She undid the latch and slowly eased the lid open. She eyed her gift and a soft gasp rose up from the depths of her throat. This was amazing. Sweet. The gesture meant more to her than anything else she could imagine. Her lips began to quiver, her heart pounded and her tears fell like heavy rain.

"It's the s-statue. My favorite p-piece of the artwork we…" She gulped and whispered, "It's from the hidden treasure we uncovered." A man reaching his hand out for the woman he loves. *"Almas Iguales. Equal Souls."*

A royal chauffeur met her at the Del Sol airport terminal, grabbing up her suitcases and guiding her toward the limousine parked just outside the entrance. She was taking a giant leap of faith coming here, offering up her heart once again. But Juan Carlos had done the one thing, given her the one gift that could change her mind. His generous gesture told her he understood her, believed in her and wanted her back in his life. She didn't see how it was possible. She didn't know what terms Juan Carlos would dictate to her when she arrived. Could she bank on his integrity? Could she trust in him enough to believe there was a solution to their dilemma?

His gift had jarred her into believing the best was yet to come. But as the hours had worn on, she'd started to doubt again. It had taken Maria and Jasmine both to convince her that if she didn't travel to Del Sol and give it one last try, she would live to regret it.

"He's been solely devoted to you since the minute he set eyes on you," Maria had said.

"Think of your time at the farmhouse," Jasmine had prodded. "How many other men would rescue feral cats and give them a good home, much less a royal palace, to make you happy? And don't forget how he battled a snake to keep you safe. He's been there for you, Portia. And he'll be there for you again."

"Go, give your love another chance," they'd both chorused.

So here she was back in Del Sol where in less than an hour, Juan Carlos would address the citizens of his country in a speech that would set the tone for his rule.

The driver opened the limo door. "Thank you." She slid inside and immediately turned, startled to find Juan Carlos in the seat beside her.

"Hello, sweetheart."

The richness in his voice seeped into her soul. She faced the most handsome man she'd ever known. His eyes were deep dark shades of coffee and cocoa, flecked with hints of gold, and he was gazing at her in that intense way that made her heart soar. His smile was warm, welcoming and filled with the confidence she lacked at the moment. Oh, how she'd missed him. A whisper broke from her lips. "Juan Carlos."

"I am glad you came."

He didn't reach for her, didn't try to touch her, and she was glad. She had to catch her breath just from seeing him. Anything more would send her into a tailspin. "I, uh, I don't know why I'm here."

He sighed. "It's because you love me."

She couldn't deny it. "Yes."

"And I love you, above all else. I have misjudged you and I am truly sorry, my love. I hope your being here means you have forgiven me."

A lump formed in her throat. How could she explain the complexities of her feelings? "I do forgive you. Though it hurt, I realized you reacted as anyone might."

"But I am not just anyone, Portia. I am the man who loves you unconditionally. And I should have recognized that sooner. I should have believed in you."

"Yes. But that wouldn't have changed the outcome. Our situation is impossible, Juan Carlos."

He only smiled. "Did you like my gift?"

Tears welled in her eyes. "It's magnificent. I was truly surprised by the gesture."

"Not a gesture, sweetheart. It's a gift from my heart to yours. And I have another gift for you. One that will make all things possible. I am only asking for your trust. Do I have it?"

She hesitated for only a moment. And in that moment, she realized that yes, she trusted him with her life. She trusted him to make the right decision. She trusted him. With. Her. Heart. She nodded.

"Good."

He took her hand and lifted it to his lips, pressing the

softest, most reverent kiss there. The sweetness of the gesture left her floating on air. "I have missed you."

Their eyes met then. His were unflappable, determined, loving. She saw everything she needed in their brown depths. Then his hands were on her, cupping her face, his thumbs stroking her cheeks as his gaze flowed over her face. She was out of her depths now, living in the moment, heat crawling up from her belly to lick at her. When his lips rained down on hers, devouring her mouth in a kiss to beat all kisses, tremendous hunger swept her up and carried her away.

His groans matched her unbridled sighs. "I cannot live without you in my life," he murmured between kisses.

"I feel the same," she whispered, as he dragged her farther into his embrace. She was nearly atop him now. His hands were in her hair, his tongue sweeping through her mouth, their bodies trembling, aching.

"We have arrived, Your Highness," the driver announced through the speaker. They'd arrived? She didn't remember them taking off.

Juan Carlos stilled. "All right," he said to the chauffeur.

They had indeed arrived at a secluded private entrance in the west wing of the palace.

Juan Carlos sighed heavily and pulled away from her. "One day, we will finish this in the limo."

"I'll look forward to that." Her eyelid fluttered. Heavens, another unintended wink? She was hopeless.

Intense heat entered his eyes and a savage groan rumbled from his chest. "You are a temptation, Portia," he said. He took a second to smooth the hair he'd just mussed. The care with which he touched her and gently pulled tendrils away from her face sent shivers down her spine. Then he smiled wide and destroyed her for good. "You will attend my speech?"

"Yes." That was why she had come. His only request

was that she be in attendance when he spoke to the press and his fellow countrymen. Her flight had been delayed and there was a moment when she'd thought it an omen. A moment when she almost turned back. But Portia wasn't going to run from the truth any longer. No matter how bad. No matter that her life would be forever altered. She had gotten on the plane ready to hear what Juan Carlos seemed eager to say. He would be giving the speech very shortly. "I will be there."

He nodded, satisfied, and the door on his side of the car opened. The driver stood at attention waiting. "You'll be driven to the palace lawn now," he said to her. "I will see you very soon."

Then he climbed out of the car and was gone.

Juan Carlos stood tall and erect at the podium looking out at the crowd that had gathered on the palace lawn. Dressed regally in a dark suit and tie, he scanned his audience. Luis and Eduardo flanked him on either side, on the lookout for signs of danger. News crews from Del Sol's three television stations were in attendance, as well as reporters and journalists from far and wide. Portia saw Juan Carlos now, as the king surrounded by people who banked on his every word. He was a model citizen, handsome, refined, a man to be admired. He was the king of his people. The press loved him. Even more, they loved the idea of him *with Portia*. Who didn't love a good fairy tale?

Her stomach ached. She had no idea what he was going to say, but it was important to him that she hear him say it. There was no doubt she loved him. And she was fairly certain of his love for her. So she stood in the front row, but off to the side somewhat with Maria and Alex Ramon. Maria slid her hand over hers and squeezed gently. God, how Portia needed that show of support right now. Her legs were two rubber posts, holding her up only by sheer stubborn will. She swallowed as Juan Carlos tapped the mike, ready to begin his speech.

And when he spoke, his voice came across clear, strong and confident. Tears of pride pooled in her eyes. He addressed the crowd, garnering cheers as he began his speech. Then he graciously spoke of the future, of how he planned to work alongside the parliament to better the country. He spoke of helping the needy, working with charities and letting the people of Alma have a voice.

He seemed to seek her out of the crowd and as those gorgeous dark eyes landed on her, her breath caught in her throat. He trained that killer smile on her once again. How unfair of him to have such power over her, to stop her breathing with a look, a smile.

All eyes in the crowd seemed to turn her way. She was no stranger to the press, to having people recognize her, but today, she wanted no such attention. She'd rather be invisible.

Maria squeezed her hand again, giving her silent support. Portia inhaled and began breathing again.

"I have one more announcement to make," he continued to his audience. "Actually it is the reason I have called you here. I have made a decision that will change the ways of the monarchy for the better, I hope. For decades past, those in power, the honorable men and women who held the highest rule of the land, often did so out of duty. But with their duty often came great sacrifice." Juan Carlos glanced at Portia again briefly and then went on. "Many true loves went unheeded. Many of those loves were lost to baseless marriages, unions that held no great affection. The sacrifice was thought to keep the bloodlines pure. I have called you here today to say that my rule, this monarchy, is one that looks forward to the future, not backward at the past. It is time to bring the monarchy into the twenty-first century.

"As you know, Portia Lindstrom and I are to be married. Our engagement was swift, yes, but when it's right, you know it deep in your heart." His fist covered his heart and he awarded the crowd his beautiful smile. "And I am here to tell you it is right."

His eyes sparkled and he sent her a look filled with so much love, Portia's heart did somersaults. "Recently, it's come to light that Portia is not the true princess of Samforstand. In fact, she has no royal bloodlines at all. She came to me when she learned this news from an elder in her family. It seems there was much confusion about the legal heirs to the throne after the chaos and hardships of World War II.

"My family went through great hardships at that time, as well. Many of you here today know all about the recent trials and tribulations my family went through to find the true heir to the throne. Our great-grandmother's recently discovered letters proved to all of us the high price that was paid to keep to the letter of law when it came to royal protocol. In those letters we learned that her son, king Raphael Montoro II, and his direct descendants were not the rightful heirs to the throne, and thus am I standing before you today, a Salazar, as your king.

"Similarly, Portia has discovered the truth of her family's past and now needs to move forward with her life. But I will not allow mere decorum to once again steer the Montoros' destiny toward a tragic outcome. We will not let history repeat itself. We will not sacrifice our love in the name of an outdated custom. Portia Lindstrom is here today, as my fiancée, and princess or not, she is the love of my life and will become my wife."

Juan Carlos put out his hand. "Portia? Will you join me here? Be by my side."

The crowd was stunned into silence. Cameras angled her way, shots were snapped off by the dozens.

"Go," Maria whispered. "He is changing a centuries-old tradition for you. Don't leave him waiting."

She blinked, coming to grips with what had just happened. The depth of his commitment astonished her, delighted her and sent her hormones into a tizzy. She caught Eduardo giving her a smile and an encouraging nod from behind Juan Carlos. She smiled back.

Maria was right; she couldn't leave the king waiting. Not for another second. If he could do this for her, then she wouldn't hesitate to show him her love. With him by her side, she could conquer anything. She wasn't a wimpy princess. Well, she *wasn't* a princess at all, but she wasn't wimpy, either.

Her head held high, she stepped forward and made her way to the podium. As she reached it, she took Juan Carlos's outstretched hand and gazed into his eyes. In them, she saw her life, her future. The details were negotiable, but the love, that never wavered. She loved him. She would always love him. Thank God, King Montoro of Alma was a determined man.

Juan Carlos pulled her close and there before the world, bruised her lips in a kiss that left no one doubting their king's commitment. "Juan Carlos," she murmured. "Everyone's watching."

"Are they?"

Cameras clicked like crazy and she had no doubt this epic scene would go viral.

When Juan Carlos broke off the kiss, he nudged her tight to his side to present a united front and turned to the crowd. "Portia is a wonderful, bright, talented woman and in the days and years to come, you will all see in her what I see. I ask only that you welcome her today. Give her the same chance you gave me."

The crowd was silent and Portia's heart plummeted. And then a sole cheer rang out from a man shouting his support. And then another cheer went up and another, in a show of loyalty. And soon, the entire gathering displayed their acceptance as boisterous cheers and booming applause echoed against the palace walls, the citizens of Alma giving the king their allegiance.

They had accepted her.

Portia couldn't keep a wide, teary-eyed smile from spreading across her face. She was grateful for their support, but she was certain that even if the crowd had turned hostile, nothing would have deterred Juan Carlos. He had her back, and that was the best feeling in the world.

The speech over, Portia walked off with Juan Carlos. "I love you, you know," she said, winding her arm around his waist and leaning her head on his shoulder.

"I do know, but I think I'll need to hear you say it about a thousand times. Tonight?"

She nodded. "Tonight." She lifted her lips to his. "Do you think you can make me say it a thousand times?"

He laughed. "Oh, I know I can. Just let me alert the chauffeur we'll be needing the limo soon."

Her eyes went wide. "Juan Carlos, you don't play fair!"

"Sweetheart, I play for keeps. Princess or not, you're a royal temptation that I can't live without."

"So you're keeping me?"

"For as long as you'll have me."

"Forever, then. It's settled."

"Settled," he said, grinning as he picked her up and twirled her around and around.

She floated on air.

And her feet never did touch the ground again.

Epilogue

One month later

Juan Carlos couldn't stop grinning as he held Portia in his arms and danced to the royal orchestra's rendition of "Unforgettable" under hundreds of strung lights and a moonlit sky on the grounds of the newly restored farmhouse. This place that Bella and James would someday call home was where Juan Carlos and Portia had found love, too, and it seemed fitting to have a small intimate exchange of promised vows here in front of their close friends and family. His new bride dressed in satin and ivory lace, with his mother's diamond wedding ring sparkling on her finger, was the most beautiful woman on the planet.

"Are you happy?" he asked, fairly certain his answer was found in the sky-blue gleam in her eyes.

"I don't think I've ever been happier."

"That's how I want to keep it, sweetheart." He pressed her close and kissed her forehead, brushing his lips over her cheeks and nose and finally landing on her sweet mouth.

"I loved our sunset wedding," Portia said. "This is a special place."

Their first dance ended and Juan Carlos swung Portia to a stop in the center of the circle of their guests, who applauded them, their dance and their marriage. Portia's elegant grace, her help in discovering the hidden artworks and her work with local charities had endeared her to the country. Even the doubters had begun to come around as she constantly proved to them that she belonged at his side. It was a good thing, too, because Juan Carlos would rather give up the throne than live without Portia.

His cousins approached. "Welcome to the family, Portia," Rafe said, his very pregnant wife on his arm. "We couldn't be happier for you both."

"It was a lovely ceremony," Emily said.

"Thank you. I've heard all about your special ceremony, as well," Portia offered, glancing at Emily, Rafe, Gabe and Serafia. "I've never attended a double wedding before."

"We wish we would've known you then," Serafia added.

"Might've been a triple wedding, who knows?" Gabe said with a teasing smile.

Juan Carlos found it all amusing. His cousins had met their wives in uncanny ways and now every one of them was married. Rafe had resumed his position as head of Montoro Enterprises and the company was thriving. Good thing, too, because Rafe's father had decided to retire in Alma. After the ceremony he'd been the first to offer his congratulations, giving Portia a kiss on the cheek and wrapping Juan Carlos in a tight embrace. Juan Carlos owed a great deal to the man who had raised him from early childhood.

Gabe, the younger of his male cousins, had finally shed his bad boy ways and settled down with his lifelong friend and love, Serafia.

"I think I just felt something," Bella announced. She took James's hand and placed it on her small rounded belly. "Here, see if you can feel the baby."

James kept his hand there several seconds. "I'm not sure," he said softly, diplomatically. "It's early yet, isn't it, honey?"

"Maybe for you, but I think I felt it." Bella's eyes were two bright beams of light. She was carrying James's child.

James kissed her lips. "I can't wait to feel our baby, too."

Portia slipped her hand in Juan Carlos's and they watched the scene play out. James had one child already and Bella was proving to be a fantastic stepmother to one-year-old Maisey. And now, their family was expanding. Juan Carlos was glad that Bella and James had settled in Alma and James was back playing professional soccer—football as they called it here—and winning games for the home team. Things had been rough there for a while between James and his father, oil tycoon Patrick Rowling. Patrick had picked James's twin brother, Will, to marry Bella. The arranged marriage was an antiquated notion to say the least, and Bella was having none of it. James was the man for her. And then Will had also found love with Catalina Ibarra, his father's maid. The whole thing had sent Patrick into a nosedive but he was finally coming around and softening to the idea that perhaps his sons could make up their own minds about their love life and beyond.

"Now that we're all here together, I have good news to share with all of you," Juan Carlos said. He couldn't help his ever-present smile from intensifying. He had his family's attention now. "I'm told by Alex and the prime minister that Alma has never seen a better year. The country is well on its way to being financially solvent again. Thanks in part to our efforts here, I might add. With the discovery of the lost art treasure, tourism will climb, especially once we put those pieces on public display. We are working to that end. Since the state of Alma is now finally secure once again, a sizable portion of the Montoro fortune has been repatriated. It has been decided that the money will fund a new public school system named for my grandmother Isabella Salazar."

"That's wonderful," Bella said.

Rafe and Gabe slapped him on the back with congrat-ulations.

"If it wasn't for Tia Isabella's determination to see the Montoros return to Alma in her lifetime—and those let-ters I discovered—none of this would even be possible," Bella said.

It was true. Juan Carlos wouldn't be king, he would never have met Portia and who knew what would have happened among his other family members. "We owe my grandmother quite a bit."

They took a solemn moment to give thanks to Isabella. And then the orchestra music started up again.

Couples paired off and moved onto the dance floor.

Little Maisey Rowling had woken up from her nap. Wearing pink from head to toe, she was sitting on the front porch playing with the palace kittens alongside Portia's maids in attendance, Jasmine and Maria Ramon.

"I owe those two women a dance," Juan Carlos said to Portia. "If not for them, you may never have come back to Alma. Actually, I owe them much more than that."

"Yes, but first, my love, I have a wedding gift for you. I hope it will match the one you gave me. I cannot wait another second to give it to you."

"Okay," he said, eager to please her. "I'm yours."

She tugged him to the back of the house, to the garden area that was in full bloom, despite the late fall climate. Oh, the miracle of royalty that made all things possible. She sat him down on the white iron bench and then took a seat beside him.

"Juan Carlos," she began, taking his hands and hold-ing them in her lap. "You have given me your love, a new family and a beautiful palace to live in."

"You deserve all those things, sweetheart."

"But there's one thing missing. One thing I want and hope you want, too."

He had no clue where she was going with this. He had everything he wanted. "Have you found another brood of cats to adopt?"

She shook her head and grinned, her eyes beaming with the same glow he'd seen in Bella's. His heart stopped beating. He gathered his thoughts and came to the only conclusion he could.

"You're not?"

She nodded now, bobbing her head up and down rapidly. "I am."

"We're going to have a baby?"

"Yes!"

A glance at her belly gave him no indication. "When?"

"Seven months from now."

Carefully, he pulled her onto his lap. "I'm…I'm…going to be a father."

"Yes, you are."

He curved his hand around her nape and brought his lips close to hers. "You're going to be a mother."

"Yes."

The idea filled him with pride. His Portia would give him a child. It was the best gift in the world. His mouth touched hers reverently and he tasted the sweetness of her lips. "I couldn't be happier, sweetheart."

"I'm glad. Our baby will grow up in a home filled with love. Neither one of us knew our parents for very long. But now, we will have a family of our own. It's quite unexpected…"

"It's all I've ever wanted, Portia. For us to be a family."

"Really?"

He nodded. His throat constricted. His emotions had finally caught up to him today. His life had come full circle—the orphaned boy who would be king, married to his heart's desire, was to have a family all his own now.

There was no better kingdom on earth than for a man to share his life with the woman he loved.

He and Portia were two of a kind.

Almas Iguales.

Equal souls.

* * * * *

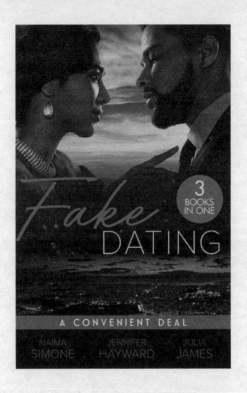

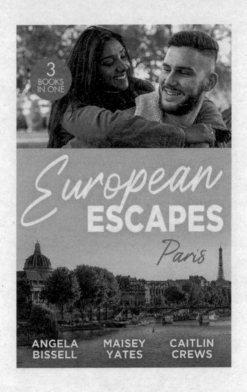

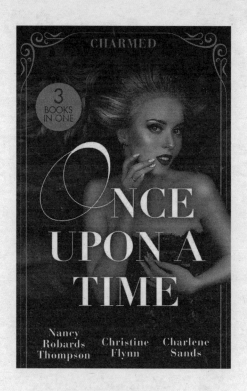

MILLS & BOON

THE HEART OF ROMANCE

A ROMANCE FOR EVERY READER

MODERN

Prepare to be swept off your feet by sophisticated, sexy and seductive heroes, in some of the world's most glamourous and romantic locations, where power and passion collide.

HISTORICAL

Escape with historical heroes from time gone by. Whether you passion is for wicked Regency Rakes, muscled Vikings or rugge Highlanders, awaken the romance of the past.

MEDICAL

Set your pulse racing with dedicated, delectable doctors in the high-pressure world of medicine, where emotions run high and passion, comfort and love are the best medicine.

True Love

Celebrate true love with tender stories of heartfelt romance, from the rush of falling in love to the joy a new baby can bring, and a focus on the emotional heart of a relationship.

HEROES

The excitement of a gripping thriller, with intense romance at its heart. Resourceful, true-to-life women and strong, fearless men face danger and desire - a killer combination!

From showing up to glowing up, these characters are on the path to leading their best lives and finding romance along the way – with plenty of sizzling spice!

To see which titles are coming soon, please visit

millsandboon.co.uk/nextmonth